SOUL MATES

USA TODAY BESTSELLING AUTHOR
ELLIE WADE

DEDICATIONS

Bared Souls

This book is dedicated to my dad, whom I miss every day.

To all the gentle souls.
May you be stronger than your demons.

Kindred Souls

To all of you that loved Bared Souls and requested I write another
book for
Alma—this is for you.

BARED SOULS

ELLIE WADE

PROLOGUE

ALMA

From the very start, he told me that he'd destroy me. He warned me that he'd rip my heart out. He might not want to, but it would happen. And I believed him.

I knew he wasn't lying, and yet I loved him anyway.

There are many types of love. The raw, deep, soul-crushing love is rare. I craved it, that connection. I wanted him and all that entailed.

Despite everything that happened, even now, I wouldn't change any of it.

For a love to have the capacity to destroy you, it has to be extraordinarily powerful—and that kind of love is impossible to walk away from.

Regardless of the consequences.

He loved me fiercely, and I loved him back.

CHAPTER 1

ALMA

"This is you." Amos nods toward the tan metal door.

At first glance, the color seems drab and depressing, but I shake that negativity from my head because *this is college*. I'm finally starting my life. Everything about the next four years is going to be epic. Drab door be damned.

I position the box I'm holding on my hip, securing it with one arm. My free hand extends out to my side toward my best friend. He repeats the motions with the box in his grasp and takes my pinkie in his.

"This is it." He grins, our pinkies entwined between us—our eternal sign of our best-friend status.

I've been waiting for this day for years, ever since Amos told me about the magical place called college so many years ago. The first eighteen years of my existence were ... interesting. My parents brought a huge set of challenges to the mix.

I, Almalee Hannelda Weber, named by my wannabe-hippie

parents, was raised by immature humans with a love for illicit substances. My parents had been mere babies during Woodstock and not yet in middle school when the whole peace-and-love era fizzled out in the early 1970s. Yet there aren't two people who would look more comfortable driving around in a lime-green Volkswagen bus with bright flowers painted all over it than Alman and Lee-Ann Weber.

My dad, Alman, was a first-generation American with parents who had immigrated here from Germany in the 1960s. My mom, Lee-Ann, was a first-generation American as well. Her parents had come here from Venezuela around the same time.

They combined their first names to get mine, and my middle name is the combination of both of my grandmothers' names—Hannah and Esmerelda.

Utter geniuses, my parents.

They love me, in their own way—though I've been reminded many times that I was an oops baby—but they love their free lifestyle more.

My father's priorities can be summarized by his two tattoos. The largest across his chest are the symbols for peace, love, and marijuana. Then, he has a band of ivy and daisies around his arm with my mother's name scattered throughout the design.

Lee-Ann's philosophy on motherhood can be summed up in her favorite anecdote that she brings up anytime she's reliving the story of my birth, and that is, "The first thing I told those doctors was that they'd better tie my tubes the second after they pulled that baby out, so I'd never risk having another." She labels her emergency C-section as a gift because it allowed her to get the tubal ligation for less money since the doctors were already in there.

It is what it is, and I love my parents. They love me the best they can even if I did practically raise myself. I'm just so grateful that the sweetest little boy lived next door from me, growing up. Without Amos, I'm not sure where I'd be.

I'd probably be living on a naked commune. I'm not exaggerating when I say that my parents have taken me to enough naked camps in my life to scar me for life. One wouldn't think that such a thing existed, especially with children in attendance, but I'm here to tell you that they do. Truthfully, I would never walk in my parents' shoes. I was born, wanting to be what they weren't and to do everything with my life that they hadn't. I saw early on that I wanted more. It wasn't something that had been taught to me. I just knew inherently that I needed more in my life.

I've worked hard to get here. Neither parent attended a teacher conference or asked me if I did my homework even once throughout my schooling, and I still graduated with perfect grades. Amos and I were co-valedictorians of our graduating class. Years of hard work got me a full-ride scholarship to EMU, Eastern Michigan University. It's not the most prestigious school in the state, but it's completely paid for, room and board included, and it ranks really well as a teachers college, which is my degree of choice. On top of that, it's only about a twenty-minute car ride away from the University of Michigan, which is the most prestigious college in the state and where Amos is going.

I was also accepted into the University of Michigan but was offered very little scholarship money. The fact is that they don't need to hand out academic scholarships because the brightest students in the state are all clamoring to get in anyway, and many—like Amos—can afford it.

"All right, let's hope she's cool." I release my smallest finger from his and open the door to my dorm room.

A petite blonde sits on a futon, painting her toenails and bopping her head to the music coming from her earbuds. Her smile widens when she spots me. She puts the nail polish brush back in the container and jumps up from her seated position, removing her earbuds as she stands.

"Oh my gosh! Hi." She quickly closes the distance between us and extends her hand. "I'm Quinn. You must be Almalee. Am I saying that right?" she says rapidly, her entire demeanor bubbly and sweet.

"Just Alma is fine, and yes." I return her smile.

"I'm so glad you're here. I was beginning to worry that you weren't coming. My parents moved me in a couple of days ago, and it's been lonely. I come from a family of seven, so I'm just not used to being alone for so long." She rolls her eyes and shakes her head. "Look at me." She raises her hand and moves her fingers against her thumb in the *blah, blah* motion. "I can't shut up. It's a problem really." She giggles at her own expense. "Let me help you." She reaches for the box in my hand and carries it over to the side of the room that's empty of any personal belongings.

The room isn't much larger than my bedroom at home. There's a twin-size bed and a plain wooden dresser on each side of the room. In between the two beds is a bright pink futon sofa.

I'm sure Quinn brought it. She has also supplied the area with a small refrigerator, a microwave, and some colorful lamps.

"I hope this side of the room is okay with you. It honestly doesn't matter to me. We can switch if you want. Also, these beds do stack into bunk beds, but I didn't know if you were a bottom or top bunk kind of girl, so I just figured this setup was our best bet."

I grin, so happy that my roommate is nice. I was terrified of getting some evil witch, and Quinn is seriously like the exact opposite of my worst fears. She's gorgeous with her bright green eyes, big smile, and long blonde hair. She's like a perky Barbie doll but shorter and with normal proportions.

"Everything looks great," I reassure her. "I would've been here sooner, but we spent a day getting this guy moved into his dorm." I hook my thumb back toward Amos. "This is Amos. He's attending U of M."

She nods. "Oh, nice. Pretty close then."

"Yeah," I agree.

Amos sets the box that he's holding down and extends his hand out toward Quinn. "It's nice to meet you." He shakes her hand.

"You too!" she replies.

"Well, I'm going to go get the rest of your things," Amos says to me.

"I'll come help," I offer.

He shakes his head. "No, stay here. Start unpacking. I got it."

"Are you sure?"

He smiles warmly. "I'm sure."

After he's left the room, Quinn turns to me, her eyebrows raised. "Um, please don't take this the wrong way, and I hope I'm not being too forward, but your boyfriend is, like, the hottest guy I've ever seen in my life." She bites her lip.

I can only chuckle. "He's not my boyfriend," I tell her. "Life-long best friends."

"Seriously?"

"Seriously."

"You know who he reminds me of? I used to watch this show called *Private Practice* with my mom, and he looks just like the hot doctor on the show."

"Taye Diggs? Yeah, he gets that a lot." I press my lips together, fighting a grin.

"Oh, he's so dreamy. I'm sorry. I must sound like an idiot. I told you I was lonely."

I wave her off. "It's fine. He is absolutely gorgeous and the nicest human I know."

"Does he have a girlfriend?" she inquires a bit too enthusiastically.

"No," I tell her.

"That's surprising," she says as Amos enters the room with two boxes stacked in his arms.

He sets the boxes next to the others. "Only one more load, and then that's all." He shoots me a smile before leaving again.

"I don't have much stuff," I say to Quinn. "Mainly clothes. I'm really glad you brought the futon and appliances. That was nice of you."

"Oh yeah, absolutely fine. It's all hand-me-downs from my older sister's time in the dorm. She's a junior at Central Michigan University, but she's sharing an apartment with some friends now, so she didn't need any of it anymore."

"That worked out," I say.

"Yeah," Quinn agrees.

I quickly start putting away my clothes. The sooner I'm moved in and settled, the sooner I can walk around campus with my schedule and get my bearings. I want to know where all of the buildings are and how long it takes to get to each one.

I'm kind of an obsessive planner. I suppose it stemmed, once again, from growing up with my parents. I never knew what to expect with them. So, I liked being able to control what I could, when I could. It tamed my anxiety and brought a calmness to my life that was lacking at home. School is my domain. It's where I shine.

Amos returns with the last of my things.

"You want to go grab some dinner?" Amos asks. "Then, we can walk around campus and find your classes."

He knows me so well.

My stare drops to the pile of stuff I have to put away.

"You have two days to get that organized. You have time." He chuckles. "Plus, you have to eat."

"Okay, you're right." I turn to Quinn. "You want to grab some food with us?"

"Sure. You know, I had takeout from this local restaurant that was so amazing. It's only a block away if you want to go there."

"Sounds good," Amos says. "Let's go."

CHAPTER 2

ALMA

*I*t's a hot August day with extra humidity, like most typical Michigan summer days. Growing up here, I've come to realize that residents must stay for the autumn and spring. The winters are long and frigid, and the summers are so muggy that one's lips sweat.

Trucks with sofas and boxes are parked in front of the dorms. Parents are all around, wistfully aiding their child with move-in day. We pass a father lugging a large chair, who looks unimpressed. His scowl and sweat-soaked face give the impression that he'd be willing to sign his child out of his life for some air-conditioning. Right past him is a mother hugging her daughter tight; tears are falling down her cheeks as the daughter tries to pry herself free.

I look up to Amos, and he simply grabs my pinkie with his. We stay this way until we reach the restaurant.

The mom-and-pop Italian restaurant, Giovanni's, is fairly

empty, as it's still a little before the dinner rush. There are plastic green vines with plump, shiny grapes draping the walls around the restaurant. The fake foliage circling the hostess area carries a layer of dust, which, I'm going to be honest, freaks me out. Hopefully, the kitchen cleaning crew is more competent than the dining room cleaners.

"Three, please," Quinn tells the hostess, who proceeds to seat us right away.

I open up my menu to read as Quinn tells us, "So, I ordered the focaccia bread in the appetizer section. It came with fresh basil and tomato and melted mozzarella. It was to die for, and I'm really craving it again, but I also want to try something new, you know?"

"The mushroom risotto sounds good too," I point out.

"It all sounds good. That's the problem," Quinn adds.

The waitress takes our order, and Quinn opts to try something new. Before the waitress walks away, Amos adds the focaccia bread appetizer for the table.

"Aren't you the sweetest?" Quinn gives Amos a flirty look, which had I not told her that he and I were only friends earlier would have been a bit of a betrayal.

I haven't known my new roommate for long, but I'm usually a pretty good judge of character. I'd say Amos would be lucky to date her. She seems so sweet.

What if my bestie and college roommate got married?

Perhaps I'm jumping the gun a bit.

"So, what are you planning on studying, Alma?" Quinn asks.

"Teaching. Probably elementary ed."

She nods in approval. "Well, Eastern is a great school for teachers. What about you, Amos?"

"I'm going to apply to the College of Business after I get my prerequisites finished," he answers.

"Oh, nice. Yeah, U of M has one of the best business

programs in the country. My grandpa went there years ago, so we hear about his alma mater all the time," she muses with a warm expression.

"What about you?" Amos inquires before taking a sip of his iced tea.

"I don't know, honestly. I figure I have two years to get the basics done, and hopefully, I'll have decided by then." She shrugs.

"Oh, tons of students do that. You have time," I add.

"So, you two have been best friends since you were young?" Quinn asks.

I glance toward Amos and smile.

"Yeah, my dad's grandparents left us their house when they passed. I was seven. We moved in next to Amos and his parents," I say.

Amos looks to me. "The first time I met Alma, I was riding my bike up and down the sidewalk past our houses the summer before second grade. There was this barefoot girl with long, wild hair just sitting in her front yard, making mud pies, and her mother was belting out a ballad in Spanish. Her voice could be heard all the way down the street." He chuckles at the memory.

I nod. "Yeah, she was singing along with her favorite Mexican band, Maná," I offer that detail as if Quinn would know who Maná is. I'm betting she doesn't.

Amos continues, "So, I stopped my bike in front of her. She had mud up her arms and smeared across her cheek. I asked her where she was from, and she told me she was a little bit of this and that and was from all over. She said she was a mutt. I found that so cool because my dad would say the same thing about our dog at the time. Her name was actually Lacy, but we called her Mutt. I thought it was a term of endearment, so I started calling Alma here Mutt too."

"Oh my gosh, that's so cute!" Quinn says.

"He did. For most of our childhood, I answered to that name. He sat down cross-legged in front of me and started building a mud hut of some sort. It was cute. We talked, and then he blurted out that his mom named him after the cookie she was eating when she went into labor. So, I called him Cookie."

"Mutt and Cookie? You two must have been quite the pair." Quinn giggles.

"We were." I nod. "We've done everything together since then. Neither of us is close with our parents, and we are only children. So, he is my family."

"I think that is so sweet. I love it." Quinn clasps her hands together.

The conversation continues. We learn about Quinn's large family from Northern Michigan. Her parents have five children, all girls. Quinn is right in the middle. She tells us what she's heard about campus life. She wants to pledge a sorority this coming fall.

"We should do it together! It would be so much fun," she tells me.

I try not to grimace. "I don't think sorority life is my jam," I say.

"Why?" She raises an eyebrow.

"I'm more of a *stay home and study* kind of girl, I guess."

"There are smart girls in sororities. From what I hear, each one is known for something different. There is the studious sorority, the slutty one, the party one, the nice-girl one ... you know."

"Why would anyone join any of them but the smart and nice one?" I chuckle with a shake of my head.

Quinn waves her hand. "I mean, how much of that can we believe? It's just the stereotypes of each one. I bet they're all great."

"Maybe. We'll see." I opt to give her hope instead of shutting her down immediately, but I just can't see myself in a sorority.

I excuse myself to use the restroom. As I enter the restaurant's waiting area, I pull my cell phone out of the back pocket of my jean shorts. There are no missed calls or texts. I'm not surprised, but I'd be lying if I said I didn't wish my parents would care a little more than they do. A simple *Hope you got settled in at school* text would've sufficed.

I gasp in surprise as I bump right into someone. An apology leaves my mouth as I lift my eyes from my phone.

"I'm so sorry." I look up to see an angry scowl and take a step back. "I'm sorry. I was … I'm sorry," I repeat like an idiot.

"Yeah, you should probably look where you're walking. It helps." His voice is clipped.

I shake my head and step around him before speed-walking to the restroom.

"What a jerk," I grumble as the restroom door swings behind me. A hot-as-hell one, but a prick nonetheless.

Why are all the beautiful ones such assholes? No, that's not true. Amos is beautiful.

I only saw him for a second, but his appearance had such an effect on me that the mental picture in my mind is crystal clear. Disheveled chestnut-brown hair, striking blue eyes, a strong jaw, and full lips, and so tall. Though, with my height at five feet two inches, most men are tall next to me.

Pulling in a breath, I clear the thoughts of the guy next to the hostess stand.

I mean, I said I was sorry.

After washing my hands, I head back toward our table.

The dude is gone, and Amos and Quinn are standing in the lobby area, chatting.

"What about the check?" I inquire.

"Amos paid for the bill before I knew it. I tried to give him money for my meal, but he wouldn't take it," Quinn says.

I squint my eyes and smirk in Amos's direction. "Yeah, he has a way of doing that."

"It was my treat. It's not a big deal. You ready?" he asks me.

"Yeah, let's go."

Amos has been taking care of me my whole life. Someday, I hope to repay him for all he's done. As we walk back to the dorm, a shadow of loneliness invades my heart. I'm not ready for him to leave. Twenty minutes away is nothing, but it's farther than he's ever been. I don't know if I'm ready to be without him.

CHAPTER 3

ALMA

*A*mos sticks around and helps me put the rest of my clothes away. Then, the two of us walk around campus with my class schedule in hand. I have all day tomorrow to explore before classes start on Monday, but I like Amos here with me.

The temperature has dropped, and the wind has picked up, making it a pleasant evening for a walk.

"You know, Quinn has a thing for you," I tell him.

"She's not very stealthy, that one. I kind of figured." He chuckles.

"Why haven't you dated anyone—ever?" The question leaves my mouth as I suddenly realize that fact.

Amos is such a catch. I know he's had interest.

"Why haven't you?" he answers me in question.

I pucker my lips and throw him a mock glare. "You know why. I needed to focus to get away from there. I needed scholarships, not relationships. I couldn't let anything jeopardize my future. Not some high school boy who wouldn't matter in the long run, you know? No one stays with their high school sweetheart, so risking my grades over a boyfriend wasn't an option."

"Same reasons for me," he replies.

"You didn't need scholarships," I state since his parents have money.

"I needed good grades to get into Michigan though," he retorts, and years of memories and his obsession with getting into his dream school surface.

"True. So, are you going to date now?" I ask.

He shrugs. "Maybe. If I find someone I want to date. I still have to get good grades to get accepted into the business school."

"Yeah, but you can do both."

"Perhaps. I guess we'll see. Why the sudden dating talk?" he questions as we turn the corner toward my dorm.

"I don't know. I just don't want you to be alone." My voice trembles with the last word as I realize the fear of loneliness for both of us weighs heavily on my heart.

Amos stops. "Alma, look at me."

I look up into his deep brown eyes.

"I'm only twenty minutes or a phone call away. You're not alone." He reaches down and hooks his pinkie with mine.

"I know. It's just going to be different." My bottom lip quivers as my eyes fill with unshed tears.

I can't believe I'm feeling this way. I've wanted to be at college for as long as I can remember, and now that I'm here, I'm afraid. I never realized how dependent I was on Amos's support. He's my person. He's had my back for so long. I always thought I was incredibly strong and determined, but standing here now, I'm wondering if it was all a facade. Perhaps it was Amos that kept me strong.

17

"I'm going to miss you not being next door," I admit.

He brings the hand not holding mine up to my face and swipes the pad of his thumb across my cheek, collecting a rogue tear. "You don't have to miss me because I'm not leaving you. Ever. It's you and me for life, Mutt. I'll always have your back and be your sounding board. I'm your biggest fan and your number one ally. A twenty-minute car ride isn't going to change anything. You are going to rock this college thing. You're going to make new friends and impress the hell out of them, as you have with me all these years. You are kind and smart and beautiful. People are drawn to you, Alma. You won't be alone. Just be yourself, and you'll be fine. You're going to love it."

I let out a sigh. "You're right. I'll be fine. You'll be fine. It'll be great."

"There's the spirit," Amos says with a sweet smile. "Do you want me to stay longer?"

"No, you should go. I'll go inside and get to know Quinn a little more. She seems nice. Don't you think?"

He nods. "Yeah, I think she's a good person. You lucked out. The verdict is still out on Matt," he says, referring to his room-mate. "You're good?" he questions.

"I'm good."

"Call me if you need anything."

"I will," I promise.

Leaning in, we bring our fisted hands and locked pinkie fingers up to our mouths, and we each kiss the area of our hand where our thumbs cradle our pointer fingers and then release our grasp. It's the best-friend greeting that we came up with when we were ten, and it's stuck.

I turn toward the dorms, and Amos walks toward his car. Before entering the building, I give him a final wave. *God, I'm going to miss him.*

* * *

"Amos is gone?" Quinn asks when I get back in the room.

"Yeah, he had to go back. He told me to tell you good-bye."

"Aw. Sweet." She takes a step toward me, her green eyes wider than normal. "Well, while you were out, I spoke to some of our neighbors."

"Really? Are they cool?"

"They seem like it, but the exciting part is that they told me about this huge frat party happening tonight. Kind of a kick-off-the-year party. And I think we should go!" She claps her hands together with a squeal.

"A frat party? I can't. No," I stammer, kicking off my flip-flops. I head toward my bed and fall onto it with a bounce. Draping my forearm over my face, I repeat, "I can't."

"Please, Alma. Please," Quinn begs. "I've been going crazy here. I don't know anyone, and I've been so bored. It's the weekend before school starts. Please? It will be so much fun. We don't have to stay long. Maybe we'll meet some new people. Plus, you don't have homework yet, so there's no excuse."

I sit up and lean against the wall.

"The idea of a party makes me really uncomfortable," I tell her honestly. "My parents are huge partiers and always had people over, drinking and getting high. The idea of being like them makes me sick to my stomach."

"Okay," she says reassuringly. "I see your point, and I understand your hesitation, but let me play devil's advocate, if I may. First, from what I know of you in the five hours since I first met you, I'm guessing that you are nothing like your parents. Just because your parents drink and get high doesn't mean you have to. I'm not getting high. No way. You can enjoy a college party and not be like them. So, at dinner, you told me that you got a full-ride scholarship here, right?"

I nod.

"Did your parents get full-ride scholarships to college?"

"No. They didn't go to college."

She throws her hands up. "That's my point. You're nothing like your parents. You're responsible enough to go out and have fun without ruining your future. It's just a party, not a jail sentence. I promise. Plus … it's going to be so much fun," she whines the last sentence in a desperate plea. "And I don't want to go alone. I know from enough teen movies that a girl going solo to a frat party isn't a good idea. We need a buddy system. For me?" She puts her hands up in front of her in a praying stance and waits, eyes wide.

"I've known you for five hours. I can't believe your *for me* speech is breaking me." I smile at Quinn.

She gasps, "So, is that a yes?"

"I suppose," I groan.

She claps. "Yay! I'll take it."

I slide across my bed so that my feet are dangling off of the side. "So, what do we wear to these things?"

"Anything really." Quinn gives me a once-over. "Your jean shorts are cute. Maybe trade out the baggy T-shirt for a tank top? Then, add some hoop earrings and a little lip gloss, and you're good to go."

"I have a black tank top."

Quinn nods in approval. "Oh, yes. You can't go wrong with black." She begins rifling through her closet. "You're always welcome to borrow anything of mine too. We're both blessed with short-girl genes." She grins and looks over her shoulder at me. "And we're about the same size."

I agree that we're around the same height, but Quinn has a much more slender body than I do. I was gifted with my mom's hips and chest. I'm quite certain that my ass wouldn't fit into anything of Quinn's unless it was made of a stretchy material.

20

"Thanks. I'll just go with the shorts and black tank top," I say as Quinn pulls a leopard-print miniskirt from her closet.

"Too bold?" she asks as she holds up the small piece of fabric.

"No, I like it."

I throw on my top and carry my small makeup bag over to a makeshift vanity area that Quinn has set up. There's a hot-pink crate sitting in front of a full-length mirror. A variety of curlers, straighteners, and hair wands rest atop the crate and a large bin of makeup.

We're fortunate that our dorms have in-room bathrooms, but I like that this area is outside of the bathroom. I've never had to share a bathroom before, as I had my own at home, but I'm thinking if we used the bathroom for getting ready and everything else it is used for, we'd never leave.

"I really like this area," I tell Quinn.

"Thanks. I just figured, it frees up the bathroom for showers or whatever. Plus, the bathroom is always so humid. Our curls might have a chance if we get ready out here." She's right in that the bathroom is a small space with cement brick walls. There's not a lot of ventilation, and it still seems muggy from her shower earlier.

"I can tell that you grew up with girls," I say as I pull a brush through my long brunette hair. "You have everything. I barely know how to apply mascara correctly, let alone what this is used for." I hold up a metal wand.

Her smile is warm. "I'm going to have so much fun, teaching you how to use everything. You're like the little sister I never had."

"You have two little sisters," I deadpan.

"I know, but they knew the ways of makeup and hair at an early age by watching their older sisters. You, on the other hand, know nothing, and that is why you're the little sister I never had."

"Okay," I say on a laugh.

"I'll give you some beachy waves for tonight. Sound good?"

"Sure."

I sit as Quinn works her magic with my hair.

"Your hair is so thick and healthy and holds curl amazingly well."

"That's good," I answer. "I've never really done anything with it besides the occasional trim."

"I have hair envy," Quinn sighs. "Mine is so dry because of my obsession with being a blonde."

"Your hair isn't natural? It looks so good."

"Aw, you're sweet," she says while wrapping another strand of my hair around the heated wand. "No, I have brown hair and not with any of the gorgeous auburn highlights that you have, just plain mousy brown. Or that's the way I remember it at least. I've been dyeing my hair blonde since I was twelve."

"There, perfect." Quinn steps back, admiring my hair. "A couple touches to your face, and you're ready."

I apply a swipe of mascara and lip gloss and throw my feet into some flip-flops before staring at my finished look in the long mirror. I look older and, honestly, really good. I'm so used to seeing my makeup-free face and my hair in a ponytail. One coat of mascara makes my brown eyes seem huge.

"You are so hot," Quinn tosses me a compliment. She's really good for one's ego. "Seriously, you have this sexy, hippy Shakira vibe going on. You sure you don't want to wear one of my skirts?"

"Uh, I'm good, and thank you, though I hate my hips."

Quinn just shakes her head. "Figures. Everyone always wants what they don't have. I would kill for your curves."

"I think you're perfect," I tell her.

"Exactly my point." She smacks her lips together in front of the mirror. Her plum lipstick makes the green of her eyes stand out. "We're both perfect the way we are, and yet we both wish our bodies were different. It's the classic female self-deprecation that runs rampant in our society. I'm trying to be better with that, but it's hard, you know?"

She tosses her lipstick into a small black purse and peers at the contents inside. "I've got gum, money, cell phone, lipstick, and ID. Anything else?"

"Sounds about right." I tap the back pocket of my jean shorts. "I have my ID, money, and phone."

"Well, if you need gum, let me know. I have plenty. Never know if you're going to be kissing someone tonight." She raises a brow with a smirk.

I gasp, "I'm not kissing anyone."

"Never say never. Now, let's get out of here before we set the room ablaze. We're too hot to stay in one place for too long. Fire hazard."

I laugh. I think Quinn is exactly what I needed.

CHAPTER 4

ALMA

$\mathcal{T}$he fraternity house is a few blocks from campus, so it's within walking distance. The music coming from the party can be heard from a block away. People are congregated on the lawn around the old, large house, talking, laughing, and goofing around. Some linger on the expansive front porch that wraps around the building. Others can be seen through the windows on all of the levels.

My heart starts to race, and I'm wondering if I made a bad call. This is so far out of my comfort zone. Just as my steps begin to falter, Quinn grabs my hand and leads us through the group of people on the grass.

"Let's go inside and check it out," she suggests.

As we enter, a high-pitched squeal in the form of Quinn's name can be heard. A tall brunette with a messy bun atop her head closes in on us.

"You came!" she cheers.

"Hey! Yeah, we did. This is my roommate, Alma." Quinn introduces me to the girl and then addresses me, "This is Bethany. She and Gabby live across from us."

Bethany and I greet each other, and then she says, "Do you guys want a drink? Then, I can show you where everyone else is."

"Sure!" Quinn answers for the both of us.

We follow Bethany into the kitchen, where a group of guys stands around a metal keg, filling up red Solo cups with the amber liquid.

"There's beer or this punch." Bethany motions toward the large plastic tub that sits on the counter, filled with red liquid.

"What's in that?" Quinn asks.

Bethany shakes her head. "Who knows? But it's good!"

"I guess I'll go with the mystery punch," Quinn says, grabbing a Solo cup and filling it. "Alma?"

I shake my head. "I'm good."

"Come on, just try. You don't have to drink it all." She pushes the cup toward me.

I reluctantly take it.

Cups in hand, we follow Bethany as she winds us through people standing around. She takes us to a back room, away from the speakers blaring music so loudly at the front of the house. The music can still be heard, but it's not as deafening. This seems to be some sort of a game room. There's a pool table in the center, a card table in the corner, and a dartboard on the wall. Several couches face each other in a makeshift seating area, and as we approach, cheers ring from that area, welcoming Bethany back.

"And I brought friends. This is Quinn and Alma," Bethany introduces us.

I wave casually and squeeze in next to Quinn on the edge of one of the couches.

I take a sip of my punch. I have to admit, it's decent—better than I thought it would be. A grin teases my lips as a thought comes to mind. *What if it's just a big tub of generic-brand Hawaiian Punch? How funny would that be?* That's what I'd do if I were part of a frat house and hosting a party. I have to assume that alcohol is expensive. *Why provide it for the masses? Let them trip over each other, thinking they're drunk, when in reality, they've only consumed a load of sugar.*

My thoughts prompt me to drink more. When I lower the cup from my mouth, my breath hitches as piercing blues steal my gaze. The guy I ran into earlier is sitting on the couch across from me, his eyes burn into me accusingly. I swallow and pull my eyes from his, turning toward Quinn.

What a creep.

I take another sip of the juice. Quinn is regaling the group with some story, and several people are cracking up at her tale. I missed the first part of it, and now, she's talking about chickens and Superman ice cream. I'm trying to figure out how those two connect when, against my better judgment, I chance a glance back toward the weirdo. He's still staring, and I don't like it.

I stand from the sofa and dart from the room. After navigating my way back toward the kitchen, I refill my cup with the sweet liquid and take a sip. Standing in front of the screen door that leads toward the back deck, I take a few moments to people-watch. I know it's only my first night at college, but I still feel like an outsider, looking in.

"Wondering what you're doing here?" a male voices my insecurities from behind me, and I startle.

Turning around, I find the grumpy douche standing behind me, an evil smirk across his ugly—fine, gorgeous—face. A slight shadow lines his square jaw and chiseled cheekbones, making my insides flip in betrayal.

"What?" I snap at him.

"Why'd you come here tonight?" he demands.

"Why'd you?" I retort.

"This doesn't seem like your scene," he says flatly, not an ounce of concern present in his tone.

"Why do you care? And why are you even talking to me?"

He might be right. Perhaps I am a fish out of water here, but it's not his place to say anything about my life and choices. I have a reserved personality by nature, but I never back down from a bully. When I feel wronged in a situation, I gain courage.

I've been fighting for myself for almost nineteen years. Exquisite DNA doesn't give anyone the right to talk down to someone else.

Quinn's voice breaks our staredown. "Alma, you okay?"

He takes Quinn's presence as his cue to walk away.

"What was that all about?" she asks me.

"I don't know. I ran into him at dinner earlier, and he has a chip on his shoulder for some reason."

She nods. "He's definitely perfected the dark and moody type, hasn't he? Do you know who he is?"

"No," I answer.

"His name is Leo Harding. He's the son of the actor Victor Harding," she says in a hushed tone.

"Really?"

Victor Harding is a huge actor, very popular. I heard he lived in a rich Detroit suburb.

"Yeah."

I raise my eyebrows. "And he goes here?"

"That's what I'm told," Quinn answers.

It doesn't make sense that Leo would choose to attend Eastern Michigan when he could go anywhere. I'm sure there are few schools that his influential father couldn't buy his way into.

"From what I can tell, every girl here is obsessed with him," she says. "He is pretty hot."

"Yeah." I can't deny the obvious.

He has that *bad boy meets star quarterback* air to him. Sexy and brooding with a quality that makes him seem irresistible. He's tall, lean, and muscular. His chestnut hair is short with just enough length on the top to allow it to fall in adorable chunks across his forehead.

"But he's an ass. Good looks don't give you a free ride to be a dick."

"That's true," Quinn agrees without much conviction.

We top off our drinks and make our way back to the group. Besides our neighbors, Gabby and Bethany, there are several other girls and a handful of guys. They all seem nice enough.

"We should play Never Have I Ever," someone suggests.

"Have you played before?" Quinn asks me.

I shake my head.

"We'll go around in a circle, saying something that we've never done. If you've done what the person says they haven't, you take a drink. It's really easy. You'll catch on right away," Quinn whispers to me.

Bethany starts. "Never have I ever had sex on a boat."

A few people drink.

Oh, so it's this kind of game. Great.

"Never have I ever had a threesome," Gabby says.

A couple of people bring their drinks to their lips.

Some guy named Josh says, "Never have I ever eaten sushi."

One person takes a drink while someone in the group groans, "Lame," followed by, "Dumb," and other disapproving sentiments.

Josh just chuckles. "What? I haven't."

"Never have I ever had sex with two different people on the same day," a girl named Jess states, and I hate that my eyes dart across to Leo.

He takes a long gulp from his cup.

Pig, I think.

When he stops drinking, his gaze is narrowed in on me. He smirks as if he knew I'd be looking to him. I pull my eyes away as quickly as I can.

"Never have I ever participated in a threesome that included double penetration," a guy named Ethan says, and another girl squeals and throws something at him.

I lower my gaze, staring into my cup of punch. I've never heard of whatever it is that this Ethan guy says he hasn't done, and I don't want to know. I don't have any desire to see who's done it and who hasn't. Despite never having heard the term before, I think I can figure out what it means, and my brain just can't handle that.

The game proceeds, going around from person to person, each *never have I ever* is some version of where or how the speaker hasn't had sex. I don't miss that Quinn drinks a few times but not for any of the truly vulgar ones. I hope no one catches on that I haven't drunk once.

Honestly, it doesn't bother me that I haven't had sex yet. I'm eighteen, not forty. I have time. It's not like I'm against it or saving myself for marriage. Finding someone to hook up with in high school wasn't a priority.

Although I haven't drunk once during the game thus far, the room is starting to wobble around me, and my head is getting fuzzy. So much for my Hawaiian Punch hypothesis. There's definitely alcohol in this cup.

My mind clears when Leo's voice breaks through my senses.

"Never have I ever sat at a frat party and played a game about sex when I've yet to have it."

Lifting my face, I zero in on Leo. Unsurprisingly, he's staring right at me.

"What?" he says to the group, though his gaze is on me. "No one's drinking. No virgins in this room?"

A few people snicker—at me or just in response to Leo, I'm not sure, and I don't care. I'm over this party.

I lean in toward Quinn. "I don't feel the best. I think I'm going to go," I whisper before standing and walking out of the room as fast as I can.

Quinn calls after me, "Wait, Alma."

Once I'm out of the game room, I stop my retreat and turn to face Quinn.

"I'll come with you," she says. "I don't want you walking home by yourself."

"Do you want to go?" I ask her.

She wears a slight frown. "Sure, I guess. I was having fun. But we're a team, right? I'm not letting you leave to walk back by yourself."

"It's fine," I tell her. "Just three blocks. You shouldn't have to end your night early because of me. Come back with Gabby and Bethany later. I've never really been drunk before, and whatever is in that punch isn't sitting right with me. I just need to go to bed, I think." I press my lips together in a grin.

Her eyes widen in response. "Well, if you're feeling sick, I'm absolutely not letting you walk home by yourself. No way. It's fine, Alma. There will be other parties."

"I'll walk her home." His voice comes out of nowhere.

Quinn and I both whip around to look at Leo.

"What?" I shriek.

"I'll walk you home. I was getting ready to leave anyway." He takes another step toward me.

"No," I protest. "I'm fine. I don't need you to walk me."

Quinn places her hand on Leo's forearm. "I'll go with her. Thanks anyway though."

Leo's eyes dart from me to Quinn. "What's the issue? I know you don't want to leave," he says to Quinn. "Your groupies back there, Bethany and Gabby, are practically crying over your departure. Just go back and have fun. I'm heading out anyway. I don't understand what the problem is. I said I'd take her. I'm not going to touch her." He says the last sentence like the idea is almost repulsive.

"Whatever. I don't care," I grumble.

"You're okay with him walking you back? Are you sure? I promise I don't mind," she says to me.

I plaster the most reassuring smile I can muster. "It's fine. Go have fun. Just please be safe and come back with the girls."

"Okay, I will." She pulls me into a hug. "I'll see you later." Before I can respond, she's skipping back to the game room and most likely the sex drinking game, which Leo so eloquently pointed out I had no reason to be playing.

Without giving a second of attention to Leo, I turn and walk out of the fraternity house as fast as my unsteady legs will carry me.

CHAPTER 5

ALMA

"*I*t's like watching a baby deer walk for the first time." Leo laughs behind me as I stomp off across the fraternity lawn.

"What?" I halt.

"You. You're all wobbly and stuff. Let me guess. You're the token sheltered girl from a small Midwestern town. You've never been touched by a dude, and tonight was your first taste of alcohol. I bet your dad's a preacher or some shit."

"Yes, and I'm also forbidden to dance." I glare. "You busted me. I came straight to college from my home in the *Footloose* VHS tape."

"Feisty. I like it."

I turn back in the direction of the dorms. "I couldn't care less what you like, and you're wrong about me."

"Oh yeah?" He doesn't sound convinced. "About what part?"

"And so what if I don't drink much? A tipsy college student is hardly abnormal. I'm sure you sleep with one on the daily."

"Is that your idea of a burn?" he questions, now keeping step beside me. "How much did you drink anyway?"

"Like, a cup and a half. Hardly anything. Not a big deal."

"I know it doesn't taste like it, but that shit is strong."

"Like you care," I snap. "Why are you following me—again?"

I pick up my pace, focusing extra hard on not tripping over my flip-flops. *Have these shoes always been so floppy? Also, why are the streetlights becoming blurrier, the closer I get to the dorm?*

"Why did you decide to go here?" I ask Leo.

"What do you mean?"

"This college. Why? I know who you are, by the way. Quinn told me earlier."

I don't know why I'm talking to him, and yet I can't seem to stop.

"Oh, you know who I am? Who's that, Alma? Tell me who I am." His words are clipped, his voice angry.

The tone of his voice causes me to pause and not say anything else about his family, fame, or money. I shouldn't have said it to begin with. What does it have to do with anything?

I quickly change the subject. "There's my dorm. I'm safe. You can go."

He ignores me and keeps walking at my side.

I don't say anything else as I step inside the building. Holding on to the railing, I climb the steps to the second floor. There seems to be a lot more steps than before. When I open the door of my hallway, I'm breathing heavily.

I can't wait to go to bed. This has been an emotionally and physically exhausting first day.

When I reach my door, I throw my hand in a wave behind me. "Bye now."

As I unlock the door, Leo pushes it open wide and steps in before me.

"What are you doing?" I ask, startled.

"Calm your tits. I'm not going to touch you." His eyes pierce mine. "Come in."

Against my better judgment, I step into my dorm, letting the door slam behind me.

"I'm not … I'm not doing anything with you. So, you can just go," I stammer.

Leo lets out a dry chuckle. "Number one: I can go back to the party and have the pick of pretty much any girl I want there, and I wouldn't have to ask twice. Why would I chase you? Number two: who said I wanted you in the first place? Have I done anything indicating that I want in your pants? Because I don't. Don't flatter yourself."

I hate that his words sting. I wish they didn't. They shouldn't. But they do.

"Number three," he continues, "if I wanted you—and that's a big *if*—all I'd have to do is ask, and you'd gladly give me your virginity. With zero protest."

"That's not true," I argue.

"Yes, it is," he hisses. He opens up our mini fridge and pulls out a bottle of water. "Here, drink this. All of it."

"No." I glare at him.

He can't just come in here and boss me around.

"As someone who drinks a fucking lot, I can tell you that you're going to feel like utter shit tomorrow if you don't drink that." He plops down on the futon.

With a sigh, I chug the water until it's gone. "There. Now, go."

"Lie down on your bed and close your eyes. Tell me if your head starts spinning."

"Why?"

"Because if it does, you need to go make yourself puke. I'm not leaving you here to choke on your vomit."

"Why do you even care? And I told you, I'm fine. I didn't drink that much."

I grab a pair of cotton shorts and a T-shirt from my drawer and lock myself in the bathroom. I take a long time, getting ready for bed. I start with a shower. The water feels good, and I happily wash the ick of the night off. I decide tonight is a perfect time to condition my hair, so I apply the deep-conditioning treatment that needs to soak on my hair for ten minutes. As I wait the allotted time, I shave and scrub every inch of skin. After the shower, I brush and floss. Getting through flossing only proves I'm not drunk, just tipsy. Leo's worry, or whatever that was, is misplaced. After filing my nails and applying lotion, I finally gain the courage to leave the bathroom. He'll definitely be gone.

I fully expect an empty room when I emerge from the bathroom, ready for bed. Instead, I find Leo still sitting on the futon.

"Why are you still here?" I hold back a whine. "I'm going to bed. I promise, I'm fine. Can you please go now?"

If Leo thinks I'm going to let him watch me sleep, he's delusional.

He doesn't argue though. He simply stands and walks toward the door.

"Wait," I call out before he opens it. I take a few steps toward him.

Yes, he's been throwing attitude and dirty looks my way since I first ran into him, but maybe I judged him too harshly. He did just walk me home and made sure I was okay, just as he'd promised Quinn he would.

"Thank you," I tell him sincerely.

He surprises me by taking a step toward me until we're separated by a fraction of space. His breath is warm against my skin. His scent—a combination of spice, sweetness, and intoxication—fills my lungs.

"For?" he says in a husky whisper, inching closer.

I swallow. "For getting me back safely and making sure I was okay. Maybe you're not such a bad guy after all."

He bends, closing the gap between my face and his. Stopping a breath away, he asks, "Maybe I'm not such a bad guy after all?"

My tongue peeks out of my mouth, licking my lips. As I feel his breath against the skin of my face and the warmth of his body so close, my heart picks up speed. I don't like him. Yes, he did something kind, but I don't want him. And yet I can't quiet the pounding of blood through my veins, heating my body as it rushes faster and faster.

Clamping my eyes shut, I pull in a deep breath in an attempt to steady my mind. My brain tells me to step back and instruct him to leave. Something else makes me stay put and keep quiet.

"Alma," Leo whispers my name. The sound from his lips is tantalizingly hot.

"Yeah?" The lone syllable comes out airy.

"Do you want me to kiss you?" His lips are so close now, hot and inviting, and I can almost feel them. Almost.

Do I want him to kiss me?

The truth is there under my tongue, but I'm too scared to set it free.

Leo cradles my face in his hands. "Open your eyes. Look at me." His demands are quiet and needy.

So, I do.

His deep blue eyes are so close and beautiful as they search mine. "Do you know what I thought when I first saw you in that restaurant today?"

I can't speak.

"I thought that you were the most beautiful, sexiest woman

I'd ever seen. Do you know that about yourself? Do you understand how insanely gorgeous you are?"

I'm having a hard time processing the words leaving his mouth and the sincerity in them. I shake my head.

I can't think.

He continues, "And then I find out that not only is your appearance perfection, but you're also smart and innocent and kind—well, at least to others." His lips tilt up in the smallest grin.

My chest hurts, and my body hums with want for this man standing before me. I feel like my insides are melting with burning need.

I can't move.

"Can I kiss you?" he asks.

This time, I find the courage to answer, "Yes." It's barely audible, but it's there.

His hands slide from my cheeks to my hair. He runs his fingers through my wet locks and grasps the strands as he pulls me closer. His tongue traces my lips, so soft. A whimper escapes my mouth, and I gasp, embarrassed of the sound. There isn't time to think on that, for the second my lips part, Leo enters.

I can't breathe.

My mouth moves against his, and I allow my tongue the freedom to dance with his. It's intimate and raw, warm and sweet, and hot and desperate, all at once. Standing on my tiptoes, I circle my arms around his neck and pull him closer. I need him closer.

I can't get enough.

The kiss is demanding, and I give it all I have. He sucks my bottom lip and catches my moans in his mouth. I could spend the rest of my days kissing Leo. My fingers caress the nape of his neck, and I push my body against his, knowing that if he asks, I'll give him everything.

Leo pulls away and drops his hands from my head. I ache at the loss.

"Was that your first kiss?" he asks.

I nod.

"I thought so." His voice is labored.

I take a step toward him, and he extends his arm, halting me. Rounding his shoulders, he stands tall. The air in the room changes, growing colder somehow. I cross my arms over my chest, confused.

This time, when Leo speaks, all desire is absent from his voice. "You see, Alma, I am such a bad guy after all. Stay the fuck away from me. If you see me on campus, turn and run the other way. Are we clear?"

I open my mouth to respond, but no words come, and I close it, pressing my lips together, willing myself not to cry —not yet.

Leo rolls his eyes with a shake of his head and turns to leave.

"Predictable." He chuckles dryly, and then he's gone.

CHAPTER 6

LEO

"*D*amn it." I thread my fingers around the nape of my neck and groan into the night sky. "What the fuck!"

An empty Mountain Dew can sits atop the pavement, and I kick it.

What was I thinking?

I've lost my ever-loving mind tonight. I would fucking destroy a girl as sweet as Alma.

I need to hit something. I need to hurt someone. I need to fuck someone.

I know what I need.

I meant what I said to her about being the most beautiful woman I'd ever seen. She is. God, she does something to me I can't explain. I would love to take her tight, little body and fuck her so hard.

Her ass.

That long brunette hair with auburn highlights, so thick and soft. Visions of waking up with it splayed across my chest come to mind, but I shake them off.

No.

Everything about Alma is perfection—from her flawless tan skin to her round doe eyes to the dimple on her right cheek. I knew from the second I saw her that I needed to hate her. It's the only option. It's the only way that works for her. A prick I might be, but I can't bring myself to ruin her, and I would. God, I would. It would be easy too.

I'm not sure what Alma's been through, but it's something. She has a different air about her than other girls. Her eyes hold determination and pride. I'm not going to break her for fun because it wouldn't be. For maybe the first time, I don't care about the challenge. Hell, not that I'd have much of one, given her eagerness tonight.

I don't know Alma enough to care about her, but I do. The warning bells that come along with that fact are louder than the rest. I can't develop feelings for her, and she definitely can't catch any feelings for me.

The party is still going strong when I return to the frat house.

"Hey, man. You okay?" my best friend—only real friend— Ethan asks when I get back.

"Yeah, just looking for someone," I answer.

"You sure?"

"I'm sure." I offer him my fist, and he pounds it.

"All right, man. Let me know if you need anything," he says as a drunk girl hiccups and wraps her arms around him.

He shrugs with a knowing smirk, and I shake my head.

"I'm going back to my place."

"Sounds good. See you later," he tells me before allowing the chick to lead him somewhere.

I make my way back to the room where we were playing

that idiotic drinking game before. Alma's roommate is way too giggly, and I spot Mike eyeing her.

"Hey." I get her attention.

"Hi," she says cheerfully.

"You and your friends need to leave."

"What?" She looks to me in question.

"You need to head back to the dorms. Grab your friends and go."

"Why? Is something wrong with Alma?"

She sounds legitimately concerned, and my suspicions are verified. She's not some whore like half the girls here. She's good, like Alma—which is why she needs to leave. I'm not leaving her here with vile creatures like Mike.

"Get the fuck out. Now." I raise my voice, staring her and her friends in the eyes.

"Jeez, okay," the girl next to Alma's roommate says. "Let's go, Quinn. I'm tired anyway."

"Okay, me too," she agrees.

Her eyes keep darting up to me, as if she's waiting for me to do something else. I could make a scene if I wanted. I excel at wreaking havoc, but as long as Quinn leaves, there will be no scene.

I face the back couch, and Sasha eyes me with a heated expression. She makes a show of licking her sucker, which I know is a drug-spiked lollipop. I close the distance between us.

I snatch the sucker from her hand and put it in my mouth. She pouts.

"I came back here to get you. Want to head to my place?"

Her mouth curves into a smile. "Yes, please."

"Let's go." I hand her sucker back and walk out with Sasha on my heels.

I live in a house across the street from the frat house. I could've stayed in one of the rooms at the fraternity, but it's not my style. I hang out there often because Ethan's there and girls like Sasha can always be found in abundance, but I need my own place.

I don't need the entire three thousand square feet of space the Victorian house my father bought and renovated for me has, but it is what it is. My house used to belong to a sorority years ago. Now renovated, it's a kick-ass bachelor pad I don't deserve.

"I'll meet you in my bedroom," I tell Sasha once we're inside the house.

"Okay," she agrees and flitters off.

In the kitchen, I open one of the drawers and retrieve a pill bottle, shaking out a couple of the white tablets into my hand. I toss them into my mouth and rinse them down with a swig of whiskey.

Sasha is naked and ready on my bed when I enter the room. This isn't her first rodeo.

CHAPTER 7

ALMA

I lie in bed, facing the wall for what seems like forever. The sun has been up for hours, but I have no reason to get out of bed yet. Quinn is still sleeping. I can hear her soft breathing. She stumbled in not too long after Leo left last night, but I pretended to be asleep. I didn't feel like talking.

I'm still so confused about last night and the kiss. For a minute, he was amazing and sweet, and then the next second, he was back to being an ass. If he's just a jerk, fine, but why did he have to kiss me and play mind games like that? How did I go from hating him as he glared at me before embarrassing me during the drinking game to wanting him to kiss me? And I did want it. Just as he'd told me I would.

It was just a kiss, and I can even rationalize it by telling myself that it didn't mean anything. I'm positive that's the case for Leo, but it was my first kiss, and I wasted it on someone like him.

His question made me feel ill.

"Was that your first kiss?"

Why did he ask me that? How did he know? Maybe I sucked. I wouldn't know if I did. I have nothing to compare it to. It'd be horrible if I turned out to be a pitiful kisser.

I can't believe my first kiss was given to such an ass.

Deciding I can't possibly lie here for another second, I quietly roll out of bed and make my way to the bathroom. I throw on some shorts and a T-shirt and brush my teeth.

Tomorrow, classes start.

That's why I'm here, I remind myself, not for some douche bag of a boy. I run a brush through my hair and pull it back into a ponytail before exiting the bathroom.

Quinn is sitting up in bed, her back against the wall. She's looking down, a grimace evident on her face.

"Good morning," I say.

"Do you have to yell?" she grumbles, looking up with a pained grin.

"That bad?" I shoot her a sympathetic smile.

"Worse."

Thankfully, I feel fine today. Quinn surely drank more after I left and probably didn't hydrate.

"I'm sorry. Can I get you anything? A water?" I offer.

"Yeah, I should probably drink some," she answers, and I snag a bottle of water from the fridge and hand it to her. "Can you get me some Tylenol? My head is pounding."

"Sure." I walk back to the bathroom and search through the cupboard for the Tylenol. Bringing back two pills, I drop them in her hand.

"How was your walk back with Leo?" she asks, and I freeze before reminding myself to chill.

"Eh, fine."

Call me a coward, but I don't want anyone to know about the kiss. It's just so humiliating.

"Did anything weird happen?" she questions.

I feign looking for something over by my dresser. "No. Why?"

"It's just … when he got back to the frat house, he was such a jerk. He seemed angry, and he yelled at me to leave."

"He yelled at you and made you leave?" I look at Quinn, my eyes wide.

"Yeah, it was strange." She takes a sip from the water bottle.

"Well, the impression I got is that he's a jerk. So, I wouldn't take it personally."

"You're right."

"How was the party after I left?"

"It was fun. I wish you could've stayed a little longer, but I had a good time with the girls."

"Good, I'm glad."

A knock sounds at the door, and I look to Quinn. "Are you expecting anyone?"

She shakes her head. "No."

My heart races as I step toward the door, and I'm ashamed to admit why. A familiar smile greets me.

"Amos?" I shriek, and I wrap my arms around his body, hugging him tight. His hands are full of various bags, so his hug is awkward. "What are you doing here?" I grin and take a step back.

The sight of my best friend fills my soul with a contentment that's been lacking since a broody boy's lips stole my kiss hours ago.

He raises the bags in his grasp. "I come bearing gifts, and I missed you."

"I missed you too," I say as I step to the side to allow him entrance. "What's in the bags?"

He steps inside and places the bags on my bed. "Well, my

roommate was telling me about this amazing Chinese restaurant by our campus. It got me thinking about the last time we ordered Chinese. You remember?"

"The day I got the letter from Eastern, saying everything would be covered for me for the next four years, and you surprised me with a picnic in the park with all of my favorite Chinese dishes? Yeah, I definitely remember." I grin like a fool.

That day will always be on the highlight reel as one of the best days of my life because, in that moment, I knew that I was free. On my own, I had made it. I would get a degree, be someone great, and make a difference in this world. All regrets that I'd had about my childhood no longer mattered because I knew that as soon as I stepped foot on this campus, life would be different. My journey would be on my terms, and my parents couldn't sabotage anything ever again. That letter was my golden ticket, and that picnic was the best celebration.

"I needed to see you." His voice is full of emotion. "We celebrated the future of this place together, and now, we need to celebrate your arrival in the same fashion."

"You're too good to me," I say.

"Where should we have this picnic?" he asks.

"Well, Quinn is feeling under the weather, and with her headache, the sun might push her over the edge."

"It's true." Quinn grins weakly.

"So, let's just have it here," I suggest.

"Works for me." Amos removes a blanket from one of the bags and fans it out on the floor between the two beds. He removes the white takeout containers and places them in the center of the blanket along with some plates and sets of plastic silverware.

"I have grape or red." He holds up two six-packs of Fanta pop.

"Ooh, grape, please," I say.

"I'll take a red," Quinn says and slides off of her bed onto the blanket.

Amos and I follow suit and sit cross-legged on the soft material across from Quinn. We start serving ourselves.

"So, how was your first night?" Amos asks.

"It was good. We went to a frat party," I tell him.

"You did?" He sounds surprised. Then, he looks to Quinn in understanding. "Ah, hence the pounding headache."

"Yes, exactly," she says.

"Did you drink?" he asks me. His tone isn't accusing, only curious.

"Some, not as much as Quinn," I tease. "The party was okay. There were lots of people and loud music. We played a drinking game, and I left early."

"You walked back by yourself?" he asks.

"No, a friend walked back with me." That is the loosest use of the word *friend* imaginable. "What did you do?"

"I went to Pinball Pete's, this cool vintage arcade place, with Matt and some other guys. Then, we ordered pizza. Pretty chill," he says.

"Oh, nice. So, Matt's getting better?"

"I think so. I don't know. The verdict is still out on him." Amos lets out a dry chuckle.

"Well, not everyone can have as cool of a roommate as me." I toss a piece of a crab rangoon in my mouth and wink at Quinn.

"I wasn't very cool last night. I drank too much and let you leave without me. And worse yet, I sent you home with the rudest guy on campus. I'll get better though." She grins.

"You went home with a guy last night?" Amos asks.

"No." I shake my head. "This guy at the party, Leo, heard that I wanted to go home. Quinn didn't want me to walk alone. So, he offered to escort me. He walked me back the three blocks and left. It wasn't a big deal."

"Just be careful. Not everyone's intentions are good," he warns.

"I know. It was fine. I promise," I reassure him because I know he worries about me.

The three of us chat about random stuff, and Quinn starts to come back to life with some food in her belly. Seeing Amos today is just what I needed. It reminds me of who I am and why I'm here.

Worrying about what some guy thought about a kiss isn't even on my scale of importance. By the time Amos leaves, I'm centered. I feel good and ready to start school tomorrow. As usual, Amos gave me a gift that I hadn't even known I needed.

CHAPTER 8

LEO

*A*bandoned buildings with shattered windows take up the eighty-two-inch TV screen. As I sit on the couch, elbows resting on my knees, my thumbs and index fingers push the buttons on my controller at a rapid speed.

"Okay, Leo, right there. We're making a run for it," Ethan yells.

My avatar follows his across the screen.

"Oh my God. Holy shit. Look at my health."

"Dude, I have no more fucking shields," I groan. "You know they're probably going to be waiting for us, right?"

"They know where we are," Ethan says.

Our avatars are hiding in a hollowed-out building.

"What are we going to do, just sit here? We could just hide out for five minutes to inevitably die," I say.

"Shit, dude. Don't you have class?" Ethan asks.

I spare a glance at my phone to see the time. "Yeah," I grumble.

Truth be told, I don't know if I'm going to be able to make it two more years until I get my business degree. Freshman and sophomore year almost killed me—or I should say, I almost killed myself—multiple times. My close calls can only be blamed on myself and my inability to make good choices.

My mother's voice—like a nagging, high-pitched parrot—rings in my ears. *"Make good choices. Make good choices."*

What does she know about good choices?

Fuck good choices.

In the history of my life, what has doing the right thing ever gotten me? More shit. Whether I do what I'm supposed to or the opposite of it, I'm constantly deflecting buckets full of shit. My existence is shit, and this whole *get your business degree* facade I have going here is a joke.

I have enough money in my trust fund to live comfortably for the rest of my life. I don't need my father to provide me with a career. I have zero passion to aid him in anything, let alone align with him in business. My father, retired heartthrob of an actor Victor Harding, decided purchasing a dozen local businesses—from restaurants to golf courses to manufacturing plants—was what he should be doing in retirement. Harding Enterprises is to be run by his two sons. One of whom is capable and one of whom is me.

This idea that my dad has of me getting a degree in business, so I can be COO of Harding Enterprises is idiotic. The COO job is mine whether I get a degree or not. Everyone knows that anything important is learned on the job anyway. My textbooks contain nothing that will be of any use down the line.

And who decided running a company is what I should be doing for a living? I'm the last person who should be in charge of anything of importance. Besides, Stephen—who would allow himself to be fucked up the ass with a shampoo bottle if it meant he'd earn an extra dollar on a deal—is doing just fine. Greedy fuck. As big of an asshole as Stephen is, he should be in charge of all of my dad's investments. Not me.

The one saving grace is that my dad allowed me to pick any college I wanted, so I chose Eastern since my one and only friend was here. Growing up with as much money as I did, it's hard to make real friendships. I should know since it's only happened once.

"I'm going to skip it," I tell Ethan, keeping my eyes on the large screen.

"Bro, it's the first damn week. You'll be skipping plenty soon enough. Go to class." He shuts off my Xbox console just as I was downing an enemy.

"Damn it!" I complain.

"Go to class," Ethan repeats.

"Fine." I shove my phone into my back pocket and throw my backpack over my shoulder. "Lock up on your way out."

"Always do," Ethan calls out as the front door slams behind me.

I pull up my schedule to remind myself what class I'm supposed to be heading toward. *Right, Econ.*

Then, I see her.

Fuck.

I stop moving, and I stare, taking her in.

She's sitting on the grass, her back against a tree and a book in her hand. It's not a textbook. It could be required reading for a Lit class, or she's one of those people who reads for plea-sure. I knew she was a nerd the second I laid eyes on her. A beautiful, innocent, boring, lame-ass nerd.

And yet I stay in place, incapable of movement as I watch. Her face carries so many expressions, and they change as she reads. What she's reading now must be humorous because her lips tilt up in a grin, and I can't turn away. She's stunning. I can read her face like a book. This one couldn't keep a secret to save her life, I'm sure of it. The way she wears her emotions so boldly for the world to see is something that I love about her.

Hold it. Back the fuck up. *Love* about her? Wrong word choice.

Let's try ... find intriguing about her.

On Saturday, she told me everything I needed to know without saying a word. I knew she was into me. It was clear she wanted to kiss me, and I was shocked when I saw the fact that my lips were the first to touch hers written all over her face.

Knowing that I'm the only person to wrap my tongue with hers and feel those soft lips against my own is a turn-on for sure. I wonder how many firsts she'd give me. Hell, I know she'd give them all to me. I'd be lying if I said I didn't want to take them from her, too, but I can't. As much as I'd enjoy it, I can't.

Innocence isn't something I take.

I'd break a girl like Alma. I might be an asshole, but I'm not cruel. Even someone like me has limits, and she is clearly mine.

Yet why can't I walk away? What is it about her that pulls me in with such intensity? Why am I still staring at her like a fucking creeper?

As if she can read my thoughts, she raises her gaze and captures me in it.

The sight of me standing here, staring, definitely startles her. Her breath hitches, but she doesn't look away, and I can see it on her face that she doesn't want to.

Interesting.

After the way I left things in her dorm room, she should be angry. My intention after all was to make her mad and hate me. She seems almost ... expectant.

I walk toward her.

Bad choice—here I go again.

As I close the space between us, she whips her face to each side, as if hoping to find someone next to her, someone else I'm walking toward. Though she knows exactly where I'm heading.

I stop a foot from her, and she tilts her face up to study mine.

"Hey," I grunt.

"Um, hi." She frowns.

"How's your first week going?" *What in the actual hell am I doing right now? Small talk?*

Her face hardens. "Why are you talking to me?"

And she has a backbone, ladies and gentlemen. Fuck, if that doesn't turn me on.

"Why wouldn't I?" is the best I can come up with.

She closes her novel and slides it into her backpack before standing up. She rounds her shoulders, her back straight. She can't be much over five feet two, so I'm still looking down on her.

" 'Stay the fuck away from me. If you see me on campus, turn and run the other way,' " she repeats the words I spoke to her after our kiss. "So, let me ask you again. Why are you talking to me?"

I shrug, my face unbothered. "Because I can."

"I gotta go," she says hastily before taking a quick step around me.

I grab her arm. "Wait."

She squints and glares at the spot where my fingers are wrapped around her arm.

I quickly release my grasp and hold my palms out in apology. "Sorry. Can you wait just a minute?"

"Why?" she snaps.

53

"Because ..." I pause to gather my thoughts. "I wanted to ask you if you've tried the world's best chili-cheese fries."

She raises an eyebrow. "What?"

I hitch my thumb in the direction of the main street that runs past campus. "There's this place, Coney Island, just a couple of blocks down, and my man, Luca, makes the best chili-cheese fries. So, I just think you should try them ... maybe now. With me."

"You want to go grab some food? Together?"

She seems confused, and I don't blame her. I have no idea what's going on.

"You have to eat, right?"

She looks toward the large brick building to the right that houses the campus cafeteria. "I was just going to grab something with my meal plan."

"Seriously, nothing in there will hold a candle to Luca's fries. It's my treat for being an asshole on Saturday and all other times to come."

"So, it's an apology for Saturday and future times when you'll be an ass?"

"Yeah."

"Why don't you just not be a dick?" she questions, holding back a smile.

My lips form a slight pucker. "I can't help it. It's what I do, but I'm admitting that what I said Saturday was wrong, and I'd like to apologize over a plate full of fries ... and who knows? Perhaps, we can be friends."

"Friends?"

"Yeah. Why not?"

"Okay," she answers quietly with a shake of her head, as if she can barely believe she's agreed to hang out with the guy who screamed at her a few nights ago.

I can't believe she's agreed to come with me either.

We've taken a few steps toward the road when regret starts

to surface. It's only a matter of time before it will scream within. This isn't a good idea, and I'm fully aware of that fact. However, I'm incapable of stopping it. I need to see her, to be by her.

Maybe I could do the friend thing with her.

As much as I want it, I know it's a lie.

CHAPTER 9

ALMA

*L*eo is silent as we walk toward the restaurant. There's a nervous energy encircling us. It's like we're surrounded by one of those glass plasma globes that you see at science museums. There are strands of electric currents shooting out from us in all directions, and everyone around us is immune to it. However, if I were to reach my arm out or step out of place, I'd be shocked with a volt of electricity that would bring me to my knees. I just know it.

"So, you were coming from class?" I ask an obvious question. *Smooth, Alma.*

He hesitates. "Uh, yeah, Econ."

I nod. "I was just reading. Nothing for school, just a romantic comedy. I'm done with classes for the day." Word vomit spills from my mouth, and I hate myself.

Leo doesn't respond.

We reach the diner, and he opens up the door. I step in, and a man greets us from behind the counter.

"Leo, my boy! My favorite customer!" the man shouts with a large grin.

"Please, old man. You say that to all the kids." Leo waves him off and takes a seat.

The gentleman places two red plastic cups of water down in front of us a second after we sit. He pulls two menus out from under his arm and sets them before us. "Just in case you want something different," he says to Leo. "This is the first time you've brought a lady friend."

"Stop being creepy, Luca, and just bring us two plates of chili-cheese fries and two Cokes." He hands his menu back to Luca with a small grin before turning his attention to me. "Do you want anything else or something else to drink?" He tilts his head toward each shoulder, stretching his neck. "I'm sorry. That was rude."

"No, fries and a Coke are fine." I give my menu back to Luca as well.

"You got it," Luca says before heading off.

"You come here a lot then?" I ask Leo.

He nods. "Yeah. Honestly, the food is great, and Luca's a good guy. He lost his wife and only son in a car accident my freshman year. It's sad. So, if you know any single middle-aged women, send them in. I think he's lonely."

Leo's words are so surprising. The conversation is almost normal and shows a side of him I never imagined.

"So, you're a matchmaker in your free time?"

"I have many talents." His words are suddenly deeper, and I take a quick drink of my water.

Luca comes back with our drinks and food. "Enjoy, friends."

"Thank you," I tell him as he retreats back behind the counter.

"So, each fry needs some chili, cheese, ranch, and ketchup." Leo loads up a French fry with all of the fixings on his fork and takes a bite.

"Ranch and ketchup too? Isn't the point of these fries the chili and cheese?" I eye him skeptically.

"No." He shakes his head. "Trust me, you need the ranch and ketchup."

"Okay." I load up my fork in the same manner as Leo and try a bite. "So good." I stifle a moan as a burst of flavor fills my mouth.

Leo full-on smiles, and it's a devastating event. Sullen Leo is the most handsome man I've ever seen, but happy Leo is more than my heart can take.

"I told you," he says with a modest shrug.

We chat about our majors. I tell Leo that I want to be a teacher, and he tells me that he's going to help his dad run all of his pet projects. It sounds like Mr. Harding buys businesses like some women buy shoes. He tells me that he chose Eastern because his best friend goes here, which makes sense. I'd have attended U of M to be with Amos if I could've afforded it. The meal is … normal—well, as normal as time spent with Leo Harding can be.

I can tell he's on his best behavior, and yet there's still an edge to him, a darkness that keeps parts of him hidden. I'm still not sure why I agreed to this in the first place.

Does Leo really want to be friends? More importantly, do I?

I eat as many fries as I can manage but have more than half the plate left when I'm finished. Leo cleans his plate.

"Do you want some of mine?" I grin.

"Nah, I'm good."

"You sure?" I shoot him a smirk.

"Hey, this is the first thing I've eaten all day. Stop judging."

"I'm not judging. I was just kidding. And it's six o'clock. Why haven't you eaten anything today?"

"Busy," is his only response.

He holds his wallet under the table and pulls out a bill. Folding it, he slips it under his plate. He was trying to be sneaky about it, but I caught sight of the hundred-dollar bill before it was concealed under the dish.

"Let's go," he says, standing abruptly from the table.

"Leo," Luca calls out when the bell above the door chimes as we open it.

"I'll see you tomorrow, old man," Leo says playfully as we exit.

On instinct, I walk in the direction of my dorm room. Leo doesn't offer much in the way of conversation. There were parts of this … *date* that were normal, fun even. Yet the moment's pregnant with silence with distinct reminders of the inherent awkwardness between the two of us. There's some connection between us—I can't deny that—but where does it go from here?

Leo follows me up the stairs of my dorm and to my door, a sickening sense of déjà vu present. I open the door to find the space empty. Quinn's probably at the dining hall for dinner.

I drop my backpack on the floor and turn to address Leo standing in the doorframe. "Thank you for dinner. I appreciate it, and apology accepted."

"What?" Leo lowers his gaze toward me.

"You said dinner was an apology for Saturday." Uncertainty fills my thoughts.

Leo pulls in a breath. "Right."

"So, I guess I'll see you around," I say softly.

"Yeah, okay," Leo answers and extends a hand toward my face before tucking a strand of hair behind my ear.

The movement is so foreign and intimate and out of place. Or maybe it's not out of place at all in this weird back and forth that Leo and I have going.

"Alma, I'm sorry." Leo takes a step toward me, and I retreat backward, the dorm door closing behind him.

I swallow. "I know. You said that. It's fine. Water under the bridge."

Leo closes the distance between us and takes my hands in his. "I'm sorry for taking your first kiss and then ending it that way. I'm not a good person, but that's not an excuse. You deserved better."

"It's ..." I start to say before Leo raises his finger to my lips.

He shakes his head. "It's not okay."

My heart thrums in my chest, a desperate, intoxicating rhythm. I'm finding it hard to inhale enough air. Leo's finger scalds my lips. They ache and demand more.

His hungry blue eyes speak to me, and I understand because they mirror my own.

The desire that I feel for Leo right now is visceral. It's all around me. It burns in my lungs with every breath I take. It pulses in my heart with each beat. It rolls around in my gut, where electric shocks pulse, shooting waves of lust to my groin. I feel dirty and wrong. Close to insanity. Wanting Leo's touch doesn't make sense, and my mind knows this, but my head is no longer in control. My body wants him, if only for a kiss. Damn the consequences.

My tongue peeks out of my mouth, and I lick the tip of Leo's finger. I want to hide in shame at the movement until Leo's eyes go wide, and his lips part, his breath heavy. A sense of power comes over me.

I flick my tongue against the pad of his finger again and suck. He releases a heady groan.

"Alma"—his voice is husky and raw—"you don't want to do that."

I bite the tip of his finger.

He rips his finger from my mouth and roughly cradles my face between his hands. He turns me around and walks us backward until I'm against the door before crashing his lips against mine. This kiss is different than before. It's needy. It's desperate. Just more. And I love it.

My lips move against Leo's like they've done it a thousand times. My tongue meets his stroke for stroke. His groans echo mine. He threads his fingers through my hair, and mine attempt to grab any part of him that will keep me on earth, for I'm floating away on a high like never before.

The firmness of Leo's need for me pushes against my stomach as his pelvis thrusts against me, riding on a wave of lust. I swallow his moan. Searing my skin with his touch, he splays his hand across my belly and pushes it under my shirt before cupping my breast.

I hiss, and a whimper escapes. The skin beneath his palm has never been touched by anyone before. He pulls my nipple between his fingers, and my body hums in pleasure.

Leo removes his lips from mine and takes the bottom hem of my shirt in his hands. "Can I?" he asks breathlessly.

I'm not sure what he's asking, but I nod. Whatever it is, the answer is yes.

He lifts my shirt and bra, and without warning, his tongue flickers against my puckered nipple. I shudder, and my entire body tingles as his hot, wet mouth circles and sucks with sweet abandon.

I cry out, my head hitting the door. Leo licks, kisses, and sucks my breasts until I'm so turned on that my body fills with molten lava. Then, he pulls away and drops my shirt. He leans his forehead against mine, and our breaths dance as our breathing calms.

"I alone have your kisses, and now, I've taken second base," his lips whisper against mine before he steps back.

Grabbing my hand, he pulls me from the door and opens it wide enough to step out.

The door closes behind him, and he's gone, leaving me alone in my room, wondering, *What in the hell just happened?*

CHAPTER 10

ALMA

*T*he next two days dragged by. I found myself scanning my surroundings every time I was on campus, hoping to see Leo.

I haven't heard from him since he left my room after Coney Island. There's a part of me that's happy he didn't go storming off after kissing me, telling me to leave him the fuck alone. There's another part of me that's wondering where to go from here.

We never exchanged numbers, so I'm not surprised he hasn't called, but he obviously knows where I live. I'm trying not to be upset that he hasn't stopped by, but I've never done any of this before. I'm guessing to guys like Leo, second base isn't that special but just a casual boob-sucking.

"Ugh!" I groan into my pillow.

Truth is, he doesn't owe me anything. We didn't say a word

about commitment or even dating. We kissed and then … *God, was that hot.*

What is wrong with me?

I should be happy that Leo hasn't called. Clearly, I can't resist the guy, and it's evident that he's not dating material.

Chalk it up to completing the first week of college with some new experiences.

As far as how the first week of college went, I love my classes and my professors. Quinn and I get along so well. I chat with Amos every night, and he's happy and doing well too. I got to experience my first kiss, and bruised ego aside, I do have that.

Quinn comes out of the bathroom. A towel is wrapped around her hair, and a cloud of hot steam follows behind her.

"Were you talking to yourself out here?" she asks.

"No."

"I thought I heard you yell or something. Anyway, I just got a text from the girls, and there's another party tonight." She presses her lips together and smiles, her big green eyes opening wide.

I simply grunt in disapproval.

"Come on. Last time wasn't that bad. Tonight, you'll know even more people, and it will be a little easier. You have all weekend to do your homework, though I'm pretty sure it's all done anyway."

"You know it's not my scene," I reply.

"What do you mean? You did great last time. Plus, it's no one's scene until it is."

"I don't feel like drinking," I say.

"Then, don't drink, and I promise to drink less so that I'm not a total downer tomorrow."

I sigh, "Okay, fine."

"What?" Quinn laughs. "That was easy. I thought you'd put up more of a fight."

"I just figured you'd win anyway, so I should save my energy for tonight." I grin.

"Good call. I would win anyway." Quinn giggles. "All right. Now, to decide what we're going to wear!"

It's true that Quinn can talk anyone into anything. She's extremely persuasive. It's part of her charm. Though I can't pretend like a certain sulky hottie didn't weigh on my decision. It'd probably be best if I didn't run into him tonight, but I'm hoping I do.

* * *

"Do you think this is what every weekend will be like?" I ask Quinn as we approach the large frat house.

We're seriously entering the same scene as last weekend. Clusters of people are congregated on the lawn, drinking. There are some smaller groups on the porch, smoking. A bunch of guys stand before us, cheering raucously. Couples are scattered throughout, making out. It feels identical to last week.

"I don't know. I bet less people will be outside once winter comes," she adds.

"Ooh, what a change. Can't wait," I kid.

"You're feisty today." She chuckles.

"I feel feisty. Maybe I will have a couple of drinks."

"That's the spirit!" Quinn approves.

I let Quinn talk me into wearing one of her short black tube dresses while she opted for a hot-pink pleather one. The black dress is stretchy and clings to every curve. Quinn says we look hot, but it feels strange. Especially now that guys on the lawn are checking us out as we walk by.

We head to the kitchen first for drinks and then to the game room, where the group of people we hung out with last week are sitting around, minus one. Leo's nowhere to be found, and I can't pretend I'm not bummed. I wanted to see him. As stupid as that makes me, I wanted to. The extra bit of makeup I wore, this dress, and my curled hair were in part for him. Pathetic, I know.

I actually put forth effort to get to know some of the people we're hanging with. Since my roommate is a social butterfly, I either need to up my game and come out of my shell a bit or spend many weekend nights in our room, alone.

The conversation goes from college football to what bands are coming to Detroit this fall and who wants to go to what concert. There's chatter about rush coming up, which is where all of the fraternities and sororities host potential recruits over a week of activities and decide which among the interested they deem acceptable to receive an invitation to join their group. Quinn and the girls rank the sororities in order of interest based on what they've heard about them so far. I use the time during this particular conversation to count my teeth with my tongue.

Gabby gets my attention. "What sororities are in your top three?" she asks me.

Tilting my head to the side, I answer, "You know, I don't think sorority life is for me. I'm going to pass on that one."

"No," Gabby and Bethany groan in unison.

"Don't worry," Quinn says to them. "I'll get her to change her mind."

I laugh. "You're persuasive, Quinn, but even you have your limits. You can tell me all about it though, and I'll be there in spirit." I tap her leg before turning to the guy on the other side of me. "Where's the bathroom?" I ask him.

"The cleanest one is upstairs to the left. There is one by the kitchen, but I wouldn't use that one if I were you." He scrunches up his face.

"Okay." I chuckle. "Thanks for looking out."

I tell Quinn I'll be right back and snake my way around the people dancing until I find the steps leading upstairs.

"On the left," I repeat his directions to myself as I get to the top of the steps.

There are a dozen wooden doors lining the hallway to the left.

Great.

Approaching the first door, I knock, and when I don't hear anything, I try to open it. It's locked.

Okay, next.

I rap my fist against the second door and listen. I can't hear anything, except the thumping bass from downstairs. I turn the handle, and the door opens wide.

It's not a bathroom, and it's not empty.

I gasp, bringing my hands to my mouth. Leo is sitting on a sofa against the far wall of the room. A girl is kneeling on the floor before him, her blonde head bobbing up and down against his crotch. Leo looks to me and squints his eyes, as if he's bringing me into focus. A lazy smile spreads across his face, and I shake my head, stunned. Quickly, I take a step back and close the door.

Seconds pass, and I'm frozen to this spot, my hand clinging to the metal doorknob. I try to make sense of what I just witnessed, and as it becomes clearer, my panic increases.

Finally, I pull my hand from the doorknob and hold it to my chest as if it burned me.

I have to get out of here.

My bottom lip begins to tremble, and I know that the tears aren't far behind. Retreating toward the steps, I race down them as fast as I can without falling on my face. I push past the drunk dancers in the living room of the house and dart toward the front door.

Once outside, I stumble on my shoe before yanking them

off. Sandals in hand, I run back toward the dorm. The quicker I put space between Leo and me, the better.

I hate him. The thought comes to me as my tears finally break free.

Hot streams of betrayal fall down my cheeks as I sprint up the steps to the second floor and down the hall to my room.

As the solid door closes behind me, I sink to the floor and allow my sobs to come. It's stupid. I'm stupid. Of course he's the type of guy to get random blow jobs at parties. Of course he's the guy who sucks on a girl's breasts and moves on as if it meant nothing because to him it didn't mean anything. Of course he appeared charming at Coney Island, only to morph back into a womanizing player later. None of this surprises me in the slightest, and yet my heart aches.

I don't understand why I feel so broken. I've always been so strong. I've had an impenetrable wall around my heart my entire life. The only person who's been allowed in is Amos. It's easy to avoid heartache when the world is locked out.

Leo kissed me twice, and I opened the steel gates wide, optimistic that the moments we'd shared meant something. To me, it did.

I'm a hopeless romantic and a fool. *What did I think this was? A romance novel? Bad boy meets innocent girl and falls in love? Soul mates, butterflies, and a happily ever after?*

Yeah, I hate Leo, but in this moment, I think I hate myself more because he's never pretended to be a good person. I'm the idiot who hoped he was.

CHAPTER 11

ALMA

*A*fter my tears cease, I make my way to the bathroom and step into the scalding shower. I allow the hot water to wash away the makeup, the curls and hair products, and mainly the shame. I've never been one of those girls who wanted to save all of my firsts until marriage, but I suppose I always thought that those moments, when they happened, would mean something.

Clean and dressed, I respond to Quinn's frantic texts and let her know that I'm home safely and tell her to have a good time. Next, I call Amos. He picks up on the second ring.

"Hey, Mutt. How are you?" he greets me cheerfully.

"I'm okay. I'm good," I add the last thought quickly so as not to worry Amos, but he knows me too well.

"What happened?" he asks, his voice concerned.

"Nothing. Something," I stumble on my words. "I'm fine. It's nothing. I don't know."

Do I want to tell Amos about everything that's happened over the past week? True, I usually tell him everything, but we've never really chatted about this type of stuff. Then again, neither of us has had this type of stuff to chat about.

"I'm just having a bad night, and I wanted to hear your voice," I tell him.

"I'm coming over," he says.

"No," I protest. "You have that paper due Monday."

"It's fine. I have the rest of the weekend to work on it. I'll be there in thirty."

Amos hangs up, and I lie in bed, waiting for him to get here. Life was simpler when my hormones were in check. And starting now, they are. Everyone says that college is where you truly figure out who you are, so I try to give myself some grace. It's impossible to find oneself without some snags along the way.

I listen to my latest song obsession on repeat until Amos's knock sounds at the door. Springing out of bed, I run to open it. It's barely open before I throw my arms around Amos's back and hug him tight.

"I missed you," I say into his chest.

"I missed you too. And I come bearing gifts."

I know it's something sweet. My parents don't have many scruples, but they are surprisingly strict on the food that they allow in their house. LSD is fine, but processed sugar is criminal. Nothing says comfort food like a kale and quinoa salad, which is why Amos became my official sugar dealer. Every sip of pop or bite of chocolate was supplied by him.

I steeple my hands in front of my face expectantly. "Can't wait." I grin.

He reaches into the paper bag at his side and pulls out some chocolate-covered raisins, a king-sized Twix, gummy bears, and ...

"You found the sharks!" I exclaim.

The gummy sharks are blue with white bottoms. Truthfully, they aren't better-tasting than any other gummy candy. We just never seem to be able to find them in the stores. So, the occasions that we get our hands on them is cause for celebration.

"I know. I was pumped when I saw them."

"Where did you find them?" I ask.

"Just a little convenience store on campus."

"Sweet." I open the bag of sharks first and plop down on my bed.

Amos sits beside me. "So, you ready to talk?"

"Yeah," I sigh.

Then, I tell him everything—the parties, the kisses, the attraction, the date, and the blow job. I hold no information back. As I speak, I'm taken aback by how easily the information comes out. At first, I was ashamed, but the more I share, the more I want to share. Telling someone I trust all about my regrets over the past week makes me feel lighter, as if now, I don't have to carry the burden on my own.

Amos listens and doesn't interrupt. He's always been the best listener. When I've finally finished telling him every detail, he takes my pinkie in his.

"First of all, you did nothing wrong. You have absolutely nothing to feel bad about. But I need you to promise me that you'll steer clear of this guy. He's bad news, Alma. A good guy doesn't treat others like that."

"I know," I agree.

"I'm glad you told me. You know you can share anything with me—always. I'm on your side, no matter what." His smallest finger squeezes mine.

"I know that too," I say as the dorm door opens, and Quinn walks in.

"Hey! It's A-squared." She laughs, tossing her purse onto the floor.

Ann Arbor, the city that houses the University of Michigan, where Amos lives, is often referred to as A-squared by the college students.

"You know ... Amos and Alma—two *a*'s," she explains with a hiccup.

I smile. "You should drink some water," I tell her.

She points her finger at me. "Good idea."

"Did you have fun?" I ask.

She grabs a bottle of water from the refrigerator. "Besides the part where I was freaking out because I thought my roommate was abducted?" She disapprovingly waves her pointer finger in the air.

"I'm sorry. Next time, I'll tell you I'm leaving, okay?"

"You'd better. It was not fun, worrying. I gotta pee." She hurries to the bathroom.

Amos chuckles beside me.

"Can you stay?" I ask him.

"Of course."

Quinn returns from the bathroom. "You know what would be really good right now? Taco Bell! Oh my goodness, I would marry someone for some Taco Bell."

"We can get Taco Bell tomorrow," I tell her. "You should finish that bottle of water."

She gives me a thumbs-up. "Good idea. You're so smart."

"Hey, Quinn. You don't mind if Amos sleeps over, do you?"

Her lips tilt into a grin. "Of course not. A-squared is always welcome," she says as she plops onto her mattress.

"You've been roommate approved," I whisper to Amos.

"That's if she remembers tomorrow." He says.

"True."

Amos gets up and turns off the lights before sliding in behind me. He wraps his arm around my middle and pulls me in tight.

I feel safe and loved ... and happy. Sleep comes quickly.

* * *

AMOS HANDS me the big Taco Bell bag and a package of gummy worms.

"Tacos and gummy worms! You're the best," I wrap my arms around his body, and hug him tight. Amos understands my love for all gummy candy. But there's something about the sugary worms that I'm obsessed over. He thinks I'm silly but I swear they taste better than the bears. "Are you sure you can't stay and hang today?"

"I wish I could, but I do have that paper to write," he says with a sigh.

"I know. I've kept you long enough. Maybe we can hang out next weekend?" I offer.

"I hope so." He grabs my pinkie in his, and we kiss our fists in our good-bye ritual. "Bye, Quinn," he says.

"Bye! Thank you!" She waves from her bed before he closes the door behind him.

I turn to face Quinn and hold up the bag. "Hangover food at your service."

She grins and claps her hands. "At least I feel better than last week. I think the water helped."

I hand her a burrito, and she opens it before applying several packets of Mild sauce.

Rolling her burrito up, she takes a big bite. Her eyes roll back. "I could live off of this stuff," she moans.

"Same," I agree as I take a bite of my bean burrito.

"Amos is a keeper, I tell ya. Why aren't you two together?" she asks.

Her question startles me.

"What do you mean?"

"Like, have you thought about dating him before? And if not, why? He's the perfect man."

I think on it. "Honestly, no. I've never looked at him like

that. I know he's beautiful, smart, and kind. I mean, he's clearly a catch. Maybe I've felt attracted to him a few times in my life, but he's too important to me. Relationships mess things up. Amos is the only constant in my life. He's all I have. I could never risk doing anything that would jeopardize our friendship. Love is a gamble, and Amos is the one thing I'd never bet on losing." Just talking about it makes my heart ache. "Plus, he's like my brother. I don't see him like that. He doesn't see me like that either."

"I get it." Quinn nods. "So, you wouldn't be jealous if he had a girlfriend?"

"No, I'd be happy for him."

"What if his girlfriend were me?" She raises an eyebrow, and I almost choke on my mouthful of burrito.

I swallow. "Is there something I should know?"

She shrugs. "No, not yet. I figured you were secretly pining for him, but if you're serious that you're not, I might go after him."

I grin. "I'm serious. There's nothing going on between us. If you want to put the moves on him, go for it. Just promise me it won't be awkward between us if he doesn't reciprocate." I don't see him falling for Quinn, but I can't tell her that and hurt her feelings.

"Oh, of course not. If he's not into me, that's cool, but I don't see that happening," she says with confidence.

"Someone's a little cocky," I tease.

"I know what I have to offer."

"He'd be lucky to have you. Anyone would."

We each hold our water bottles up in an air cheers.

"So," Quinn says with a wag of her eyebrows, "let's talk rush week."

I throw my head back and laugh. "Oh gosh ... let's not."

CHAPTER 12

LEO

*S*he comes to me in my dreams, and it makes me feel like a giant pussy, but I secretly love it. It's been a month since I last saw her. An entire thirty days has passed since my mouth was on her.

Her lips. Her moans. Her tits.

My cock stands at attention.

Damn it.

I promised myself I'd start going to classes again today. Grabbing my phone, I check the clock, fist my hand around my dick, and close my eyes. In the darkness, she's there—her small frame, curvy hips, and juicy ass. She looks to me with those round russet eyes of hers, framed by long lashes and so full of emotion. Her full lips make an appearance too. I could kiss, lick, and suck them all day.

I jump into the shower and then throw on some clothes. I

haven't gone to classes in four weeks. My brother, Stephen, sent me over a "doctor's note" for my professors, letting them know I had a severe case of mono and needed to stay in bed for a month.

I've "come down with mono" at least twice a year since starting college. Usually, the professors waive the work I missed while I was "sick." I've been spiraling out of control this past month. It's a pattern with me.

I can be okay for a while, and then I'm not. There's a constant hole in my chest, void of all the things I can never have—respect, happiness, love. When life throws something my way to remind me who I am, I self-medicate and escape. I'm fucked up for weeks straight. I'm an equal opportunity addict. There isn't a substance I haven't abused. I have very little recollection of the past month other than my dreams of her.

Though I have to admit that she just might be my trigger. With her, I want more, but that will never be my reality. The weight of that is a hard pill to swallow. I am who I am. A beautiful girl isn't going to change that.

I grab a muffin and an energy drink on the way out. I have no idea why there are muffins in my house. God knows I didn't go shopping. It was either Ethan or my mother—probably both. I'd be dead without Ethan—that much is true.

I only have two classes today, and I'm glad.

Business Statistics is first, and the professor calls me up after class. "Mr. Harding, I'm sorry to hear that you've been ill. Are you doing better?"

"Getting better every day. Little by little," I say in a pathetic voice, one that I've mastered for this exact situation.

"Good, I'm glad. I just wanted you to know that I've waived all of the assignments we had over the past month. You have enough to focus on with getting healthy. If you can, just complete the assignments from here on out."

"Absolutely. Thank you so much," I tell the professor and walk out.

English Composition is next, and this professor, a woman —Professor Gilbert—is a real bitch. I didn't miss this class in the least. She, too, calls me up after class.

"Mr. Harding, so glad to see you up and around. I wanted you to know that you have exactly a month to make up all of the work that you missed over your little break."

"But—" I start to protest.

"Your fake mono note might fool everyone else, but you're not fooling me. I've looked into your records and spoken to your previous professors. I know this is a pattern with you, and I'm not buying it. You will make up everything you missed within a month, or I'll fail you. Furthermore, I've signed you up for tutoring. You'll have a minimum of twenty hours of tutoring to help make up for the class time that you missed." Her voice is cold and firm.

"You can't require that," I hiss.

"Oh, yes, I can. It's the least I can do. I know your type. You think the rules bend and change around you. Well, that's not the way the world works, Mr. Harding. If you want something in this life, you have to work for it. If you'd rather not retake this class with me next term, you'll have to show me that you know how to do the work." She stacks up a pile of papers on the desk and slides them into her leather briefcase. "Any questions?" Her voice is perky, and her lips press into a tight smile.

She's gloating. She knows she has me by the balls, and there isn't a single thing I can do about it.

"No," I grumble.

The urge to fight her on this is strong, but she's right. She can prove that I'm a screwup and make this a lot worse for me.

"Great," she says a little too cheerily, extending her hand with a paper in her grasp toward me.

I grab it from her.

"I looked at your schedule, and I took the liberty to sign you up for your tutoring sessions. The first one starts in an hour. The tutoring offices are located on the second floor of the library. You'll see the room number for your first session. Work hard and good luck."

With that, she walks out, and I flip her off as she exits.

What a bitch.

I weigh my options. Telling this broad to fuck off and dropping her class sound appealing. I could always take another English class next semester. However, there's a big chance that if I do that, she'll inform the rest of my professors and possibly the school that my doctor's note is fake. If all of my professors make me catch up on a month's worth of work, it will be tough. Plus, if the school looks into years past and discovers that I do this every semester, there could be repercussions. Could they take two years of credits away? I don't know. I have less than two years of school left. I need to finish and move on with my life.

I can manage twenty hours of tutoring. I've been through worse.

Before my scheduled hour, I grab some coffee from the commons and then make my way toward the library on foot. It's the building that's the farthest out from the central part of campus. I could drive, but the walk gives me time to let go of some of my anger with Professor Gilbert, myself, and life in general.

With ten minutes to spare, I reach the library and take the steps to the second floor. *Room 204 A*, the paper reads. I scan the plaques beside each office door for their numbers. I contain my annoyance and open the door.

What. The. Fuck?

Alma is sitting at the lone table in the room, reading a book. When she hears me enter, she looks up, and her smile breaks. Her eyes go wide, and her lips part.

"What are you ..." she asks quietly.

"I'm meeting a tutor here."

She shyly raises her hand. "A tutor."

"What?" I snap.

"I'm a tutor here. It's my job. This is my tutoring office—204 A. Are you scheduled to be here? Now?"

"No, I'm just strolling through the library, opening doors for the fucking fun of it," I bark, immediately regretting my tone.

She shakes her head and pushes back from the table, standing. "I don't think this is a good idea. You should sign up with someone else."

I look down to the paper in my hand and see that every session is in this room. I toss the paper toward Alma. It falls to the table, and she picks it up.

"Are those all you?"

Her eyes move across the paper. "Yeah," she sighs.

I drop my backpack on the table with a groan and drag my fingers through my hair. "Just great."

"There are other tutors," she explains. "We can find someone else who fits in your schedule."

I think of Professor Gilbert and know I don't have a choice. "Listen, this isn't my idea of fun either, but I have this professor up my ass, and if I screw up these sessions, she's going to fail me. Maybe you could just sign the paper saying I was here for all the slots, and we'll call it good."

"I can't do that. It's unethical. I could lose my job if anyone found out, and I need it."

I fall into one of the chairs. "Fine. Teach me. Whatever."

"Um ..." Alma sits back down across from me. "What class are you in here for?"

"English."

She releases a breath of air, seeming relieved. "Oh, good. I love that subject. I was afraid you were in here for Business or

Econ or something. I mean, I would've made it work, but they aren't my favorite," she says rapidly.

I suppress a smile. I love how she talks fast when she's nervous.

Stop. No. Not doing this again.

Remember your month-long binge because of this chick? No. Not going there—ever.

She's not worth it.

Hell, she is. I know she is.

It's me who's not.

CHAPTER 13

ALMA

"You look cute," I tell my roommate, who's sporting a colorful jogging suit and pigtails. "Where are you off to?"

She's been so busy with sorority activities that between our class schedule, my tutoring job, and her social life, I barely see her.

She leans toward the mirror and puts on some hot-pink lipstick. I could never pull off such a bold color, but on Quinn, it just looks adorable.

"Our new pledge class is painting the kiosk, and then we're going to play flag football against the other sorority pledges," she tells me with a smack of her lips.

"That sounds fun."

"Yeah, I'm excited. You're off to tutor Hottie McIssues?"

About a month ago, I ended up telling her all about Leo. I figured if I wanted Quinn and me to be true friends, then I needed to open up to her about real things. Plus, I wanted her to understand why I planned on avoiding the frat parties.

Quinn hasn't been hanging out at the frat house either with all of her sorority activities and social events.

After talking with Quinn and Amos about Leo, I knew I had to just forget about him, and I did for the most part. My homework and project load kicked up a notch the second week of school, and I had little time to worry about what Leo was doing. Turns out, eighteen credit hours is a lot of work. I was hired by the university as a tutor about a month ago. I needed some spending money, and I enjoy it. I've been so busy that I've only seen Amos once. We text daily and talk on the phone every few days, but I still miss him.

I promised myself that any free time I had was going to be spent on people who mattered, those who loved me. I'd be lying if I said I didn't secretly hope to run into Leo on campus just to get a glimpse of his beautiful face. I don't want or need him, but I still crave him. I just pretend I don't.

I look to Quinn and sigh, "Yeah … his appointment is in thirty minutes."

"Well, be strong and don't put up with any of his shit," she says with a huff.

"I won't," I promise.

Two days ago, after he plopped down at the table and agreed to allow me to tutor him, he didn't say another word until the end. The entire hour was spent with me talking to him about his assignments, him typing up what we discussed, and him staring at me like I smelled. His face was twisted into this weird grimace the whole time.

I still haven't figured that one out, though there's a lot that I can't figure out about Leo Harding.

Before walking out at the end of the hour, he looked over his shoulder and said, "See you Wednesday," and that was the extent of his communication.

"See you Wednesday."

And, now, it's Wednesday, and I have to meet him at the library. I really don't want to, but I kind of do.

Quinn and I walk out of our dorm together. Once outside, I tell her to have fun.

"You too but not too much." She shoots me a wink, and then she's skipping toward the kiosk.

I hitch up the straps on my backpack and start toward the library.

"Where are you heading?" a familiar voice asks with a hint of a smile. He walks in step beside me.

"The library," I answer, not wanting to play his games.

"What a coincidence. Me too," Leo says, much more cheerful than he was on Monday.

I detest charismatic Leo. It's hard to hate that guy when he turns on the charm.

I look straight ahead as Leo keeps pace next to me. I'm going to my office. We're going to talk about English for an hour, and then I'm leaving. I'm not getting involved in the weird hot and cold that Leo's such a fan of.

"I'm sorry," he says suddenly, and it catches me off guard.

"For?"

"For leaving your room after kissing you and never contacting you again. Know that it has nothing to do with you. I have issues."

That's what he's sorry for?

"Yeah, okay …" Disapproval weighs heavily on my words. "It doesn't matter. It was two kisses. You don't owe me anything. We're good. I'm just surprised that's what you're apologizing for."

"What do you want me to apologize for?" he asks.

"Nothing. It doesn't matter."

"I'm getting the impression that it does. You're being very huffy."

"I am not."

"Ooo-kay," he drawls out. "Just tell me what it is that you want an apology for. We have nineteen more hours together. Wouldn't it be better if we didn't have this animosity between us?"

"There's no animosity. And you don't owe me anything. The entire student body could give you head, and it wouldn't be my business. You do you, Leo."

"What are you talking about?" he replies gruffly.

I can't stop myself. "Was it uncomfortable for me to see that girl giving you a blow job? Sure, of course it was. But that's not your problem. I'm the one who walked into the wrong room. It's not like you meant for me to see it, not like it would matter, considering we're nothing."

"Wait." Leo grabs my arm and stops walking. He steps in front of me, and his expression seems pained. "You saw a girl sucking me off? When?"

"At the frat party the weekend after ... you know"—I look down—"we kissed."

"No," he says more to himself than me.

"You know I did. You looked right at me," I snap.

"Alma, I'm sorry. I ..." He raises his arm, his hand cradling the back of his neck. "I don't remember that."

"What do you mean, you don't remember?"

"I was fucked up. I don't remember most things from when I'm wasted. I am sorry that you saw that. I never wanted you to." His beautiful blues look upset, and I find myself believing him.

"It's fine. Whatever, right?"

"Yeah," he answers softly, and we continue walking toward the library.

Once inside the study room, Leo pulls out his binder and laptop, and we work on one of his assignments.

"You have a lot of missing assignments," I note.

"Well, I missed a lot of school."

I want to ask him why, but it's not my business. *What Leo does in his free time isn't my concern.* I repeat that thought over and over in my mind.

"How's your first month of school been? Are you liking Eastern?" Leo asks, and I snap my head toward him, raising an eyebrow.

Who is he trying to be? Sure, the questions are normal enough if they came from anyone else's mouth, but coming from Leo, they seem odd, forced.

"What's going on? I don't understand this back and forth. You're interested in me, and then you're not. You warn me away from you, and then you're kissing me. You're sweet, and then you're short with me. Now, you're asking generic questions about my time at Eastern like you're some distant family member inquiring about college life. You give me whiplash, and I can't do this with you anymore. I'm not cut out for this." I motion my hand between us. "I can't be friends or anything else. I'm going to work with you on your English assignments, and that's all."

"You're right," he simply agrees and directs his attention back to the laptop.

His two-worded response bothers me. I pretend that I don't want him to fight back, to say something—anything—that would make sense. I pretend that I wanted him to agree with me. I pretend that everything in me doesn't want to reach out and grab his hand, just to feel his skin. I pretend because admitting the truth would be a betrayal of who I am and who I want to be.

I close my eyes and breathe in through my nose in an attempt to calm my nerves.

Leo's typing stops.

"What are you doing?" he asks me, his voice hoarse.

I snap my eyes open. "What?"

"Why are your eyes closed?"

"I was just thinking. It's nothing." I wave my hand in front of me.

Leo's face falls, and it causes my chest to ache. He looks at the time on his phone and packs up.

He stands to leave, and I follow suit. He grabs ahold of the door handle but doesn't turn it. Instead, he drops his hand and spins to face me.

"Do you feel this connection between us?" he asks.

"No," I lie.

"Well, I do, and I hate it—not because of you, but because of me. You see, Alma, even if I wanted to, I can't be with you. Can't ... do anything. You're off-limits. Because I see you. Maybe you don't believe me, but I do. You're kind and good and smart and beautiful. I'm none of those things. In fact, someone like me would ruin those things in you. I would destroy you, Alma. I wouldn't want to, but I would. And that's why, no matter how many times I see you in my dreams, I can't run to you when I wake because I'd hurt you."

He presses his lips into a line and pulls in a breath through his nose. I simply stand across from him, silent. I can't find words to say in response. I'm at a loss.

"I'm finding it difficult to be around you. When I'm my typical asshole self, I end up feeling bad for treating you that way. Though, when I try the friends route and you gift me with a smile, I want you even more, and that shit hurts. Being around you hurts, Alma, and I don't know how to make the pain stop." He flattens his palm against his chest.

The rawness in his words resonates down to my soul.

"Leo." His name is a whisper.

His hand leaves his chest, and he presses his finger against my lips.

He drops his hand. "I'm sorry," he utters quietly before turning and walking out.

CHAPTER 14

ALMA

The lines of trees beyond the cut pastures are vibrant with beauty. The ever-changing colors of autumn are my favorite. The sun shines bright in the pristine blue sky. Today is perfection. Warm and windy, it's one of the days that Mother Nature gifts us Michiganders to keep us here. She's smart, that one.

I stare out the passenger car window, dreading what's to come. I'm spending one of our rare perfect days at the place I hate the most—home. I won't exactly be in my family's house for long but Amos's. But those walls hold little love too.

It's Amos's mother's birthday, and his father insisted he drive back for her birthday dinner. Amos asked if I'd accompany him, and of course, I couldn't say no.

Catching myself wondering what Leo is up to on a day like this, I attempt to force his gorgeous face out of my mind.

It doesn't matter what he's up to.

I'm hoping that, eventually, I'll be able to have a thought that he doesn't interrupt. I've seen Leo a total of six more times over the past few weeks at our twice-a-week tutoring sessions. Since his declaration of—well, I'm not sure of what exactly, but since his beautiful and broken words, it's been okay. We meet at the office, we keep our talk strictly about his schoolwork, and we leave.

Easy.

All right, it's anything but easy, but it's doable. I only have to make it through twelve more hours of sessions.

"You're quiet today," Amos says as he takes the exit off of the highway leading home.

"Just tired." It isn't a total lie.

"Yeah, me too. You told your parents that you're going to be home today?" he asks.

"I texted them. No response." I'm honestly not surprised. Technology isn't my parents' thing. Their cell phones aren't charged half the time.

"I guess they'll be home, or they won't."

"Yeah."

Amos's knuckles bend as he grasps the steering wheel tight. He squeezes the hard plastic in a revving motion, and I know he's getting nervous as we approach our street.

"As for dinner, we're going to eat and leave," he tells me.

"Absolutely," I reassure him. "You know what? If your dad crosses the line, we're going to get up and leave right then. You don't have to be his punching bag anymore. You owe him nothing."

"He's paying for my college," Amos adds quietly.

I sigh, "Yeah, that's true. But still … he can't just say hurtful things to you anymore."

My words carry no weight though. Amos isn't going to risk getting cut off when he's only two months into his college career.

We pull into his driveway, and he puts the car in park and turns it off. I reach my left pinkie toward him, and he wraps his right pinkie around mine.

"We'll be fine." I give him a reassuring smile.

"I know. We will." He nods once before exiting the car.

I grab the gift bag and bouquet of flowers in the backseat and shut the door. I spare a glance across the driveway to my house, and it looks just as forgotten as the girl who left it. The exterior has been untouched since we inherited it from my grandparents. The landscaping is withered, and the weed-choked grass needs a cut. My parents couldn't care less about curb appeal, and it shows. I fight the urge to grab the mower from the garage, but it's not my problem anymore.

"Do you want to say hi to your parents now or later?"

"Later."

A sweet aroma hits us as we step into Amos's home. His mother is a talented cook, and my stomach growls on instinct. At least the visit won't be all bad.

"Baby." His mother comes into the hallway, wearing a white apron.

"Happy birthday, Mom," Amos says, extending his hand to give her a gift bag.

She smiles and hugs him. "I've missed you." She clings to Amos, and in this moment, my heart breaks for her.

Mrs. Davis is a good person. She's always been kind to me, but she's never stood up for Amos. And as I watch her hold onto Amos as if her life depends on it, I realize that she's a victim too. Now, she's trapped here with her husband, alone.

She opens her eyes and smiles at me. She extends a hand in my direction. I clasp her hand in mine, and she squeezes gently. Finally, she releases Amos and puts his present on the small table in the hall.

"Happy birthday," I tell her and give her the bouquet of gerbera daisies—her favorite flower.

"Thank you, Alma." She takes the flowers. "Thank you for coming, both of you. Let's go put these in some water."

She starts for the kitchen, and Amos and I follow.

"It smells so good," I tell her.

"I made all of Amos's favorites. Barbeque ribs, brisket, mac and cheese, greens, and corn bread. Then, for dessert, I made coconut cake."

"Sounds great, Ma," Amos says.

"Amos," Mr. Davis's voice booms.

We both turn to face his dad, standing in the entrance to the kitchen.

"Dad," Amos says, his voice void of emotion.

"I see you brought the hippie," Mr. Davis grumbles.

Amos starts to step forward, but I grab his hand, pulling him back.

"Good afternoon, Mr. Davis," I offer in greeting.

Eat and get out of here, I repeat our objective in my mind.

It doesn't matter what Mr. Davis thinks of me. Fact is, I don't think highly of him either. He's never physically harmed Amos or Mrs. Davis that I know of, but his verbal and emotional abuse is hard to take. I recall once, after a particularly brutal tongue-lashing from Mr. Davis, Mrs. Davis told Amos that his father's dad was worse and that Mr. Davis said what he said because he wanted Amos to be the best, to be successful and strong.

The thing is that Amos is all of those things, not because of his father, but despite him.

We sit down to eat, and I take a bite of Mrs. Davis's mac and cheese. I have to stop myself from groaning aloud. She once told me that the secret to making anything delicious is to double the butter in all recipes. I thought she was kidding, but now, I'm not so sure.

"You look like shit," Mr. Davis says to Amos. "You haven't been confusing your priorities, have you?"

"No, I haven't," Amos answers.

"What are your grades?"

"All *As*," Amos says.

"They'd better be," Mr. Davis grunts, looking like he wants to say more.

I realize, as he stews over his plate with a grimace, he doesn't know what to harp on Amos about anymore. Insults have been slung at Amos in the name of his future throughout his entire childhood. However, now, Amos is exactly where his father always wanted him to be.

"You'd better not screw it up," Mr. Davis snaps.

"I won't," Amos replies.

"You still need to get accepted into the business school."

Amos nods. "That's the plan."

Mr. Davis glowers. "Don't embarrass me. Remember what's important and don't fuck it up."

I take a large gulp of my sweet tea to stop my mouth from saying something that will make it worse for Amos. Maybe, someday, someone will tell Mr. Davis where to shove it.

"Shall we do cake? We should do cake." Mrs. Davis jumps up from the table and hastily begins to clear the plates.

After cake, Mr. Davis leaves the dining room, and we let out a collective exhale.

"We should go, Mom," Amos tells her.

"So soon?" she protests, her lips sinking into a frown.

"I'm sorry. I wish I could stay and visit with you, but we have to get over to see Alma's parents and then get back. We have classes tomorrow," he explains.

"I know you do, and I'm proud of you. I just miss you," she says.

"Call me this week when Dad's out, and we can chat freely. Okay?" Amos takes his mother's hands in his.

"Yeah." She nods and wraps her arms around his middle. "I love you, son."

"I love you, Mom."

I thank Mrs. Davis for a delicious dinner, and Amos and I bolt for the front door. Once the door is closed behind us and we're standing on the porch, we both sigh.

"One down, one to go." I grin.

"Yeah, let's get this over with." He entwines my pinkie with his, and we cross the driveway to my childhood home.

I knock on the front door, but there's no response. I open it and walk in. A wave of stench smacks me right in the face, and I step back with a shudder. The smell is overwhelming—a combination of smoke and garbage.

I kick the cardboard boxes to the side. My parents have always been slobs, which is why I'm borderline OCD about a clean environment.

"Lee-Anne?" I call my mother's name. She's never allowed me to call her mom. *"Vati? Papa?"* I call out for my father. He's always had me address him in his native German.

The house is quiet.

"Lee-Anne? Vati?" I call out again.

No response.

In the kitchen, there are plates of half-eaten food on the counter, and the garbage can is overflowing. Drug paraphernalia are scattered about. I continue past the kitchen, and that's when I spot them.

"Ew," I gasp and cover my mouth as I turn toward Amos.

He wraps his arms around me to shield me from the view.

I only saw them for a second, but the image of my naked parents passed out on the couch is seared into my brain forever.

"Let's go," Amos says as I keep my head buried in his chest. He leads me out of the house.

Once we're clear of the horrors of my home, I open my eyes and inhale a breath, grateful for air that doesn't coat my lungs with bile.

"Let's get the fuck out of this town." Amos pulls me toward the car.

"God, yes," I groan in agreement.

I can't say I'm surprised. It only ever resembled a home because of me. My parents have always cared more about epic highs and fuckfests more than they care about me. At least when I was living there, they attempted to keep their activities to the second floor of the house. Now that I'm gone, I guess every inch of that place is fair game.

Amos pulls out of his driveway and heads east, toward my new home because, let's face it, I'd rather live in that small dorm room for the rest of my life than ever call my parents' house home again.

"Do you think they're worse?" I ask Amos.

"It's hard to tell," he says. "Maybe they are, or maybe they've always been that bad, and they tried to shield you from some of it."

"That's a sobering thought." I let out a dry chuckle. "I don't want to come back here."

"I don't blame you. Maybe, someday, they'll get their act together, and you can have something resembling a relationship with them. But if they don't … you'll be okay. You're not alone."

"I know," I respond.

I've never been alone. Amos has made sure of it. I don't need countless people to love me to be okay. I just need one. As long as I have one, I'll be fine.

CHAPTER 15

ALMA

$\mathcal{A}$mos pulls up to the dorm. "With midterms coming up, I won't be able to hang out for a while," he says.

"I know. I'm busy too. We'll chat soon," I say as we lean toward the middle in our good-bye ritual.

"You're okay, right?" Amos asks as I pull the handle on the door.

I turn back with a reassuring grin. "I am. You?"

"Always," he replies. "Love you."

"Love you." I step out and shut the car door. I watch Amos's taillights disappear around the corner.

"Hey."

His deep timbre startles me, and I release a yelp, holding my hands to my chest.

"Oh my God, Leo. You scared me."

"I'm sorry." He attempts to hide a smile.

I playfully roll my eyes. "I see that."

"What are you up to?" he asks.

"Nothing. I went home for the day. I just got back."

"How was that?" he inquires.

"Not worth talking about," I respond before saying, "What are you doing? Why are we … talking like this?" I'm not trying to be rude, but this kind of normal conversation isn't us.

Leo ignores my question and instead asks, "Are you dating that guy?"

It takes me a second to understand what he's asking. "Amos? No, he's my best friend from home. Would it matter if I were?"

"Maybe." He shrugs.

"Well, it shouldn't."

"I suppose you're right."

He's taken a step closer to me now. I can smell the cologne or body wash he used, and it's intoxicating.

"I'm going inside," I tell him in a rush, eager to get some space between the two of us.

"Wait," he blurts out. "I really need your help with something school-related."

"What?" I quirk up an eyebrow.

"A paper that's due tomorrow."

"You need help with an assignment. Right now?" I ask slowly.

"Yes, please. It's really important. I didn't know who else to ask."

He seems sincere, but I'm having a difficult time with trusting him. I am his tutor, not that I'm required to make Sunday evening house calls. Though the thought of hanging out with him is intriguing.

"Okay," I say.

"Really? Okay, great. Do you need to grab anything, or should we just go?" He points behind him.

"Let's just go."

I walk in step beside Leo as we get farther away from the dorms. I should be scared, going anywhere with him since he's a loose cannon, but I'm not.

"Did you have a good weekend?" I ask to fill the silence.

"I guess. I just hung out at home and played video games with Ethan."

Leo turns onto a street with several restaurants. He slows in front of an ice cream shop.

"What are we doing?" I ask.

"It's one of the few warm days we have left this fall. I figured we should stop for some ice cream." He walks toward the ordering window.

"This isn't a date, Leo," I hiss under my breath.

"I know. What would you like?"

I roll my eyes. "A scoop of mint chocolate chip in a cone."

"Waffle or cake?"

"Waffle." I pucker my lips.

"Good choice." He winks.

"We'll have two large mint chocolate chip in waffle cones," he tells the girl taking our order.

He pays and then hands me the cone.

"This is huge, Leo. I said, one scoop. I'll never be able to finish this."

"Eat what you want, and then I'll finish the rest." He says, taking a bite of his ice cream.

I walk alongside him. "Please tell me you've eaten something today."

He chuckles. "Yes, I've eaten today, but there's always room for ice cream."

We stroll down the side streets of Ypsilanti until we're across from the fraternity house.

"You live at the frat house?"

"No, I live here." He veers toward a huge Victorian house

that sits on the corner across the street from the fraternity house.

I follow him up onto his porch. "Who do you live with?"

"No one," he replies.

"This whole house is yours? It's huge."

He opens the front door, and I step in.

"Your cone is huge. My house is huge. Seems to be a theme. Maybe I'll show you something else that's huge a little later." He quirks up an eyebrow.

"That'd better not be a joke about your ..." I halt my sentence. "Homework. Show me your homework," I instruct abruptly, reminding myself why I'm here.

I adore charming Leo, but I'm not getting sucked in this time.

I hand him the rest of my ice cream cone. I can't eat another bite. "I'm stuffed," I say.

He takes it from me, walks over to the island in the kitchen, tosses it into the sink, and turns on the garbage disposal.

I do a slow turn around the room, taking it all in. It's like something out of a magazine. The whole first level has an open floor plan. One can see across the living room and past the kitchen to the dining room on the other side. Contemporary artwork adorns the light-gray-blue walls, creating a kaleido-scope of colors reflecting on the shiny wood floor, and a leather sofa faces a flat TV screen so grand that it could pass as another wall.

"That TV is ..."

"Huge." Leo grins, handing me a bottle of water.

"I can't believe you live here. I've never seen such a beau-tiful home, and you're what ... twenty?"

"Just turned twenty-one actually."

"When?" I ask.

"Yesterday," he states.

"Oh my goodness. Happy birthday! And you just sat around, playing video games? Did you have a party or see your family or anything?"

Leo sits on the couch, and I follow suit, sitting a few feet away.

"Nah. I hate when people make a big deal about things like that—at least when it pertains to me. Honestly, I despise most people, so being forced to hang out with them would be the worst birthday gift ever. I hate parties."

I shake my head. "I know that's not true. I've seen you in action at a couple of parties."

"I said, I hate parties. I never said I hate getting fucked up. There's a difference." He takes a sip from his water bottle before screwing the cap back on and setting it on a slate-gray end table in front of us.

"Oh, right."

Our conversation from weeks ago surfaces, and I remember when he told me that he was so messed up that he didn't remember seeing me walk in on the girl giving him a blow job. Suddenly, my ice cream isn't sitting very well.

"I didn't get wasted yesterday," he tells me. "In fact, it's been a while. I'm trying to be better."

"Why?" I ask because I need to know.

"There's something I want more than a high, and I don't think she's a fan of illicit substances."

I swallow, finding it hard to breathe. *Why is he doing this?*

"We really should get to your assignment." My voice quivers, and I swallow a gulp of water.

Leo scoots toward me on the couch. "Tell me what you want me to do." His voice drops an octave, making him sound hoarse and sexy.

"What?" My voice cracks.

"Tell me what you want because, Alma, I can't go on like

97

this. I have you every time I close my eyes. You're there in my mind, and it feels so good. Yet, when I open my eyes to face reality, you're gone, and we're in this weird limbo, where all we can talk about is commas and other fucking punctuation. I want you. Period. I don't give a shit where the apostrophe goes."

I squirm in place, suppressing a smile. "Apostrophes are important." I raise my gaze, chancing a glance at his beautiful face.

He takes my hand in his and runs his thumb over my palm. "Alma," he pleads, and I have this intense, immediate need for him.

"I don't know." I look down.

With one finger, he lifts my chin to meet his eyes, and his intoxicating gaze traps me, like it does every time. He closes the gap between us and crashes his lips with mine. He kisses me, and I kiss him back. It's no longer a question. I want—no, I *need* to kiss him. I blame it on the hormones and need running through me, but I want to lose myself to him in every possible way. His lips send me spiraling into a haze of lust and desire.

He boxes me in with his arms, and his lips continue their sweet assault. He kisses me thoroughly until my entire existence is nothing but want.

He moves his palm beneath my shirt, and I squirm at his touch, his hands hot and searing. I want him to brand me so that he never forgets that I am his and he is mine. That's what this has all been leading up to. We both know it. We can't say we didn't try to stay apart, but the pull between us is too strong.

He works to unbutton my pants before pulling down the zipper of my jeans. I breathe heavily as his fingers drag across the skin above my panties.

His nose nuzzles against my ear before he whispers, "Tell me to stop."

I ignore his command.

"Alma, tell me to stop." His voice is almost pained as one of his fingers dips beneath the elastic of my cotton underwear. He gathers my need for him and teasingly glides his finger over my opening.

"No," I whimper, my hands clinging to his sides.

A guttural sound leaves his throat, and he kisses my neck as his finger enters me. My hips push up against his hand on instinct, and I moan into the lust-filled air.

"Leo," I cry out as his fingers work faster.

"Say it again," he pleads.

"Leo." His name is a breathless plea for more.

I ache for a release I've never felt but one I know he can give me.

He removes his hand, and I groan in protest.

"I want to taste you," he declares, his dark gaze on me. He rips my jeans and panties off in one fluid motion, and he slams his face between my legs, flicking my clit with his tongue.

I release a cry as his hands grasp my thighs, and his tongue works its magic.

"Yes! Oh my God, Leo," I yell, frantic for him to keep doing what he's doing because a warmth, a sensation is building in my core, tickling its way through my entire body. It aches but so good.

I run my fingers through his hair and hold his head tight to me. He growls against my sensitive skin, almost primal. My hips rock as heated chills shoot through my limbs. Releasing a half-sob, I cry out as I'm assaulted with enormous jolts of pleasure.

Leo licks until my body stops shaking. I open my fingers, freeing my grip on his head, and my arms fall to my sides, heavy. He kisses up my body and lies beside me, circling his arm around my stomach.

"Stay with me tonight," he implores, his words almost desperate. "Just to sleep. Please."

"Leo ..." I hesitate with a sigh.

"Please?" he asks. His breath pebbles my skin. He kisses my neck.

"Okay," I agree.

Leo climbs off of the couch and hands me my panties. I sit up and put them on, leaving my jeans on the floor. He swoops me into his arms and carries me upstairs. I rest my head against his chest, the rhythm of his heart beating a gentle stroke against my cheek.

He sets me on the bed and removes everything but his boxers. "I have extra T-shirts if you want," he offers.

"Okay." I nod.

He removes a black T-shirt from one of his drawers and hands it to me. I quickly remove my bra and top and throw his shirt over my head. It falls to my thighs.

"I have an extra toothbrush too." His words are timid, and I get the sense that he thinks I'm going to bolt at any minute.

I should run and fast, but I don't want to. I search deep within myself to find that voice that will steer me in the right direction, but I'm met with only acceptance. My truth is simple: I want to stay here with Leo.

Leo's in the master bathroom, leaning over the sink, brushing his teeth. The muscles of his back are mesmerizing, and I force myself to look away. He hands me a new toothbrush, and I squeeze the toothpaste on the bristles and bring it to my mouth.

He watches me in the mirror with a shy smile. I grin back.

After brushing my teeth and using the bathroom, I shoot Quinn a text to let her know that I won't be back tonight before I climb into his king-size bed. He gets in after me and moves toward me until his front is pressed against my back.

Wrapping his strong arm around my waist, he draws me in tight against him. He cradles me, our bodies a perfect fit.

I'm comfortable, warm, and sated, and sleep finds me fast.

Just as my dreams are pulling me under, his voice, full of sorrow, whispers, "I'm sorry," into my hair.

CHAPTER 16

LEO

$\mathcal{W}$hen I wake, she's gone, but the smell of her still lingers on my sheets—a reminder that she was here. Last night proves I'm a bigger asshole than I thought I was. I'm going to taint her innocence with my bad intentions.

I've been a semi-functional human being for three weeks. Why do I think that's sufficient enough to pursue someone good, like Alma, when I've lived twenty-one years of being straight wrong? I'm weak. My father made sure I knew that at a young age. I'm not strong enough to walk away, not from her. So, I've convinced myself that I can be better—for Alma.

Maybe I can hold my shit at bay for a while, but it will creep back up. It always does. The level of baggage that someone like me brings to the table will drown her and beat her down until she breaks.

Yet I'm selfish. I'm an asshole, and I want her. Scratch that. I need her. I don't understand why she has such a strong hold on me, but I'm positive I can't walk away now. Not anymore.

Grabbing my phone from the end table, I check the time. *Shit.* I'm going to be late for my first class. Old me would've said, *Fuck it,* but new, phony me knows it's better to show up late than not at all.

I have several classes to get through, and then I'll see her at tutoring. I wish I could see her now, but I'm positive she's already in her class.

* * *

As I GET CLOSER to Alma's tutoring office, I wipe my palms against the front of my jeans. I'm nervous as hell to see her. *What if she's come to her senses? More importantly, why am I a weak-ass whiner when it comes to Alma, and why am I not bothered by that fact?*

I turn the handle and step in. Alma's already here. She stands from the table as I close the door behind me. She's nervous too. I don't blame her. She never knows what she's getting with me. Angry? Jaded? Aloof? Kind? Charming? I treat her differently every time I see her, but that ends now. After last night, I decided that if she wants me, then I'm going to pursue her because I'm a selfish fuck.

I drop my backpack on the floor and step toward her. "You were gone this morning."

"I had class." Her voice shakes.

"I had a great time last night." I cup her face in my hands.

She releases a breath, relieved. "Me too."

Bending down, I pull her face to mine and kiss her. She splays her hands against my abdomen and leans into the kiss. I pull away and place a kiss on the tip of her nose. A small smile forms, lighting up her brown eyes. With the sun shining in through the long windows of the office, I can see tiny flecks of gold scattered within her irises.

"We really should exchange cell phone numbers," I say, dropping my hands from her face. "I wanted to text you all day."

"Yeah, it'd be helpful," she agrees, more upbeat than she was moments ago.

We swap phones and type in our numbers.

Pulling up her name, I type, *I miss you*, and hit Send.

Her phone buzzes, and she reads the text, a wide smile crossing her face. "I'm right here."

"I know, but I miss your lips."

She playfully smacks me. "Later. We should probably do some work. I am getting paid to help you after all."

"Later?" I tease, quirking an eyebrow.

"Maybe, if you're lucky. Now, get out your work. Focus."

I do as commanded and let Alma help me on an assignment. To be fair, she pretty much does the work, and I stare at her. Have I mentioned she's the most beautiful woman I've ever seen?

"I think we've done enough. Let's go back to my place and order dinner," I suggest, tossing my laptop into my backpack.

She chews on the inside of her lip. "I don't know."

"What are you afraid of?" I ask her.

She chuckles dryly. "Honestly? You."

I nod. "That's fair. How about this? We'll order some dinner, chat, hang out a little, and if you want to go back to the dorm, then you go. No pressure."

"If I want to go back?" She eyes me in question.

I opt for the truth. "I slept great with you there with me. If you wanted to stay the night, we could just sleep again. I promise not to hit it home."

She looks to me, confused, and I explain, "I'm just saying, I've rounded first, second, and third, but I won't hit a home run until you want me to." When her eyes bulge out and her cheeks turn red, I throw out, "If you ever want me to."

"Just go." She motions toward the door. "I'll do dinner. That's all I'm committing to right now."

We leave the library together.

"What do you feel like eating?"

"I've really been craving Thai lately."

I search for a local Thai place on my phone. "Perfect because I know the best Thai place."

"You seem to know all the best places to eat."

"Well, when you do nothing but eat out for two and a half years straight, you learn," I say.

"I can cook for you sometime," she offers.

I tilt my face down to see her. "You can cook?"

She grunts, "Yeah. Growing up, if I didn't cook, I didn't eat. So, I learned quickly." I wait, hoping she continues, and she does. "Taking care of a child didn't come naturally for my parents. So, I pretty much raised myself. I figured out right from wrong by watching what my parents did and then choosing to do the opposite."

This little peek into Alma's childhood throws me off. I assumed someone as put together and, well, perfect as she is must have had amazing parents. She's even more impressive to me now.

"Tell me something else about your childhood," I urge.

"There's not much to say. It wasn't great. My parents and I aren't close. I spent my childhood working my ass off to get out of there. The only person who truly loved me is my best friend, Amos. He's the guy you saw dropping me off yesterday."

"I'm sorry. That kind of sucks," I tell her.

"Eh, it is what it is. Others have it worse."

"Yeah, I suppose they do."

We walk past the frat house and cross the street. I unlock my front door and stand aside, inviting Alma in.

We drop our backpacks, and I order the food.

She takes a seat on the couch, and I plop down beside her.

"Come here." I pull her head into my lap. "Tell me more. I want to know all about you."

"What do you want to know?" she asks as I run my fingers through her long hair.

"How'd you meet Amos?"

Her face lights up as she talks about her next-door neighbor. There are mud pies, cookies, and mutts involved. Gummy sharks and secret meetups are mentioned. I listen and continue to play with her hair. I much prefer this conversation to the one about her parents. The way that she talks about Amos, I can only be grateful that she has him. She deserves to be loved, and I'm glad she found such a great friend. Her bond with Amos is like mine with Ethan, though admittedly, she and Amos seem closer. Ethan and I don't have special pet names and handshakes with each other because ... well, mainly, because we're dudes. Girls are always extra like that.

"Why do you want to be a teacher?" I ask.

"To make a difference. I want to be a mentor to kids who might not have support at home. I had Amos, and thankfully, I can learn easily. But what about the kids who don't have anyone and have learning challenges? What are their options? Everyone deserves someone to cheer them on in life. I can be that for them, you know? Plus, I really do just love learning and teaching. Education is fun for me."

"You're an odd one, Alma."

"That I am. You think you can handle me?"

"I'm going to try." I grin down at her. "Did you know that *Alma* means soul in Spanish?"

She nods. "Yeah, my mom's parents were from Venezuela. She speaks Spanish."

"Really? What's your whole name?"

"Almalee Hannelda Weber."

I choke on a laugh and cover my mouth. "Almalee Hannelda? Man, that's a mouthful. Your parents really did hate you, didn't they?" I kid.

"I told you." She shrugs and then goes into the story of her name, which is fascinating.

I like the idea her parents had of combining names, and even though her name is different, it fits her perfectly. She's unlike any woman I've ever met, and she should have a unique name.

"It fits you, your name," I say. "You could never be an Emma, Olivia, Ava, or Sophia."

"Why? I could pull off a Sophia"

"Nah, they're too common, and you're anything but." I tuck a strand of her hair behind her ear.

She blushes and changes the subject. "Enough about me. What's your story? Start with this house. No one your age has a house like this."

"My dad bought it for me."

"Pretty nice dad," she says.

"He's anything but. He's a horrible person. Money doesn't mean you're good, and it definitely doesn't mean you're happy." My tone is harsher than I intended.

"I'm sorry. I didn't mean—"

I cut her off, "It's fine, Alma. It's just that my dad is one of the worst humans alive, and my mom and brother are right behind him. I'm not close with my family either. But that's the difference between us. Where you used your adversity to make you a better person, mine gave me an excuse to be worse."

Now, I get it. I am the darkness that lurks in the shadows, and she is the light. My shadow of a soul can only exist where there is light. Without her, I'll keep slipping into the blackness until I can't find my way out. Alma, with her soul of goodness, is my one chance at anything resembling happiness, and I know that I'm selfish enough to take it.

CHAPTER 17

ALMA

The scream jolts me awake, and I fling off the blankets in a panic as I gather my bearings.

His voice is pained as he cries, "Please, no! Please, stop! Stop! No!"

His agony is visceral, and tears well in my eyes at its sound.

Leo.

I spin in bed to face him. "Leo." I grab ahold of his shoulders and shake him. "Leo, you're dreaming. Wake up."

His body is rigid, petrified as he whimpers, still trapped in the nightmare playing in his head.

"Leo!" I scream, desperate to free him from the demons.

He gasps and bolts up into a seated position. His chest heaves as his vicious breathing calms.

"Alma?" he murmurs, confused.

"I'm here," I reassure him, bringing my palm to his cheek. He leans into my touch. "It was just a nightmare. It's okay."

"Alma?" he utters my name again.

"It's me. I'm here." I pull his head against me and brush my fingers through his sweaty strands.

"Please don't leave me," he implores, terror saturating his words.

"I'm not. I'm right here." I kiss his forehead. "Shh," I whisper. "I'm not going anywhere."

He lies back down against his pillow. "I need you," he sighs before sleep pulls him under.

I scoot in next to him and wrap my arm around him. My fingertips drag lightly against the skin of his forearm, and I listen to his deep breaths.

What has this beautiful man been through?

My heart shudders as I think about what kind of trauma would cause that level of pain. The raw hurt that radiated through his cries was evidence of his torment.

I'm unable to fall back asleep, so I lie here. Listening. Thinking.

The past couple of days have been great. Leo's been normal and kind. I can't help but get my hopes up that things could be real between us. It's clear that we're drawn toward one another. The crazy attraction we have is palpable, a tether between us that keeps us connected. I don't understand it, but it's there. I feel it every time I think of him.

Last night, we sat at his table and did homework together, like a regular college couple would do. He was true to his word that he wouldn't pressure me to do anything sexually. We kissed and cuddled and kept our clothes on. As much as I love when he touches me, I need to know that we're more than that. The second that Leo's hands and mouth are on me, I can't think straight, and I question if what I'm feeling is real or simply lust.

I want to be with Leo. Perhaps it's a bad call, given our history, but I can't deny that I do. I need to trust that he's in it, truly in it with me. I need stability, and I'm terrified of falling in too deep with Leo because he seems to thrive off of chaos.

My phone buzzes on the nightstand, and I hurriedly reach over to turn it off. Leo grumbles behind me, waking up.

"Morning." He nuzzles into my hair.

"Morning. Sorry, I didn't mean to wake you," I say.

"It's fine. I have class too. How'd you sleep?" There's no hint of the fear from his nightmares in his voice.

"Good. You?"

"Great, because you're here," he answers, his arms wrapping me into a hug.

Tilting my body back so I'm facing him, I ask, "What are we doing here? I mean, obviously, this is all new to me. I just need to know where we stand."

I hold my breath, waiting for his response.

"You want to have the talk now?" He chuckles.

I shrug. "Yeah, or soon."

I get the feeling that while this is my first experience with something resembling a relationship, it's Leo's first experience as well. While he's more seasoned in other areas, I think he's new to the whole dating thing. That thought both elates and frightens me. Maybe he's not cut out for monogamy, which would suck because my heart couldn't take anything but fidelity.

"Are you worried?" he asks.

"A little bit," I admit. "I'm not cut out for casual hook-ups, Leo. I need to know where you stand before I get in too deep."

He kisses my forehead. "How about this? You are the only girl these lips will touch." He peppers kisses down my cheek to my neck. "You are the only girl these fingers will touch," he breathes against my ear as his hand glides into my panties.

Two fingers enter me, and my body hums as he pushes them in and out. He presses his thumb against my bundle of nerves as his fingers continue their movements, making me feel things I can't even explain. I claw at his arm as the sensation in me builds.

"Leo," I pant.

He nibbles on my earlobe. "Yeah, baby?" His husky whisper is warm against my neck, causing a torrent of goose bumps to erupt across my skin.

My hips greedily rock into his hand.

"Oh, you're so responsive, Alma. You and I are going to have so much fun."

My breath hitches, and I cry out as my body convulses.

Leo kisses my face, neck, and collarbone as I come down from the incredible high he just gave me. He shuffles under the sheet and removes his boxers.

"Now, my hands will own you." He kisses my palm. "And your hands will own me." He moves back the sheet and leads my hand onto his length.

I gasp, staring at my grasp on him. He's soft and silky against my palm, and touching him there is fascinating. My heart beats wildly against the walls of my chest.

"I don't know what to do," I admit weakly.

He lets loose a seductive grin. "Just move, baby." His voice is hoarse.

I strengthen my grip on him and pump my hand up and down. Leo's eyes roll back, and his tongue peeks out to lick his lips before he pulls his bottom lip in between his teeth. I work my hand faster, encouraged by his body's reaction to my touch. His leg muscles flex, and his breathing goes ragged.

Without opening his eyes, he slips a hand under my nightshirt. Cupping my breast in his palm, he groans and pushes his pelvis up into my hand. I squeeze harder and pump faster. I moan as he pinches my nipple between his thumb and forefinger. The feel of his hand on my breast and the sight of his body coming undone are intoxicating, and pulses shoot up between my legs, as if I might come again just from this experience alone.

"Alma." My name leaves his lips as hot white liquid covers my hand.

I don't stop moving until he drops his hand from my breast with a sigh of pleasure.

His gaze, happy and sated, captures mine. He cradles my face between his hands and pulls me toward him until our lips meet. "That was so good, baby," he says between kisses. "Promise me all of your firsts. I want them all."

"Okay." I kiss him.

"Promise me." He pulls my lip, and I moan into his mouth.

"I promise."

His lips press against mine one more time. "Let's get cleaned up."

"I really need to run back to the dorm and take a shower before class," I say.

"Take one here. I'll take it with you." He quirks an eyebrow.

"I don't think I'm ready for that." I force a laugh.

Our wet bodies, completely naked? Yeah, I'm definitely not ready for that.

"All right, fine." He kisses the top of my head. "You shower here, and I'll grab a shower in one of the other bathrooms."

"Okay," I agree.

Leo leaves me alone in the master bathroom, and I struggle to shower quickly because this is the most incredible shower I've ever experienced. It's like my own personal massage.

After I've showered, I throw on my clothes from yesterday and look at the time. If I hurry, I can make it back to my dorm for a clean change of clothes and still get to class in time. If these sleepovers become a regular occurrence, I need to think about leaving some clothes here.

Leo is in the bedroom, showered and dressed, when I exit the bathroom.

"You ready?" he asks with a tilt of his lips.

"Yeah. I have to stop at my dorm on the way to change my clothes."

We retrieve our backpacks from the living room and head out.

"How about I grab us some coffee and breakfast while you go change? I'll meet you at your dorm and walk you to class."

"Okay." I smile like a fool, so happy.

"Do you want a muffin? Egg burrito? Breakfast sandwich?" he asks.

"I'll do a scrambled egg and veggie burrito," I say.

"Great. See you in a minute." Leo hurries off toward the diner, and I walk toward the dorms.

Quinn is still sleeping when I get back, so I quietly change in the bathroom.

"Hey. Where were you last night?" she asks, half-asleep from her bed when I exit the bathroom.

"I have a lot to tell you." I grin as a soft knock raps against the door. "I'll fill you in later."

She stretches her hands over her head. "Sounds juicy. Can't wait."

I open the door to see Leo standing there.

"Ready?" he asks, handing me an insulated to-go cup of coffee.

"Yes," I say, closing the dorm door behind me.

We're quiet as we walk to my first class while we each take bites of our breakfast burritos. I'm not sure if it tastes incredible because of the situation I'm in—happy with Leo—or if it's legitimately the best burrito in the world, but I have to stop myself from groaning with every bite.

As we approach my first class, I stop and face Leo. "I just want to clarify," I state. "I am only kissing and touching you, and you're only kissing and touching me."

"Yes." He nods.

"So, basically, what you're saying is that we're dating. I'm your girlfriend, and you're my boyfriend." I chuckle as Leo's face twists into something resembling pain.

"Would we use those terms though?" he protests, scrunching up his face.

My head falls back in laughter. "Yes, we would. Unless you want to take back the first part and give me free rein to kiss some—"

He halts my sentence by abruptly pressing his fingers to my lips.

His stare is predatory. "Do not finish that thought, Alma."

"So then, you're my boyfriend?" I quirk up an eyebrow.

He rubs the back of his neck. "Yeah, fuck it, I'm your boyfriend."

"Great." I giggle and stand up on my tiptoes to kiss him.

He kisses me several times—short, chaste kisses—and I love every one.

"I'll see you later." He kisses me once more.

"Bye." I spin toward the building, and if not for the hot coffee in my hand, I would skip the entire way.

CHAPTER 18

LEO

*a*fter finishing my last class of the day, where my douche bag of a professor decided to assign an additional paper for shits and giggles, I pull out my cell phone to text Alma.

Dinner?

Her response is almost immediate.

I'm just going to grab something from the cafeteria. I have to tutor in thirty minutes.

When will I see you?

After? I work until 8 tonight.

Okay.

So, you want me to come over to your place?

Unless you want me to finger you in front of your roommate, I'd say that's a good idea.

Leo! So vulgar.

You love it. Don't pretend you don't.

Whatever. ;-)

See you tonight.

See you! xo

I resist the urge to tell her that I miss her and that I've been thinking about her all day. I already agreed to a label this morning. There's only so much new-relationship shit I'm comfortable with in one day.

I do miss her though. It's stupid really. I've managed twenty-one years without her, but now that I have her, I can't go an hour without wishing I were with her. I wonder if she'd quit her tutoring job if I just gave her a bunch of money. I have plenty, and she obviously needs it, but I have a feeling that if I offered Alma money and asked her to quit her job, she'd be pissed at me. She seems like the type of girl who likes working and making her own way. Nah, I think it's wise to wait a bit before offering her money and asking her to give up her independence to spend all of her free time with me.

Damn, I'm needy AF in a relationship. Who knew?

On my way past the frat house, I stop by to see Ethan. He's in his room, sitting on his bed, laptop open.

"Hey. What are you up to?" I ask him.

"Hey, man. Not much. Just finishing up these discussion questions for my Lit class," he says.

"I was gonna order a pizza. Want to eat and play some Siege?" I ask.

"Yeah. Sounds dope. I have, like, three more questions, and then I'll head over."

"Okay." I nod and turn to leave.

"Meat Lovers!" Ethan calls from his room as I descend the steps.

"Got it," I yell back.

Exiting the frat house, I cross the street as I pull up the pizza place's website and quickly input our order. Sliding my cell in my back pocket, I dig for my house key when I see that my front door isn't all the way closed. I know I closed and locked it this morning.

I hesitantly push the door open and step in. I scan the space for the high-ticket items. My computer, video game shit, TV—it all sits untouched. So, I wasn't robbed.

There's movement upstairs. I grab a knife from the kitchen and take the steps two at a time. Leaning back against the hallway wall, I inch my bedroom door open.

"What the fuck, Tiffany?" I yell when I see her sprawled out on my bed, naked.

"Hey, sexy," she coos, rubbing her fingers in between her wide-open legs. "I brought you a present." She tilts her head toward the end table, where a clear bag of white powder sits.

She's clearly already started without me. Her pupils are so dilated that her baby-blue eyes are almost black.

"Fuck," I mumble, putting the kitchen knife on my dresser. "How did you get in here?" I snatch up pieces of her clothing from the floor.

"Your spare key, of course, silly. Now, come fuck me. You haven't called for a while. I miss you—your cock especially."

Tiffany was one of my regular fuck buddies. She and I had a lot in common. We liked to get messed up and screw. She was never clingy or needy, which made her a great lay. A couple of months ago, I would have been balls deep in her already, but I'm trying to change.

Her limbs start to quiver as she works her fingers faster, masturbating on my bed.

I throw her pile of clothes at her. "Stop. Get dressed. Get out." I pick up the baggie of powder. "Take this with you."

"Are you serious?" she asks, confused.

"Yes, Tiff. I'm seeing someone. You can't just let yourself into my house and take your clothes off. Get dressed. Now."

"Leo," she whines.

I know she's horny as fuck, but that's not my problem.

"Now!" I bark out. "I need you gone."

"Fine," she gripes.

As soon as she's off my bed, I pull off the sheets and comforter. I have to wash them before Alma comes over.

Before leaving the room with the pile of sheets in my arms, I turn toward Tiffany. "Don't come back. If you let yourself into my house again without my permission, I'll call the cops."

"Asshole," she growls.

Inside the laundry room, I shove the linens into the washing machine and add extra soap. The thought of Alma's beautiful skin anywhere near Tiffany makes me physically ill. I turn the washer to the Deep Clean and Sanitize setting and start it up.

Ethan's setting up the Xbox when I return from the laundry room.

"Tiffany sure ran out of here fast," he notes, humor in his voice. "Things not go well in the bedroom?"

"She fucking broke in here and got naked on my bed. I came home, and she was just in there, rubbing herself off," I scoff and shake my head.

"And?" He snickers.

"And I made her leave."

"Why?"

I look to Ethan with a scowl. "What do you mean, why?"

He raises his hands in confusion. "You love that shit. You told me that she was the best fuck you've ever had."

"I'm not into her anymore."

"What?" Ethan asks in disbelief, and I ignore him.

"I have a girlfriend," I say casually as the doorbell rings.

Grabbing my wallet, I pull out a couple of fifties and open the front door. The delivery dude hands me a large pizza and a two liter of Coke. I press the fifties in his hand and kick the door closed behind me.

I toss the pizza on the table and fetch two glasses from the kitchen cupboard.

"What do you mean, you have a girlfriend? Who are you? And what have you done with Leo Harding?" Ethan jokes.

"You know Quinn, that tiny blonde? I think she came with Gabby and Bethany to the first frat party. She's a Sigma now."

"Oh, yeah. She's hot."

"Well, not her. You remember her roommate? Little tan brunette? She didn't stay long that first night."

"If I recall, you made fun of her virginity, and she stormed off," Ethan says, quirking up a brow.

"Yep, her."

"That's who you're dating?" He seems shocked.

"The very one."

"Why? She doesn't seem like your type."

I grab a few slices of pizza and throw them on a plate. "Oh, she's not. She's way too good for me, but I'm really into her. So, it is what it is." I shrug, sitting on the sofa.

Ethan sits across from me with a plate full of pizza. "Have you slept with her?" he asks before taking a big bite.

"Actually slept? Yes. Fucked? Not yet."

"Just be careful, man," he tells me through a mouthful of pizza. "Girls like that are different. They break and don't bounce back like the Tiffanys of the world, you know?"

"I know. I'm not going to break her." The words feel like a lie.

He shakes his head. "Okay, well, cool. If you're happy, I'm happy for you."

"I'm trying," I say.

"Well, good. You deserve it, man."

CHAPTER 19

ALMA

*T*he past three hours of tutoring ticked by at a snail's pace. *Is this what dating Leo is going to be like? Counting down the moments until I can see him again?* I'm sure it will settle— a little at least. It's new and exciting now, but eventually, kissing him won't be such a novelty. Maybe.

I stop by the dorm to grab a change of clothes, so I don't have to do it in the morning if there's not time.

"Hey, stranger." Quinn sits atop her bed, flipping through a magazine.

"Hi," I say, so excited she's here.

"Was that Leo's voice I heard in the hall this morning?" Her eyebrows rise in question.

I knew this was coming.

My throat bobs with a swallow, and I answer without hesitation, "Yes. We're dating."

"You're dating?" Her voice squeaks.

I hold up my hands. "I know what you're going to say. Yes, he's rough around the edges, but I've really gotten to know him, and he's so great." I steeple my fingers in front of my face, my grin wide. "I think he's been through some heavy stuff, which gives him that rude exterior, but when he lets his walls down, he's so wonderful. I really like him." I say the last part in hopes that she won't chastise me too much.

I know what she's thinking, and I know what Amos is going to think when I work up the nerve to tell him. Leo was a jerk to me—on several occasions. I shouldn't be with someone like that. But I know Leo, and those asshole moments of his aren't who he is.

"I don't know what to say." Quinn frowns. "I don't want to rain on your parade because I can see you're really excited, but I'm worried about you."

"I promise, it's good. He's different than he was. I'm being careful and taking it slow, so I don't get hurt." Perhaps that last part is a bit of a stretch. In Alma world, things are moving at record speed.

"Well, I'm not your boss. You know what's best for you, and as long as you're sure you're being careful ... and I get it. He is, like, so hot." She fans herself.

I'm relieved that the roommate interrogation wasn't as bad as it could've been.

"I know, right?" Opening my dresser, I pull out some clothes for tomorrow. "What are you up to tonight?"

"You're looking at it. What about you? Are you packing?" she asks, amused.

"Going to go hang out with Leo."

"So, just bringing clothes in case your hangout lasts all night?" Quinn chuckles.

"Yeah, something like that." I say. "Let's got out this weekend if you're free."

She nods. "Okay. Sounds like a plan."

I say good night to Quinn and then start toward Leo's house. The closer I get, the more excited I become. God, I'm pathetic.

Reaching Leo's front porch, I knock, and he calls out for me to enter. I step inside, and he's sitting on the sofa with his friend Ethan. They're both holding video game controllers in their hands.

"One second, babe. I just have one more ... boom." He makes the explosion noise, sounding triumphant as Ethan grumbles.

"Fucker," Ethan says under his breath and sets the controller by the console. "See ya," he says to Leo and starts toward me. "Bye, Alma." He winks before walking out the front door.

"Bye." I wave, and Leo comes toward me.

He cradles my face and presses his lips against mine.

"Hey, beautiful," he says in greeting as he kisses me. "How was your day?" He takes a step back.

"Good. Long. Yours?" I ask.

"Long," he responds. "Are you hungry? There's some pizza left."

"No, I'm good." I set my backpack down on the dining room chair.

Leo steps around me and locks the front door before turning off some of the living room lights. "Let's go relax. If you want to turn on the TV up in my room, we can do that too. First, I have to grab my sheets from the dryer."

"You wash your own sheets?" My question is accusing. "I figured you had a housekeeper."

Leo playfully pinches my side. "I do actually have a house-keeper. Yes, she normally washes my sheets, but I'm capable as well. I'm not an idiot."

"I didn't say you were." I smile. "I'm pleasantly surprised.

Fun fact: I'm kind of a neat freak," I tell him as he reaches his arms into the dryer and pulls out a wad of white linens.

"Oh yeah?" He heads toward his bedroom, and I follow.

"Yeah, my parents are slobs, like straight-up hoarders. Growing up, I was the one who kept the house clean, and it kind of became a bit of an obsession. As I've mentioned, my childhood was a little rocky. Keeping a clean house gave me something that I could control. It calmed the turmoil around me."

Leo laughs. "You and I certainly have very different coping mechanisms."

He throws the bottom sheet on the bed, and I walk around to the other side to help him tuck it under. "So, tell me the story of Ethan. You said he's your best friend. How did you meet?"

"You have to swear not to make fun of me or throw out any rich-boy jokes," he says seriously.

I shake my head. "I wouldn't do that."

"Well, Ethan is the son of our former housekeeper. His mom cooked and cleaned for my parents. She was on staff full-time. So, when he wasn't in school, she would bring Ethan along. We just hit it off. He's a really good guy and the only person who has never tried to take advantage of me or exploit me in some way because of my family. He's like a brother to me."

"I'm glad you have someone like that in your life. Everyone needs one person they can rely on. So, you're closer to him than you are to your brother?" I tuck the top sheet under the bottom corner of the mattress.

"God, yes. I hate my real brother."

"That's sad."

Leo scoffs, "Not really."

Bed made, he walks around it until he's in front of me. He tucks a strand of hair behind my ear. I love it when he does that. It's such a little gesture, but it makes me feel like what I'm doing here with Leo is real, and I so desperately want our relationship to be real.

"Take a bath with me?"

"What?" My question comes out squeaky.

"Please?"

I press my lips together. "I'm not sure. It feels so intimate. I don't know if we're there yet."

"Please. It will feel so good. I'll close my eyes if it makes you feel better. I won't look." His grin is mischievous and so sexy.

"Yeah, right. Okay, fine."

"Yes?"

"With bubbles," I demand.

"Bubbles. You got it." He nods in agreement.

I follow him into the bathroom. There's a grand claw-foot tub to the side. Leo's a tall guy, and I bet even he has extra leg room in this thing. It's gigantic. He turns on the water, running his hand underneath the faucet to test for warmth. Steam starts to billow out from the tub, and he drops some lavender bath salts and an iridescent soap from a glass container into the water.

"Bubbles." He holds up the container of shimmery liquid.

"Perfect," I say.

He plays music on low volume through the Bluetooth speakers. Then, grabbing a lighter from the bathroom drawer, he lights some candles and turns off the bright lights.

"You've done this before, haven't you?" My insecurity leaves my mouth before I know it, and I immediately regret my question.

He sets the lighter down and stands before me. "No, I haven't. I've had sex before you but never anything romantic or sweet. You're the only one I've ever wanted to go slow with. You might not have all my firsts, Alma, but you'll have a lot. You'll have the ones that matter."

He places his finger beneath my chin and tilts my face toward his. "Are you okay?"

I smile weakly. "Yeah."

His kiss is sweet and soft.

Pulling his mouth away from mine, he grabs the hem of my shirt and tugs it up over my head. He peppers kisses across my shoulder as he removes each bra strap. He pecks across my collarbone as he unhooks my bra in the back and lets it fall to the floor. Kneeling before me, he unbuttons my jeans and kisses along my hips as he pushes the jeans down.

He slides his finger under the elastic band of my panties, causing goose bumps to break out across my skin. "Should I close my eyes?" He tilts his face up to gauge my reaction.

I simply shake my head, causing him to smile. He pulls down my panties. They fall at my feet, and I step out of them. His stare remains on me. He studies my face as I react to his movements. He runs a finger along my opening, and I pull in a sharp inhale. With a sly smile, he pushes a finger into me, and I hiss in pleasure.

"So wet," he growls as he pushes a second finger inside me.

I grab on to his shoulders as his fingers work in and out. Without releasing my stare, he leans closer, extending his tongue until it's flicking the perfect spot, mirroring the actions of his fingers below. Watching him pleasure me this way magnifies the intensity of his movements, and before I know it's coming, an orgasm hits me, hard and strong. Leo holds me up with his free hand as my body shakes, and I cry out.

Leo removes his fingers from my opening and puts them into his mouth, sucking. I open my mouth in a gasp.

He chuckles. "Perfect."

He rises from his knees and makes quick work of removing his clothes. When he's standing naked before me, I take in his body from his face to his feet. He's everything, an Adonis. I splay my hands across his chest and run them down his abs, feeling the chiseled lines of his muscles.

"Do you approve?" He grins knowingly.

I bite my bottom lip and nod.

"Come on," Leo says, humor lining his voice.

He grabs my hand and leads me toward the tub. The bubbles are floating on top of the water. Leo leans over and turns off the running faucet. We step in and sink into the hot water. I lean back against Leo's chest, and he runs his soapy hand up and down my arms and shoulders. He makes me feel so cherished.

"Tell me one of your dreams," he says into my ear before kissing my shoulder.

"I want to be a mom. I want to have at least three kids, maybe more. The idea of raising a beautiful, kind family with my soul mate has been my dream since I was young. I want my kids to know that I love them and that I wanted them. I need them to know that they're valued and special and perfect, just the way they are," I say, running my palms against Leo's knees at my sides.

"So, you want to be the mother that you didn't have," Leo observes.

"Yeah, I guess so," I admit.

"That's a good dream." He kisses my hair.

"Do you want kids?"

"No." His answer is immediate, and it crushes my heart.

"Really?" I ask again, hoping that his response will somehow be different.

"I wouldn't be a good dad. I'm too fucked up. I wouldn't do that to a child. It wouldn't be fair. Plus, I don't see myself here long."

I sit up and spin around to face him, and water splashes over the side of the tub. "What does that mean?"

"I can't see a future. You can imagine yourself getting

married and having a family, right? I'm sure you can see your-self growing old with your husband and rocking on the porch swing, right?"

I nod because I can envision all of that. I can't see the details or the faces, but I can see the life I'll have someday.

"When I think about my future, all I see is blackness."

"Just because you can't visualize it doesn't mean it's not going to happen, and you can change your mind about kids. Most twenty-one-year-old guys aren't ready for kids, but it doesn't mean you'll never be. If you don't think you're good enough to be a dad, then change," I argue, almost furious.

I want to cry; I'm so mad. *How can he just write off his future in such a cavalier manner? How has he already given up on happi-ness and a family? What am I even doing here? I feel myself falling for him, and for what? Heartbreak?* Because that's where it's heading.

"I have to go." I start to stand, and Leo grabs my arms.

"Wait, no," he says desperately. "Don't go."

"What are we doing here?" I demand, sitting back down in the water so the bubbles cover my body.

"I don't know," Leo responds. "What do you want me to say?"

I open my mouth to yell, but then I close it and gather my thoughts. "I understand that people date and break up all the time in college. I'm not delusional enough to think that the first guy I date will be the one. But with each boyfriend, there has to be the chance that he could be it; otherwise, what is the point of going out in the first place? I'm not looking for a hook-up. I don't need you to take my virginity and then dump me. If you're telling me right now that you're a hundred percent sure that there is no future for us, then I'm out."

"What do you want from me, Alma? You're the first girl I've dated—ever. We've been together for two fucking days. You want a marriage proposal now? I can't give that to you. I'm trying to be open and honest with you, and you're giving me shit? You're insane," he spits out.

"Ugh," I groan, standing from the tub and stepping out. I grab a towel from the shelf and wrap it around me. "Clearly, I am insane for thinking that anything between us could work." I snatch my clothes off of the floor and storm out of the bathroom.

Leo gets out of the tub. "Just wait," he barks out.

He follows me into his room, a towel wrapped around his waist. Water drips from his chest. "Let me get this straight. You're mad because we've been dating for two days, and I can't tell you that I'll marry you someday?"

"No! I'm mad because you're telling me that there's no future for you or us. I don't need a definite, but I need a possibility. What's the point of being together if there's no chance we'll work? Why go through all of these emotions and share these experiences that I'll never get to have for the first time again if there's no future? I'm not going to risk falling in love with you if there isn't a chance. That's not fair to me!"

Leo runs his fingers through his wet hair. "I'm new to this too. Not only am I new to relationships, but caring about someone is also a new experience. Cut me some slack, Alma. Damn it, I'm trying."

I see the torment in his eyes, and I want to hold him. I know he's trying.

Pulling the towel tighter around my chest, I sit on the end of his bed. "I'm scared," I tell him. "I'm so scared, Leo." My voice trembles.

He sits beside me. "Of what?"

"Of you. We've had this connection for a couple of months now. Yes, the relationship part is new, but the attraction isn't. When I'm with you, I feel so good. You make me feel so good. I'm afraid of losing that feeling, of losing you. Losing you now would be heartbreaking. Losing you a year from now would be devastating. I don't know how I'd recover from that," I say with a sigh.

"Alma, I don't know what a year from now will look like, but I'm trying. For you, I'm trying. That's all I can do. That has to be enough."

"I know." I lean my head against his arm.

"I can't promise you forever, but I can promise you today. I'll cherish every part of you today, and tomorrow, I'll keep trying to be better ... for you." He sets his open hand palm up on my leg. "Is that enough for you?"

I place my hand atop his and thread my fingers through his. "Yeah, it is."

In this moment, I realize that I'm already in too deep. It's a very real possibility that Leo can't give me tomorrow, but I need him enough to settle for today.

CHAPTER 20

ALMA

"We're not original at all. You know that, right? We're going to be those cliché sexy kittens at the Halloween frat party. There will probably be another twenty girls dressed just like us," I say to Quinn, her face deep in concentration as she draws whiskers on my face with black eyeliner.

"You'll be the hottest," Leo comments from my bed, where he's sprawled out, looking at his phone.

"Yes, we will!" Quinn cheers in agreement. "Listen to your boyfriend. He knows. There might be other kittens at the party, but none of them will be as gorgeous as us. Plus, you can't beat a two-dollar costume."

Quinn found us black kitten-ear headbands and fishnet stockings at the local dollar store. Paired with two of her skimpy black dresses and some dark makeup and whiskers, we are pretty sexy.

"It's not too late for you, you know," Quinn says to Leo. "We could make you a pirate or a rock star. Oh! You could wear a white button-down shirt and underwear and be Tom Cruise from *Risky Business!*"

"Yeah, I'll pass," he deadpans. "Halloween isn't my thing."

"Have you ever seen *Risky Business?*" I ask Quinn.

"No, I'm not a fan of old movies. Movies that came out before we were born are all grainy and stuff. But ... that scene where he slides across the floor in just a shirt is classic. People would know what that costume was. Stay still," she commands while circling the eyeliner around the tip of my nose.

"Are you almost done?" Leo asks.

"Shh," Quinn warns him. "You can't rush perfection."

"Clearly, but if you want to make it before Halloween is over, we should get going," Leo states.

"Leo Harding, you will wait." Quinn glowers toward Leo, and I can't hide my smirk.

Over the past couple of weeks, I've been making an effort to hang out here with Leo sometimes. I would've hated it if Quinn had been the one to start dating someone and left me alone all of the time.

The time spent here in our tiny little dorm room has been good for me too. Sometimes, it's hard to put things in perspective over at Leo's semi-mansion. College relationships aren't meant to have that much room or privacy—along with a king-size bed and bubble baths in a claw-foot tub.

It got too deep, too fast. One minute, I was kissing a boy for the first time, and the next, I was yelling at him because he couldn't promise me that he'd marry me. It wasn't fair to Leo or myself.

After our fight the night of the bubble bath, I realized that I had to make a change. As much as I crave alone time with Leo and love playing house with him, I'm eighteen. This entire life

—college, roommate, parties, job, boyfriend—is an adjustment. I almost sabotaged it before it even really started.

A knock sounds on the door. Quinn and I exchange expectant looks. Everyone we know should already be at the party. Quinn opens the door, and there stands Amos in a fighter pilot jumper and aviator sunglasses.

"Oh my gosh!" I stand from the crate I was sitting on and rush over to Amos. "What are you doing here? I thought you were going to a party in Ann Arbor." I throw my arms around him, hugging him tight. I haven't seen him since we went home for his mother's birthday.

"I was, but I missed you." He kisses the top of my head, and I release my hug, taking a step back.

"We were just talking about Tom Cruise!" Quinn says gleefully.

"What?" Amos seems confused.

"Tom Cruise. *Top Gun*. That's who you are, right?" she asks.

"Oh." Amos looks down at his costume, as if he forgot he was dressed up. "I was just going for a fighter pilot. But, sure … we can say *Top Gun*."

Quinn claps. "Oh, good. I love that movie."

"I thought you didn't watch '80s movies?" I eye her in question.

She rolls her eyes. "Everyone's seen *Top Gun*, Alma."

"Hey, I'm Leo. Nice to officially meet you."

I stiffen when Leo's voice sounds from behind me. I start to panic. For a second, I forgot that he was here.

"Yeah, you've heard all about the new boyfriend, right?" Quinn says with a grin.

"Oh, you're dating Quinn?" Amos says, extending his hand to shake Leo's.

Leo drops his hand before Amos can shake it and grabs my waist, marking his territory. "No, Alma," he growls.

Crap. Crap. Crap.

I was planning on telling Amos about dating Leo, but it just didn't come up. I wanted to explain everything to Amos when I saw him in person. This is not how I saw it going. *Ugh.*

"So, we should probably get going. My makeup is done, right?" I ask Quinn.

"Yeah." She clears her throat. "You're good."

Leo stands behind me, unmoving. His muscles are tense as fury simmers beneath his skin. I understand why he's upset, but I wasn't hiding him from Amos. I just didn't get around to telling him yet. I'll explain that to Leo later. For now, we should get going. The awkwardness in this room is suffocating.

"We should go!" I snatch my small purse off of my bed and step into the hallway, extending my hand toward Leo.

He takes it with a scowl.

Quinn locks our door, and she and Amos follow behind Leo and me. Tilting my head back, I shoot Amos a nervous smile. Quinn—bless her heart—is regaling him with some random story. That girl can talk—a skill that is easing my nerves at the moment.

Once inside the frat house, Leo drops my hand and walks ahead of me, disappearing into the crowd of costumes.

"I guess we should get a drink," I call back to Amos and Quinn.

We make our way to the kitchen and fill three red Solo cups with whatever alcohol-infused punch they're serving this time. It's always a little different.

"I wasn't trying to hide anything. I wanted to explain everything in person. Sorry this is so awkward," I say to Amos.

We leave the kitchen and follow Quinn into the game room. I haven't been to one of these parties in a while, but the couches in the game room seem to still be our designated spot.

"Is he good to you?" Amos questions.

I nod. "He really is. We got off to a rocky start, but things have been great, and he's different. I'm really happy."

"Okay, but please be careful. He rubs me the wrong way," Amos says.

I chuckle and take a sip of my drink. "He has that effect on people, but I promise, once you get to know him and he lets his guard down, you'll see him differently."

Amos doesn't respond, and I know he's still skeptical of the whole situation, but he'll come around when we can talk without yelling to each other over the loud music.

"You look really good as a fighter pilot," I tell him with a wink.

"You pull off a cat pretty well yourself." He nudges my knee with his.

I look down to my barely there black dress. "Yeah, this is all Quinn." I shake my head.

We chat with the group we're sitting with and watch as a few play beer pong on the table beside us. There's a semi-innocent game of Never Have I Ever, where only half of the questions are sex-related. I try not to worry, but Leo still hasn't come back from wherever he stormed off to.

"Hey, Alma!" Quinn leans toward me. Her big green eyes aren't as focused as they were when we got here. She evidently hasn't been nursing the same cup of punch the entire time, like I have. "Do you care if I steal Amos away to dance? You'll dance with me, right?" She directs the last question to Amos.

"Of course not! I'm going to go track down Leo anyway," I say over the music. "Have fun, Cookie!" I laugh at the uneasy expression on Amos's face as Quinn pulls him onto the living room dance floor.

The house is exceptionally packed tonight. There's nothing like booze and costumes to bring the college kids out of their shells. I wind my way through all of the rooms on the first floor, looking for Leo but come up short.

I'm relieved when I spot Ethan filling a cup by the keg in the kitchen.

"Hey! Have you seen Leo?" I ask.

"Hi. Yeah, he's up in my room. Third door on the right." Ethan nods his head toward the stairs leading to the second floor.

"Thank you."

I step around a couple practically doing it at the base of the stairs and hurry up the steps. Taking a deep breath, I take hold of the handle and push Ethan's door open. Leo is sitting on a futon, his eyes shut and his head tilted back. A girl who decided to dress as a prostitute for Halloween is sitting on his lap, sucking a lollipop.

"Leo," I say, and he jerks his head up.

"Oh, look! It's my secret girlfriend. We don't tell people that we're dating though because I'm such a fuckup. Little Miss Perfect is embarrassed to be with me, you see?"

I'm assuming he's saying all of this for the hooker's benefit, but she's completely zoned out.

"Can you please give us a minute?" I say to the girl in Leo's lap.

She looks at me, confused.

"She said, get the fuck out, Stacy!" Leo tilts his legs, so she slides off onto the futon. "Get out," he barks, and she rolls her eyes before standing and walking out.

I shut the door behind her. "Is she going to be okay? She seems off."

"She's fine."

"Were you doing anything with her?" My voice is hesitant, and I'm terrified of his answer.

"No. She, unlike the only person you care about in this world, knows that we're dating," he grumbles, and I notice that his words are slurred.

"Are you drunk?"

"Something like that," he huffs.

"So, you get mad at me, and the first thing you do is get wasted?"

"I don't know. You talk to that guy every single fucking day, and I just never came up?" he snaps out a question in response to my own. "Are you that fucking ashamed to be with me?"

"No, of course not. I was going to tell him."

"Well, if it were important to you, you would have."

Leo is different. His voice is off. His eyes don't seem to be able to focus on me. His entire demeanor has changed, and it makes me uncomfortable.

"I don't like you like this," I admit.

"Yeah, well, I don't like you very much either."

I stand, staring at this beautiful, broken man, and I don't know what to do. *Should I leave? Should I stay?* We're so different. Maybe I'm just kidding myself in all of this. We've been happy for three weeks, and now, we're fighting again.

I contemplate my next move, failing to realize that tears are falling down my face until Leo points them out.

"I'm sorry." He rushes toward me and pulls me into a hug. "I didn't mean to make you cry. I'm sorry, Alma. I'm sorry. I just love you so much, and I want you to love me back."

I stiffen at his words. "You can't tell me you love me for the first time when you're wasted, Leo. That doesn't count."

"I do love you, Alma. You're the only woman I've ever loved. Love me back," he pleads.

"Let's get you home. We'll talk tomorrow." I wipe my cheeks, removing any trace of mascara-coated tears.

I text both Quinn and Amos to let them know that Leo's not feeling well and that I'm taking him over to his house. In my text to Amos, I apologize and promise that we'll hang together soon. I know if I go and find Amos downstairs, he'll see that I've been crying and worry. I don't want him to be concerned when, moments ago, I was telling him how amazing Leo was.

"You'll stay with me, right?" Leo's question makes him sound like a little boy.

"Yeah, I'll stay."

I lead Leo down the stairs, and we exit right off the back door in the kitchen. Once we're across the street, I unlock his door, and we go inside. I'm grateful to have space between me and that party. I can't say I've ever had fun at one of them.

We brush our teeth together in the bathroom, and I make sure that Leo drinks some water. Once in bed, I don't allow him to kiss me, but I let him hold me. He tells me he loves me again, but I feign sleep. The thought that perhaps love isn't enough echoes deep within my soul.

CHAPTER 21

ALMA

*L*eo wakes, screaming from another nightmare. I calm him down, and he holds me while drifting back to sleep. He doesn't seem to remember the night terrors in the morning, which is probably a blessing for him. Though I can't get his tortured cries out of my mind.

Sleep evades me for most of the night. My brain won't stop weighing all the options. The blatant differences between Leo and me keeps me tossing and turning, but the glaring truth makes me stay—and that's that I love Leo. I do. I'm drawn to him on a spiritual level. It doesn't make sense, and I can't always put words to our connection. Just like faith, love is hard to prove, but when it's present, it's impossible to ignore. I feel it. I believe it. I need it.

I need Leo.

Sleep doesn't come, so I decide to get up. I'll go back to the dorm to shower and get ready for the day. I have a feeling that

Leo will be sleeping off his choices from last night until at least the afternoon.

I leave him a note in case he wakes before I return and start toward the dorm. This outfit felt cute and sexy last night, but in the morning light, I probably look like Leo's friend Stacy.

Relieved to be back at my room, I unlock the door and step in. Gasping, I drop the keys, covering my mouth. Quinn is lying naked in her bed with an equally bare Amos draped around her. His tight ass facing me.

Half-asleep and confused, he rolls away from Quinn and toward the door, giving me a full-frontal show.

"Oh my goodness!" I hold my hand out to block him and squeeze my eyes shut before quickly stepping back out into the hallway and closing the door.

Wow. I did not expect to come back to that.

There's some commotion inside the room, and then Amos opens the door before closing it behind him.

"I'm sorry. We didn't mean for you to come home to … that." He rubs a hand along the back of his neck. "We just fell asleep after."

I slide down the hallway wall and sit on the questionable carpeted floor. Amos sits beside me.

"You and Quinn had sex?" I ask.

"Yeah, we did."

"You lost your virginity with my roommate?"

"Yes. Are you mad?"

"No," I say hesitantly. "Shocked, I guess. I didn't know you were into her."

"Something changed last night. We were drinking and dancing and then kissing. Then, one thing led to another, you know?"

"Wow. Okay, well … are you dating now?"

"I don't know. We haven't talked about it. I guess we'll do that today."

"Right." I nod. "I'll just grab a change of clothes and get out of here, so you two can talk and whatever else."

"Don't be mad, Mutt. I'm nineteen. Do you know how many nineteen-year-old male virgins there are? It was long past due. You understand."

"I'm not mad. I told you that. And, no, I don't really understand because I love Leo and we still haven't done that. Do you even know Quinn's last name?"

"You haven't slept with Leo?" Amos asks in disbelief.

"No, of course not."

"I figured you had."

"Well, I haven't," I say with a sigh. Extending my pinkie toward Amos, I say, "Promise me we'll be fine. We won't change."

He wraps his finger around mine. "We'll always be fine. You're my *soul* mate, Alma. My family. My best friend. Others will come and go, but you and I are forever."

"Okay. Don't you forget it." My lips tilt up. "Well, I do need a change of clothes, but I can shower at Leo's and give you two some time to do whatever it is that you want to do."

"Thanks." He stands and takes my hand, pulling me up.

"Was it good?"

"Amazing. I don't know why I waited nineteen years. It was …"

I hold up my hand, halting his thought. "I'm not ready for details yet." I chuckle.

"Fair enough."

We venture back into the room. Quinn is sitting on her bed in a loose T-shirt and cotton shorts. Her legs sway nervously over the side of the bed.

"Hi," she squeaks when I enter, eye makeup from last night smeared across her face.

"Hi. I'm just grabbing some clothes and heading back over to Leo's."

"Are we all okay?" she asks.

"We're all great," I reassure her.

I change out of Quinn's hooker dress and throw on something comfortable before grabbing another change of clothes and my backpack, just in case their day-after-sex date goes long.

"I'll talk to you both later," I say before leaving to head to Leo's again.

At least he's only a three-block walk away.

I'm not surprised to find him still sleeping when I get back. I start the shower and step in, allowing the hot water to wash off the makeup and randomness of the past twelve hours.

"Can I join you?" Leo's voice startles me.

"Gosh, you scared me. Yeah, sure."

Leo steps in and shuts the glass door. Standing behind me, he circles his arms around my front and holds me against his body. "I'm sorry about last night," he whispers against my neck between soft kisses.

I turn in his arms and press my cheek to his chest, hugging him tight. "I'm sorry too."

Taking a step back, I find the loofah and squeeze body gel onto it. Sudsing it up, I clean Leo's chest and arms.

"You probably don't remember much from last night, huh?" I ask, swiping the loofah over his shoulder.

"Not much, no. Well, besides when I confessed my love for you."

I stop cleaning him and look up to see him grinning down toward me.

"Oh," is all I can say.

"I do love you, Alma. Like, a crazy amount." He cradles my face in his hand and lowers his lips to mine, the bewitching kiss affecting me to the point of dizziness.

"Really?" I breathe.

"Definitely."

I part my lips, and his mouth closes in on mine. The kiss is slow and teasing.

"I love you too," I say against his lips, causing him to smile wide.

We make out under the hot spray of the water until my skin starts to crinkle. I pull my mouth away from his, and my lips, sore from the intensity of the kiss, miss his almost immediately.

"I've been wanting to try something, but I'm scared. I've never done it before." I swipe the wet strands of hair away from my face. "I want it to be good for you."

"What is it that you want to try, babe?" Leo asks, rubbing the pad of his thumb against my bottom lip.

I swallow. "I want to kiss you ... down there."

Leo's arousal grows harder against my stomach. "I want that too." His words are gruff and husky.

"Can you help me? Tell me what to do."

Leo chews on his bottom lip and extends an arm against the shower wall, steadying himself. He nods in response to my question, and I drop to my knees.

Grabbing the base of his shaft, I slide his length into my mouth as far back as I can manage.

"Suck, baby," Leo instructs, and I comply. He hisses as I move my head back and forth, suctioning my mouth and swirling my tongue around him. "Stroke the base with your hand. The part that won't fit in your mouth."

I do as Leo said, spurred on by the sounds coming from his mouth and the needy movements of his hips.

"Just like that," he groans, pumping into my mouth as he chases his orgasm. "Alma." My name is a prayer on his lips, and he threads his fingers through my hair. "Baby ... fuuuuuck," he moans as warm, salty liquid squirts into my throat.

I gag a little. With the combination of him pounding against my throat and his cum filling it, my gag reflex is set off.

Pulling my mouth from him, I close my lips and focus on swallowing. Leo wraps his hands around my arms and pulls me up from the tiled floor.

"You okay? I meant to warn you in case you wanted to finish with your hand."

"It's fine. I liked it," I tell him, and it's true. There's nothing sexier than being the cause of your lover coming undone like that. The power is intoxicating. "How was I?"

"So good." He kisses my forehead. "You are amazing."

"I won't make you wait much longer," I say because the reality is that I really want to have sex with Leo. There's just a small part that's holding out because I feel like I should.

"Alma, baby … I will wait for you forever. There is absolutely no rush, okay? Plus, I think we're having plenty of fun with the way things are right now. Don't you?"

"Yeah," I agree.

"Then, don't worry about it. When you're ready, I'll be here. Until then"—he drops to his knees and inserts a finger inside of me—"I'll be here," he growls before his tongue licks between my legs.

My eyes roll back, and I hum in approval.

CHAPTER 22

LEO

$\mathcal{I}$ can't wipe the smile from my face as I listen to Quinn and Alma's banter in the kitchen.

"Is it done?" Quinn says to Alma.

"I don't know. The red thingy hasn't popped up. So, I don't think so," Alma notes.

"Why are you buttering it?" Quinn's question is clipped.

"To keep it moist. I saw someone do it on a cooking show once."

"But it's never going to finish cooking if you don't keep the oven door closed, you know? You're letting out all the heat," Quinn says as calmly as possible even though it's obvious that Alma's methods are driving her crazy.

"You're right." Alma pushes the turkey back into the oven and closes the door. "I think the potatoes need a few more minutes before they're ready to be mashed," she tells Quinn.

"Yeah, they're not ready yet," Quinn agrees, stirring something on the stove.

Meanwhile, Ethan, Amos, and I are sitting in the living room, staring at the giant TV, watching our professional football team, the Detroit Lions, lose.

Alma had the idea to host Friendsgiving at my house since Ethan, Quinn, and Amos are going home to see their families for the holiday in a few days. Apparently, Alma usually spends Thanksgiving with Amos's parents, but he told her that she didn't have to go this year, and she was relieved. From what I've heard, his dad's a real asshole, though I'm sure he doesn't hold a candle to mine.

My family is celebrating America's day of thanks in St. Lucia. Nothing says that you're grateful like an out-of-country vacation on a beach. It's perfectly fine by me, to be honest. I would've canceled on my family's Thanksgiving dinner anyway. Now, I get to stay home with Alma without having to shoot my mother a text with a complete lie as to why I can't come.

The past month since Halloween has been incredible. Thanks to all the fucking that her roommate and bestie have been doing in their dorm room, Alma is back to spending most nights with me. Alma and I, on the other hand, are still not fucking. But I can't complain. She makes me come at least twice a day with her hand and/or mouth, so it's been pretty great. We've been spending so much time on third base that it's practically home at this point.

Alma and I have started to get each other off in the most random places lately. It's become the best game. I know her clit so well that I can have her violently shaking in less than a minute. Three days ago, she sucked me off during one of my last prescribed tutoring sessions. Now that I know orgasms are included, I'm going to miss studying in that little room.

"I'm going to grab a drink. Either of you need a refill? Beer? Pop? Water?" I ask the guys.

They both decline, so I start for the kitchen.

"Smells great, ladies. Sure you don't need any help?" I offer, though we all know I'm just trying to be polite. I can't even make Kool-Aid on my own.

"Nope, we're all set," Quinn says. "Thanksgiving is an art at my house. With six women, we have it down to a science."

I have to agree that she's stirring the contents of that pot like it's her God-given mission. Alma, on the other hand, seems to be faltering a bit. She's attempting to roll out crescent rolls, though she appears to be almost punishing the poor dough. There's a streak of flour across her nose, and it about does me in.

She told me a couple of months ago that she was a decent cook. Something about if she didn't make the food, she didn't eat. But I'm guessing the meals she made when she was young were simpler.

"So, your parents don't celebrate Thanksgiving, right?" I ask Alma, teasing, wondering if she's ever made this type of food in her life. She told me once that they didn't do holidays, so I already know her answer.

"No. Remember, they don't do holidays and definitely not Thanksgiving," she says.

"Why's that?" Quinn asks.

"In the words of Lee-Anne, pilgrims are greedy murderers." She shrugs.

"Wow. That's lovely. With every tidbit I learn about your childhood, I become more curious as to how you even survived." Quinn laughs before yelling, "Oh shoot." She moves the pan off of the stovetop.

I take what appears to be a burning mishap of some sort as my cue. "Alma, can I borrow you for a sec? The washing machine's messing up. Something's up with your clothes. Were they all pink before you started the load this morning?"

"What?" Alma gasps. "No!"

"Go, go. I'm fine," Quinn says, peering into the pan.

I follow Alma toward the back of the house as she hurries toward the laundry room. She stops inside and throws open the washing machine lid. I close the door behind us.

"They look fine," she notes.

Stepping behind her, I wrap my arms around her and slide a hand down her pants. She's wearing stretchy black yoga pants today. Second to a skirt, these are the preferred bottoms that she wears.

"Leo," she chastises. As my finger slides into her, she loses some fight. "I have to help Quinn."

"I think she'll be fine for a minute. You, however, need to relax. Aren't you a good cook?"

"Yeah," she answers. "But Quinn's like a drill sergeant in there. I've never seen her so bossy. She's stressing me out."

"Let me help you." I run my other hand up her sweater and under her bra. I pinch her nipple while the other hand alternates between her entrance and her clit.

"Leo," she whispers, pushing her head back into my chest.

"Does it feel good, baby?" I kiss the skin at the nape of her neck.

"Mmhmm." She rides my finger.

I pinch her clit. She turns her face to the side, and my lips meet hers. I capture her cries in my mouth as she comes undone.

"Feel better?" I kiss her again when her body has calmed.

"Much better." She grins. She turns in my arms and reaches for the button of my jeans.

I grab her hand, halting her progress. "Later." I chuckle. "Quinn might have a coronary if you're gone too long."

"True," she says. "I love you." She stands on her tiptoes and presses her lips to mine.

"I love you."

She checks herself over before opening the laundry room door.

"Wait," I say.

She turns back to me.

I lick my thumb and rub it across her nose. "You have flour on your nose."

She giggles. "Thanks," she says and steps out.

As I walk back to the living room, I hear her tell Quinn that it was a false alarm and the clothes are fine.

"False alarm, huh? Interesting. Your cheeks are pretty red there," Quinn calls Alma out.

"Really? I don't know why." Alma washes her hands in the sink.

"Oh, I think you do," Quinn teases.

"You'd know since I haven't been able to enter our dorm room at night for a month." Alma chuckles.

"Touché. You got me there." Quinn grins. "You're going to burn the potatoes, by the way."

"No, I'm not. They're going to be perfect."

Their playful bickering continues, and I turn my attention back to the game on TV.

A while later, the five of us are seated at my large dining room table. A feast of food sits in the center of the table, and it all looks and smells delicious. We raise our crystal glasses filled with champagne, and Alma toasts to good friends and good food.

The food is incredible, and I make sure to tell the girls that repeatedly. I can't remember the last Thanksgiving meal I had where I wasn't high on something. This entire dinner is a whole new world for me. I have other friends besides Ethan.

I'm fucking in love with a girl. And, damn … has stuffing always been this tasty?

I suppose being sober has its perks.

"What's the secret ingredient in these mashed potatoes, Quinn? Fucking ecstasy? They're incredible," I say.

"Those are all Alma," she answers.

I internally kick my ass for having doubted Alma's culinary skills. The urge to ask Alma to marry me on the spot and feed me mashed potatoes for the rest of our days surfaces, but I push it down. Instead, I shove another bite of the starchy masterpiece into my mouth.

"They have sea salt, fresh ground pepper, butter, sour cream, milk, cream cheese, and a little garlic. They're totally not healthy, but my parents would've been fine with having kale smoothies for Thanksgiving, if they celebrated, so I go a little overboard on some of the dishes. I actually adapted it from Amos's mom's recipe. She doesn't add the garlic or cream cheese."

"Alma's potatoes are better than my mom's." Amos shoots Alma a reassuring smile.

"Thanks. Though to be fair, his mom is an incredible cook."

"She is, but so are you," he tells her.

"And so is Quinn," Alma adds, and Amos quickly agrees.

"Well, thank you, ladies. This is really nice," Ethan says.

"You're welcome," Quinn answers. "So, during Thanksgiving dinner, my family likes to go around the table and have everyone say something that they're thankful for this year."

I scoff, "God, your family sounds so nice and normal."

Quinn grins. "I'll go first. I'm thankful for my awesome roommate, becoming a Sigma Sigma Sigma—the best sorority on campus—for meeting new people, and for my mom's new job."

Ethan says, "I'm thankful that I finally saved enough money to buy a car and that my dad's cancer is in remission."

"I'll go!" Alma says. "I'm thankful for Eastern and my scholarship, for being a short drive away from my bestie, for a job that I love, friends that I love, and new experiences with people that I love." Her eyes catch mine.

Amos says, "I'm thankful that I aced my midterms and currently have a 4.0. I'm thankful for the new people I've met and for a mutt of a girl who crashed into my life, covered in mud, years ago."

Alma smiles across the table to Amos. I find it odd that he isn't thankful for Quinn—without whom, he would only be getting action from his hand—but whatever. If he's dumb enough not to feign being thankful for her, that's on him.

"You have to say something, Leo," Quinn says.

"Alma," I answer simply.

She will forever be the answer to anything good in my life.

CHAPTER 23

ALMA

"*A*re you sure you don't want me to go home with you? I don't mind. I feel bad that you have to face your dad on your own," I say to Amos over my half-eaten plate of eggs.

He shakes his head. "No. You'll have more fun here. Plus, I don't think it will be that bad. What does he have to yell at me about? My grades are perfect."

"I know, but I'm afraid he'll find something."

"It will be fine. I swear," he says before taking a drink of his coffee.

It's been a while since Amos and I have had a meal alone together. He stayed over with Quinn last night, but she had to get up early to go help her mom and sisters cook the food for Thanksgiving. Many of the local restaurants are closed, but Luca's Coney Island is open, and his breakfast food is just as good as the chili-cheese fries that Leo's obsessed with.

I'm a little confused with Quinn and Amos's relationship. They love to be together, especially to have sex, but he doesn't seem to miss her when she's gone, and vice versa. I crave Leo every second that I'm not with him. Heck, I'd never tell Amos, but I'm missing Leo like crazy right now.

I ask Luca for a large chili-cheese fry with a side of ranch and ketchup to go, and he smiles down at me knowingly.

"Your mom sure will be happy to see you. Give her a hug for me, okay?" I say to Amos.

"I will," Amos says, snatching the bill from Luca before I can grab it.

"Let me pay for my meal or Leo's takeout at least."

"The fries are on the house," Luca says, clearing our plates.

"See, the fries are on the house. No worries." Amos hands Luca some cash and wishes him a happy Thanksgiving.

"Thank you, Luca. Hope you have a great day," I tell him before Amos and I head out, the bell of the diner chiming as we exit.

I walk Amos to his car and say good-bye before heading the other direction, back to Leo's house.

He's still in bed when I get back.

"I come bearing gifts." I hold up the white plastic bag containing his fries.

Leo scoots up in his bed until he's sitting against the padded headboard. "You're awesome."

He takes the bag from me and pulls out the large Styrofoam container.

"How was breakfast?" he asks through a mouthful of fries.

"Good. He's on his way back home."

"You want to stick with our plan for the day? It's not too late if you want to do the Thanksgiving dinner thing with just the two of us."

"No, we had a big dinner last weekend. Takeout and a movie marathon sounds perfect."

"I just want to make sure you're happy." He dips a fry in ranch and then ketchup and tosses it into his mouth.

"Or do you want Thanksgiving food, so I'll make those potatoes again?" I quirk up a brow.

"I would do almost anything to have them again."

I shake my head with a grin. "I can make them for you every weekend. It's not hard."

"Ah, babe, that would be incredible."

"Okay, it's a plan." I pull off my shirt and head toward the bathroom. "Finish eating and then come join me in the shower. Afterward, we'll put on jammies and veg on the couch all day. I say we watch *The Notebook* first."

"I was thinking maybe *Endgame*—you know, the Avengers," Leo calls from the bed.

"No way," I say in response, turning on the shower. "You said my pick."

"Your idea of a great movie is some sappy, romantic crap?" he groans.

"Today it is."

Before I step into the shower, Leo grumbles, "Fine, but only because I love you."

WE SPEND the day watching all of my favorite romance movies and order Chinese takeout for dinner. Snuggled up next to Leo on the couch, I reach onto the coffee table and grab the fortune cookies included with our meal.

I hand Leo his. "We have to read our fortunes. That's the best part," I exclaim.

"Okay, ladies first," He nods toward the cookie in my hand.

I remove it from the wrapper and crack it open. Taking the small rectangular paper in my hand, I read aloud, "You may love many people but only one will burn into your soul forever." I stare at the paper for a moment, re-reading the sentence in my head. "Wow."

"That's deep," Leo says.

"Yeah," I shake my head with a grin. "They're usually not that serious. Now, I want to know what yours says."

Leo snaps his fortune cookie in half and pulls out the paper. "To truly find yourself you should play hide and seek alone."

I chuckle. "I don't know if that one is supposed to be meaningful or silly."

"Not sure. Maybe both," Leo shrugs. "Let's trade. I want you burned into my soul."

"No way," I hold the paper against my chest. "I'm keeping this one."

"You keep your fortunes?"

"The ones that I like. I put them in my journal or on my vision board. This one may get framed," my lip tilts up into a smile.

"Oh, yeah?" Leo's beautiful blue eyes sparkle with happiness.

I lean toward Leo and place my lips against his. "Yeah, I think so."

Today was a perfect day. There were no roommates or parties, homework or classes ... just Leo and me. My world is the best when it's just the two of us and no outside distractions.

Leo's in bed, scrolling through his phone, when I enter the bedroom after brushing my teeth.

He smiles and sets his phone on the nightstand. "Ready?"

"Yes." I turn off the light and climb into bed, wearing one of Leo's shirts and my panties.

Leo, clad in just his boxers, wraps his arm around me, and I nuzzle up against him.

"Thanks for a great day," I say. "I think this has been my favorite Thanksgiving of all time."

"Same," he says and kisses my temple.

His warm skin under my palms, the smell of his body wash —clean and woodsy—and the sheer perfect nature of the day have me wanting every part of Leo. Who knew I'd fall so hard for the rude guy I ran into at that Italian restaurant on my first day here? It's unnerving, just how much I feel for him.

Sitting up slightly, I swing my leg over his abdomen until I'm straddling his middle. I reach for the hem of my shirt and pull it over my head.

"Well, isn't that an incredible sight?" His tongue wets his lips, and his gaze darkens as he takes me in.

Raising his hands, he cups my breasts and tugs on my nipples. A zing of pleasure shoots down my body, and I hum, rocking my hips against him.

"Oh, baby. You want to play?"

I nod slowly and drag my fingers down his chest.

"Take off your panties and straddle my face." His voice is hoarse.

I freeze. "What?"

"Come here. You'll like it."

I crawl up Leo's body and hold my center over his lips. His warm breath brushes against my heat, and I push into him. He softly kisses me there, and my legs quiver. My hands grip the headboard to steady myself.

"Just move where it feels good," Leo instructs from below.

My head falls back, and I groan as his greedy tongue licks me. My body tightens as his finger pushes up into me, and his tongue continues its voracious dance.

"Ah," I gasp.

The sensations are overwhelming, and I thrust my hips, wanting more. Leo curls his finger, and he licks harder. I moan, rocking faster as a flush of fireworks explodes throughout my body.

Leo slows his tongue as I slump against the headboard

when I come down from my high. I swing my leg off of him and fall on my back.

He peppers kisses up my arm and across my chest before he reaches my mouth. "How do you feel?"

"Amazing." Lifting my arm, I thread my fingers through his hair. "I want you," I say.

"You have me." He kisses my lips.

"I want you … inside of me. Now."

"You're ready?" he asks. "Are you sure?"

"I'm sure. I don't want to wait anymore." I reach my hand into his boxers and wrap my palm around him.

He removes his boxers and traces a path of kisses over my mouth, down my chest and my stomach, and against the sensitive area between my legs. I'm panting with want.

"Leo," I moan, pulling him up.

He grabs a condom from the bedside table and slides it over his length. "I'll go slow. Tell me if you want me to stop."

I hold his shoulders as he positions himself at my entrance.

He slides in slowly. "Are you okay?"

I nod against his chest. There's only a slight stinging. He pushes in further.

"Are you ready?" he asks.

I nod, pulling his face to mine. I kiss him as he thrusts his hips and moves all the way inside of me. His mouth captures my cry at the sharp pain. He stays still, waiting for me to get used to him, and then he starts to move again. Each passing minute tips the scale a little bit further from the pain.

Grabbing ahold of his butt, I pull him toward me and grind against him. The uncomfortable sting is still present, but the rest feels good. His tongue enters my mouth, and I kiss him hard, my love. He's gentle and attentive and everything I could have asked for my first time.

He pushes into me one last time and groans as he trembles

against me. He pulls out and tosses the condom in the trash. He lies behind me and kisses my shoulder.

"I love you," he says.

"I love you," I answer.

"I promise tomorrow will feel so much better."

"It was good. I enjoyed it," I say.

"Then, just wait until tomorrow and the day after that. It'll blow your mind." He kisses the back of my head.

"Tomorrow and the day after that?" I tease.

"You're going to want to do it all the time, and I will gladly be your willing partner."

I smile, pulling his arms tighter around me. Twisting my head to the side, I kiss his arm, and entirely content, I fall asleep.

CHAPTER 24

LEO

*L*ife with Alma is an adventure of the blind leading the blind. Had it not been for Amos, my beautiful girl wouldn't have experienced the emotional connection needed for childhood development. And while I had most traditional childhood experiences, I was so closed off to the world that I didn't take the moments in. Alma walked through life, craving it, all while I hid from it. We're two broken beings, trying to be whole, and maybe together, we are.

The past few months with Alma have been the best in my life. I never thought I would truly love someone or need someone in the way I love and need her. Perhaps our shattered pasts are to thank for us coming together. None of it makes sense, and yet it's entirely perfect in its dysfunction.

If I were a complete cheeseball, I might say that she completes me or some shit. I haven't fallen to that level of lameness, so I'll leave it simply stated—I love her. As deeply as a person can love another, I love Almalee.

Today is Alma's nineteenth birthday, and as we're only two weeks out from Christmas, I planned a day of holiday festivities for her. Based on the sex this morning after revealing my plans, it was the best gift I could've given her. On the list of things her parents didn't do, right after loving their daughter, they also didn't celebrate holidays, so today, we're celebrating.

I pull into the Christmas tree farm's parking lot.

"I'm so excited." She bounces on the passenger seat.

"This is a first for me too. My parents are all about the fake trees. The real ones would've been too messy for my mother." I step out of the car and close the door.

There's a wooden fence separating the tree farm and the parking area, and each tall wooden post has a large red felt bow attached. Strings of white Christmas lights loop across the length of the fence, creating a festive feel.

"It's like a Hallmark Christmas movie. Everything is so pretty," Alma exclaims as I meet her in front of the car and thread my fingers through hers.

I check in at the office, pay, and am handed an axe. We stroll out toward the lines of evergreens.

"So, are you thinking short and fat, tall and thin, or a Charlie Brown one? What's your ideal tree?" I ask her.

"Ooh, a Charlie Brown tree sounds fun. What's that one look like?" She wraps her free hand around my arm and leans against my side as we walk.

"You've never seen *A Charlie Brown Christmas?*"

"No."

"Well"—I smile with a shake of my head—"a Charlie Brown tree is basically a sad little branch with a couple of smaller sad branches on it." I search the ground and find a suitable replica from the cartoon classic. "Like this."

"Oh." Alma giggles. "Maybe not. That's just pathetic. What's the point of a tree like that?"

"That is the point. That it's sad and pathetic."

"I don't get it." She tilts her head back and looks up to me.

I lean in and kiss her temple. "And now, we're adding *A Charlie Brown Christmas* to our evening agenda."

"Oh, that sounds fun."

"Maybe not fun but clearly needed. Every child has seen that cartoon."

"Not every one." She shrugs. "Oh, what about this one?" She releases my hand and skips over to a bushy evergreen.

"I like it. Are we calling it then?"

"Yes. This is the one," she confirms, and I walk toward the tree. "Wait. Before you cut it down, let's get a selfie."

We stand in front of our first Christmas tree, and Alma holds her phone out, taking pics.

"Can you do it? Your arm is longer, so you can get more of the tree in the background."

I take the cell phone from her, clicking a few pics. "Good?"

"One more."

I hold the phone back out and smile as Alma kisses my cheek, and I snap the photo.

I return the cell phone to her. "All right, let's do this."

After the pine tree is cut, wrapped, and tied to the top of my car, we start back toward Ypsilanti and my house.

Prior to the Christmas tree farm, I'd taken Alma to a seasonal store to pick out holiday decor for both the interior of my house and the tree. There was much debate on what theme to go with—and by debate, I mean, Alma talking out loud to herself. Pink and silver almost won out, but since this is her first time Christmas decorating, she ultimately decided to go with traditional, hence the bags of everything green and red that the store carried piled high in the back seat and filling the trunk.

160

Shopping isn't how I'd normally prefer to spend a Saturday —or any day really. Online shopping is definitely my preferred method. But Alma makes even the most mundane tasks enjoyable. She makes the former chore of simply living worth it.

She's my reason. She's five foot two inches of beauty, brains, and spunk, and she makes everything better.

Holiday music plays softly through the speakers as we decorate my main living area.

"Christmas is officially my favorite holiday." Alma beams, hooking glittery red bulbs onto the tree branches. "Let's do this every year, okay?"

"Yeah." I grin.

Something deep within my chest aches. The thought of Alma here in my house a year from now is an incredible feeling. I never realized how much love hurts. There's a thin line between love and pain.

"I can see why people start decorating after Halloween. It just makes me so happy."

"Hold up. We are not going to be the people who put up our Christmas decorations on November 1. Those people are crazy." I shake my head.

"So? I bet they're happy."

"Well, you can't get a real tree if you decorate too early, or it will be dead by Christmas," I offer some logic.

"We could put up a fake tree first, and then in December, we'll get a second real tree. People can have two trees, you know?"

"Yeah, I know." I smile. "Whatever you want, babe."

Truth be told, if Alma wanted to celebrate Christmas fifty-two weeks a year, I'd do it. She can have whatever the hell she wants.

"Let's string popcorn!" she gasps. "That's a thing, right? Making strings of popcorn and draping it around the tree. I swear I've seen that before."

"Yeah, it's a thing."

"Sweet. We can do that and watch that Charlie Brown show you were telling me about."

"Sounds like a plan."

Just then, the sounds of voices ring outside the front door, and I watch Alma's face as she figures out what's happening.

"Carolers?" she shrieks, and her reaction is exactly as I pictured it when I set it up with Quinn earlier.

I follow Alma to the door, and she opens it, a giant smile plastered to her face. She leans back into my chest and listens as Amos, Quinn, and a dozen of Quinn's sorority sisters serenade us with Christmas tunes.

After they've finished a few songs, they come inside for cocoa and cookies. Yep, I bought hot chocolate and cookies for this occasion. I'm a regular-ass Martha Stewart.

"Thank you so much. That was awesome," Alma tells Amos and Quinn.

"It was Leo's idea," Quinn says.

"Well, thank you. I loved it."

"Happy birthday, Mutt." Amos hands her a small gift bag and pulls her into a hug.

"Thank you," she says to Amos, and the genuine joy on her face is everything I wanted for her today.

Alma's soul is so pure and good. She deserves nothing but happiness.

The carolers stay for an hour but then head out for some big sorority social event they have planned with another fraternity. As Quinn's date to the event, Amos leaves as well.

It's been a long, busy day, and with most of the decorating complete, I stream *A Charlie Brown Christmas*. Alma snuggles up against me under a fleece throw on the couch.

"I love you," I tell her and kiss the top of her head.

She sits up to look at me. "I love you. Thank you for the best day."

"I'm glad you liked it."

"I loved it, truly loved it." She holds a hand to her chest, her bold brown eyes filling with tears. "It was one of the best days of my life."

I swipe a lock of hair away from her face. "The way I love you makes me think I can be different."

"What do you mean, different? You're perfect just the way you are. I love you for you."

I hold her face in my hands and bring her lips to mine. Fact is, Alma doesn't know me. Pretending to be someone I'm not is exhausting, but if it means I get to keep Alma, I'll do it forever.

She reaches between us and undoes the button to my jeans. I quirk up a brow.

"I guess we could make the day a little better," she teases.

"There's always room for improvement." I snag a condom from my jeans pocket before kicking them off.

Alma yanks off her leggings and tosses them on the floor. She straddles me, my fingers dig into her hips, and when she slides her heat over me, a hiss escapes my lips. As I enter her, she circles her hips again and again, tormenting me.

"Baby …" I take her nipple into my mouth and suck hard.

She fists my hair and starts to ride me.

"I love you," she groans into the lust-filled space.

"I fucking love you," I tell her as she picks up speed.

I will love you forever.

CHAPTER 25

ALMA

*T*he waves of restless energy radiating from Leo are so palpable that the tiny hairs on my own arms buzz with nerves. He white-knuckles the steering wheel. The melancholy music drifts from the car speakers, a creepy soundtrack to this solemn ride.

Leo's childhood is still very much a mystery. He keeps the lock good and tight on those memories, never sharing them with me. And I've never felt that I should request that he does. Maybe it's not my place to ask. The regular night terrors and screams that steal his sleep tell me enough.

I've shared everything with Leo. He knows all about my past—the good and the ugly. I'm not embarrassed of where I come from. Had I been able to choose, I might've chosen different parents, but I can't regret them. Their choices and their actions, or lack thereof, made me who I am. I fought damn hard to get here, and I'm proud. I'm living proof that one can rise above their circumstances to be better.

Yet I can't pretend to know what it's like to walk in Leo's shoes. Trauma isn't universal, and no one will experience it or navigate through it the same way.

Leo is taking us to his parents' mansion, a thirty-minute drive from school. He says that Christmas is the one day a year he's obligated to spend with his family, but if it makes him this unhappy, then why? Why go through this? We should be at home, starting a Christmas Day tradition of our own. He offered me an out, but I want to be with him, today especially.

"We don't have to go." I reach my hand out and rest it atop Leo's thigh.

Christmas morning has never been a cause for celebration in my life, as my parents deemed it a commercial holiday, as useless as the rest of them. A fat, jolly man in a red suit, a bunny with a basket, love notes, or even green shamrocks weren't a thing in my house. Sure, each holiday came with a special tradition that existed solely between Amos and me, but all the rest was just noise.

Now that I'm out on my own, I want to start new holiday traditions. Leo has been so wonderful these past couple of weeks, making sure that I get to experience everything that this holiday has to offer. It's been truly magical for the first time in my life. I finally understand the commotion around Christmas, and now that I'm an adult, I will never *not* go all out for it again.

I think back over the past two weeks—the decorations, the movies, the lights, making and frosting Christmas cookies, all of it—and there's no way I could be disappointed in the slightest. However, I'd be lying if I said I hoped for more today.

"Can I ask you a few questions and not have you get mad at me?" My request is idiotic, but so is Leo's palpable anger. Better safe than sorry.

He forces out a sigh. "I'm sorry. You know this has nothing to do with you or us. I just really hate going home."

"Because of your family?"

"Yeah."

"But aren't you getting your business degree, so you can work with your dad and brother? How is that going to work if one meal gets you this worked up?"

"I don't know, honestly. I'll be mainly working with Stephen. Dad doesn't do much with the businesses anymore."

"So, you're cool with your brother?"

"No, he's an ass."

Leo takes a corner a little too fast, and I hold on to the door for support.

"So, why are you going to work with him? Why not do something else with your life? Something that will make you happy."

"I don't know what makes me happy—besides you, that is. I don't have hobbies or interests or passions. I don't fucking care about life in general—or at least, I didn't. But I have to do something. I can't just sit in my house, playing video games and living off of my trust fund. It's always just been expected that I follow this path, and I didn't care enough to argue. Now, I don't know."

"Life's too short to be unhappy, Leo. You deserve to do something that brings you joy."

"Doing you brings me joy," he deadpans.

"Well, I'm not going to pay you for your services. That's illegal," I say, attempting a joke. "So, you should probably think about another career." I reach my hand over the center console and place it on his thigh. "You're lucky in a way because you can do whatever you want even if it doesn't pay well. You don't have to choose a career based on income, like so many others do."

"Real lucky," Leo drawls out.

"You know what I mean," I say softly.

"Yeah, I do. And you're right; maybe I should think about another career."

"I think you should."

He places his hand atop mine. "Let's just get through today. Thank you for coming with me. My mom is excited to meet you, by the way."

"I'm always here for you. You know that. And really? What does she know about me?" I'm suddenly nervous, realizing that I'm meeting my boyfriend's parents. I mean, obviously, I knew that coming into today, but that's big.

"That you're perfect."

"Well, great. Then, she's sure to be disappointed," I kid.

"No one could ever be disappointed in you, babe."

THE HARDINGS' estate is exactly how I pictured a millionaire ex-actor turned business mogul's property to be. The brick house is more expansive than my entire dorm. The landscaping alone probably cost more than most people have in their retirement account. Even with the snow covering the ground, the trees, stone fountain, and ornate statues are impressive. Why do rich people always have some sort of statue in their yard?

"Who is that statue of?" I ask Leo.

He huffs out a laugh. "I have never cared enough to ask."

He pulls around the circular drive and parks the car in front of the grand entrance, a wooden door with beautiful glass work.

He grabs the gifts and then extends his hand toward mine. I take it.

"Help me get through dinner, and then we'll get out of here." He squeezes my hand.

"Of course." I stop along the stone walkway. "Look at me," I tell Leo.

He turns toward me, and I cup his cheek with my free hand.

"It's going to be fine." I stand on my tiptoes and press my lips to his.

"Okay," he utters as we continue up the steps.

Leo opens the door and steps inside. I force my expression to remain calm even though I want to squeal at how beautiful this home is. There's a Christmas tree in the foyer that's probably taller than my parents' house, and every branch is decorated with an opaque white ornament and white lights. It's stunning, right out of a magazine.

Past the foyer and into one of the living areas, there's another magnificent Christmas tree, decorated in rose and gold accents.

A gorgeous woman who looks like the female version of Leo greets us with a large grin. She's wearing a cream pencil skirt, a loose white blouse, and heels that match her skirt.

"Leo, honey. So good to see you." She kisses his cheek.

"Mom," he replies coolly.

"You must be the beautiful Alma who Leo's been hiding from us. He's not a big sharer, my boy, but I knew you must be special if he was bringing you home for Christmas. Welcome. We're so glad to have you here." She pulls me into a hug.

I nervously look to Leo because I want to hug her back, but I don't want to release his hand. When I thought about Leo's mother, I pictured someone different, someone colder.

"Thank you for having me. Your home is beautiful. The Christmas trees are just stunning," I tell her.

"Oh, thank you. Yes, I love Christmas decorations. We have seventeen Christmas trees up. I'll give you a tour later, so you can see them all. The designer did a fantastic job this year. Come. Everyone is this way." She starts across the foyer, and Leo and I follow.

Seventeen? I mouth to Leo.

Leo just rolls his eyes, not impressed.

Mrs. Harding leads us to the room with the rose-and-gold decorated tree. A man, who I know must be Mr. Harding, sits in a big leather chair, drinking amber liquid from a crystal tumbler. He doesn't get up from his chair but nods in our direction, a scowl on his face. Another much younger man who resembles Leo's father walks toward us with a super-model on his arm.

"Leo," he says coldly.

"Stephen," Leo responds with a bite.

Man, this family dynamic makes me and my parents seem somewhat normal. We know how to talk to each other—when they're sober at least.

"Hello, I'm Alma." I extend my hand, and Stephen shakes it.

"Hi, I'm Caterina, Stephen's wife. You can call me Cat." She smiles warmly, and I'm relieved that the women under this roof seem kind.

"Come sit." Mrs. Harding motions toward the white sofas.

I take a seat, and Leo leaves me to fill a drink from the decanter that sits atop a metal table. Leo fills his almost to the top before taking a long swig. Fear fills my belly, and I wipe my palms against my dress.

"Careful, Leo," Mr. Harding warns, his voice low and menacing.

"Fuck off, Dad," Leo responds.

"It's Christmas, asshole," Stephen adds. "Keep your shit together."

We haven't been here ten minutes, and my chest hurts. My heart hammers wildly, and I bite the inside of my cheek so hard that I taste blood.

"How's school?" Mr. Harding asks, his voice monotone.

"Fine, not like you care," Leo grumbles.

"If he didn't care, he wouldn't ask. Do you always have to be such a dick, Leo?" Stephen gripes.

"Caring isn't a prerequisite for actions in this house. There are many things that are said and done, and none of them are a result of compassion," Leo utters, his icy blues staring out the window. His entire demeanor is cold.

"It's Christmas," Leo's mother sighs. "Can we all please try to be civil?"

"Sure, Mother." Leo turns from the window and sits beside me on the leather sofa. "How's work, *Dad*?" Leo asks in a snide voice.

"Good, of course. Your brother has an incredible mind for business. Stephen, tell Leo about the deal you made last week."

"While you all talk business, I'm going to give Alma a tour," Cat says sweetly, standing up.

"Oh, that's nice of you." Mrs. Harding smiles toward her daughter-in-law.

I glance at Leo. I'm not sure I should leave him right now.

"It's fine," he whispers and squeezes my knee gently. His smile is forced, but I stand and follow Cat anyway.

When we're out of earshot, she says, "The tension in there, right?"

"Yeah, it's a lot. Is it always that bad?" I ask.

"Pretty much. The Hardings are definitely dysfunctional. They're so broken, I don't know if they can mend it." She leads me into the library.

"Wow. This room is amazing. Who's the book nerd?" I ask. My fingers caress the leather-bound covers of a row of classics.

"No one." She chuckles. "It's all for show. Most things in this house are."

Her last sentence almost sounds like a warning, but before I can ask her what she means, she continues walking, and I follow.

"I would be in here all the time if I lived here," I say. "I love books. So, how long have you been married to Stephen?"

"Three years. We met four years ago at one of my shows in Prague."

"Your shows?"

"Yeah, I was a model."

"I thought so," I say, hoping she knows it's a compliment.

We enter a room that has floor-to-ceiling windows, some fancy chairs, and lots of plants.

"What's this room for? Does anyone use it?" I wonder.

"I've never seen anyone in here, but I imagine it'd be a great place to read a book, if that was the sort of thing anyone here did." She grins. "I know Stephen seems like an ass, but I assure you, he has a good heart and a kind side. The men of this house don't bring out the best in each other, if you haven't noticed."

"Yeah, I got that impression."

Cat's heels stop clicking against the tiled floor, and she spins to face me. "Are you and Leo serious?"

I squint my eyes in confusion. "Um, yeah."

"So, you love him, and he loves you?" she clarifies.

"Yes, very much," I state, still wondering where this line of questioning is heading.

She lets out a relieved breath. "Good. I'm so glad. He needs someone to truly love him." She peeks over my shoulder, as if she's afraid someone is listening. "I need to talk to you but not here. If you're sure about your relationship with Leo, I think there are some things you should know that might help"—she pauses, as if trying to find the right words—"you understand him a little better."

"Is it bad? Should I worry?" I pull in a breath. "You're kind of freaking me out, Cat." I attempt a chuckle, but it falls flat.

"You're safe and fine … it's nothing like that. I just know some things that I'm sure Leo hasn't told you, but I think you should know."

"Is it about his nightmares?"

Her hand goes to her chest, and she looks distraught. "He still has those?"

I nod.

"Let me see your phone," she whispers. "We really can't talk here."

I hand over my cell, and she inputs her number. "Call me this week, and we'll do lunch."

A loud crash of glass shattering echoes from the other room.

"Oh shoot," Cat sighs.

"What?" I grab her arm, panicking.

"I think Christmas dinner is over—at least for you. Such a bummer." She frowns, and I know she means it. "Call me this week." She nods and squeezes my hand.

"Alma!" Leo roars.

"Bye!" Cat calls as I run past her toward Leo's voice.

CHAPTER 26

ALMA

I chase after Leo, not even bothering to wave good-bye to his family, and follow him out the front door. I weave around the stone work on the ground, so my heel doesn't get caught in one of the seams. The perfect ending to this failed dinner would be a trip to the emergency room.

"Leo," I urge him to slow, but he doesn't seem to hear me.

He jumps in the driver's seat of his Porsche. I slide into the passenger side and buckle my seat belt as he speeds out of the drive, rocks and snow spraying out behind us.

As we approach the end of the Hardings' property, the back of the car fishtails, and I press my hand to the dash to steady myself.

"Leo! Slow down!" I demand.

He's still lost in his head.

"Slow down, or let me out right now!" I grab his arm to get his attention.

His eyes dart toward me.

"Please, stop this," I plead.

His brutal stare softens as my gaze holds his for just a second. He resumes a normal speed as we pull onto the main road. His fingers wring around the steering wheel, and his chest heaves.

"What happened? Are you okay?"

"Same shit that always happens, Alma. Same. Fucking. Shit." He hits the steering wheel with his palm at each word.

"Hey." I massage the back of his neck. "It's okay. You don't have to go back there. We're gone. It's just me and you now."

He nods once, his eyes focused on the road.

"Do you want to talk about it?" I ask hesitantly.

"No." His answer is final.

I don't press him further, though I keep my hand on his leg, so he knows that I'm here if he needs me. The thirty-minute drive back to Leo's house feels longer, as the entirety of it is spent in an awkward silence and palpable anger.

Once parked in his driveway, I hurry out of the car and follow him up the steps. Our fluffy Christmas tree twinkles with lights in the front window, and sadness hits me. So much for starting new traditions today.

I jog after Leo as he takes the stairs up to the second level, two at a time. He yanks off his tie and jacket and drops them to the floor. I remove my heels and shimmy out of my skintight red dress. Rifling through my bag, which I refuse to unpack here even though I stay here most nights, I locate my reindeer fleece jammies that I packed just for today. I'm meeting up with Amos later tonight for our Christmas tradition, but until then, jammies it is.

Before I can put on the pajamas, Leo is behind me, his bare chest rising and falling against my back. "I need you, baby." His plea is pained.

"I'm here," I reassure him.

He splays his hand against my back and presses me against the bed. I hear the condom wrapper before Leo nudges my feet further apart with his. He thrusts into me in one quick motion, and I yell into the comforter. He fills me so completely, taking me intense and harsh. He grips my hips, almost bruising me as he pulls me back against him, my body meeting each of his thrusts with force. Harder and faster. I whimper into the mattress, the soft material catching my cries. It's so unlike anything we've done before. There are no words of love, just immediate need, and I find it ... hot.

Each time he pounds into me, I feel as if I were going to rip open but I want more. My orgasm hits, fierce and quick. My body shakes with satisfied tremors, and Leo bellows his release.

"Oh, baby." Leo twists my body to face him and kisses me. His tongue swirls with mine, and he pulls my lip between his teeth.

He removes the condom and tosses it in the trash without taking his mouth from mine. "I love you, Alma. I need you so much, baby. I love you. I need you." His words of adoration break my heart.

"I love you, Leo. I'm here." I run my fingers through his hair, pulling his face closer to mine.

"Promise me," he begs. "Promise me, Alma."

"I promise, Leo. I promise," I swear against his lips. I have no idea what I'm promising, but whatever he needs, I'll give it to him willingly.

He reaches over to the bedside table and grabs another condom foil. Ripping it open, he quickly puts it on and enters me again. This time, he makes love to me, his tongue in my mouth mirroring the movements below. I squeeze his ass, urging him deeper inside of me. He feels so good. I'm glad that Leo was my first, and I pray that he's my only. There's never been two people who fit this well together. He is everything to me. I don't have all of the pieces to the puzzle, but it doesn't matter. What I have—what Leo's given me—is enough. The parts that he wants to keep hidden from me are his, and if he doesn't want to share them, that's okay. He's enough, just as he is.

We come undone together, and he falls atop me, his body slick with sweat. I trace light circles across his back as our breathing slows.

Rolling off of me, he discards the condom and grabs another.

"Are you serious?" I say in disbelief.

He sits back against the headboard. "Come here." He motions.

I crawl toward him and straddle his lap before sinking onto him.

"Yeah," he breathes. "Faster, baby."

I ride Leo until my thighs burn. His face is a contortion of pleasure and peace, and the sight makes me bounce faster. If this is how Leo releases the pain, then I'm all in. This, I can do.

He buries his face into my chest as he growls and thrusts his hips into me, releasing into the condom.

"Fuck," he moans. "I could fuck you all day, baby."

"I see that," I say, humor in my voice as I roll off of him.

"You didn't come that time. Let me make it up to you." He rolls atop me, pressing me back into the bed as he kisses down my body.

"Leo, I'm fine. You don't have—" My protests are silenced when he starts to lick my most sensitive area.

When I'm beyond sated and my limbs feel like jelly, Leo kisses back up my sensitized skin. "Let's take a shower," he says.

"Okay." I grin lazily, running my fingers through his damp hair.

Before walking to the bathroom, he grabs another condom

packet. "You really need to get on birth control," he says with a smirk.

"Shower sex? Seriously?"

"It's my new Christmas tradition. Getting lost in you."

* * *

LEO LEAVES the bathroom first as I wrap a towel around my wet hair. Looking up to the fogged bathroom mirror, I see he's written *I love you* on the reflective surface.

The sentiment is adorable, but the clean freak in me cringes. "You know the oils on your fingers will stay on the mirror in a smudge until you clean it off."

"So? Then, I'll be reminded of you every time I look in the mirror. Or at least, until the cleaner comes." He chuckles.

I secure the towel around my chest and brush my teeth. Once finished, I pull a brush through my hair. All the sex has made me sleepy. I'd love to curl up on the couch and watch Christmas movies with Leo, but I know Amos is on his way.

"I'm kind of tired, so I won't be gone long," I say as I wipe the mascara that I had on for Christmas dinner at Leo's parents' off from under my eyes with some makeup remover.

Leo stands at the entrance of the bathroom. "You're leaving?"

The tone in his voice sounds off, and I turn to face him. "I mean, I'm supposed to meet up with Amos for our Christmas thing, but if you need me, I could call him and reschedule."

"No." He shakes his head. "Just go. I'm fine."

"Are you sure?"

"Yeah. You have plans. It's cool."

"We're just going to exchange gifts. I won't be long," I reassure him.

"It's fine. Just go."

He retreats from the bathroom and starts for downstairs.

His words said one thing, but his body language said another. I don't feel good about leaving him, but I did make plans with Amos.

Grabbing my cell from the bedroom, I call Amos.

"Hey! Merry Christmas! I'm almost to your dorm. I'm about five minutes out."

"You are?"

"Yeah. We're still on, right?" he questions.

"Yeah, of course. I'll see you soon."

I hurry and put on my jeans and a sweatshirt. I'll be gone an hour, tops. I shouldn't feel guilty about that. This has been planned, and Leo's known about it. I love Leo, and I want to be here for him, but we have to have normal boundaries too. I can't drop plans with my oldest friend because Leo's in a mood. It wouldn't be fair to any of us. That's not how life works.

It will be fine.

CHAPTER 27

ALMA

*C*ampus is eerily calm tonight. Most houses lie dark. The fresh snow is undisturbed in the yards. I suppose most people my age are home with family on Christmas. It's surreal, passing the places that are usually loud and alive but are now peaceful and blanketed in white.

I walk slower, absorbing this winter wonderland. My footsteps alone crunch into the sidewalk snow, and I can't help but feel like this gift of serenity is for me. After an unusual and completely random day, the calm nurtures my soul, and I cherish it.

As much as I complain about the snow and cold of my state, I have to admit that a fresh snowfall is one of the most amazing things. It drapes the world in a fresh beginning, a seasonal reminder that anyone can start anew. Chaos can be silenced. Ugly can be hidden.

"There's my Christmas Cookie." I smile wide at the sight of my best friend leaning against the brick of the building.

"I could've swung by and picked you up, you know?"

"I know. I enjoyed the fresh air." I swipe my badge over the keypad to unlock the entrance door, and we step inside. "How was home?" I ask as we walk up the stairs.

"Fine." The response is less than enthusiastic. "Mom sent some leftovers back for you. Remind me to give them to you later. They're in the car."

"Oh, yay! That's awesome. Did you see my parents?" I ask while opening up the door to my room.

"No, didn't see them. Did you hear from them at all?"

We step inside the room, and Amos sets down his gift bags. Quinn went home for the two-week holiday break and took every piece of clothing and bed linen with her to wash. Without her half of the room covered in clothes, the space seems bigger.

"I called and left a message and then a text. No response. I'm not surprised." I shrug.

There's a look of pity in Amos's eyes, but I ignore it.

"So, candy or presents first?" I ask, clapping my hands together.

"Always candy. We need to eat while opening our presents, silly."

I retrieve Amos's wrapped gift from beneath my desk and sit across from him on my bed. He dumps a bag of candy atop my comforter.

"Ooh, clearly, your mom misses you. This is double your normal stocking load," I say, picking up a chocolate-covered marshmallow Santa. "Chocolate-covered marshmallows are my favorite." I sigh and take a bite.

"I know they are." Amos grins and opens a Reese's Santa. Chocolate-covered peanut butter is his favorite.

From our very first Christmas as friends, when Amos

found out that Santa didn't visit my home and my parents didn't believe in sugar, he's been splitting his stocking candy with me. We exchanged handmade gifts that first Christmas too. I had made him a pencil topper out of aluminum foil. It was supposed to be a robot, but looking back, I realize it was just an aluminum foil blob. He had made me a bracelet, constructed out of some of his mother's multicolored craft string. It was a pathetic, thin, little, braided bracelet, but it's still one of my favorite possessions.

I have a shoebox full of everything meaningful in my life in the top drawer of my dresser. I have spelling bee medals, photos, certificates, and the gifts from Amos—including that bracelet.

"Oh, Dove! Grab your fortune," I tell Amos as I take a foil-covered chocolate and unwrap it. "Mine says, *Love is the only true adventure*," I read from the inside of the wrapper. "Aw. Sweet. What's yours?"

Amos unwraps his chocolate and reads it. "*You are exactly where you need to be.*"

"Perfect. I'm in love, and life with Leo is never boring; that's for sure." I chuckle. "And you are kicking ass at the college of your dreams and making your life goals come true. See, the Dove gods know."

"They haven't failed us yet," Amos agrees.

"Speaking of love, do you love Quinn?" I pop another chocolate in my mouth.

"I'm not sure. How do you know? I mean, I definitely like her, and the sex is great."

"Sex isn't love." I shake my head, a slight smirk on my face.

"I know that. That's why I'm not sure. I enjoy being with her and look forward to seeing her when we're apart, so maybe I do love her."

"I think if you did, you'd know. It's undeniable."

"For you, it is. Maybe, for me, it's different."

"True," I agree. "Well, are you ready for your presents?"

"Plural?" Amos quirks up a brow.

We've always agreed to just do one.

"It's all connected." I hand him the first box. "These were like my trial run. So, they don't count as the gift."

He pulls off the wrapping paper and opens the top of the box, revealing blue-and-yellow crocheted squares.

"They're pot holders! In Michigan's colors. I learned to crochet!" I grin wide.

"I love them." He holds up one of the squares. "And when I am out of the dorms and have pots ... I will definitely use them. Or ... I could use them like coasters or something."

"Okay, well, as I said ... those were my practice. So, open the next one."

He opens the next box and pulls out the scarf I made him.

"I looked up a pattern and everything. I tried to copy a scarf that's for sale at the Gap, so you'd actually wear it, you know? If you don't like it and don't want to wear it, I'll totally understand. But I had fun, making it."

"You did a great job, Mutt. Truly, I love it, and I'll absolutely wear it."

"Aw, yay!" I bounce on the bed. "I'm so glad."

"Your turn." He hands me the gift bag.

I pull out a book—or more accurately, a journal, daily devotional, and planner, all in one. Amos drew out monthly calendars for the year to come along with places for my to-do lists, quotes, and thoughts. He doodled designs on each page. I've always thought he's so talented with his art, but he rarely uses his drawing skills because art has never been valued in his home.

Tears fill my eyes as I turn the pages. Each page is better than the next. He hid little gems throughout—from memories to our favorite quotes to little drawings.

"This is incredible." I'm in awe. "It's almost too beautiful to use. This is so thoughtful, and your pictures … I just love them so much. Thank you."

"You're welcome. You'll use it, right? Don't just put it in that shoebox of yours. It's meant to be used."

"I don't want to ruin it."

"Alma," he drawls out my name.

"Fine, I'll use it. Cross my heart." I continue flipping the pages. "I'm going to mess it all up with my daily scribbles."

"Good. That's the idea." He smiles warmly. "You want to stream a movie or something?"

"No." I frown. "I'm sorry. I have to get back. Today wasn't a good day."

"What happened?"

"I'm not entirely sure. You know how Leo has some unspoken issues with his family. Well, we went there for dinner, and his sister-in-law was showing me around. The next thing I know, there was a glass smashed, and Leo and I were speeding out of the driveway. He won't open up about anything pertaining to his family. I'm not sure how to help him, but he was pretty bummed when I left tonight."

"I'm sorry. I understand," Amos says.

He divides his Christmas candy into two piles and tosses half of it in my gift bag. The gesture warms my heart.

"I would invite you over, but it's not a good time."

"I'm fine, Alma." He places his hand on my knee. "Plus, with Quinn gone for a couple of weeks, I can get caught up on my reading."

"Your reading?" I raise a brow with a smirk.

"I mean … have I read every book in the world? No." He chuckles and gathers his crocheted gifts in his arms. "I can drop you off."

"Thanks." I leave my journal on my bed but make sure to grab the bag of candy before heading out. "Speaking of books, you should've seen Leo's parents' library."

"Incredible?"

"Oh, yeah. We're talking *Beauty and the Beast* amazing."

"Really?" His curiosity is piqued. "Disney quality?"

I nod, my eyes wide. "Yes, and … they don't even use it!"

We exit the building and walk toward Amos's car.

"That's a shame."

"I know, right?"

CHAPTER 28

ALMA

I pull a long breath of the cool night air into my lungs, the crispness refreshing. Turning the door handle, I step inside.

"I'm back," I say into the foyer and kick off my boots.

A handful of gifts sits beneath the Christmas tree, the reflection of the lights bouncing off the shiny paper. I completely forgot that Leo and I still have gifts to exchange. A large smile finds my lips.

"Leo," I call out.

I do a quick scan of the main level before heading up the stairs. When I reach the top and look for him, I find he's not in his bedroom or bathroom.

"Leo!" I search through all of the spare rooms and come up empty.

Maybe he ran out to grab some food.

I shoot him a quick text.

Hey, babe. I'm back. Where are you? xo

I return to my reindeer jammies and snuggle under a blanket on the sofa while flipping through the DVR. There are a few holiday shows and cartoons that we've yet to watch. I turn on one of the old original holiday cartoons. Leo said that he's not a fan, as the Claymation characters freak him out, so I know he won't mind if I watch it without him.

When I don't hear back from Leo, I call his cell phone, and I'm sent straight to voice mail. I've been back for an hour now, and there's been no word from him. I'm starting to get worried. His Porsche is missing from the garage, so wherever he went, he drove. Given the snowy state of the roads and the fact that a sports car doesn't have the best traction on slick pavement, it adds another level of worry.

"Where are you, Leo?" I grumble and click off the TV.

Leo was right; those Claymation cartoons are just creepy.

I text Leo several more times and send a few texts to Ethan as well. I don't know what else to do.

Around midnight, Ethan calls me back.

"Hey! Do you know where he is?" I screech into the phone.

"No. I haven't heard from him today. When's the last time you saw him?" Ethan asks.

I tell Ethan about me leaving for an hour to meet up with Amos and coming back to him gone.

"So, you both went to his parents' today?"

"Yeah, earlier."

"How'd that go?" he asks with a tone indicating that he already knows.

I tell him everything.

There's a sigh on the other end of the line. "Alma, he's fine. He'll be back at some point."

"What do you mean, at some point? Where is he? You don't think he's in danger? I shouldn't call the cops?"

There's silence on the other end of the line, save for Ethan's quiet breaths. I'm under the impression that he's keeping something from me.

"What is it? Please tell me, Ethan. I'm literally freaking out with worry," I plead.

Ethan sighs. "Alma ... it's not really my place. All I'll say is that, he does this, and he'll be back."

"He does this?" I snap. "What does that mean?"

"His dad has a way of setting him off and getting under his skin. Leo has been known to take off for a few days after a confrontation. Their relationship is toxic, and Leo doesn't always ... handle it the best. I wouldn't worry. He'll be back. He just has to cool off."

"He just left without telling me. Where would he go? What is he doing? This doesn't make any sense."

"I'm sorry. Leo's life is complicated."

"Yeah, I get that, Ethan, but how am I not supposed to worry about him? And why would he just leave without a word or a note or anything?"

"I'm really sorry, Alma. I'll come back to school tomorrow and look for him, okay? Just try not to worry and get some sleep."

"Okay," I say, resigned. "Call me tomorrow."

"Will do. Night, Alma."

"Night, Ethan."

The line goes dead, and I stare at the cell phone in my hand, processing everything Ethan said. Not only was he not surprised, but he also wasn't even worried, and that part unsettles me the most. I know that Ethan's loyalties lie with Leo, but there's something he's not telling me.

Tears flow freely, cascading down my cheeks as my heart rips open. This entire situation is disturbing, and with every beat deep within my chest, my doubt whispers that nothing is going to be the same again.

* * *

ETHAN COMES BACK FROM HIS PARENTS' house the day after Christmas and looks for Leo "in all his usual spots," whatever that means. He doesn't find him but assures me that Leo's fine and he will come back when he's ready.

Now, I'm just furious. I get that there's a lot of stuff going on within Leo's mind that he's not sharing with me, but to just disappear like this is so selfish. He has to know that I'm worried sick about him. I would never put him through this torment. He has to have seen my texts and listened to my voice mails. I just don't understand.

* * *

ON DECEMBER 27, two days after I last saw Leo, I break down and call Amos in tears. If I'm being honest, I didn't want Amos to know. I wanted Leo to return with a good explanation and for everything to be okay. Admitting what's been going on the past two days makes it real, and I'm afraid it's not something Leo and I can come back from. I love Leo more than I ever knew was possible, but I have to love myself and know my worth.

I exit the dorm, stepping into the chilly air as Amos walks up the shoveled, salted sidewalk. He opens his arms, and I fall into them. I cry into his puffy down jacket, and he holds me close.

"You should've called earlier, Mutt." He kisses the top of my head.

"I know. I'm just embarrassed. This is all so stupid. Who does this, Amos?" My tearstained face looks up to my best friend, and I can see the pity in his expression. The pity in his eyes is why I avoided calling him in the first place.

"Try not to think about it. Your imagination could be

making it worse than it is. Maybe there's an explanation that will make sense." Even as he says it, neither of us believes his words. "Let's go eat. What do you feel like?"

"Pasta," I say. I need something good and heavy and carb-filled to hold me down as pieces of my heart feel like they're breaking off and floating away.

"Perfect. I drove past an Italian restaurant on the way here. It looks locally owned, so I bet it's good."

"Okay," I agree and follow Amos to his car. "What have you been up to the past couple of days? No roommate. No Quinn."

Amos starts the car and pulls out of the parking lot. "It's been nice. It's kind of cool to be on campus when most everyone is home."

I nod. It wasn't long ago that I was thinking the same thing.

"I actually watched this documentary online that was originally filmed for PBS." Amos launches into the details of what he learned, and I rest my head against the glass of the car window, listening—or trying to.

Then, I see it.

"Stop!" I yell and sit up, looking toward the house we just passed. "That's his car! That's Leo's Porsche!"

Amos turns in the next side street and pulls over. "Are you sure?"

"I'm positive. That's Leo's car. I know it is. The paint job is custom." I strain my neck to look down the road toward the house. "We have to go there and check."

"I don't know if that's such a good idea." Amos shakes his head.

"Please. I have to know."

Amos blows out a breath. "Okay."

He completes a U-turn and heads back in the other direction before pulling into the driveway next to Leo's car. The house is a small brick ranch. It's an older house, the wear and tear on it evident. The person who lives here hasn't kept up on its maintenance. A gutter has broken away from the roof and swings in front of the small bay window. The bottom of the front screen door appears to have been chewed off by an animal, a large dog presumably. The place gives me the creeps, but I step out of the car anyway.

"Alma"—Amos hesitates beside the car—"are you sure about this?"

"Yeah." My voice comes out steady, more confident than I feel.

Amos stands beside me as I knock. No one answers, and I knock again. Finally, the door handle turns, and the door is opened a crack.

I'm hit in the face with an awful stench—dirt, smoke, sweat, and rot—almost knocking me over.

"What do you want?" a woman with a gruff voice asks.

"Is Leo here?"

"Who's asking?" the woman questions.

"His girlfriend, Alma. I just have to see him for a minute. Please."

She doesn't respond but opens the door wider and retreats back into the house. I shoot Amos a look, and the two of us step inside. I fight the urge to cover my nose with my shirt and step deeper into the dreary place.

The first thing I see when we enter the living room is a girl riding a man in the corner on a reclining chair. I gasp at the couple having sex right out in the open. The place is a pit. There are empty beer cans, wrappers, pipes, and drug para-phernalia everywhere. A half-dozen people sit on the dirty plaid couches around the room, clearly drugged out on something.

I scan the room, trying to take in what I'm seeing, and my chest aches when I see him. He's sitting on a love seat to my right, wearing the same clothes I last saw him in. His cheeks seem sunken in, and purple bags are prominent under his dead eyes. He stares at me, assessing but lacking emotion. He's a hollow shell of the man I know. The Leo I love is gone.

I cover my mouth as bile rises in my throat, and I gag, clenching my stomach. Amos grabs my arm and pulls me out of the house, shutting the house door when we step into the winter air. I fall to my knees, dry-heaving. My stomach is empty, so nothing comes up save for the acidic bile. Tears blur my vision.

I release a heart-wrenching scream. Amos lifts me from the ground, and I cry against his chest as he leads me to the car. My pain and heartbreak are the only sounds as Amos drives back to the dorm.

CHAPTER 29

LEO

*S*he was here. Alma, my soul. She was here. Beautiful and brave and gone. I didn't try to stop her because she should go. She's always been too pure, too good for someone like me. I was selfish in believing I could keep her.

I wanted to be better. For her, I did. For the briefest of moments, I thought that maybe I could. Yet I've never been brave, and I've never been strong. I've always been a coward, running.

The demons pull me down every chance they get, and I let them. I allow it because it's easier to be lost to oblivion than drowning in pain. It's easier to check out than fight. I know because I've been losing the battle my entire life. I'm exhausted, and I can't do it anymore.

She'll thank me someday. She'll realize that because I love her, I had to let her go. She won't see it yet, but she will. The greatest gift I can give her is a life without me.

CHAPTER 30

ALMA

I unplugged the lights of the Christmas tree, turned off the lights in the house, left my set of keys on the table, locked the door, and closed it tight. As I walked away with tears in my eyes, I promised myself that I'd never go back there.

Never.

I cried in my room for two weeks. Amos brought me food and held me most nights. He's the only person I'd trust to see me in such a desperate state. He knows my soul in and out, as I know his. He's all I have in this world—a fact that's clearer now more than ever.

How can I trust love when the sentiment is thrown around so easily? Leo claimed to love me, but in the end, he didn't. I gave him everything, and he left me broken and exposed. I hope I never love again. When I'm in it, it's magical, but when it leaves, the agony is unbearable. I'd give up the past three months to not know what this pain feels like.

Classes started up again a month ago, and since then, I've gone through the motions. I get up. I go to class. I complete the assignments. I go to the next class. I show up at work. Most of the peers I tutor are probably scared of me, but I get paid whether I smile or not.

I take a lot of walks in the cold. February is a horrible month, freezing and miserable. Amos and Quinn think they're doing me a favor by retreating to the bathroom to screw in the shower, but the shower is just on the other side of the wall from my bed. I can hear everything. So, as soon as they enter the bathroom, I go for a walk.

I just want to be okay again. I want to stop hating Leo, as I've realized that hate is awfully close to love. It's an intense and all-encompassing emotion. I'd give anything to simply not care. Indifference is the goal, and I pray I get there.

It's been an hour since Amos and Quinn got into the shower, and I can no longer feel my toes, so I head back.

"Where've you been?" Quinn asks me as I enter our room.

"Just walking."

"It's below zero out there. You're going to freeze." She pulls a straightening iron through her hair.

I want to tell her that the numbness from the bitter temperature is a welcome sensation, but I've been trying to be less of a downer lately, so I simply say, "I don't mind the cold."

"Well, now, you have to hurry and get ready," she says.

"For?"

"A party."

I shake my head. "I'm not going to a party, Quinn."

"Please," she begs. "Amos is going. It's not at Ethan's frat house, so there's no chance you'll see *him*. My sorority is throwing it with another frat. It's going to be so fun. It's in the basement, and it's a glow-stick party."

"What's that mean?"

"Everyone wears black. It's going to be completely dark, except for whatever glow sticks you wear. So, if you want to just chill and not draw attention, you can wear a glow bracelet only." She dangles a package of glow sticks, as if the fact that wearing one would somehow change my mind.

"No," I state and plop onto my bed.

"You really need to start living again, Alma," she says.

"No," I repeat.

"Fine." She throws the package of glow bracelets onto the dresser. "Then, we're not going either. You're alone too much. We'll stay here with you."

"I like being alone," I argue.

Quinn throws her hands up in frustration. "That's the problem. You shouldn't. Everyone needs people, Alma. You're letting him win. Is that what you want? For him to win? It's been six weeks, and you mope around here like Eeyore all day. He's moved on. You need to as well. That's why we're staying here with you."

"I agree. We're not leaving," Amos finally speaks up. "Plus, I could use another shower."

With the last sentence, he looks at me as my mouth falls open.

I throw my pillow at him. "Jerk," I say in jest.

He knows me too well. Truth be told, I'd rather hang out at a party in some dark corner by myself than listen to Quinn and Amos have shower sex again.

"I'll wear black, but I'm not doing my makeup or hair. I'm going as is." I motion to my plain face and messy bun.

"That's fine. I'll accept those terms." Quinn holds back a grin. "Can we compromise on you brushing your teeth?"

I shoot her a mock glare. "Well, now, you've just gone too far."

Amos and Quinn laugh, and I grab a pair of black yoga

pants and a black sweatshirt and amble toward the bathroom. I put on my attire for the evening and brush my teeth.

I know Quinn's right. I can't mope around forever. Leo might have stolen my heart, but I can't give him everything else. I still have three and a half years of college left. I need to start living again.

* * *

AMOS DRIVES us to the frat house. It's a little farther out from campus than the rest of the sorority and fraternity houses. It's one I've never been to before. As we park, a few girls in tiny black dresses and glow necklaces saunter up the drive toward the large house.

Quinn bends and cracks the plastic glow items to activate their light and hands them out to Amos and me.

"I'm just going to do a bracelet." I wave off the extra pieces she's trying to hand me.

"Okay." Quinn doesn't press the issue. "I'll put the rest of yours together to make a belt for me. Won't that be cute?"

We each take one of Amos's arms as we walk toward the back door, where everyone seems to be entering. There are black lights flanking the steps that lead down to the basement. Quinn was right; it's dark down here, save for the glowing items.

"Let's dance!" Quinn pleads, pulling on Amos's arm.

"Go dance," I say over the music. "I'll be over there." I point toward the far corner of the wide-open basement.

Quinn pulls Amos over to the area where the most people are dancing, though it seems like everyone is just dancing everywhere. I wind myself through the dancing bodies and over to back of the space. I smile faintly when I see an empty barrel in the corner. I sit on it with a sigh of happiness.

Yep, this is living.

It's cool to see what everyone has done with their glow items. Many just wear them as necklaces, bracelets, and headbands. Though some more daring people have constructed skeletons or phallic items. A few girls have glowing circles around their boobs—always classy. One girl has at least a dozen glow wands sticking up from her head in some sort of an intriguing bouquet or firework display. One guy has his in the shape of an arrow pointing toward his crotch. He gets an A for effort for sure.

I continue to people-watch and zone out to the music with my back pressed against the cement wall. I wouldn't say it's fun, but it's a step in the right direction.

I feel *him* before I see him. The hairs on my arms rise, and my stomach immediately feels ill.

"Alma," he says hesitantly, and I freeze.

Do I run? Yell? Ignore him? I don't know. Why is he here?

The decision is made for me because I literally can't move. I'm frozen to my spot on the barrel, terrified to breathe or speak.

"I thought you might be here. I knew Quinn's sorority was cohosting, and I wanted to see you."

He sounds like himself, the Leo I loved. But I can't stop picturing the man I thought I knew sitting in that disgusting house with purple bags under his eyes.

I close my eyes, and my body shudders at the memory.

I pull my legs into my chest and bury my face. The movement seems immature, but I don't care. I can't face him.

He continues, "You don't have to say anything, and I'll leave in a second. I just had to tell you that I'm so sorry. You probably don't believe me, but I am. I am sorry for all of the hurt I caused you. I'm sorry for not being stronger. I'm sorry that you had to see me like that. I'm sorry that I let you love me. I should've never walked you home all those months ago. I should've never kissed you. None of it. I was selfish, and I thought I could have you. I was wrong. I'm sorry."

I'm trying to understand his words, and I hear the remorse in his voice, but so much of what he's saying doesn't make sense. Tears fall onto my pants, and I keep my face hidden, afraid of seeing him, terrified of breaking.

"I guess that's all." The raw emotion in his voice crushes me. "I hope, someday, you'll understand that I do love you. I don't love anyone else, Alma, not even myself. But I'll always love you."

I feel him turn away from me, and I lift my tear-soaked face. "Why?" I say into the darkness.

Leo turns back toward me.

"We were perfect," I say. "Why'd you do that when we had everything?"

"You are perfect," he retorts, his heartache palpable. "I am nothing."

My lip trembles. "You were something to me."

A slow song starts, and the ache in my chest grows. The first notes of "If the World Was Ending," by JP Saxe and Julia Michaels, echo against the basement walls. I've been listening to this song on repeat over the past month every time I need a good cry. To me, it speaks to two people who desperately love each other but can't be together. The music connects with my heartbroken soul.

Leo extends his hand, barely visible, save for the glow band around his wrist. Without thinking, I take it, and he pulls me into his arms. He holds me, and I cry against him as we sway to the melancholy music. He smells like Leo, a mixture of his natural scent and his body wash. It's intoxicating. I breathe deep, committing the way he smells to memory. My arms circle his body. I want to remember what it feels like to have him in my arms. He's always been so much bigger and taller than me, larger than life as he captured my heart. The way he holds me and how I melt into his body, it's pure magic. It's undeniable chemistry, and this is the last I'll feel of it. This dance is our good-bye song.

Leo kisses the top of my head, his lips lingering, and his chest swells as he breathes me in. His arms squeeze me tight, and my body shakes against his as I cry. The slow song is over, but we remain in this tortured embrace. My battered soul clings to his for several more fleeting moments, and I break as he pulls away.

"I'll never forgive you." My lip trembles.

He swipes a tear-soaked strand of hair away from my face. "I'm counting on it," he says before walking away.

CHAPTER 31

LEO

I rush out of that basement as fast as my feet will carry me, needing to get distance between me and her. Getting into my car, I slam the door and repeatedly bang my palms against the steering wheel.

Seeing her was a bad idea. She looked so lost and frail, sitting alone in the corner of that basement. I'm sure her annoying roommate dragged her out against her will. She clearly wasn't in the partying mood. I shouldn't have gone. I know that, but she deserved some sort of good-bye, an explanation. Though I'm not sure if I adequately conveyed either.

I drive back to my house, the one I haven't been to since Christmas Day. After my two-week bender, where I should've OD'd and died ten times over, I checked into a treatment center to detox and get clean—again. My life is a revolving door of shit. I'm in a constant state of fucked up or fighting to stay sober. It's one or the other ... all the fucking time.

I wish I were provided with coping mechanisms like other people seem to have, but I wasn't. Sometimes, shit gets so heavy that I need to escape or I feel like I'm going to die. I'm suffocating in the hell that is my life.

None of this is a recent self-discovery. I've always been completely aware of my issues, but I was selfish enough to think I could change for her. I pulled her into my shit, knowing deep down that I would crush her with the idea that maybe love would be enough.

Her love couldn't save me because I'm irredeemable. Love is a fucking joke. It just gives you false hope, makes you think you can do the impossible, and then makes your lows that much heavier.

I pull into my driveway and park in the garage. Disappointment surfaces at the fact that my house is still standing. Part of me was hoping the Christmas tree would catch fire, so the whole place would burn down. It would've been easier to start over that way. I know that every piece of fabric is going to smell like her. Every surface that I ever made love to her on is going to make me hurl.

I step inside and flick on the lights. She's everywhere. Her water bottle is on the edge of the sink. The blanket that she covers with while watching TV is in a crumpled pile on the couch. I can only imagine how long she sat there, snuggled in that blanket, waiting for me to come back.

The pine tree is completely brown, and most of the needles have fallen to the ground. The strands of lights swoop around the sad branches. Our presents remain untouched under the dead limbs. I wipe a pile of dead pine needles from a small gift and pick it up. My name is scrawled across the top of the package in Alma's writing.

I pull off the metallic red paper, and there's a note.

Leo,

New tradition. I'm going to get you an ornament for our tree every year. So, when we're old and gray, we'll have years of memories and love hanging from our tree branches.

I love you, more than I knew was possible. I'm yours forever. I promise.

Love,

Alma

I remove the box lid to find a flat ceramic ornament with the selfie of Alma and me at the tree farm printed on it. She chose the picture where she's kissing my cheek and I'm smiling like a happy fool.

A fool nonetheless.

A new level of rage hits me. Fury at myself and my father and my life. I hate myself more than ever. I want to scream and cry and escape into oblivion, where I can't feel the pain. I want to burn this whole fucking house down.

I fold the note, put it atop the ornament in the box, and place the package in my back pocket. With one jerk, I pull the dead tree to its side, and I drag it out onto the front lawn. I head back into the house and grab everything that reminds me of her and heave it from the house. I toss every blanket, towel, and linen she's ever touched into the pile. My T-shirts that she's worn and a chair she rode me in make it to the heap. It takes an enormous amount of strength to maneuver my king-size mattress down the steps and into the front yard, but I manage to get that in the pile as well. I can never sleep in that bed again.

Retrieving a can of gasoline from the garage, I douse the evidence of her and set it on fire. In a few minutes, I'll hear sirens, and I'm positive I'll be ticketed for this giant bonfire in my front yard, which is undoubtedly breaking a slew of fire zoning rules. Though, by the time it's put out, she'll be gone, and I'll be able to move on.

Remembering the box in my back pocket, I pull it out, set to toss it in the flames. My hand trembles with the small gift in my grasp. Its contents are too painful.

I need to let her go.

I need to let her go.

I need to let her go.

As the police cruiser stops in front of my house, I shove the box into my back pocket.

CHAPTER 32

ALMA

*M*y good-bye dance with Leo set me back a bit in my healing process. It did less to make me not want him and more to remind me how much I still loved him. After the night of the glow-stick party, there have been no additional run-ins with Leo, which my brain would say is good. Yet the organ that speaks the truth—my heart—would admit the sadness that goes along with that fact. Plus, I hate how the last time I saw him was in such a dark place. I could barely make him out.

That tidbit is hardly important since I scroll through the pictures of us on my phone daily and feel sorry for myself. The pictures are my Leo patch. I can get through the day without him as long as I get a glimpse. Just a glance at his smile or his eyes or his lips. I need just a brief snapshot to see his face and the happiness and love on it as he looks at me—a reminder that I was loved and it was real, if only for a moment.

There are only two weeks of school left, and I'm freaking out. I've been working as a tutor all year to save money, but I still only have enough for about a month's rent. A full-ride scholarship with room and board is great during the school year, but the dorms close for the summer, and I'm expected to leave.

There's no way I can go back home. I've spoken to my parents twice this year. My father called me once because he couldn't remember the password for the cable app. My mother called to ask if I remembered where we stored the duffel bags because they were going to go stay with some friends in a hippie commune out west for a while. Neither conversation was meaningful, and though I tried to give them some details about my life here, it didn't seem as if they were interested.

If they're still out west, it could work. I'd just have to clean up the house so that it was livable, but who knows if they're still there or when they'll be back? Heck, I wouldn't be surprised if they never went in the first place. They aren't the most reliable in their travel plans. The point is that I can't count on them, and I definitely can't survive a summer with them.

It's difficult to get a job off of campus without a car, and I can't keep relying on Amos to take me everywhere. He'd do it, no questions asked, but that's not fair to him. At this rate, if I'm not careful, I'm going to be bunking up with a crack dealer in the worst part of town. The options that I can afford are limited.

I scroll through my phone, searching online for nearby apartments to rent. There are a bunch of summer leases available because a lot of students go back to their families for the summer, but all of the apartments for lease are two or three bedrooms. Seeing that Quinn and Amos—my only real friends—are going home for the summer, I need a one bedroom, a cheap one.

A text comes through on my phone. It's Cat. She's been texting me on and off over the past couple of months, asking if we can meet but I always tell her no. She has definitely been persistent. I know she means well and is trying to help, but Leo's no longer in my life, so his family shouldn't be either. I don't have the right to know anything that Leo hasn't told me himself, nor do I have a reason to get involved.

Please, Alma. Just meet me for a quick bite.

I'm driving through Ypsilanti in a bit.

Just tell me where to meet you.

I'm not going to give up until you talk to me.

It's important. Pretty please.

Her texts come through in rapid succession. I don't have time to respond to one before she's texting again. She seems desperate to speak to me. I let out a groan and type back.

Fine. I'll meet you at Luca's Coney Island, but then that's it.

Thank you, Alma! See you soon.

I grab my purse and head out. The walk to the diner is quick, and before I know it, I'm pulling the door open and finding a seat.

Maybe I should've offered to meet her somewhere else. This place will always remind me of Leo. Fear courses through me as I wonder if I'm going to run into him here. Though he's seemed to have dropped off the planet, and I know because I've looked. Every time I walk across campus, my eyes scan for him. Every party Quinn drags me to, I look. He's just gone. This school isn't that big. There's no way our paths wouldn't have crossed, even once, since February.

"Hello, my lady! Good to see you. Is my favorite customer meeting you here today?" Luca greets me, setting down a plastic cup of water in front of me.

"No." I shake my head. "I'm meeting someone else. Have you seen Leo lately?"

"Not for many months," Luca answers with a frown.

His answer doesn't surprise me. I knew Leo was gone. I felt it.

"Hey, Luca"—I look around at the packed diner—"you aren't hiring, are you?"

"Why? You want a job?" He smiles wide.

"Well, I desperately need a job." I nod, folding my hands in front of me.

"You're hired. My waitress Sally just quit."

"Really?" I gasp and stand to hug him. "Thank you!"

"Come in tomorrow, and we'll get the paperwork completed and your schedule set."

"You don't know how much this means to me. Thank you so much, Luca."

"Thank you." He pats my hand and scurries off to another table.

The bell above the door chimes, and I look over to see Cat walking through the door. She waves when she spots me. I wave back and can't help my smile. She's just so nice. How she got mixed up with the Hardings, I'll never understand.

I greet her when she reaches the table, and she pulls me into a hug.

"Thank you for meeting me, Alma. You look beautiful," she tells me, though I think she's just being polite.

"You too," I say because it's the truth.

"What's good here?" she asks, looking over the menu.

"Everything. Though Leo's favorite is the chili-cheese fries." His name burns as it leaves my lips, but I swallow the hurt.

Luca returns to the table, and we both order the chili-cheese fries.

"Should I just get to it then?" She quirks a brow.

"That'd probably be best."

"Well, as you know now, Leo has addiction problems," she says softly, as if it pains her to admit it. "Stephen tells me that Leo's been abusing substances since he was twelve. The other thing, the information that I wanted to tell you on Christmas ... well, the thing you have to understand is that my husband loves his brother, but there is so much hurt between them that he doesn't know where to start to mend it. You might see cruelty in Stephen, but it's simply frustration. Anyway, I'm getting off track." She waves her hand in front of herself.

I realize that she wanted to tell me that little tidbit about Stephen because I had seen the way he was around Leo and I wasn't impressed. She assumes that I have a bad opinion of her husband, and she's right.

She continues, "Okay, so Stephen told me that when Leo was very young, his father would take him to the basement and"—her eyes fill with tears—"abuse him."

"What kind of abuse?" I ask.

"Physical ... and sexual." She swallows a lump in her throat. "When it first started, Stephen heard his brother screaming and didn't know why, so he went looking for Leo and found their dad raping him."

"What?" I cry, tears falling from my eyes.

Cat dabs her tears with a napkin. "It happened a lot. Stephen heard Leo's screams for years, but he was told to never go down to the basement again, or it would be him. He was afraid."

"What about his mom?"

"She knew. She was afraid too."

My tears fall freely, and the anger wells up in my chest. This isn't the type of information that I can process here. I'm going to start yelling in this diner, and I need to get out. I run for the door. Cat chases me out.

"Alma, my car's here." She points to a BMW parked toward the corner. "Come sit and talk to me."

I follow her to the car and sit in the passenger seat. Once the door is closed, my sobs come. I cry into my hands, rocking back and forth. My chest aches for Leo and the little boy inside him who was stolen.

"I can't believe this." I shake my head. "When did the abuse stop?"

"When Leo was ten, he tried to kill himself, and it stopped after that."

"Who was there to protect him?" I scream, snot and tears covering my lips. I wipe the back of my arm under my nose. "His mom should've protected him! Stephen should've stopped it! Why is everyone hanging around Mr. Harding like nothing happened? This is sick! I hate them all."

"I know." She cries silently beside me as I fall apart. "I've been trying to understand it. They're all victims, Alma, in their own way. They've chosen to pretend it didn't happen and carry on with their lives. His mom is weak; that's just who she is. Stephen was a child too."

"I guarantee you that Leo hasn't forgotten it! How could he? They all ruined his life. And you all are just over there, having dinner with a child rapist?"

"It's a challenging situation. Despite the trauma, they're still a family. I think people have this innate desire to stick together. Even Leo still comes around for holidays. As outsiders, looking in, it's hard for us to understand the messed up dynamics."

"I'll never forgive them." My chest heaves. "Why are you telling me this now? You know Leo and I aren't together anymore. I love him, and I understand now why he might turn to drugs to cope with his demons. But I can't be with an addict. I was raised by addicts. I won't be a part of that life. I *can't* be a part of that life."

"After Christmas, Leo signed himself into rehab for a month. Then, he saw you and started spiraling, but instead of turning to drugs, he got help. He wants to be better, Alma. He's been in rehab and therapy for four months now. I'm the only one he allows to visit. His room is barren. There are no personal effects, except for an ornament of the two of you. You're kissing his cheek."

"I had that made for him for Christmas."

"He doesn't know that I know, but when he went to the bathroom, I found a note you had written him peeking out from underneath his pillow. He's only had two personal items in his room all these months, and they're both from you. He loves you, Alma. He doesn't think he's good enough for you. He's afraid of failing you, but he loves you, and I know you love him."

I swallow and swipe the back of my hands across my cheeks. "I know he does. I know he loves me, but I can't save him."

"He's trying to save himself." Cat's voice trembles with sadness. "He's trying so hard. Just love him back. He deserves to be loved."

I cup my face with the palms of my hands and cry. I almost can't process what I've learned in the past few minutes. No child should have to go through what Leo did. I can't imagine the pain that an experience like that has on a person. How does anyone survive that? It's not fair. I'd live my childhood over a hundred times if I could save Leo from his.

Forever seems to pass as I fall apart in Cat's car. She doesn't say anything else and allows me my grief. When my tears run dry and my chest physically aches from too much despair, I ask Cat to drive me the two blocks back to my dorm.

She pulls up alongside the walkway leading to the building.

"I'm sorry. I know that information broke your heart, but I love Leo. I want him to be happy, and I think you're his shot." Cat pats my knee.

"I have a lot to think about. I can't promise anything."

"I know, and you have to do what's best for you. I understand that. But I can tell you that Leo is better than I've ever seen him. He's putting in the work. He's trying. People beat addiction. People survive horrible pasts."

I nod and smile weakly. At least Leo has his sister-in-law to love him since he has the worst family in the world. I feel incredible gratitude toward her.

"Thank you for loving him."

She sniffles and bobs her head as a tear falls. "He'll be home on Saturday."

"Okay," I say before stepping out and closing the door. It's not an answer, good or bad, just a word, but it's all I have.

CHAPTER 33

ALMA

*T*he rest of the week passes in slow motion. Every time I think about Leo, I start to cry. I'm sure my professors are worried about me at this point. I can't help it. I'm an emotional wreck.

I met with Luca and apologized for skipping out on our dinner, promising that I'd pay him for the wasted food. He refused to take my money. Instead, we worked out my work schedule. I'll be starting next week.

Amos has been busy with his end-of-the-year school load, so I haven't seen him in a couple of weeks. Quinn has been immersed in school and sorority activities, so she hasn't been around much either. I'm grateful for the extra alone time. I need time to process all this. I've decided that I'm not telling anyone what Cat told me. It's Leo's history, and he wouldn't want others knowing. I don't blame him either.

I've gone back and forth all week on what I should do. Of

course I want to run to him and hug and tell him that he's loved. But I'm scared. A repeat of Christmas is inevitable, and I can't make it through that again. If I know anything, it's that you can't change people. I could love Leo with every fiber of my being for the rest of my life, and I wouldn't be able to change him.

I know myself enough to know what I deserve, and it's not a life of loving an addict. We've been apart for over four months. I'm finally functioning. I just need to move on.

According to Cat, he came home today.

I need to move on.

I imagine him alone in that house, and I yearn to hold him.

I need to move on.

He has Cat and Ethan. He'll be okay.

I need to move on.

We can't be together. I know that deep down in my soul.

I need to move on.

I throw on my shoes and run out the door. I'm going to move on. I will. I just have to make sure he's okay first.

His house looks different, though I can't put my finger on why. Maybe it's just for the simple fact that I haven't looked this way since our last dance. I step up onto the front porch. Pulling in a fortifying breath, I knock.

A moment later, Leo opens the door.

He's as beautiful as ever. He's wearing a pair of gray sweat-pants and a black T-shirt that clings to his biceps. There's a small amount of stubble on his square jaw, and it's intoxicating. His blue eyes are bright and clear, content. He looks good and healthy.

"Hi," I say.

He scans my body, as if he can't believe I'm here. His eyes hold mine. "Hi."

The silence between us is uneasy. Uncertainty taints the air.

My body wants to go to him. Goose bumps pebble on my skin as I'm innately drawn toward him.

He shakes his head, as if breaking a trance, and steps to the side, allowing me entrance. "You can come in. I was just cleaning."

"You're cleaning?" I attempt a lame joke.

"Yeah, well, I left the place a mess."

I step inside and look around. Random cushions are gone from the couch, and a couple of chairs are missing. I want to ask him what happened, but I don't.

"Cat told me that you would be back today," I say instead.

"Yeah, when I saw you here, I figured."

"She loves you. I like her a lot."

He nods. "Yeah, she's a good one."

The mention of Cat brings back all of the information that she told me and the emotions that came with it. Then, seeing Leo here in the flesh and thinking of him as a boy, I break. I gasp as I start to sob.

"I'm sorry," I cry.

He wraps his arms around me, and the contact feels so good.

"I'm so sorry."

Tears soak his shirt, and he leads us to a part of the couch with cushions. We sit, our arms clinging to one another. I apologize over and over through my tears.

I'm sorry for what he's been through. I'm sorry for not understanding. I'm sorry for showing up here when we're both just trying to move on. I'm sorry that he's the one comforting me when it should be the other way around. I'm sorry that life isn't fair and that two people who love each other as much as Leo and I do can't be together. I'm sorry for it all.

"Shh. It's okay," he says quietly, his words broken, and I realize that he's crying too.

We hold each other for what seems like hours until our tears abate.

"I'm so proud of you," I tell him, pulling away from his chest so he can see my face when I say it. "Getting help takes a lot of strength."

"Thank you." The corner of his lips tilts in a grin, but he still looks sad. "I'm sorry that you had to see me like that. I know what you've gone through with your parents, and I never wanted to hurt you. I think that's the part that's haunted me the most—what you must've gone through, seeing me like that."

"It's okay," I reassure him, swiping my thumb across his cheek to catch a fallen tear.

"But it's not, Alma. It's not okay."

"Maybe it's not, but I'm okay."

"Because you're so strong. It's one of the things I love the most about you." He presses his lips in a tight line.

"You're stronger than I could ever be, Leo."

He forces out a dry laugh. "But I'm not. If I were, we wouldn't be here, like this. I wouldn't have ruined everything."

"I never would've survived, having to walk in your shoes." My lip trembles, and fresh tears surface. "I would've died."

"I've wanted to die most of my life, but I'm not strong enough to do that."

"Stop," I beg, placing a finger against his lips. "You're here for a reason, Leo. You're kind and good. You care about others. You love fiercely and boldly. You're tough, and you've fought your entire life just to keep breathing. The darkness in your past isn't your fault. You are so good." I hold my hand over his heart. "You deserve happiness. You deserve love. Don't let anyone take that from you. They've taken enough."

"You're the best thing to ever happen to me, Alma." He leans his forehead against mine. "I don't think you know how much

I love you. I would fight my way back from hell a thousand times to see your face again."

"I love you too, Leo. I always will."

"I know I ruined what we had, and I'll regret that forever. But know that I will never love anyone else but you. You are the only woman who will ever be allowed in my heart. I lost you, and I'll live with that, but having you for the time I did, no matter how brief, will keep me going. You are the love of my life."

His words are a confusing mixture between a good-bye and a plea.

"I don't think I can ... I'm scared."

"I know. My issues are a hard limit for you, and I get that. I take the blame for ruining it. I understand why you can't be with me, but I just want you to know that I'm taking sobriety seriously this time. I'm trying so hard. I don't want the darkness to win. I want to dance with you in the light."

"I need time to figure things out, Leo."

"Okay, I get it. I can wait, for forever even. If you can't ever trust me again, then I accept that, but I'm still going to love you. I don't have a choice in that. I wasn't planning on coming to you or saying any of this. I was just going to stay clean and love you from afar. I respect your wishes. I do. But now, you're here, and when I'm with you, I can't seem to keep my mouth shut."

I let out a small chuckle. "Well, I tried to stay away too. It seems we both have issues."

"Will you stay with me tonight?"

"Leo ..." I drawl his name out.

"I just want to hold you. Clothes on. No expectations. I promise. Please. One night?"

Against my better judgment, I nod. "One night."

He leads me up to one of the spare bedrooms.

"What's wrong with your room?"

"I'm waiting for my new bed to come in."

"What happened to your old bed?" I question.

"It caught on fire," he states as if a bed catching fire were a normal occurrence.

"Oh my gosh!" I exclaim.

"Yeah," he sighs and directs me into a spare bedroom.

We climb beneath the covers, and Leo wraps his arm around me, holding me close to his body. Months of longing and exhaustion and so many tears weigh heavily on me, and here, in this space of our shared breaths, it all goes away. Sleep takes me, and something resembling happiness fills my heart.

CHAPTER 34

LEO

*Y*eah, turns out, I can be a noble, decent human being for about a day. Twenty-four hours hits, and I'm ready to sell my soul to have her back. I meant what I told Alma yesterday. I hadn't planned on going after her. I knew she didn't want to get back together. I'd told myself that I was strong enough—selfless enough—to leave her be. Apparently, I'm not.

Last night, I slept better than I had in years. I needed to fall asleep with Alma in my arms. Her scent still on the sheets was the wake-up call I needed.

When I finally woke, she was gone but had left me a note, telling me once again that she was proud of me. While that's all well and good and I appreciate the sentiment, there was no mention of immediate future plans. No *I'll see you tonight*, and that's not going to fly.

Yeah, I know I'm a fuckup. Alma is smart to be hesitant. But

I'm not going to fail her again. I put in the work, and I will continue to put in the work for the rest of my life to be good enough for her because she's it for me. And while she could definitely find better than me, she'll never find someone who loves her more.

CHAPTER 35

ALMA

*a*s I near my dorm room, I can't help thinking back to
August when I first approached the formally drab
brown door. Our once-brown door is now a colorful collage of
our life this school year. Quinn has covered the space in a
patchwork quilt of pretty scrapbook paper. There are pictures
and quotes affixed to the vibrant colors. Every time I come
home, it just makes me happy. There's not a roommate around
who could top my year with Quinn. She's perfect in her
bubbly, obnoxiously adorable way, and I'm going to miss her
desperately. I can't believe there's less than two weeks left of
my freshman year.

Everyone says college is life-changing, but for me, it truly
is. I'm not the same person I was eight months ago.

I've loved. I've lost. I've gotten a job. I've let my parents'
lack of interest in my life stop bothering me so much. I've
made real friends. I really do enjoy the company of Quinn's

sorority sisters and the girls we've met in our hall, but mostly, I adore Quinn. I love her in the way I'd love a sister. We haven't spoken about her plans for next year, but I have a feeling she's going to want to live with her sorority sisters, which will leave me with a brand-new roommate.

A wave of oregano, basil, and Parmesan cheese hits me when I open the door to the room. I step inside, confused at the sight that awaits.

"What's all this?" I ask Quinn, who sits on her bed, her legs dangling from the edge.

In the center of the dorm room is a table with a burgundy linen tablecloth. In the middle of the table is an arrangement of electric votive candles surrounding a large pillar candle. There are half a dozen plates covered with silver domes to keep the food beneath warm.

"You tell me. It's for you. These guys just came and set it up and said they'd be back later to clean it all up. Don't forget those." She nods toward my bed, which is covered in fancy white pastry boxes.

On the bedside table is one of the most beautiful bouquets I've ever seen. It's a wild and artsy arrangement of purples and pinks—daisies, tulips, roses, lilies, and sweet peas. In front of the bouquet, leaning against the square vase, is a letter with my name on it.

I snatch it up and open the envelope. There's a handwritten note inside.

Alma,

The first time I saw you was in Giovanni's. You came barreling into me while looking at your phone. I was so taken aback because when your body connected with mine, I felt this chemistry between us. You were wearing jean shorts and a baggy T-shirt. Your hair was up in a messy ponytail, strands falling, framing your face. You were clumsy and awkward, a little sweaty, and by far, you were the most beautiful woman I'd ever seen. I was immediately terrified of you and the power I knew you'd hold over my heart. After you apologized and went stumbling toward the restroom, I left without waiting for my food because I couldn't deal with seeing you again. From that initial moment, I knew you were special, and I was sure we'd be amazing together. But I also knew me, and I couldn't risk it.

An instant connection like ours isn't something most people find in their lifetimes. Yet we had it. Destiny isn't something I buy into, but you make me want to believe. From the first second I saw you, I wanted to believe in more.

I've seen you, all of you, from the beginning. I miss you more than I can convey. My soul aches when I'm apart from you. I'm far from perfect, but I want to try for you. I want to be a man who deserves to be loved by you.

Enjoy your dinner. I sent every dessert on the menu on account of your sweet tooth. ;-)

I love you forever.

Leo

I look up from the note in my hand, tears in my eyes.

"It's from him, isn't it?" Quinn sighs.

I nod, running my fingertips over the flowers.

"He's a smooth talker, Alma. Don't fall for it. You can't change him. Remember that."

I look to her with pained eyes. "I know," I say.

But I know him. She doesn't. She can't possibly understand.

"Have dinner with me?" I grin awkwardly before scrunching up my nose.

She claps her hands together. "I thought you'd never ask!"

Quinn and I sample all of the dishes until we can't eat another bite. Then, we taste all of the desserts until our stomachs are round with food babies and we have the sugar sweats.

"He did it. He killed us. That was his evil plan all along," Quinn groans from her bed, holding her stomach.

"It's pretty cool that he didn't even eat with us that first day, but he ordered everything we ate. That dinner with you and

Amos the day I moved in seems like forever ago. And that mushroom risotto is still one of the best things I've ever tried."

"Yeah, well, he had half the menu delivered, so it was probably luck. And I'm not going to lie; the guy has good taste. Everything that he puts effort into, he excels at. I'm not surprised he ordered all of our favorites."

He does have good taste. I'm not going to dispute her there.

"Can you pass the tiramisu?" I groan, extending my hand between our beds.

"You can't possibly eat any more." She chuckles.

"Just one more bite."

After the servers come to retrieve the table setup and dishes, I pull out my phone and send Leo a two-worded text.

Thank you.

* * *

THE NEXT DAY, I come home after tutoring to another enormous and incredibly gorgeous flower bouquet and a gift basket filled with candy and at least a dozen envelopes. I read the hand-addressed envelope first.

Alma,

The second time I saw you was the same night after Giovanni's. You had swapped out your baggy T-shirt for a tight black tank top and showed up at the frat house with Quinn. You were ridiculously out of place, which I loved, and even more beautiful, which I hated. I adored that the party life wasn't your style because as much as I was a slave to it, I hated it. Your innocence was refreshing and drew me in more.

I wanted to scare you away. I wanted you to hate me. You were the light to my dark, the good to my evil, the pure to my tainted soul. You were everything that I wanted but nothing I should have.

After I walked you home and kissed you, it was over for me. I knew then that I had to make you hate me because you would always

223

be irresistible to me. I was terrified that the parts of you that I craved would be destroyed if you let me in.

At that first party, before the drinking game started, you were chatting with some girls about local concerts. Detroit showcases all sorts of incredible artists. I hope you enjoy them all.

I love you forever.

Leo

I begin opening the envelopes that rest between the loads of sweets. Each one contains concert and stadium tours tickets to the shows scheduled in Detroit this coming summer and fall. The variety is eclectic. There's pop, rock, country, rap, old school, and even a reunited '80s hair band. I can't contain my smile because it's so me. I'm the type of person to belt out Britney Spears's "Baby One More Time" one moment and then "The Dance" by Garth Brooks the next. I don't have a favorite genre of music. I simply appreciate amazing songs.

The gift is so thoughtful and expensive, though I know the financial aspect isn't important to Leo. He has money and enjoys spending it on those he loves.

Loves.

Sigh.

His note is beautiful, and each word hurts my heart. I love him. Of course I do. I'm so confused. I see that he's trying. He went to rehab. He's seeing a therapist. He's showing me that he's ready for us now. Yet I'm still terrified. I'm trying not to blame Leo for the choices he made due to the trauma of his past. But the truth is that he did make them. We all handle trauma differently, and Leo turned to substances to dull his pain. What if there's always a part of him that will crave the utter numbness that drugs bring? I won't be able to handle it. Sometimes, two people can love each other more than anything and not be right for one another. I don't know if that's us, but most days, it feels like it is.

Folding Leo's note, I place it back in the envelope, kiss it, and then hold it against my heart.

I don't know, Leo. I will him to understand.

I place his words in my top drawer, on top of the letter from yesterday, and grab my new work clothes. I get dressed in black pants and a white button-down and retrieve the apron from the hook beside the door. After a day of classes, homework, tutoring, and now emotional stress in the form of an ex-boyfriend, concerts, and chocolate, I'm completely exhausted.

I'd give anything to take a hot shower and crawl into bed, but I have to make money. Luckily for me, the diner is open eighteen hours a day, so there are always times that I can work in a shift. Luca has been amazing this week, letting me choose my own schedule. I'm hopeful that I'll earn enough in tips the next couple of weeks that, paired with what I've already saved from tutoring, will afford me a place for the summer.

I snatch a Twix from the gift basket on my bed and smile as I head out. I might not have all of the answers, but I'm filled with hope that things will work out for the best.

CHAPTER 36

LEO

I've sent flowers the past ten days. I've purchased meals from every restaurant we've ever been to and had them delivered. I've all but bought out the candy selection at the local store.

Maybe she's in a sugar coma?

I've gone through all of our past conversations, and any interest that she's ever spoken about, I've organized a themed gift around it. Yesterday, I sent her a box filled with Sharpies, gel pens, planners, a calendar, sparkly notebooks, color-coded tabs, and anything else the office supply place had that would speak to Alma's incredibly organized side. If I know her, it's her favorite gift so far, and yet the only reply I've received is a text that read, *Thank you. I just need time.*

All I know is that my hand permanently aches from the amount of love notes I've written her, detailing every moment of our time together because I remember all of it—every outfit, every smile, every touch, every minute. The fact that more time is passing and we're not together is enough to send me over the edge, and yet I'm not going there. Instead, I'm going to meetings, therapy sessions, and getting together with my sponsor, Ollie.

I'm fucking running to relieve stress. What the hell have I become? My therapist, Dr. Tucker, tells me that workouts release endorphins that make one feel good—a natural high, if you will. Clearly, he's never done hard drugs because they don't compare. You know what else gives one a natural high? Sex. And I'm not having that either.

My days are spent trying to better myself and begging Alma to love me. That about sums up my life. There are only a couple of days left of school, and I'm not sure what she's doing for the summer, so I'm starting to feel desperate. I don't know what else to do. I fucked up. I know it. Alma knows it. Everyone who knows me knows it. So, my options are limited.

I can buy Alma the fucking world and rip my heart open for her to see, and she still doesn't have to love me back. I can't make her do anything. Her feisty spirit and willpower have always been two of my favorite things about her, but I'm not loving them so much anymore.

I scan the pictures of Alma and me in my phone, hoping that one of them sparks some more gift ideas. I'm running out of things to send her. I'm a phone call away from buying her a car because I know she needs one badly. I'm afraid that gift would do more to push her away from me than toward me. She's accepted all of my gifts thus far, but I think she'd see a car as too much. She's prideful, my little firecracker. Her success is her own, and I don't want any of my gifts to make her feel less than.

Closing out of my phone, I stand from the couch and head for the door. I need food. The extreme amount of exercise makes me hungry all the damn time. I normally have my meals delivered, but a change in scenery is needed. The walls of my house feel like they're closing in every second that she's not there.

Luca's chili-cheese fries always make things better. The bell chimes when I open the door. Her deep browns widen when they see me, but a smile doesn't find my lips. *Why is she here?* She looks exhausted, beautiful as always but completely beat. She has bags under her eyes, and the sight almost causes me to lose my shit. *What in the world is going on?*

I inhale deep and take a seat. This was going to be a carryout run, but now that I've seen her …

She sets a plastic glass of water down in front of me. "Hey," she says softly. "The usual?"

"You work here?"

"Yeah."

"Why?" I attempt to keep the edge out of my voice, but I fail as the question comes up clipped and demanding.

She chews on her bottom lip and sighs. "I need the money, Leo. I'm out of the dorms in three days, and I need more than I've saved with tutoring."

I take her hand in mine, and she flinches before the corner of my lips tilts up slightly. I endeavor to make my words communicate the concern I feel but not the anger over the fact that she is struggling and didn't come to me.

"You look really tired, Alma."

She has to know I would do anything for her.

"It's just the past two weeks. I've picked up hours with tutoring to help students study for exams and complete final projects. Plus, I'm finishing my own assignments and studying for exams. Then, I've been working here as much as I can because I only have three days until I need to find a place. You don't have to worry about me. I haven't gotten enough sleep as usual, but classes are almost over. I'll be fine."

I don't say everything I want to say. I want to yell and tell her that she's killing herself when I could be helping her. It would be nothing for me to help her. She shouldn't be picking up extra tutor shifts. She shouldn't be working here. She shouldn't be stressing about money when I would give her everything if she'd take it. She should be studying for her exams, getting extra sleep, and enjoying her last weeks as a freshman. I'm so fucking livid at her, at me. *How did I not know she was struggling?* I didn't know because I've never wanted for a dime my entire life. It didn't even cross my mind that she was stressing out about the dorms closing. I'm such an asshole.

I want to scream all of these things, but I don't.

"You know you could've asked me for help." The ache in my voice is unnerving. "I would do anything for you." I run my thumb across the palm of her hand.

"I know you would, but it's not your problem. I'm capable."

Fuck that. It's not my problem? And of course, she's capable. That's not the point.

"How many exams do you have left?" I ask evenly.

"Two tomorrow and two Friday, and then I'm done."

My eyes catch a glimpse of the sparkly gel pens lined up in her apron, and I have to hold back the cheesy grin. I knew she'd love them.

"Good." I release her hand with a gentle squeeze and say, "I'll just have my regular, please."

My food comes, and I eat as I watch Alma flit around to the rest of the customers. She's so flipping cute. God, I love her. When she goes to the back to retrieve some ice, I wave Luca over.

"How's my favorite customer?" he greets me with a grin.

"Not good," I snap under my breath. "You're working Alma to death. Can't you see that she's exhausted?"

"Leo, my boy, I'm only trying to help her. She seemed desperate for money, so I gave her a job. I let her pick her own hours." Luca wipes the palms of his hands against his black apron.

"I know you're trying to help her, but I'll make sure she has enough money this week. After I leave, I need you to tell her to go home early tonight. Tell her that you're overstaffed for the next two days and have to cut her shifts. She has exams to finish, and she's not sleeping because of this job. I will come in and work for you if her absence leaves you in a bind. Just please tell her to go home and not come back for at least two days. Please?"

Luca nods. "Okay, I can do that, and I'll be fine. As I said, she picks her hours. I was only trying to help."

"You're a good person, Luca. Thank you."

Luca leaves to attend to customers, and I write Alma a note on a napkin.

Alma,

I'm not giving this to you for any reason other than your excellent service. Your server skills are the best I've seen. Once again, this is your tip. Nothing more. My fries were delicious, and my server was exquisite.

Rock your exams.

I love you forever.

Leo

I pull out the cash in my wallet, a little over two thousand dollars, and leave it beneath the napkin. With a nod toward Luca, I walk out.

CHAPTER 37

ALMA

*A*mos steps into the room, and instinctually, my arms fly around his neck. He picks me up and spins me around. My leg knocks over a stack of boxes.

"Oops." I giggle as he sets me down. "We did it!"

Our hands meet in a high five.

"One year down," he says with a huge grin. "How were your exams?"

"Good! I think I aced them all. How about you?"

"Pretty sure I aced mine too," he says. "So, Quinn's at her last exam, and then we'll celebrate?"

"Yep, dinner and then a party before she leaves for home tomorrow. She just left, so we should be finished moving before she's done. It'll only be one car load." I pick up the boxes that my foot just kicked to the ground.

"So, the new place is close?"

"Yes. I got this little studio apartment about a block away.

I'm surprised I found one so easily at the last minute, but I guess a bunch of places become available at the end of the year with people changing their summer plans and stuff. It's less than a block from work too."

I leave out the part about Leo's tip, but with the money I saved and Leo's money, I was able to pay for all three summer months up front and have plenty to spare. I plan to continue to work at Luca's. Maybe I'll save enough this summer to buy a car.

I haven't seen Amos in a while with the end-of-school craziness. We've both been so busy, and come to think of it, I'm not sure he and Quinn have spoken much. I don't really pry since I'm friends with both of them. If there is trouble in paradise, I'm sure my advice would be biased somehow.

Amos starts collecting my clothes, which I've shoved into big garbage bags, and places them by the door. "I think Quinn and I are cooling off," he says, as if reading my thoughts.

"Yeah?"

"We haven't seen each other in a long time, and to be honest, I don't miss her, you know? We had a lot of fun this year, but I don't know if it's deeper than that. Maybe we're best as friends," he says.

"With benefits?" I quirk up a brow, causing Amos to laugh.

"If she wants. I mean, I'm down." He shrugs with a smug grin.

I'm sure they'll have all sorts of benefits flying around after the party tonight. They'll probably be needing the shower for a good long time.

Amos glances at my bed and notices all of the gifts and baskets on it. He squints and walks over. "Is this stuff from …" His voice trails off as he picks up the envelope stuffed with concert tickets.

"Yeah," I respond immediately. No use in denying it.

Amos's face jerks toward mine, his eyes angry. "You're not back together with him. Are you?"

"No." I shake my head with a glance toward my feet.

"Alma, please tell me you're not thinking about going back to him." His voice is stern but pleading.

I let out a sigh. "I don't know."

"You don't know?" His voice rises an octave, and honestly, it's the first time in my life I can remember that happening. Amos is always cool as a cucumber, especially with me.

I raise my palms, urging him to calm. "Don't get upset. I don't know. There are a lot of things that you don't know about him. A great deal of information has come to light fairly recently that's changed the way I think of him. He's a good person, Amos, and he's sorry. He was in rehab for months, and now, he's in NA—Narcotics Anonymous—and seeking help. He's better ... and I miss him."

Amos closes his eyes and rubs his temples. "I can't believe you right now." He shakes his head before looking to me, confusion in his stare. "You grew up with druggies, Alma. You know what that life is like. I get that you miss him, and that's okay, but you're not weak. You're the strongest person I know. You're better than Leo in every way. Don't sell yourself short. You saw him. We both did. You know what he was involved in. It made you literally sick. Don't forget that because I'm telling you right now that an addict is always an addict. It's just a matter of time before he slips again. You deserve better than that, and you know it. Getting back together with Leo isn't just getting back together with the parts you love. It's all of it. You'd be dating that person we saw high as a kite in that crack house because ... that is who he is."

I shake my head. "It's not though." My voice trembles. "You don't know him."

"Yes, I do. I think it's you who's forgotten what a monster he can be." Amos paces the room. "Please don't take him back,

Alma. I'm begging you. He will break your heart over and over again. I know you loved him, and that's hard to get over, but you have to be strong."

"I'm sorry. You just can't understand. There are things about him that you don't know, and I can't tell you. He's a good person, and he loves me more than anyone else could possibly love me."

"Are you fucking serious right now?" Amos shouts, and I take a step back.

He's never yelled at me or been this angry with me our entire lives. The rage explodes from him, filling the room with a tension so thick that I'm choking on it. It's hard to pull in a deep breath. I start to cry as anguish squeezes my heart. I understand his anger, but I can't promise him that I won't go back to Leo because I honestly don't know.

Amos flinches when I take a step away from him and shakes his head, his fists clenching at his sides. He looks to me, broken. "You have a really warped idea of what love is. I thought I knew you, but you're different. I don't think I know you anymore." He steps toward the door.

"Wait," I cry. "Please don't go."

"I have to leave, or I'm going to end up saying something I'll really regret. Once words are spoken, they're out there forever. Some words are really hard to forgive, Alma." He opens the door and leaves me alone—something he has never done.

* * *

QUINN RETURNS to the room a couple of hours later to find me crying and eating my weight in chocolate.

"Oh my gosh! What's wrong?" She rushes toward me.

I tell her everything, and she just listens, her arm around me as I snot on her shoulder. It's an overwhelming feeling to have Amos mad at me. We've never been in a fight, and I'm not entirely sure how to handle it.

"That explains it," Quinn says when I finally finish.

"What?"

"Well, I got a text from Amos, telling me that he can't make it out with us tonight and that he enjoyed getting to know me this year and wishes me well."

I raise my head from Quinn's shoulder and look to her. "He broke up with you via text?"

She laughs. "I think so!"

"So tacky!" I let out a chuckle and wipe the tears from my cheeks. "What a jerk." The last statement feels like a betrayal, and I immediately want to take it back.

"Eh"—she flicks her wrist, swiping her hand in front of her —"we weren't really serious. I mean, we were crazy in lust over one another, but I didn't love him. He's a good guy, and he gave me company this year. It was fun while it lasted. He doesn't owe me anything."

"He is a good guy. Though he hates me now, so …"

Quinn pushes my arm. "He doesn't hate you. He could never. He loves you to death. He's just worried for you—and honestly, with good reason."

"Please don't," I beg, not wanting to argue with my other best friend on our last night together.

"I'm not." She pats my leg. "You know how I feel about it, but ultimately, it's your life. Only you can make the decision. I'll support you either way, and so will Amos once he chills out a little."

"Thank you." I place my hand atop hers and squeeze. "See, why can't Amos be as levelheaded as you?"

"He loves you more. You pull this shit in a few years, and we'll have words," she says with attitude, causing me to laugh.

"I'm going to miss you."

"Same. What are you going to do next year? I'm feeling really guilty."

Quinn broke it to me that she signed a lease at the sorority house in the fall.

"Same as I did this year. Move into the dorms with a new roommate. I'm sure the university will pair me up with someone cool. They did a good job this year."

"You'd better not love your new roomie more than me," Quinn says with a huff.

"I can't promise." I grin.

"Um, yes, you can because no one is going to replace me. And you'd better promise to hang out with me next year."

"Of course I will. We'll hang out all the time."

Quinn looks around the room at my bags and boxes, the ones that Amos was going to help me move.

"First of all, don't worry about your stuff. When my dad gets here tomorrow, we'll load your things up and drop them off at your new place before we pack up my boxes. My dad will be happy to help."

"Thank you," I say because I thought I was going to have to walk my stuff over box by box, which would have been awful.

"Now, secondly, we are going to go all out tonight. I'm talking hair, makeup, outfit ... all of it. It's the last party of the year. We're ending the year, looking hot. I mean, we're always hot," she clarifies, "but irresistible."

"Irresistible. Got it." I feign excitement because even after being Quinn's roommate for eight months, parties still aren't my thing. But hanging out with her is, so I'll suck it up.

"Thank goodness you're not majoring in acting." Quinn giggles.

"What? I'm super excited."

Quinn hops off of my bed and starts thumbing through her closet, which she hasn't even started packing up yet. "You're not, but I don't care. I'll take it."

CHAPTER 38

ALMA

"*H*uh," I say out loud to my empty apartment. My boxes and bags of clothes are piled in the small living area, and save for that pile and myself ... the apartment is empty. Completely empty.

Coming from the dorm life, I didn't even take into consideration that the girl I subleased from would be taking all of her furniture and, well, everything else. There isn't so much as a plastic fork left in the kitchen.

"How much does a girl really need?" Apparently, talking to myself is my new thing now that I'm without a roommate.

I don't need much, honestly. I can get an Uber to the dollar store and get some paper plates, plastic silverware, and frozen dinners. At least there's a built-in microwave. I can sleep on the floor. I have a blanket and pillow. It will be like camping. I don't need a chair or TV. Most of the summer, I plan on working, and when I'm not, I can lean up against the wall and read.

Totally doable.

I haven't heard from Amos, which sucks.

Quinn is on her way up to Northern Michigan with her dad, which is great for her but blows for me.

I'm feeling a little lonely and lost. I'm on summer break, so I don't have any pressing homework, and I'm off work this weekend, something about Luca being overstaffed. So, I have nothing to keep my mind off of Leo.

It's almost impossible not to think about him every second of the day, but with idle time on my hands, it's hopeless. I'm not trying to be cruel or unfair to him. He deserves a solid answer. All of this *I need time* nonsense can't go on forever. I've just been scared.

Amos was right about one thing. I'm stronger than this.

I already know my answer. My heart, body, and soul have been screaming it since the day I stopped by Leo's home. I have to find the strength to tell him and be bold enough to face the consequences.

Grabbing my phone and keys, I lock up my new place and walk the block to Leo's house.

With a steadying breath, I rap my knuckles against his door. He opens after a few seconds.

He releases a sigh, happy and relieved, and I feel it down in my soul. A smile graces his gorgeous face, and he steps to the side, inviting me in. I enter hesitantly.

The space looks the same, except for some new furniture. Just being here makes my chest ache. I've missed everything about this place, but mostly, I've missed the man standing before me.

"Can I get you something? Bottle of water?" he prods, a nervous energy surrounding his words.

"No, I'm fine." I take a seat on the new sectional sofa.

"How are you?" he asks with genuine concern. "Exams? Work? An apartment?"

"Everything's good. Passed everything with flying colors. Haven't worked since the night you were in. Luca doesn't need me this weekend. And I found an apartment—about a block from here actually. Speaking of my apartment, thank you for your tip. I'd offer to pay you back, but I know you won't take it. It saved me though," I admit.

As much as I wanted to march over to Leo's house after he left me that tip, for the first time in weeks, I wasn't stressing out about being homeless. He gave me the means to find a place.

"You're welcome, and you're right. You don't owe me anything."

"How are you?" I question, and we both know what I mean.

"Well, I'd be better if you forgave me and took me back, but to answer the question you're asking, I'm good. I told you, it's different this time. I'm going to keep putting in the work to live a healthy life."

"What if we don't get back together? Are you going to relapse?" I hate even asking the question, but I have to know.

"No, Alma, I'm not." He sits down beside me and holds my hand between his. "You were right. I've suffered enough. I owe it to myself to try to live a normal life and be healthy and happy."

"Really?" I swallow a lump in my throat.

"Really, I'm okay. You don't have to worry about me or feel guilty if you don't want to be with me."

"I've been wondering something," I say. "Remember on Christmas Day, how you kept making me promise? You kept saying, 'Promise me.' What did I promise?"

Leo looks down at his lap, taking a fortifying breath before his eyes return to me, bright and stunning and broken. "I wanted you to promise that you'd always love me and not for who you wanted me to be, but for who I really was. I wanted you to promise that you'd love me enough to stay. I knew I was breaking, and I wanted to know that you'd love me when I came out on the other side. Because, Alma, I am an addict and always will be. Recovering or not, that darkness will always be there. I'm far from perfect. I've been ruined and beat down. I have a temper. I'm moody. I have no idea what I want to do with my life. I have issues. In truth, the only thing I've ever been certain about is my love for you. And I truly believe that no one could love you as much as I do. Not because you're not worthy of it, but because my love is so deep. It's all-encompassing. Everything good in me is entangled with my love for you."

"Christmas Day, I promised to love you for who you are?" My voice breaks.

"Yeah, but you didn't know."

"I think part of me always knew. I think that's why our love is so strong—because our souls are connected, bare and open. I see you, your beautiful side and your broken one. You see the same in me. I do love you for who you are. My hesitation about getting back together has nothing to do with my love for you and everything to do with me and the life I want." My eyes fill with unshed tears.

Leo visibly swallows as his gaze holds mine. "I understand that, and it's smart. I can't promise you everything that you want to hear. I can only tell you that I don't ever want to be out of control again. I can promise you that I'm going to try every single day. I will never stop fighting because a life with you is worth fighting for. And I think my fight, my best fight, will be enough. I do, Alma. But I can't promise you."

A tear escapes, and I brush it away. "You know, Amos and I used to play this game, growing up—Would You Rather? You've heard of it, I'm sure. The other day, I was thinking back to a night when he and I were lying outside in a hammock, looking at the stars and asking each other questions for hours. Most of them were silly. *Would you rather only be able to eat or only be able to drink for the rest of your life? Would you rather hiccup every five minutes or sneeze every thirty? Would you rather have no eyebrows for a year or be completely bald for a week?"*

Leo watches me intently, listening.

I continue, "Well, I specifically remember this one question from that night. *Would you rather be with your one true love for a short time and lose him or never be with him at all and be spared the pain of losing him?* As I looked up at the stars before answering, I thought to myself, *If I'm lucky enough to experience true love, then I'll take it for as long as I can get it. One day with my soul mate is better than a lifetime without him."* I taste the tears now flowing down my cheeks and over my lips. "I hope we're lucky enough for forever, but I'll take every day I can get."

"Really?" Leo asks, unsure.

"Really." I nod. "I love you, Leo. You are a once-in-a-life-time love. I'd be an idiot to let you go. And I'm so proud of you and what you've done for not only yourself, but also for us. You're so much stronger than you think you are, and I know you'll try every day for us."

"I will, Alma. I will." He peppers kisses over my face, loving away my tears. "It was all the chocolate that did the trick, wasn't it?" he kids.

I shrug playfully. "You know the key to my heart."

Leo lifts me from the couch, our lips connected as he walks us up the stairs. He pulls away, whispering, "True to your name, you're my soul mate. My one and only. Without you, my life has little purpose. I love you, baby."

"I love you." I kiss his neck as he navigates us toward the bedroom.

"And by the way, you're moving in with me. That hole of an apartment you're staying in isn't good enough for you."

"What?" I gasp. "How did you ..."

"I know everything about you. I wanted you to get a place of your own so that you'd know you were coming back to me for the right reasons. I didn't want you to have an excuse to second-guess your desire to be here. But here is where you belong. Your apartment can house your extra belongings, but I want you in my bed and in my life every single day. I don't want to miss a second with you." He sets me on his bed and starts removing my clothes.

"You're so bossy." I glare toward him, but it's all in jest. Truth is, now that I've been brave enough to admit that I need Leo as much as he needs me, I don't want to be without him either.

"You promised to love me as is," he teases, making quick work of undressing.

My mouth falls open because Leo has always been the hottest man I've ever seen, but now, he's even more buff and muscled.

"Like what you see, babe?" He chuckles at my gawking expression.

"Hell yes," I sigh, a rush of need hitting me.

"We are encouraged to work out, endorphins and shit. Since my only pastime was missing you, I've been working out like it's my full-time job."

"I approve." I grin as Leo crawls up my body and slides on a condom.

"This first time is going to be hard and rough because I've been dreaming about this for too damn long. The rest will be slow and drawn out, and I promise to pay attention to every part of you because I've been craving every inch." Leo's words are husky and dripping with want.

Threading my fingers through the hair at the nape of his neck, I pull his lips to mine as he enters me. I moan into his mouth. Nothing has ever felt better.

I am exactly where I am meant to be.

Please don't hurt me. Please don't break my heart. Please don't ruin me. I chant silent prayers in my head as he makes love to me.

I've made my decision. I am Leo's, and he is mine. Being with him was never a choice; it was my destiny. Now, all I can do is pray that he doesn't destroy me. All I can do is pray that our love is powerful enough to keep his demons at bay.

I will love him so hard and deeply that his broken soul will heal back together. Love can do amazing things, and just maybe, this time, it will be enough.

Please be enough.

CHAPTER 39

ALMA

*L*eo's arm drapes over my waist, and he pulls me closer. His bare skin is warm and silky against mine.

"Don't leave," he grumbles into my hair, his voice still gravelly from slumber.

"I have to. I'm scheduled to work a double today." I trace my pointer finger over the taut skin of his muscled forearm.

In fairness, I don't have any desire to leave Leo's bed either. The past five days have been nothing short of incredible. We've only left his bed to shower or to answer the door when our food is delivered. We've talked, laughed, and made love for hours. Existing here in this space is my utopia; he's my heaven on earth. My soul feels whole again. My lungs rejoice as I can finally take a full breath after months of struggling to find air. I don't ever want to be without Leo again.

"He'll survive without you." Leo kisses my shoulder, sending warm tingles throughout my body.

I sit up, refusing to let my desire for Leo take over. If I succumb to it, I'll never make it to work.

"He needs servers, and I need a job." I giggle as Leo attempts to pull me back down toward him.

"I need service, and I'll gladly pay you for it," he taunts, and I jump from the bed, needing distance between him.

I shake my head with a laugh. "I'm pretty sure we've established that's illegal."

"Seriously, I have money. You can have it all. I just want you," he says evenly, propping his body up with his arm.

"I know, Leo. I don't want to be away from you either, but we have to create some sort of normalcy. There are times when we have to be apart. I need to work and earn my own money. You should spend time on your online classes, work out, whatever. It will feel good to be productive, I promise."

"I disagree," he groans, sitting up against the headboard of his bed. "It will feel good to be in you."

"Later," I vow and shoot him a wink before heading to the bathroom and hopping in the shower.

"Do you want company?" he asks from outside the shower stall.

"No!" My response is instant, and it causes a deep chuckle to erupt from Leo.

"Why's that?" he asks teasingly.

"You know damn well why. I'm not going to be late."

"Fine." Humor lines his voice.

The buzz of his electric toothbrush sounds.

"I work tomorrow, but then I'm off for a few days. I was thinking that we could drive back to my parents' house on my day off. I don't know if they'll be there or not, but if so, you can meet them. Plus, I really need to make up with Amos. This is the longest we've gone without speaking in my life, and I hate it."

Amos hasn't returned one of my texts or reached out to me

since he stormed out of my dorm room a week ago. I want to be angry with him because if he was a good friend, he would support my decisions, but I know his anger comes from a place of concern. Nothing good comes from holding on to anger because of a bruised ego. He has his reasons for feeling the way he does, and I'll accept them, but hopefully, he can learn to accept mine. Bottom line is that I miss him, and I need him in my life.

"Sure. That sounds good." Leo runs the water in the sink.

"Great," I reply.

Leo's gone from the bathroom when I step out of the shower, but his words are smeared on the foggy bathroom mirror: *You are my everything.*

"Your smudges are going to stay on the mirror, you know," I call toward the bedroom, a giant smile on my face. Even the obsessive clean freak in me loves his mirror love notes.

"Good, and don't you forget it."

* * *

I'VE BEEN CALLING and texting my parents for two days to let them know I'm coming back for a visit with Leo. I haven't received a response, so either their cell phones are lost, uncharged, or out of service because they're living on some commune for the summer. My parents aren't the best thing in my life, obviously, but I still want Leo to meet them and see that part of me. They're a piece of my history, and for good or bad, they had a role in molding me into the woman I am today. I've lived through nineteen years of disappointments, and yet I still crave their attention and approval. I wish I didn't. I wish there were a switch I could simply turn off that would stop me from feeling the urge to make them proud of me ever again.

"It's going to be fine, babe. Whatever happens, it will be

fine." He reaches over from the driver's side of the car to pat my knee.

"I know. I just want them to know you and hear what I've been doing with my life. I haven't seen them since last August," I reply before remembering the other stressful aspect of this trip. "And what if Amos is still pissy? Maybe this visit was a bad idea."

"As a wise man told me just this week, you can't control the actions of others. You just need to live a life that you're proud of, and if others don't respond the way you wish they would, it's on them. You are doing the right thing here. You're reaching out to the people in your life. If they don't reach back, you'll be fine because you had good intentions, and that's all you can control."

I press my head back into the seat and stare at Leo. "Those are wise words." A smile finds my lips. "Ollie?"

"Yeah," he says.

Ollie is Leo's NA sponsor and has been instrumental in the growth that Leo has made. He's a thirty-year-old guy with tanned skin and unruly shoulder-length blond hair. He's the type of guy I'd imagine spending his days surfing in Hawaii. He's just chill. I'm so grateful to him because he has this way of speaking to Leo that resonates. He connects to and understands the darkest parts of Leo that I can't, and I'm so glad that Leo has him.

"Would it be too much to ask that my parents pretend to care? If they're there, I'll have seen them an hour all year. Anyone can fake love for an hour."

"They love you. How could they not? Maybe they don't love you in the way they should, but they care. But once again, babe, it doesn't matter. You can't change them."

"Well, someday, when I have kids, I'm going to love them so much that they'll never live a second without knowing how truly loved and important they are."

"I have no doubt you will. You show everyone you care about that you value them. It's why you're so easy to love." He taps my knee and returns his hand back to the steering wheel.

The last time I told Leo that my main dream in life was to be a mom, it started a huge fight because he said he was never having kids. He doesn't make a similar comment this time, but I'm afraid to ask him if he's changed his mind. I have enough to worry about today. Picking an argument with Leo wouldn't be ideal.

As we pull up to my parents' house, I sigh. The place looks like it did last time I was home—abandoned. The spring grass is tall in places, but then there are large areas where the grass hasn't come up at all due to piles of dead leaves from last fall still sitting and decaying.

Leo parks the car, and we step out.

"This place was once really cute. When we moved here after my grandparents passed, I remember loving it. I kept it up while I was here, but clearly, it doesn't take much neglect to really fall into disarray. I'm still incredibly thankful to my grandparents for leaving us this house. I can't imagine what my life would have been like had I been raised as a nomad, like my parents always wanted. This place and Amos as my neighbor brought me stability." I feel the need to explain this to Leo as we stand here, looking at the piles of trash on the front porch.

He extends his hand, and I take it. We walk up the steps to the house. I unlock the door and hesitantly step in. The smell of rot that hits me is almost enough to make me want to close the door and leave.

"Lee-Anne? Vati?" I call out.

"We're here," my dad's gruff voice answers.

I swallow the lump in my throat, and my heart sinks. Their absence would've been easier.

"You ready for this?" I ask Leo.

"Of course." He squeezes my hand.

Inside, we find my parents sitting in the living room, thankfully clothed this time. The smell of pot burns my nostrils, and I wave my hand in front of my face to break up the stagnant air.

"We didn't know you'd be back today," my mom singsongs, "and with a guest."

"Sorry, I called and texted. I couldn't get ahold of you but needed to come back to see Amos. So, I'm glad you're here. I want you to meet Leo."

Leo doesn't miss a beat. He steps over a pile of trash in the hall and extends his hand to introduce himself to my parents. His greeting is heartfelt, and as he smiles and shakes my parents' hands, my heart swells.

"He's quite handsome, Almalee," Lee-Anne says.

"Yeah, he is." The corners of my lips tilt into a smile.

I give my parents each a quick hug. They smell like musky body odor.

"How are you?" I ask them.

They both look skinnier than ever, and I know they're not eating enough. They both are wrinkled with splotchy skin and bags under their eyes. My mother's hair is so wispy, and her roots are gray. They appear ten years older than the last time I saw them.

"Oh, just wonderful, dear. Living life, you know? Just free," my dad drawls out, obviously stoned.

"Are you going anywhere this summer?" I ask as I navigate around the junk on the floor and back into the kitchen.

I know that this isn't my home anymore, and I shouldn't care that they're living like this, but I do. I reach into the cupboard under the sink and pull out some garbage bags.

Leo is at my side, and I caress the top of his hand in thanks and hand him a bag.

My parents tell us of the new commune that one of their

friends opened in the Upper Peninsula of Michigan. Apparently, clothing is optional, but with the deer flies and their vicious bites up there, it's recommended.

Leo and I fill seven garbage bags, and he takes them out to the curb while I clean up the kitchen. My mother sits, zoned out, while my father talks about the compost system at the camp they're going to next week. I scrub the kitchen sink. Old habits die hard, and the clean freak in me can't stand that they live like this.

When the kitchen is clean, I try to tell them a little about my last year of school. It's hard to hold their attention, and Lee-Anne's eyelids start to droop.

"Do you want us to leave, so you can take a nap?" I ask.

"That'd be nice." Lee-Anne yawns.

"Okay, well, we're going to get you some food. You have nothing to eat in the kitchen. So, just know we'll be back."

I want to tell them to keep their clothes on, but I don't. Hopefully, they do though.

Leo and I say good-bye and exit the house.

"You still love me?" I tease when we step outside, knowing it must have been a shock for Leo to see where I came from.

"I love you even more." He leans down and kisses my head. "You amaze me, Almalee."

I press my lips together and grin.

I look over to Amos's house. "Do you mind waiting in the car until I smooth things over with Amos?"

"Yeah, sure." Leo bends and presses his lips to mine, soft and sweet. "Do you want me to grab some food for your parents from that corner store we passed while you talk to him?"

"Thank you. That would be great." I run my hand along the five o'clock shadow that he has going on, and my stomach flutters. *Gah, he's so hot. All right, focus.* "Just bags of beans, rice, fruits, veggies, and bread. Maybe some peanut butter. They don't eat meat or dairy."

"No problem. I'll be back."

I supply Leo with another quick kiss and then grab the bag of Famous Amos Chocolate Chip Cookies that I left in the car. As I walk up to Amos's front door, I turn the bag of cookies over in my hand. My entire friendship with Amos is built on traditions and little anecdotes that only the two of us know. Yet, in all the years I've known my best friend, we've never established a tradition for making up because we've never had a need for one. He's never been mad at me. I couldn't show up at his door without a peace offering of some sort, so Leo and I stopped at a gas station on the way here, and I bought a bag of Amos's namesake cookies.

I knock and wait.

Amos's mom answers, and a smile graces her face. "Alma." She wraps me into a hug. "So good to see you. Let me get Amos."

She retreats, and a few moments later, Amos approaches, his hands in the pockets of his khaki shorts.

"Hey," he says, his flat expression giving nothing away.

"Hey. I come bearing gifts." I hold out the bag of cookies.

Amos takes it with a hint of a smile. "Thanks."

"Can we talk?"

He nods and steps out onto the porch. We take a seat on the top step.

"Well, either you've recently acquired a Porsche or you went back to him." He frowns.

"We're together," I state, not an ounce of regret in my voice. I won't apologize for loving Leo. "Listen, I love you so much. You are the only true family I have. I'd have nothing without you, Amos. But if you love me, then you need to allow me to make my own choices. You have to trust that I know more about the situation than you do. I know Leo more than you do.

I know my heart and what I need more than you do. It's not weakness that I took him back; it's strength. I love him enough to be vulnerable. And you know, maybe you're right. Maybe he'll hurt me, and if that happens, then I'll survive it. But maybe you're wrong, and he'll cherish me and make me happier than I've ever been. I deserve to love someone who makes me feel the way Leo does."

Amos bends the edge of the plastic cookie bag back and forth. He's quiet for a moment, thinking. "I'm scared for you, Alma."

"Me too," I admit. "But I'm also really excited to see where this life takes me. My connection with Leo isn't something I can explain to you. You wouldn't understand because you can't feel it like I do. But I'm telling you that it's everything I've ever dreamed of wanting. Leo is worth fighting for. Please just trust me and love me. If I fall, then you'll be there to catch me. And if I fly, you'll be there to cheer me on. Just be my friend." My voice catches on the last word, and I swallow hard.

I extend my pinkie finger toward him, and he takes it in his. I sigh, relieved.

"I'm sorry," he says. "I was a horrible best friend this week."

Our connected fingers rest against his thigh, and I lean my head on his shoulder. "You're the best friend a girl could ask for, Amos. I love you."

He kisses the top of my head. "I love you."

We sit this way in silence for a few minutes, soaking in the easy comfort that we've always shared.

"So, we're good?" I ask.

"Of course."

"Does that mean you'll come out to dinner with Leo and me before we head back?" My voice rises an octave, and I chew on the corner of my mouth, waiting for his reply.

"Yeah, I guess I have to get to liking the guy again."

"Yay! Okay, great."

Once Leo returns with groceries, we stand from the step, and Amos tells me that he'll meet me at the car after he lets his mom know that he's heading out. I practically skip back to the car, so happy that everything has worked out.

Leo and I drop off the bags of food in my parents' kitchen and say good-bye again.

Amos waits next to the Porsche, and I smile wide. Things are back to the way they should be, and joy explodes from my chest.

CHAPTER 40

LEO

*D*inner with Alma and Amos wasn't the way I would've chosen to spend the evening, but Alma had a huge smile plastered on her face the entire time, and for that, it was worth it. I don't hold anything against the guy. If I were him, I'd hate me too. Truthfully, I'm easy to hate.

I'd never say this to Alma, but the dude is a little boring. He's so straitlaced and by the book. I have a hard time talking to him. Plus, he and Alma almost have this weird twin thing going on. They have ways of communicating that only make sense to them, little quirks that only the two of them know about, and secret handshakes.

Their relationship is borderline creepy, but who I am to judge really? I have one friend, Ethan, and while he's the real deal, he's stood by and watched me kill myself with drugs for years. He's always been there to help pick me up when I fall, and he's always had my back. But if Alma were to start doing any of the shit I've done, Amos would pull her ass away from the mess before she could blink. He'd have her in rehab before her first hit; I'm sure of it. If that's true friendship, I'm void of it.

As much as the dude's boring-ass stories about shit I couldn't care less about make me want to sleep, he's loved Alma unconditionally since they were young. I can't deny him mad props for that. Who knows what Alma's life would look like now had it not been for him? She always tells me that everyone needs at least one person to truly love them, and they can overcome anything. He is that person for her, and I'm glad she has him.

In all fairness, Amos's mundane personality is probably triggering me more than normal because I'm fucking exhausted. I haven't slept more than a couple of hours in two days. The thing about trauma is, I can go days without thinking about it, but when the memories invade, they drop me to my knees. My mind refused to turn off over the past two nights, and there's nothing worse than experiencing it all again in my nightmares. So, I stayed awake and held Alma while she slept, focusing on everything about her that's pure and good, letting her light drown out my dark.

The old me would've spiraled at this point, but instead, I met with Ollie, my sponsor, while Alma was at work and talked it out with him. Between his words and the hours of workouts I did the past couple days, I was able to fight off the urges. The voices within me that scream so loud for an end to all of this are hard to ignore. But I do. As Ollie says, that's my life now—one day at a time. And I'll take it. I'll fight the addiction over and over again. As good as those first few moments of numbness feel after I give in and use, none of it compares to the way it feels to be loved by her. None of it. Alma is the best drug I've ever had, and unlike the others that kill me little by little, she gives me life.

We're halfway home, and time has slowed way the hell down. I just want to get back and finally sleep. I'm exhausted enough that I know my nightmares won't come. Two days of long work shifts and the anticipation of going home have Alma sleeping already, buckled in the passenger seat.

My eyelids grow heavy, and I blink hard and yawn. The headlights of the car bounce against the pavement, and shadows taunt my fatigue. I look toward the radio and turn up the current song. With my eyes back on the road, the lights ahead confuse me, taking on an abnormal shape. The red of brake lights flash, but it's too late. I slam on my brakes and swerve to miss the line of stopped cars in front of me.

Pavement and lights flash before me and then the night sky disappears from view as the ground appears out the wind-shield before that too leaves. The car jolts to a halt, landing on its wheels. There's a deafening thud and the creak of metal screeching. Glass breaking.

Mentally, I take stock of my surroundings. The sounds. The screams. The smell of grass and trees and something metallic. I will sensation to come—from my arms, legs, heart, anywhere. I'm numb, and I can't feel anything.

Did I make it?

I open and close my eyes. My head pounds. It takes a moment before I can see or comprehend what happened, and when I remember, she is the only thing that matters. I force my head to turn toward Alma, and as she comes into focus, I wish I were dead.

"Nooo!" I cry. "No! No! No! Please, God, no!" I try to reach for her, but my arm won't move, and when I look down, I see a bone protruding from my skin. "Please, take me. Please, take me," I beg. My vision blurs—I think from tears, but I can't tell. "Alma, baby, please. Alma, wake up. Please wake up."

Her shoulders are hunched, and her torso and upper body are slouched forward against her seat belt. Her hair has fallen, shielding her face, and I can't tell if she's breathing. A tree branch broke through the window. Glass shattered everywhere. The end of the branch has impaled her abdomen. I don't know how deep it goes. It's impossible to see anything with all of the blood. She's covered in more blood than I thought possible for her small frame to hold.

I'm going to lose her. This can't be happening.

Please let this be a nightmare.

Wake up!

I can't lose her.

"Alma, please." Sobs erupt from my chest, and I try to reach her again.

I can't feel her. I can't see her face. I can't see her chest moving.

There are voices. Lights. Directions called. Metal creaking.

I feel myself slipping into the darkness, and I welcome it. Without Alma, I just can't …

* * *

THE HUMMING AND quiet beeping seem familiar, and I try to place the sounds. My body hurts. A bone-deep soreness brings the memory of the accident back. My eyes pop open. I blink, taking in my surroundings.

Alma.

I try to reach for the IV in my hand to yank it out, but my arm isn't cooperating. Peering to my side, I see the cast, and the image of my broken bone comes to mind. I move my IV'd arm toward my casted one and grab at the needle in my skin with my exposed fingers. They're heavy and slow.

Fuck!

I raise my left arm to my mouth and yank at the cords with my teeth. The medical tape peels off, and the needle falls out.

Once I'm free, I try to sit up. The room starts to spin, and I lie back down. A nurse walks into the room.

"Mr. Harding. What are you doing?" Her voice is concerned as she helps me lie back.

"I need to go," I insist.

"No, you need to rest. You're just waking up from surgery. You're in no state to leave right now."

"Where is she?" I yell.

"She's right outside. Just let me get you situated, and I'll let her come in." She rubs an alcohol pad over the skin of my hand where the IV once was.

"She's here?"

"Yes, she's here. Just be calm, please." She gets to work on reinserting a new needle into my hand.

"What happened?" I ask, closing my eyes to combat the pounding in my skull.

"You were in a car accident. You broke your arm, a rib, and punctured your lung. You also have a pretty serious concussion. You underwent surgery to set and cast your arm and fix your lung. You'll recover completely, but you're going to be pretty sore for a while."

"No pain meds," I bark out.

The nurse looks over to me. "I'm sorry?"

"I'm an addict. Don't give me narcotic pain meds, please. None," I tell her firmly. I can't risk it. I won't.

She purses her lips and nods in understanding. "Don't worry, Mr. Harding. I'll mark Tylenol and ibuprofen only on your chart. Those are safe."

"Thank you."

The nurse finishes inserting my IV and then checks the machine connected to the bags dripping into the line. She helps me readjust the pillows, so I'm sitting in as comfortable of a position as possible, given my circumstances. Then, she gives me a warm smile and tells me she'll send her in.

Thank God she's okay.

There are voices outside of the room, and then the door opens again. The heels clicking against the tiled floor churn the acid in my stomach.

No.

"Hey," Cat says with a gentle smile.

"Where is she? Where's Alma?" I demand, desperate.

Cat shakes her head. "I don't know, Leo."

"Please find out. She was with me in the car. She was hurt bad." My voice cracks. "Her best friend was probably her emergency contact—Amos. He might be here somewhere. Ask everyone until you get an answer. Please. I have to know."

"Okay, don't worry. I'll find out." Cat's face shows concern and worry, but she nods once, determined, and her high heels click quicker now as she leaves the room on a mission.

CHAPTER 41

LEO

*M*y skin crawls with unease. My body aches. No doubt every inch of my skin is covered in bruises. But that pain doesn't hold a candle to the agony within my chest. Every tick of the thinnest hand on the analog clock on the wall, every second that passes brings more panic.

I won't survive if she didn't make it. I can't live in a world without her.

Guilt consumes me. All of this is my fault. I was tired and didn't see the pileup of cars in time. I overcompensated when turning the wheel, flipping the car and sending us flying into a tree. This is on me. If she dies, it will be at my hands. I did this. The truth dawns—even if she did make it, she surely won't forgive me. She shouldn't. I'm going to lose her either way.

Hot tears flow down my face, and the sting in my heart is so acute that I want to scream. I want to destroy everything around me, but I can barely fucking move. I'm useless.

She has to make it. I'll lose her, and it will be a nightmare, but she has to live. The world needs the light that only Alma Weber can shine. Alma must live.

Please. Please. Please. I pray to a god that I haven't spoken to in years. Maybe this time, my prayers will work.

The door opens, and Cat hurries toward me. "She's alive," she blurts out.

I bend my head and sob. *Thank you.*

"She's been in surgery for a long time. There were lots of internal injuries that needed to be repaired, but she's going to make it. She's coming out of surgery now. She won't be awake for a while, coming off the anesthesia, but she should be fine."

"Is she paralyzed?" I ask hesitantly, remembering the branch in her abdomen, not sure if it went clear through to her spine.

Cat shakes her head. "No, I don't think so. Nothing was said about that." She brings her hand to my face and cups my cheek. "I'm so glad you're okay. That was a pretty bad wreck."

"I'm going to lose her anyway," I utter, barely a whisper.

She presses her lips together, the corners rising slightly. "No, you're not. She loves you more than anything. She loves you as deeply as you love her. It will all work out. I'm sure of it."

I turn away from Cat, unable to respond. I hope she's right.

"Your mom and dad want to come visit you here," she says.

I whip my head to face her, immediately regretting the movement. The pounding in my head intensifies, and I close my eyes until the nausea passes. "No," I reply. "It's a lot, all of this, and I need to focus on getting better and on Alma. That's all I can deal with at the moment. I don't want them here."

"Okay, that's fair. I'll tell them. Don't worry another second about that. There is someone waiting in the hall to see you. It's Amos."

"Yeah, I'll talk to him."

"Great. I'll send him in." Cat retreats, and when she returns, Amos is at her side.

It takes a moment for me to register the raw fury coming from him. I sense it just as he lunges toward me.

He balls up my hospital gown in his fists, and his eyes pop in anger as he screams in my face, "Were you high? What were you on when you almost killed her?"

Cat pulls at his arms. "Get off of him," she cries.

"I knew you'd destroy her! You almost killed her!" Spit flies from his mouth with each word.

"Stop it! Stop this right now," Cat begs, tugging harder.

Amos steps back, and I glare at him.

"I wasn't on anything." My words are cold.

"Yeah, right," he scoffs.

"I wasn't. You want me to call in the nurse and have her read you my toxicology report? I've been clean since January. I wouldn't fucking drive her if I were messed up. Whether you believe it or not, I love her." There isn't a strong bite in my tone, as there should be, because though I wasn't on anything, I'm still to blame, and I know it. I'm not going to reveal that fact to him, but I know it all the same.

Amos shakes Cat's hands away from him. "You almost killed her," he repeats, his voice quiet, tears lodged in his throat.

"I know, and I'm sorry," I confess. "Have you seen her?"

"No. Not yet."

"Well, please let me know when she's awake," I request, hopeful that he actually will.

He's visibly less tense. His rigid body of a few moments ago has relaxed, and he looks tired. He probably hasn't slept all night.

"Yeah, okay. And I'm sorry. I shouldn't have grabbed you like that," he says with sincerity. "I've been up all night. I'm exhausted and worried about Alma, and I just assumed the worst. I shouldn't have."

"It's fine, Amos. I would've assumed too. Just forget about it."

Amos examines my injuries, his tired brown eyes giving me a quick once-over. "How are you?"

"I've been better. I feel like shit."

"Well, you look like shit too." The smallest of grins forms on his face.

"Thanks, man."

He motions toward the door. "I'm going to go back to the waiting area. The nurses know to look for me there when she wakes up. I'll see you later."

"Let me know when she's up," I say again as he walks toward the door.

He gives me a thumbs-up on his way out.

* * *

A soft voice calls my name, and I stir, groaning as my body wakes.

When I open my eyes, Cat's leaning in, her face inches from mine. "How are you feeling?" she asks.

I give her a grunt in response.

"Well, Alma's awake. I talked to the nurse, and they can attach your IV bags to a wheelchair pole if you want to go see her."

At the mention of Alma's name, I'm immediately better. "Yes." I sit up in bed.

"All right. Give me a second to get the nurse, and I'll be right back." She exits the room.

She's still wearing the outfit she showed up in last night. It doesn't look remotely comfortable, and I wonder if she's slept at all. She's way too nice of a person to be with my brother.

A minute later, Cat returns with a nurse and a wheelchair. The nurse is different. The no-nonsense, professional woman from last night has probably gone home for the day. This lady looks like she should be retired and at home, baking cookies for her grandkids. Her smile is warm and puts me at ease.

"Okay, dear. Let me get you situated here." She removes the IV pump that has fluids running and attaches the pump to the pole on the back of the wheelchair. Then, she guides my legs over the bed and helps me pivot onto the chair.

We leave the room, and she pushes me to the elevator. We take it up a few floors. Exiting the elevator, she leads me down a long hallway. Cat's heels click behind us.

Parking me in front of Alma's room, she says, "I'll be back in a bit to get you. If you need me to get you sooner, just ring down to the third floor and ask for Doris."

I thank her, and she scurries off.

Cat pushes me into Alma's room and stops the wheelchair next to her bed. Alma's eyes are closed. She's connected to IVs, like me, and I'm sure she has bandages around her middle, where they patched her up. Yet she looks peaceful and beautiful.

"Amos mentioned going to the cafeteria for some coffee. I think I'll meet him there. I'll be back soon." Cat lightly pats my shoulder and retreats from the room.

Alma seems to hear Cat's clicking as she walks out and opens her eyes. When she sees me, she smiles and starts to cry, holding out her hand for me to grab. I raise my good arm and take her hand in mine.

"Are you okay?" She sniffles.

"Yeah, I'll be fine," I say, bringing her hand to my lips. I kiss her skin, below the IV.

"Me too. I'll be fine too." She pulls in a deep breath.

I lean forward as far as I can without flipping out of the chair and rest my head at her side. "I'm so sorry, baby. This is all my fault. I'm so sorry."

"How is this your fault? It was an accident."

"I know, but I was exhausted, and I didn't see the cars in front of me in time. I overcompensated when I turned the wheel, causing us to flip. I should've been more alert. I'm so sorry. If I wasn't so tired, none of this would've happened. I know you might not be able to forgive me—" My thought is halted when Alma says my name.

"Leo," she repeats, and this time, I raise my head from the bed and look at her.

"Listen to me. This is not your fault. There is nothing to forgive because this was an accident. The nurse told me that twenty people from that pileup were seen at this hospital. You weren't the only one caught off guard. She said the initial accident happened around a bend, and people kept crashing because they didn't see it in time. You didn't do this. You hold no blame for this. Do you understand?"

"I know, but—"

"No," she cuts me off again. "No buts. This isn't your fault. I don't care if you were tired. We would've crashed just the same."

"I don't think that's true," I tell her.

I kept my exhaustion at the time of the accident from Amos because he doesn't need to know. Alma's different. I don't want to lie to her about anything.

She wipes a piece of hair from my forehead. "It is. I promise you. I know you would never knowingly put me in danger. Just forgive yourself, Leo, and let's move on. Okay?"

I'm flooded with a relief so powerful that it's crippling.

"I love you," I say.

"I love you. I'm so glad you're okay." A tear rolls down her face.

There are so many things I want to tell her, declarations of love and promises of forever. I want to crawl into bed and hold her, but we're both too sore and tired. Thankfully, we'll have time for all of that later. For now, I hold her hand and gently run my thumb over hers until her breathing slows and she drifts back to sleep.

CHAPTER 42

ALMA

*T*he ending credits roll to the cheesy romantic comedy we rented. Leo rests beside me in the chaise lounge. His head sleepily fell to my shoulder about thirty minutes ago. It's been two weeks since we got out of the hospital. Our days are spent snuggling, watching movies, napping, and ordering takeout. It's pretty awesome, to be honest.

My incisions are healing well. They don't bother me or hurt anymore. Leo still has the cast on his arm, but other than that, he feels good too. Getting in an accident was horrible, but we were lucky. One or both of us could've easily not made it. I feel very blessed to be sitting here, in Leo's arms, and really not worrying about much.

The doctor wrote me off of work and all physical activity for eight weeks, but I'm not stressed about it. Leo's taking care of everything, and as much as the strong, independent woman inside of me wants to protest, right now, it's kind of nice.

There is something that I have to tell Leo, but I'm scared. I'm terrified to tell him because I haven't truly convinced myself of it. I don't want to speak the words into existence because then they'll somehow become true when I so desperately want to pretend that they're not. But it's time, more so for me and my well-being than anything else.

Leo stirs beside me, and I turn my head toward his. His sleepy gaze is on me.

"Did they end up together?" he asks in jest.

"No, actually, she left him to move to India to train elephants, and he ended up shacking up with the senior church choir lady." I pucker my lips in a grin.

"Wow. I did not see that twist coming."

"I know, right? It was intense. Too bad you fell asleep."

He pulls me toward him and kisses my temple. "What do you want to eat tonight?"

"Gosh, I don't know. What haven't we had lately?"

We've ordered carryout so much that I'm starting to get tired of food. I'm craving something simple, a bowl of cereal or a peanut butter and jelly sandwich, but that would require ordering groceries, which seems like a lot of work, and I'm still riding the *recovering from surgery* lazy train for a little bit longer.

"We haven't had sushi this week," Leo suggests.

"Oh, yeah. I could do sushi. That sounds good."

Less than an hour later, our sushi is delivered, and I'm eating it like I haven't had sustenance in days. It's amazing how hungry one can get from lying around and doing absolutely nothing. After dinner, we warm up the rest of a pan of brownies that we got with our pizza last night. Who knew that pizza places made brownies? Leo is opening up a whole new world for me with his takeout knowledge.

The brownie fills the remaining space in my belly, and I'm finally full.

"You want to pick the movie?" Leo asks.

I frown, knowing that I could eat all the takeout and brownies in the world and it's not going to make me feel better until I acknowledge and accept it.

"What's wrong?" Leo wipes a strand of hair behind my ear.

I bite my lip and exhale through my nose. "There's something I have to tell you."

"What is it?" Leo asks, his blue eyes going wide.

"Back at the hospital, when you asked me what I went through during surgery, I wasn't completely honest with you about all of my injuries." I suck in a ragged breath, and tears start to form.

"Okay," Leo says, urging me on.

I know the words that are coming, and the closer they get to the surface, the more panicked I become. I'm terrified to speak them. I didn't realize how much so until now.

"I might never," I say on a sob, "have babies." I bury my face in my hands as my body heaves with sorrow.

When the doctor told me the news, I was in shock, almost unable to believe her.

Leo pulls me toward him with his good arm and rubs gentle circles over my back, waiting for my tears to abate. "How do you know, babe?"

I sit up and swipe the back of my hand against my tear-soaked face. "Well, when the branch drove into me, most of the damage was to my uterus. The doctor said that they tried really hard to stitch everything up and put me back together, but it will be difficult to have children because of the adhesions from all of the scar tissue caused by the abdominal trauma. She said I could possibly carry a baby if I go the IVF route, but because of the damage and scar tissue also in my uterus, I might not be able to carry either. We won't know that until later."

This diagnosis isn't the end of the world; I know this. There are millions of women who can't conceive naturally or at all. I'm not alone regardless of the path in which I got here, but it hurts. It breaks me in a way I've never been broken because having babies and a big, healthy family was my dream. Being a mother is all I've ever wanted, and the hope of that dream has been taken. It's devastating.

Leo's expression is one of sadness, and as he looks to me, I see my pain reflected in his eyes.

"I'm so sorry, Alma. I don't know what to say."

I shrug. "There's really nothing to say. It is what it is, unfortunately, it's the hand I've been dealt."

Leo squeezes my hand with his. "Alma, look at me."

I lift my stare to meet his.

"You know you can still be a mom, right? If IVF doesn't work, then we'll get a surrogate. You'll be a mom, Alma. I promise you. Your journey to motherhood might look different, but you'll get there."

"You said *we*," I state.

"What?" Leo questions.

"You said *we*. Does that mean you've changed your mind about wanting children?" I inquire, hopeful.

"I want kids but only if it's with you," he answers with a smug grin.

"But you want them? Not now, of course, but someday, you truly want them?" My heart hammers in my chest, hope returning.

Leo kisses me, his lips soft. "I want everything with you, Alma. I want to do life with you. We'll have a house, wherever you want—but definitely not across the street from a fraternity." He chuckles. "We'll have a dog or a cat—your choice. We'll have babies and raise them into well-adjusted humans. You'll have to help me with that because I don't know how one raises children to be happy. I'll coach our son's T-ball team and have tea parties with our daughter, or vice versa. Whatever they want to do, I'll love and support them a hundred percent. They'll be perfect because they'll be part of you. We'll have family game night and argue over Uno. We'll laugh loudly and love fiercely. And every night, I'll fall asleep next to you and know that I'm the luckiest son of a bitch alive."

"This is too good to be true," I say.

"What is?"

"You and everything you just said and all that I'm feeling. How is it possible to love someone as much as I love you? It doesn't seem real. We're young. What if things change?" With Leo, I feel safe enough to voice my concerns.

"The only thing that's going to change is how much I love you because just when I think I can't possibly love you more, a whole new part of my heart expands, and my love for you grows. We might be young, but this connection we have isn't something that comes along every day. It's a once-in-a-lifetime find, if one is lucky enough, and we found it. You're my forever, babe."

I throw my arms around Leo and hug him tight. He's everything I've ever dreamed about, and I found him, my one and only.

"Both," I say.

"What?" Leo chuckles.

"I want a dog and a cat."

"Anything," he says, and I know it's true. He would do everything in his power to make my dreams come true.

"You're going to be a great dad. I know you'll be incredible because you're so good at loving. All any child needs is love, acceptance, security, validation, and attention. You give all of those to me daily. You make me feel loved and safe and perfect, just as I am. You weren't raised with the things I mentioned, but you were born with a kind, loving soul. It's who you are. Anyone on the receiving end of your love is lucky. You, Leo Harding, are an amazing find."

I splay my hands across his chest, over his heart. "When you feel the darkness coming over you, remember all of the things that I love about you and use those qualities to love yourself. You deserve a happy life from here on out. We deserve a happy life—together. If you fight for yourself the way that you fight for me, then we'll get it—a fairy-tale romance, a happily ever worth writing about."

"I lost you once, Alma. I'll fight for the rest of my life so that I never lose you again. You can trust me."

"I do."

Leo's lips find mine, and I pour all of my love into this kiss. It's easy, perfect, and natural because everything I have is already his and always will be.

CHAPTER 43

ALMA

"*I* don't know what to pack."

My new gift from Leo, a glittery purple hard-shelled suitcase lies empty on the bed. He gave it to me this morning and told me to pack for a seven-day trip.

"Clothes," he deadpans from the bathroom, toothbrush in his mouth.

"Seriously, do I need outfits for cool weather, tropical weather … what? It's not as easy as just *clothes*," I mock.

He walks out of the bathroom, towel around his waist, and I become flushed. Today marks the end of my eight-week restriction against physical activity. I saw the doctor a few days ago, and she said that my body has healed nicely and that I was clear to resume normal activities on the eight-week mark, which, to reiterate, is today. Leo's bare chest causes all sorts of crazy hormones to rage within me.

"Stop looking at me like that." He chuckles. Removing the

towel completely, he grabs a pair of boxer briefs from his drawer and pulls them on. "We have places to be."

"I'm not looking at you in any particular way," I retort and glare back toward my empty suitcase.

"Okay, sure. I know your *I want sex* face, and it's not happening right now, no matter how irresistible I might be." He smirks, and I can't help but laugh.

"Whatever," I grumble. "Can you please tell me what to pack?"

Leo walks around the bed in only his boxers. He stands behind me and circles his arms around my middle. He got his cast off yesterday, and it's so nice to feel both of his arms again. Snuggling with a plaster cast is tricky and, for the most part, uncomfortable.

I trace my finger along the scar on his arm. "Does it hurt?"

"No." He leans down and kisses my cheek. "For packing, I'd do a little bit of everything. The days are hot, and the nights are cool. You will need a swimsuit and a couple of dresses for dinner."

"Fancy dresses? Like prom dresses?" I inquire.

"No," Leo says with a laugh. "Cocktail-type dresses."

"I don't really have fancy clothes, Leo. You see what I wear."

"All right. Don't worry about that. I'll take care of it. Just throw some shit in the suitcase." He kisses me again and then releases his arms before he continues getting dressed.

I finish packing and pull the wheeled luggage down the hall. Leo's on the phone with someone downstairs, and I can't wipe the grin off my face. I have no idea what he's planning, but everything he does is magical. It's going to be a great week.

"Thank you. I appreciate it," Leo says into his phone, hanging up with whomever he was talking to as I enter the kitchen. "You ready?"

"Yep!"

He takes my bag and his and loads them into his new Land

Rover. He opted for a different type of vehicle after totaling the Porsche, and I approve of the switch. I think he's more of an SUV type of guy anyway.

As Leo pulls away, I say, "How about we play a game of Twenty Questions and see if I can guess where we're going?"

"Okay," he agrees.

"Is it far away?" I ask.

"Yes-ish."

"That's not a real answer." I turn in my seat to look at him, and his face beams with jovial energy.

"Then, don't ask vague questions. *Far* is subjective."

"Fine. Are we taking a plane to get there?"

"No."

"So, we're driving there?"

"Yes, and no." Leo merges onto the highway.

"That doesn't even make any sense." I giggle.

"It makes total sense," he disagrees.

"Is it in Michigan?"

"Yes."

"Is it by water?"

"Yes."

"That was a wasted question. You know, I read that no matter where you are in Michigan, you're never more than six miles away from a body of water."

"I've heard that as well," Leo agrees.

"Okay, fine. Is it on one of the Great Lakes?"

Michigan has five huge lakes that border our state. I've actually never been to any of them, but I hear they're like little oceans with beautiful sand and fresh water.

"Yes," Leo answers.

"Oh, good. I've never seen one of the Great Lakes," I muse.

"Are you serious?" Leo's cheery tone morphs to one of concern. "You've lived in Michigan your whole life and never been to one of the Great Lakes?"

"No, we weren't a vacationing type of family."

"Ugh. That's just sad, babe. All right, new plan. You're not going back to work this summer. Instead, we're going to take the last month before school starts to visit and explore all of the Great Lakes."

"I don't know. I should really work."

"Listen, you still have money left over from what you saved for the apartment. Your dorm and schooling are paid for. What do you need money for?"

"A car," I say.

"I'll get you a car," he says without thinking twice.

"I know you would, but I want to get one for myself."

"Please don't be so stubborn. Money doesn't mean anything to me. I'll gladly give it to you. I just want to spend time with you and show you the world."

I shake my head, and my lips turn up in a grin. "Only people with money would say that it doesn't mean anything."

"Exactly, so take mine. Please just think about it. We have a month before classes start up, and then we're going to be crazy busy again. Let's enjoy the rest of the summer."

"I'll think about it," I agree.

Leaning my head against the headrest, I take in the passing view. Michigan is a stunning deep green in the summer.

"Do you want to ask more questions?"

"No, I think I've decided I want to be surprised. Knowing it's by one of the Great Lakes is enough. How long is the drive?"

"Four hours." Leo reaches his hand behind the seat and produces a plastic bag. "Road snacks for my love."

"Ooh." I look inside the bag and spot what I want first. "Gummy worms! Thanks, babe." I rip open the bag and drop the long, sugary treat into my mouth. "The half-red and half-white ones are the best."

"You can really tell the difference?" Leo asks with a tilt of his brow.

"Um, absolutely. Okay, keep your eyes on the road. I'm going to put a color in your mouth, and you tell me what you think."

"Okay," he agrees, and I stick a green-and-yellow gummy worm into his mouth. "What does it taste like?"

"Sweet. Good," Leo replies.

"Okay, take a drink of your water to clean your palate."

Leo shakes his head with a smirk but complies, taking a long gulp from his water bottle and swishing it around his mouth.

"Ready for taste test number two?" I put a red-and-white worm into his mouth. "What do you think of this one?"

"Sweet and good," Leo responds with a grin.

"Okay. Do you notice a difference between the two, and if so, which did you like more?"

"They tasted a tiny bit different, but I can't really describe how. For some reason, I thought that number two was a little better."

"Yes." I clap my hands. "Told you, red-and-white is the best flavor combo of worms."

"I shouldn't have doubted you. You are the sugar connoisseur among us." He playfully squeezes my knee.

"That I am. I know my sweets."

Four hours pass quickly. One of my favorite things about our relationship is the fact that we can talk for hours. He says he finds me adorable, and I return the sentiment. We're a good pair.

Leo parks in a lot, and I see signs for a ferry.

"We're taking a ferry boat?" I ask.

"It's the only way to get to Mackinac Island." He shoots me a wink.

I bounce in my seat and exit the vehicle. "I've always

wanted to go there," I exclaim. "Have you been?"

"Yeah, I love it," he replies.

I walk around to the back of the car, where he's opening the rear hatch, and throw my arms around him. "Thank you. I love this week so much."

He grasps my waist and kisses the tip of my nose. "It hasn't even started yet."

"I know I'll love it. You make life so fun. I'm incredibly thankful for you."

Leo stares down at me with a look of wonder, and then his lips find mine. He pulls away too quickly. "We'd better get going, so we can catch this ferry. Or we'll have to wait for the next."

"Okay." I reach for my bag, but Leo insists on carrying both.

The ferry ride is exciting. I've never been on a boat before —a little tidbit I keep to myself. I think Leo is still shocked that I've never visited any Great Lakes. The water is clear and gorgeous. Peering over the edge of the ferry, I can see the rocky white bottom.

"So, you've officially seen Lake Huron now," Leo says from beside me before kissing my temple.

"It's pretty."

"It is. So, do you know much about the island?"

"I've heard it's beautiful, but that's about it," I remark, holding my hand to the side of the ferry as the wind whips across my skin.

"Well, there are no cars. Everyone either walks, rides bikes, or takes horse-drawn carriage rides. The island itself is eight miles in circumference, so it's small. There's a path that goes around the island. We can rent bikes and explore. There are so many picturesque views. The restaurants are incredible too. It's a cool experience that is unlike anywhere else. You'll see … it's just awesome."

I sigh, happy. "I can't wait."

CHAPTER 44

ALMA

*T*he Grand Hotel and the grounds surrounding it is one of the most beautiful places I've seen. It has a majestic, antique quality with high beams, stunning ballrooms, women in dresses and men in suits, rich fabrics and colors throughout the resort that look like they belong in a 1920s mansion.

Our suite is breathtaking—old world meets new. The king-size canopy bed is a focal point with its swooping pink and white fabrics and comforter. Every detail of the room is interesting and unique. It has the Ritz meets *Charlie and the Chocolate Factory* feel to it. There's an antique white milk basin next to the wooden vanity, floral chairs, a cuckoo clock on the wall, vivid wallpaper that has a soft texture, embroidered pillows with puppies that rest on the purple sofa, and chandeliers hanging in every room.

I bend and smell the fresh vase of flowers by the bed. I turn toward Leo. "This is the most amazing place I've ever seen." I'm in awe as I continue to scan the space, finding new and interesting elements with each pass. "It feels like every item in here is an antique or handmade. I can't imagine how they decorated this room."

"It's neat. I've never stayed in this suite before, but every room in the hotel is decorated uniquely. They all have different beds, color schemes, and themes. Each room is an adventure in itself. We used to stay here a lot when I was a kid. My parents loved to vacation here with their friends. I was basically left to my own devices and could explore the island all day by myself. One of the housekeepers, Fran"—he smiles at the memory —"tolerated me or maybe even enjoyed my company because she let me tag along with her to clean rooms. It felt like a treasure hunt, seeing what each room held."

"I love it here. Let's live here." I giggle, and Leo wraps his arm around my waist, pushing me forward until we've both toppled onto the bed.

Lying on my back, facing the ceiling, I notice the pieces of crystal hanging from the chandelier are butterflies.

Leo props himself up, his face resting against his palm, looking at me. "What do you want to do first? Rent bikes and ride around? Walk downtown or around the harbor? Are you hungry?"

"You tell me. You know the place. I will love anything we do."

"All right, well, I was thinking that we could rent bikes and ride around the island tomorrow, explore, have a picnic on the beach. Today, let's walk around downtown and come back here for dinner. I forgot to tell you something else the island is known for." He puckers his lips into a smirk.

"What?" I ask, wide-eyed.

"Fudge. There are at least a half-dozen fudge shops in town.

They make it right in front of you. Apparently, Mackinac Island fudge is sold all over the world."

"OMG. This place really is heaven." I jump up from the bed, grabbing Leo's hand. "Let's go."

He laughs and follows me out of the room. We walk hand in hand along the path leading toward town. The waves hitting the rocky beaches are calming. I wrap my outside hand around Leo's bicep and lean the side of my face against his arm.

In town, Clydesdale horses pull carriages with people. Their hooves clomp against the stoned street in a happy cadence.

"Let's try this place." Leo opens the door of a candy shop, and the sweet smell of sugar and chocolate invades my senses. "I've tried all the fudge shops, and they're all delicious."

There's a man behind a glass partition, folding a pliable slab of fudge onto itself. A woman stands behind him against the back wall, a giant stainless steel pot in front of her, stirring melted fudge ingredients with a long wooden spoon.

"You can try any of the flavors, too, so you know what you want to buy."

"Really? Ooh, this could get dangerous." I laugh.

Peering into the glass case where the fudge is displayed, I read the labels. There must be at least thirty different kinds. I don't know where to start.

Leo gets an employee's attention. Her warm smile complements the bright pink-and-white striped apron that she's wearing. "Can I please try the butter pecan, chocolate, chocolate caramel sea salt, and chocolate cherry? And then she'd like to try the chocolate mint, chocolate peanut butter, chocolate pecan, and peanut butter chocolate chip."

The lady chuckles. "Do you just want to try them all?"

"Yes, please," I say. "I promise we'll buy a bunch. You can freeze it, right?"

"No problem. Yes, you can freeze it, and it lasts for a long time."

"Thank you!"

She starts to cut little chunks out of each fudge and places them on top of the glass display case.

"Let's do the plain chocolate first because it's the original," I say to Leo.

"Sounds like a plan."

I drop a square of the fudge into my mouth and groan. The fudge melts against my tongue, and the flavors are so rich and delicious. It's truly incredible.

"Right?" Leo nods, his lips tilting up in amusement. "I knew you'd love it here."

"I don't think anything can top that. It's so good."

"Try the next one. They're all so good."

I taste the turtle fudge with caramel and pecans, and as Leo said, I can't pick which I love more. We continue taste-testing until my stomach can't take any more, and we end up walking away with boxes of a dozen flavors.

Leo holds our sweet treasures as I window-shop. It feels good to walk after consuming so much sugar. The main part of town isn't that big, and then we pass a small harbor. Towering up on a hill overlooking the water is an old fort.

"Can we tour there tomorrow? I love old forts and buildings with history."

"Sure," Leo replies.

We turn around and walk through town and up to the hotel. When we're back in our room, I see three large white boxes lying on the bed.

"What are these?" I ask.

"They're for you."

"Should I open them?" I look to Leo.

"Yes." He grins.

I pull up the lid to the first box. Inside is a black cocktail dress and matching heels. There's a smaller box with a silver bracelet and earrings. A complete ensemble. "What is all this?"

"Well, there is a dress code for the dining room, and you said you didn't own anything fancy, so I had some options sent here for you."

"You had formalwear and accessories sent to an island on the same day you requested it? How?" I laugh.

"I have connections." He shrugs with a smirk.

"You are unbelievable. Thank you." I open the other two boxes, each one complete with a cocktail dress, heels, and jewelry. "I feel like a princess." I run my fingers along the fabric of the black dress.

"You should always feel special, baby, because you are."

Stepping toward Leo, I circle my arms around his body. "Thank you," I say again. "I love you so much and not because of all you buy me and do for me, but because I love you. You know that, right?"

"Of course I do." He places a finger beneath my chin, tilting it up until our eyes meet. "I do things for you because it makes me happy, and because I can, and because you deserve it. Yet I know if I were penniless and lived out of my car, you'd love me just the same."

"I would." I stand up on my tiptoes and press my lips to his. "Should we get ready for dinner?"

"I think so. Which dress are you going to go with tonight?" he asks.

"The black one."

"Good choice."

I pick up the box and make my way to the bathroom, thrilled to get dressed up and go to a fancy dinner.

I spend extra time on my hair and makeup. The dress is beautiful, elegant, and sexy, all at the same time. My long hair falls in waves down my back, and as I take in my reflection in the full-length mirror, I seem so much older. For being a *jean shorts and T-shirt* kind of girl, I do clean up nice.

I exit the bathroom. Leo's back is to me, and he's looking out the large window toward the water. He's sporting a black suit, looking like a *GQ* model. He really is so gorgeous.

Upon hearing me, he turns from the window. "Holy shit." His expression darkens, his eyes hungry.

"I hope that's a good thing," I say with a chuckle.

He steps toward me, his stare heating my skin. "You are the most gorgeous woman in the world, Alma."

"Thank you, but you need to stop looking at me like that. We have to go," I echo his words from earlier, knowing full well that he'd undress me right now if he could.

He stands before me and runs his finger down my cheek, so lightly that I can barely feel it but it sends tingles shooting down my body. He swallows and presses his lips together. There's something in his deep blue eyes that I can't make out.

"What is it?" I ask.

"I just love you so fucking much," he utters, emotion thick in his voice. "I ... I want to give you something. I had another plan, but I can't wait." He steps back and quickly retrieves a white box, a little larger than a shoebox, with a pink satin bow from his suitcase.

He comes back to me and says, "I made you something. When I was ... away for those months, they encouraged us to learn a new skill to keep our hands and minds busy, you know? So, I took up woodworking and made you this." He gives me the box.

"Ahh." I smile up to him and pull the pink ribbon. When I lift off the lid, I see a wooden jewelry box inside. There's a quote carved into the top.

YOU ARE BURNED INTO MY SOUL FOREVER.

I run my finger across the words as tears well up in my eyes.

"Do you remember?" Leo asks.

"Yeah, the fortune cookie from the night we first made love." I press my lips together, trying to keep the tears at bay. "It's beautiful."

"I feel like that fortune was written for us. You're the only person in my life that I've had this deep of a connection with. It's indescribable."

Leo takes the gift from me and sets it on the table. He opens it and removes a small box. Dropping to one knee before me and opening the lid, he reveals a diamond ring.

My hands go to my mouth as I gasp.

"My entire life has been spent searching for love, acceptance, and a sense of wholeness. Then, I find you, and you're everything. You bring so much goodness to my world. I get this feeling when we're together, and I have from the very first moment I saw you in that restaurant. It's like I can finally breathe when you're near. Almost like I'm not fully myself until I'm with you. Without you, my soul's ripped wide open—bare, vulnerable, and hurting. I'm incomplete and empty. Your soul restores mine, threading through the gaps until we're one, protected by love. I feel that our love is once in a lifetime, and I want to promise you forever. Whether we get married tomorrow or in ten years, you're it for me. I want to wake up every day, knowing that you're mine and I'm yours for always. Alma, my soul, will you marry me?"

Tears wet my face, and my heart beats forcefully within my chest. I inhale deeply, catching my breath. It's fast and a little scary, but everything Leo said is true. He's my person. He's the one, and part of me—despite everything we've been through—has always known that.

"Yes," I choke out. "Yes, I will."

Leo gifts me with the biggest, most stunning smile I've ever seen, and in this moment, I'm a hundred percent certain that this is right. He slides the large diamond on my ring finger. The band is exquisite. Platinum vines thread around my finger, ending in an incredible design that cradles the diamond, as if it were a flower. It's whimsical, unique, and amazing.

"It's perfect," I say through my tears.

Leo stands, and as if he can't wait another minute, he crashes his lips against mine. Our lips move against one another, and our tongues dance in a tango created just for us. My fingers slide into his short hair, pulling him closer. He wraps me in his arms, holding me against him.

"Room service later?" he whispers against my lips.

"Sounds good." I reach for the button of his pants as he unzips the back of my dress.

We make quick work of removing all articles of clothing and climb into bed. Leo hovers above, encasing me between his muscled arms. His length rubs along my entrance, and he looks to me in question.

He was tested for all STDs during rehab, and as for pregnancy, there's no more need for condoms.

His fingers thread through mine above my head, and I nod, granting him permission. He slides into me, and we both release a cry into the lust-filled space. He drops his forehead to my shoulder, breathing heavily as he starts to move. Having him inside of me with nothing between us is intoxicating, and I never want it any other way. And now that he's officially my forever, I never will.

CHAPTER 45

ALMA

*I*f my life were a movie, the three years following my engagement to Leo would be a series of short video clips played to a romantic song, highlighting our amazing time together. These images would show a fairy-tale life, the kind that only happens in romance movies.

Upon returning from Mackinac Island with stunning bling on my hand, I officially moved in with Leo. I kept my scholarship-allotted dorm room each year, just in case, though I never needed it. The practical side of me knew to maintain that safety net. I'd worked too hard to potentially find myself homeless.

Leo finished his business degree the year following our engagement, and two years later, I completed my teaching degree with magna cum laude honors.

We remained close with Amos, Quinn, Ethan, and Ollie and hosted dinners and game nights often. Neither of us felt the need to attend college parties anymore. Truth be told, it was never my style, and now that Quinn had a house full of girls to party with, I didn't feel bad about my stay-at-home life. Leo avoided the parties for obvious reasons. He said that they only ever served one function for him—to escape and forget—but now that he was with me, he didn't want to do either.

We volunteered often, helping in the community frequently. I tutored kids, and Leo took in every opportunity to help others where he could, trying to find his passion in life. We both agreed that working for his father and brother wasn't the right or healthy path.

We visit my parents a couple times every year—when they can be pinned down. I can't say everything is great between us. I've come to realize that they'll never change, and our relationship will always be what it is. But I still try and show up for our uncomfortable get-togethers. They are my parents, and I love them. In their own way, they care for me too.

Leo's family dynamic has remained the same. We visit once a year around Christmas—not on the actual day, but close to it. I told Leo I wouldn't have the holiday ruined every year out of obligation. Cat, sometimes accompanied by Stephen or Leo's mom, visits every few months, and we'll go out for dinner and catch up. She's definitely the glue that keeps the family connected.

When we aren't volunteering or in school, we travel. Leo wants to show me the world, and I want to see it.

BONUS CHAPTER

LEO

"Almalee Hannelda Weber," the man, who carries some important role at Eastern Michigan University, announces her name with only a minor brutalization of its pronunciation.

Amos, Cat, and I stand from our seats and shout her name, cheering obnoxiously.

She walks across the stage, wearing a green graduation cap and gown. On most of the graduates here, the color is off-putting, but on Alma, it's stunning. Green is her color. Hell, she owns all the colors. She's never not been gorgeous. Her perfect olive skin, dark hair, and mesmerizing doe eyes complement all hues.

I see her up on that stage, and my heart swells with pride. My girl can do anything.

She came from nothing with virtually zero adult support for her entire life. The two people who failed her the most couldn't even get their shit together for one afternoon and be here for her at graduation. The set of empty chairs that Alma had reserved for her parents "just in case" sit vacant beside me.

She takes the faux leather binder that holds her diploma, the one that shows she graduated with Magna Cum Laude honors, and turns to face the audience. A smile lights up her face as her gaze zeros in on the three of us that make up her cheering section. She holds me in her stare, and so much love invades every pore of my body. It's unreal how much I love this girl.

Arms pumping through the air, I cheer louder. Alma shakes her head with a grin and exits the stage.

She and I have had a hell of a four years, the past three—incredible. We experienced so much life together, exploring the world and each other. I never thought I'd ever have this kind of love. The truth is, I never thought I deserved it. Alma shows me every day that I do, and maybe one of these days, I'll believe it.

If anything in this world could fix me and extinguish the demons clawing at my soul, it would be her. My entire existence has been dark. The universe finally brought me some light. It gave me her. She's my reason to fight every single day.

And I do.

Every minute of every day is a battle to live in the light, to stay two steps ahead of the darkness that threatens to pull me back into hell. I live my life one day, one moment at a time, with Alma as my focus. She soothes my battered heart and makes me believe in the future.

My biggest fear is that the demons will outrun me. They'll catch me and drag me under. I'd give anything to forget my past, but my mind is a stubborn bitch, determined to remember every detail.

I often question why I was dealt this hand in life. What could've stopped it all? Could I have changed my fate? But these questions only stir up sadness and despair because there are no answers. Sometimes things just are as they are. No one escapes this world unscarred. We all have our own weights to carry, some heavier than others.

I'm so grateful for my life with Alma for she saved me in every sense of the word. She saves me every day. I pray she saves me forever. No one knows their future, and I hope my life with Alma is a long one. But if it's not, I can honestly say she made every second worth living, gave each moment value, and lit my soul on fire with so much love that it will stay with me forever, in this life and the next.

"She looks beautiful." Cat nudges my side.

"Yeah, she does."

Cat steeples her fingers in front of her face, wearing a huge smile. "I'm so proud of her."

"Me, too."

When the graduation ceremony concludes, we follow the mass of people exiting the auditorium. Like everyone else, we're going to meet our graduate out on the lawn. The gray clouds that hovered in a sea of overcast when we arrived have opened up to pale-blue skies. Beams of spring sunshine light up the new grass.

"Hey," Alma calls. A beautiful smile graces her face as she hurries across the lawn toward us.

When she reaches me, I lift her into my arms and spin in a circle. My mouth captures hers.

"I'm so proud of you," I say, peppering kisses against her lips.

"Thank you." She threads her fingers through the hair at the nape of my neck.

I lower her to the ground, and Cat and Amos hug and congratulate her. Amos grabs her pinky in his, and the two of them do their best friend thing. It wouldn't be nearly as cute if it were anyone but Alma doing it.

"Alma!" Quinn screeches and races over, her green graduation cap in hand.

The pair embrace.

"Where are you guys going to eat?" Quinn asks. She hitches her thumb over her shoulder, motioning toward her parents and sisters. "We're heading to Ann Arbor to the new steak house. Do you all want to come?"

"No, thanks. We're eating at Giovanni's, then heading to Coney Island for dessert," Alma answers.

Quinn furrows her brow. "Giovanni's and Coney Island? You've eaten there a million times. Don't you want to go somewhere special for graduation?"

"They are special," Alma answers.

Giovanni's is the Italian restaurant across from campus where Alma and I first laid eyes on each other. She's always loved it for that reason alone. The food, in truth, is mediocre at best, but nostalgia has a way of making everything taste better. Coney Island is a big part of our dating history as well and holds many memories. Not to mention, Luca made us promise to stop by.

I have the means to take Alma anywhere. Hell, I could've chartered a plane and flown us to any of the top restaurants in the United States to celebrate. But Alma doesn't need all that fanfare. She's truly happy with the simple things in life. It's just another reason I love her. She wants to eat at a place special to her with people she loves so that's what we're going to do.

"Okay." Quinn shakes her head with a grin. "But we're due for a girls day. We'll get together soon?"

"Definitely. Promise." Alma reaches for Quinn's hands and squeezes them.

"Call me tomorrow," Quinn says to Alma. "Oh! We need a picture. Can you, please?" She hands her cell phone to me. The pair fuss with their graduation caps, making sure the tassels aren't swinging in their faces before they wrap their arms around one another's backs and look at me with wide smiles.

I snap a few pictures of the two of them, then a few more with Cat and Amos in the photo as well. Cat takes the phone from me to take some with me in it before giving the phone back to Quinn.

Quinn throws her arms around Alma, and the two embrace for a few seconds. "I'm so glad they put us together freshman year. I love you so much," she says to Alma.

"I love you, too." Alma hugs her tighter, the pair swaying back and forth. "Send me the pics, please. And I'll call you soon."

"Okay." Quinn smiles before turning toward Amos and Cat. Each one hugged Quinn and wished her congratulations on her graduation. "See you guys later." She waves to us all, and like a blur, she hurries back toward her family.

We take more photos, and after Alma has looked through them to ensure we have enough, the four of us walk over to Giovanni's.

The place is crowded with graduates and their families. Luckily, our favorite server, Karrie, saved us a table.

"Hey, guys!" She waves us over to an empty four top in the corner of the restaurant. "I'm so glad you're here. I thought I would have to fight Oscar. He kept trying to seat people here."

"Thank you so much, Karrie. We really appreciate it," Alma says.

Karrie places menus in front of us. "Of course. Anything for my favorite customers. Can I take your drink order?"

We give her our beverage order, and she takes off, weaving through the tables to the kitchen.

"What's good here?" Cat asks.

"I love everything on the menu," Alma says. "I think I'm in the mood for the mushroom ravioli, though."

Cat continues to scan the menu. "Maybe a salad."

"The salads are good, but you have to make sure you save room for the tiramisu." I shoot her a grin.

She quirks a brow. "I thought we were going to that Coney Island place you love so much for dessert?"

"We are. Luca's going to make hot fudge sundaes with all of Alma's favorite toppings," I answer.

She shakes her head and laughs. "Then I definitely won't be ordering the tiramisu."

I shrug. "Suit yourself. But it's worth it. I promise."

My sister-in-law is the best thing to happen to my family. Cat is the sibling I always wanted but never had. I have no idea why she's still with my asshole of a brother, but I hope for her sake she finds the courage to leave. Whether she's married to my brother or not, she'll always be in my life.

"So what now?" Amos asks Alma.

She tilts her head. "I'm not sure." Her gaze flicks to me. "Leo and I have plans. We just have to figure out how to bring all of our dreams into reality. We want to help kids. Especially those who may not have an adult looking out for them. We want to provide a safe place for kids to learn and play. Give them a safe place, you know? We're still figuring it all out, though."

Amos smiles. "That sounds awesome, you guys. You'll figure it out, and it will be great."

Alma squeezes my knee under the table. "Yeah, I think so, too. What about you?"

Amos graduated from the University of Michigan last weekend.

"I have a few offers from different finance firms. Just figuring out which direction I want to go," he says.

"All local?" Cat questions.

He shakes his head. "No. In fact, a firm out in Cali has made me quite the offer, one that will be hard to pass up. I'm just not sure."

"Choose the one that you think will make you the happiest," Alma says.

Something tells me that Amos will take the job closest to Alma. He won't be moving to California anytime soon. Their best friend status is too important to him. He's been protecting her since he was a kid, so I can't see him leaving her now. In truth, their closeness used to threaten me, but now I'm so thankful she has him and has always had him. I don't know where she'd be had she not had him to love and protect her all these years. My girl deserves all the people in her corner.

Alma deserves all the love this world has to offer.

* * *

Hand in hand, we make it up the walkway to our home. Now that Alma has graduated, it's time to sell this place and move into our forever home. Living next to the college campus has been convenient, but we're ready for the next chapter in our lives. One that won't include drunk college students shouting in the street at all hours of the night.

Sliding the key into the lock, I turn and push the door open. We step inside, and I close the door behind us.

"What a perfect day!" Alma circles her arms around my neck. Standing on her tiptoes, she leans in for a kiss.

"It was," I whisper against her lips.

She leans back, and her beautiful brown eyes capture mine. "Now, we're both officially adults."

I chuckle and kiss her forehead. "I think you were officially an adult when you were twelve."

We make our way to the sofa and plop down onto the cushions. Alma lays her head against my chest. "Do you think Amos will move to California?"

"No."

"Really? Why? Did he say something?"

I drag my finger up and down her back, scratching lightly. "I just have a feeling he'll be sticking around."

"I hope so. I'd really miss him if he moved that far away."

"He'd miss you, too, which is why I don't see him taking that job."

She pushes up against my chest and faces me. "I don't want him to turn down a great opportunity because of me, though. That wouldn't be fair to him."

I tuck a strand of her hair behind her ear. "Seriously, don't stress about it. As you say, he's a grown adult. He's going to do what he wants. I just think he'll choose to stay local because it will make him happier."

She nods and lies back down against me. Her hand splays across my chest. "I can't believe I have no more exams to study for or homework to do. It's surreal. I feel as if I've been studying my whole life, and now I'm just... done. We should brainstorm about our project."

"No." I smile. "We should take the night off from thinking and just relax. Celebrate your graduation."

"Okay, fine."

I press my lips against the top of her head and pull her closer to me. "I love you."

"I love you, too."

"I'm sorry your parents didn't show up today," I say.

She shrugs. "It's okay. I knew they wouldn't. I learned a long time ago not to hold my breath when it comes to them. If I don't have any expectations, I can't be disappointed. Right?"

"Yeah." Despite her words, I know she wishes they would've come.

"Besides, I had my family there. You, Amos, Cat, Quinn. I wasn't alone."

"That's true."

We talk for a while before we decide to call it a night. It's been a busy day.

In the bathroom, we brush our teeth and get ready for bed. It's all so... normal. I never thought I'd have this type of life. Alma changed everything for me. It's incredible how one person can alter the entire trajectory of someone's life.

"I'll be right back," Alma states as I crawl into bed.

I fluff the pillow under my head. "Okay."

A minute later, Alma struts into the bedroom wearing nothing but her graduation cap.

I shoot up to a seated position, my eyes going wide at the sheer perfection of the woman before me. "What the hell..." My question trails off as I pull in a deep breath, and my heart races.

Alma continues her slow walk toward me. "You said you wanted to celebrate my graduation." She grins, biting her bottom lip.

"Fuck yeah, I do," I growl.

Swinging my legs over the side of the bed, I take in every second of her seductive entrance. She's absolutely stunning. When she's within reach, I grab her hips and pull her toward me. I slide my palms against the soft skin at her sides.

Reaching up, I flick the tassel hanging from her cap. "I like your outfit."

She smirks. "I thought you would."

"You ready to celebrate?" I remove the cap and hang it from the corner of the headboard.

Her pupils dilate, and her tongue slips out to wet her lips. She simply nods in response.

"Me too," I say right before my mouth crashes against hers.

I'm going to marry this woman, and soon. She's worn my engagement ring on her finger for three years. Now that she's graduated, it's time to officially make her mine. That conversation will come a little later. For now, we celebrate.

CHAPTER 46

LEO

I tap the tassels of Alma's graduation cap that's hanging from the headboard. Memories of her walking into the bedroom last night, wearing nothing but the cap, have me immediately hard again. She's the sexiest woman I've ever seen, and she's naked in my bed—our bed.

Leaning toward her, I kiss her bare shoulder. She smiles and releases a sleepy groan as my hand traces down her abdomen, stopping when I've reached my destination. I insert two fingers into her, and her pelvis rises from the bed to meet my hand. Pulling my fingers out, I rub them against her clit and apply pressure in slow strokes.

"Leo," she breathes.

"Morning, baby."

My hand increases speed as my fingers alternate between rubbing her sensitive ball of nerves and fingering the hell out of her. Her breaths deepen as she squirms and moans against the bed. I'm so hard, it's painful.

Bending down, I take her peaked nipple into my mouth and suck.

"Oh, Leo," she cries as her hips buck from the bed and her body starts to tremble.

Watching her come undone is my all-time favorite pastime.

My tongue flicks her nipple, and I kneel between her legs. Holding her knees back against the bed so she's wide open and ready, I enter her slowly, watching every inch of me slide into her. The visual is better than anything I've seen in my life. I grunt, primal and fierce, while Alma whimpers at the pleasure, a satisfied hum escaping her lips, and then I pound into her.

Hard.

Fast.

So fucking good.

"Leo. Yes," Alma yells, clawing at my forearms.

Her eyes roll back, and her chest arches from the bed. She loves this position, her legs spread wide. My thrusts are deep and punishing, bringing her an intense and brutal pleasure.

"Leo." My name is a strangled scream coming from her mouth, and I know she's about to explode.

I drive into her harder, chasing my own release, and when she breaks and cries out, I empty inside of her before falling to her chest, slick with sweat.

"Oh, babe." She skims the tips of her fingers down my back. "That was an incredible wake-up call."

"You liked it?" I kiss her collarbone.

"Mmhmm," she hums, sated and happy.

"I wanted to warm you up." I roll off to her side and prop my head up on my hand.

"For what?"

"I have an idea." I cup her breast in my hand, twisting her nipple between my finger and thumb. I have a difficult time keeping my hands off of her. I want to touch and please her all day long.

"What's that?" She leans forward and plants her lips against my jaw before licking down my neck.

"Let's fly to Hawaii and get married this week, on the beach, just you and me." I rub my hand up from her breast to her neck and then cup her face. "I want you to be my wife."

She kisses the tip of my thumb against her lips. "I want that too. Let's do it."

"Really?" I ask, mildly shocked that she didn't take more convincing.

"Yeah." She chuckles. "I graduated, which I'd wanted to accomplish before marriage, but now, I'm ready. I don't need a fancy wedding. I only need you."

"How did I get so lucky?" I kiss her.

She extends a hand to find my length firm and ready. She strokes me a couple of times, and our kiss deepens. I roll back onto her and enter her again. This time, it's slow and sensual. Our mouths never separate as we make love.

She's worn my ring for three years, and finally, this week, I get to add the wedding band that I had designed to lock in with the engagement ring. I can't wait to slide it onto her finger and make her truly mine forever.

* * *

It's a perfect day for a wedding, as most days in Hawaii are. I rented a house with a private beach. An officiant and photographer are here. The former because we needed one and the latter because Alma's only request was that our wedding be photographed. She wants the memory of this day in print.

I haven't seen her since our marathon shower sex this morning. Nothing turns Alma on more than being a bride. After we made love under the spray of the shower until my lips were sore and my body was spent, she left to get ready for the wedding.

Now, I'm standing here, on the pristine sand, in a gray suit. Wind blows lightly across the beach. The palms of the trees sway in a rhythm at my back, creating their own island wedding march, accompanied by the splashing of the waves and the calls of the tropical birds.

I see her foot first as she steps out of the line of palm trees and into view. Tears well in my eyes, and my chest aches. I bite the inside of my lip, holding in my emotion. She's wearing a simple dress, white and almost sheer. It hugs her chest and waist and then flows in the breeze behind her. There's a slit up one side, and her leg peeks through with every step. Her deep brown hair cascades in waves down over her bare shoulders and back. The bright sun makes her natural auburn highlights shine. She wears minimal makeup, as always, just a small amount to highlight her already-gorgeous features. Her tan skin looks utterly delectable against the white dress and beach backdrop.

Tears shine in her enchanting brown eyes as she nears. She holds a simple bouquet of pink and white lilies, and I swear she looks like a princess, a perfect and pure angel, and I'm the lucky son of a bitch who gets to marry her.

The wedding officiant gets to the important parts—simple vows and *I do*s. I told her I didn't want any fluff. Just the basics. Alma knows every part of my soul, as I do hers. We don't need poems and scriptures of love from a stranger on our wedding to tell us about commitment. We live our love story every day. It's one of forgiveness and hope and a love that transcends pain, a love that heals and gives life.

The minister says the words I've been waiting to hear, "You may now kiss the bride."

I take Alma Harding, my wife, into my arms and kiss her with every promise I have.

"How do you feel?" I ask against her lips.

"Amazing," she whispers against my mouth. Pulling my face closer to hers, she presses her forehead against mine.

"I love you more than anything in this world," I tell her.

"And I love you the same," she answers.

We sign the marriage documents and take some more photos. Then, the two party crashers leave, and it's just me and my wife.

I thread my fingers through hers. "Let's go for a walk."

"I figured you'd want to get me out of this dress as soon as possible," she teases.

"Oh, I do, but you in that dress is the best foreplay there is. I want to watch you wear it for a little while longer."

"You like it?" She picks up the light skirt and fans it to the side.

"I love it. It's perfectly you."

We kick off our shoes and walk along the sand, where the ocean laps onto the beach.

"I can't believe we're married, and I love the ring, by the way. It's incredible." Alma holds her hand up to admire the set of bands on her finger.

"I thought you'd love it."

"I do, and I love you." She kicks her foot across the water, splashing some onto my pant leg.

"Oh, really?" I raise a taunting eyebrow.

Alma giggles and starts to run, but I circle my arms around her waist, picking her up before she can escape. She kicks wildly, laughing as I walk the two of us deep out into the water.

"Oh my gosh, Leo!" Alma shrieks when we're waist deep in water. "Your suit! And my dress!" She chuckles.

"Yeah? So?" I say. "The water feels good, right?"

She spins in my arms, so she's facing me, her arms wrapped

around my neck and her legs circling my waist. "You're crazy." She presses her lips to mine.

"For you"—I kiss her back—"Mrs. Harding."

"Hmm ... that's hot. Say it again." Her tongue licks up my neck, and she pulls on my earlobe with her mouth.

I sigh, content. "I'm crazy for you, Mrs. Harding."

"Alma Harding. That has a nice ring, yes?" Her wet hands mess my hair.

"Sure does." I hold her against me with one arm while my free one finds her core beneath the dress.

She leans back, her arms extended to her sides as her back floats against the water. Her eyes are closed, but her lips part with sounds of pleasure as my fingers work. The dress floats at her sides, and she looks like an angel.

"Don't move," I groan as I undo my pants, allowing my cock to spring free.

I push the thin piece of fabric of Alma's thong to the side and enter her. Holding her hips in my grasp, I pull her against me over and over again. She remains floating on the water, sinfully exquisite. Water laps over her chest, her nipples visible through the wet, sheer fabric. She licks her lips, biting down on the bottom one as she moans.

It's the sexiest experience of my life, the weightlessness of the water and Alma sprawled before me, beautifully made for me. It doesn't take long before I'm exploding inside her.

I lift her body up, and our lips collide. I kiss her with everything I have and hope that it's enough.

CHAPTER 47

ALMA

*H*and in hand, Leo and I walk through the empty house. It's a modern four-thousand-square-foot mission-style home in Ann Arbor. It sits on a two-acre lot, which is a lot for this part of the city. The lot is wooded and serene, giving the home a more secluded feel, though the house itself is only a five-minute drive from many stores and restaurants. I particularly love the deep blue color of the exterior and the bright white trim. It makes the home seem happy, a good place to settle down.

"I love it," I exclaim. "It's perfect. It's just ... ahh ... so beautiful."

"Yeah?" Leo smiles. "I knew you'd love it."

"Do you like it?" I ask.

"I could live anywhere as long as you're there." He pulls me into a quick kiss.

I shake my head and press my lips together. "I know, but I want you to love it. It's going to be our home, not just mine."

"I do love it. It's a gorgeous house. What's not to love? So, you think we should get it?" he asks.

"Absolutely." I roll up on my toes and kiss him again.

"Great, because I already bought it." He smirks playfully.

"What?"

"It's really hard to get into this neighborhood. The house just went on the market today. I knew you'd love it, so I snatched it up before anyone else could."

I laugh. "That's a risky little move."

"Eh, I know you, babe. Plus, if for some odd reason it hadn't worked, I think we would have had, like, three days to cancel our offer. Not a big deal."

"I can't believe this is our house!" I hug Leo.

"Give me two minutes. I have a surprise for you," he says. "Close your eyes."

"Okay."

A couple of minutes later, Leo returns. "You're good."

"I can look?"

"You can look," he says.

I open my eyes and scan the living room. It's still empty. "What am I looking for?"

He smiles. "I'll show you in a minute. First, I need to make out with my wife for a bit." He steps toward me and pulls me close. His lips caress mine.

I'll never tire of kissing him.

We make out like two teenagers in a hidden corner at prom until I'm startled by the sound of the doorbell.

Leo steps away. "Give me a second," he says and goes to the front door, returning a moment later with bags of delivery.

"There's this fantastic, authentic Greek restaurant nearby." He holds up the paper bags in his hands.

"Awesome." I clasp my hands in front of me.

"Think about all the rooms in the house," he says. "Now, go to your favorite one."

"My favorite room?"

"Yep."

There are so many gorgeous spaces in this home, but I know which is my favorite. I lead Leo to the library. I love the rustic bookshelves on either side of the room and the floor-to-ceiling windows overlooking the scenic backyard.

Opening the door to the library, I gasp when I see the romantic picnic he's set up. There's a large blanket on the ground with a half-dozen pillows placed around it. In the middle of the blanket rests two meal settings with real ceramic plates and silver utensils. On every bookshelf sits a votive candle, making the entire space glow in a soft light.

"Oh my gosh, this is so pretty, Leo. Thank you." I take a seat on the blanket and place the pillows at my back, so I can lean against them. "I didn't tell you this was my favorite room."

"I knew it would be." Leo opens the containers of food and places some on each of our plates. "When I saw this house earlier and the realtor showed me this room, I immediately thought of you. I knew you'd love it."

"It's beautiful." I dip a piece of warm pita into the container of hummus and take a bite. "I can't even believe that we're both graduated, married, and now new homeowners. Part of me still feels like a child while the other part wishes I could've married you years ago."

"Well, you could have," he kids. "Three years ago, to be exact."

"Aren't you funny? You know what I mean."

"I do. I wish I had known you sooner, too, but I'm just damn happy I have you now."

I take a sip from my water bottle. "So, what's the plan now? When will we move everything over? We should have a house-warming party!" I exclaim, clapping my hands.

Leo chuckles. "Well, we can schedule the movers this week and shop around for anything else we need and move right in. Then, we'll put the other house on the market."

"Maybe some sorority or fraternity will buy it." I say.

"I doubt it. It's had tons of work done. I had the entire house remodeled. I don't think they could afford it."

"I hope that whoever buys it loves it as much as I do. It was a great first home for us," I say.

"It was," Leo agrees.

He closes the containers of food and sets them off to the side of the blanket. He crawls up the blanket until he's hovering over me. I lie back on a pillow as Leo kisses me. His hands knead my sides, and I squirm at his touch.

"Are we going to break in our new home?" I run my finger under the waistband of his pants.

"I mean, I think we should." He smirks.

I unbutton his pants in response.

QUINN EXTENDS her arms out to her sides. "I mean, I don't get it. She was probably eighty. Does she need a miniskirt? Or a backless dress? I'm not saying anything against her age, like do you and all that, but she must've tried on every single item we had. Use some discretion. If you pick up a strapless pink pleather dress and ask yourself, *Am I really going to wear this? And the answer is no?* Then, there's no need to try it on!" Quinn slumps in the patio chair and sighs, causing the rest of us to laugh.

"So, it sounds like work is going well?" Leo jokes.

"I just don't want my dad to be right," Quinn says. "He told me that a degree in fashion was a waste, and so far, the only job I can get is a glorified dressing room attendant. I'm so sick of picking up clothes that people have tried on and dropped on the floor and hanging them back up. It's doing the same thing over and over again, and I want to pull my hair out."

"Michigan isn't that fashion trendy," I offer.

"Yeah," Amos agrees. "Maybe you should look for jobs in New York City or somewhere like that."

"I know, but my older sisters are having babies, and I want to know my nieces and nephews. I don't like the idea of being so far away from my family," she explains.

"You'll figure it out, snookums," Quinn's new boyfriend, Patrick, says, handing her a drink.

She's been dating Patrick about a month, and today is the first time I'm meeting him. The jury is still out on that one. I'm trying not to be judgy, but there's something about him that I'm not sure about.

Leo stands from his chair. "I'm heading inside. Anyone need anything?"

No one comments.

"I think we're good, babe. Thanks."

"Okay." He leans down and kisses me before retreating indoors.

I love that he spent time out by the bonfire with me and my friends, but I know he's anxious to head inside to catch up with Ethan and Ollie, who we left in the game room, playing pool.

"How's your job going?" I ask Amos.

He's working for a large company in one of the richer suburbs of Detroit as a Financial Advisor. He's also taking business classes to get his master's at the University of Michigan.

"No complaints. It's interesting. Every day is different. I'm not helping senior citizens try on clubbing attire"—he smiles at Quinn—"so it's good."

"Ha-ha." She shoots Amos a mock glare. "Are you dating anyone?" she asks him.

Quinn and Amos have been friends with occasional benefits since freshman year. I'm glad that it wasn't awkward for them when they ended things. I would've hated not to be able to hang out with both of them at the same time.

"Not really, no. I went on a Tinder date last week, and it was bad. I don't understand how people do that—the whole *meeting on an app* situation. It's so impersonal and fake. I just want to meet someone the old-fashioned way, face-to-face, you know?" Amos says, taking a drink of his beer.

"Okay, Grandpa." I chuckle, hitting his knee with mine.

He squints toward me. "You have no room to talk there, Mutt. We all don't marry our first kiss."

"True." I grin.

"How is married life?" Quinn asks. She extends her hand in front of her toward the house. "Obviously, you're doing well. The house is amazing, and you seem so happy."

"It's wonderful." I press my lips together, containing the giddiness that comes every time I stop to think just how grateful I am. "I don't know. It's just perfect. I'm very lucky."

"You deserve it," Amos says.

"Thanks."

It's true what Amos said. I would suck at navigating dating life online or through apps. All of my friends have gone out with many people, and each relationship has been less than ideal. Leo's best friend, Ethan, has dated more crazy women than any one person should have to deal with.

And then there's Leo and me.

He is my one and done, and it's not lost on me how rare that is.

CHAPTER 48

LEO

$\mathcal{T}$he basketball swishes through the net.

I clap my hands in front of me. "I missed my calling," I kid.

"Yeah, it's the NBA's loss," Ollie teases. "Let's take a break. It's hotter than balls in here."

"Yeah, the air is going to be turned on tomorrow," I say as the two of us head over to the bleachers and sit down. I grab my water bottle and take a big swig.

It's crazy to think that Alma and I bought an old school. It was a small Christian school that had been fully operational until a month ago. Their student body has outgrown this place, so they're constructing a larger school a few miles away.

It's perfect for our needs. It was quite the find.

Over the last few years, I've volunteered at a lot of places, and I realized that it's good for me to help kids and teens who come from abusive or neglectful backgrounds. While I brainstormed with Alma, we came up with the idea to open up a center for these kids. It will be open after school, on weekends, and on holidays. Basically, anytime when the kids aren't in school, we'll be open if they need a place to go.

We're going to provide tutoring, which Alma is heading. There will be a counselor on staff to talk with anyone who needs it. We'll have sports, crafts, and games. Eventually, we want to provide lessons for life skills. We want a cooking room, where kids can learn to make meals for themselves and bake. We want an automotive section, where teens can learn to change their car's tire or oil. All of the life skills that parents should be teaching—how to budget money, cook, clean, hygiene, self-care, and personal safety—will be taught here.

I had a shitty childhood, but I had money, and I can't deny that wealth has its benefits. Alma didn't have the best childhood, but she had the will and determination of a goddess. We want kids and teens in the area to have people looking out for them and to have their backs even if their parents don't. We want them to always have a safe place to go, so they don't turn to other things that are dangerous.

This center has been a long time in the making. Alma and I started working on the concept of it a year before we were married. Now that we've acquired this building, we get to see it all unfold.

"So, have you decided on a name for the center?" Ollie asks.

"Yeah, we're calling it The Lion's Lair. Alma came up with it." I shrug. "She wanted it to be named after me, and apparently, my name means lion in some language—Latin maybe? And a lair is a lion's home, his safe place. It's cheesy, I know, but she likes it."

"No." Ollie shakes his head. "It's awesome, man. What you're doing here … is incredible. You're going to change lives. You're going to save kids, hopefully from ever becoming me or you and living a life as an addict. This"—he looks around the gym—"is the real deal. Good shit. I'm so proud of you and stoked to help here whenever I can."

"Thanks," I say.

I hope he's right. I hope we can make a real difference in many lives.

"You don't think working with abused kids is going to trigger anything in me? Lately, my anxiety has been high."

"Having a hard time sleeping again?" he asks.

"Yeah." I nod.

"That's the thing, isn't it? We never know what's going to help or hurt our journey, what's going to trigger or save us. I would think that making a difference would be helpful, and I know you think that, too, which is why you're doing this. Living a life of service is noble and good, you know? On the hard days, you have to go back through your steps, call me, take one day at a time. Fight for it, for the life you want. Remember why you're clean and what you have to lose. Be stronger than your demons."

"Yeah," I answer.

"You're doing good, man. So good," Ollie says.

"Thank you. I'm trying."

* * *

"I CAN'T FIND my daisy earrings," Alma calls from the bedroom, her voice a little panicked. "Have you seen them?"

"You mean, the ones right here on the coffee table?" I yell back, humor in my voice.

She comes rushing out to the living room, and her hand splays across her chest. "Oh, thank goodness." She reaches down, picks up the silver flowers, and sticks them into her earlobes.

"I don't think people are going to care what earrings you're wearing." I chuckle.

"I know, but daisies are happy and welcoming. I want today to be perfect. I want all the kids to feel welcome and their parents to sign all the waivers, so the kids can keep coming."

"They're going to feel welcome, babe, I promise. And it won't be because of your earrings; it'll be because of you." I take her cheeks between my hands and gently kiss her lips. "We've planned for this day as much as humanly possible. Now, we just need to go and enjoy ourselves. Okay?"

"Okay." She nods, pulling in a deep breath. "You're right."

Alma and I have worked our asses off the past two months, getting the Lair ready for the grand opening today. The entire place was remodeled in calm and soothing colors. We set up the different rooms. We hired counselors and instructors. We solicited donations and sponsors and got volunteers. We spoke to all of the local school counselors to help us reach out to the families and kids who needed our center the most. This place was built with all of the love, determination, and hope for the future that Alma and I possess. It's going to be great.

"We'd better go," I say, extending my hand toward hers.

"Right." She blows out a breath and takes my hand. "I'm just so nervous."

"Baby, they're all going to love it."

She bobs her head in tentative agreement and takes my hand, following me out to the car.

Minutes later, we're standing in front of the center, a large blue ribbon in front of us, as a crowd of families waits on the other side. The crowd counts down, and Alma and I cut the ribbon, welcoming everyone inside.

The Lair is set up as a carnival today—a party to celebrate the opening. Volunteers are getting parent signatures, so their kids can come back on their own another day. We have fair games on the playground, an ice cream truck handing out free frozen treats, and a cotton candy machine. Volunteers are taking families on tours of the facility. Teens are playing basketball, and the little ones are making slime. Each family is leaving with a goody bag containing some swag and treats and information about our mission.

Alma and I circle the party all day, introducing ourselves and thanking everyone for coming. The day couldn't be any better, and I'm pleasantly surprised at the turnout.

As I introduce myself to each child, I look him or her in the eye and express how happy I am that they're here. Alma is the social one between the two of us. Loving others comes as naturally as breathing to her, but I try my best to make each child feel important. I compliment art projects, smiles, and basketball form. My goal is to find something unique and special about each kid and tell them, let them know that I see them and that I care.

After the last volunteer and family have left, Alma and I stare out toward the empty parking lot, exhausted and humbled.

I turn to her when I hear a sniffle and see tears cascading down her cheeks. "What's wrong?"

"We did it, Leo. We did it. You and I, we made it happen. Our dream. We did it," she repeats herself, sentiment thick in her voice.

"I know. It's pretty surreal." I wrap my arms around her, and she hugs me tight.

"I'm so proud of us. We're going to save all the little Leos of the world who don't have anyone to save them," she cries.

I let out a soft laugh. "Well, let's start with this city and expand to the world at a later date. One project at a time."

"Deal," she says.

We lock up and get in the car to drive home.

Inside the car, Alma asks, "Are you happy, Leo? Like truly happy?"

"Absolutely," I say, preparing to pull out of the parking lot and onto the main street. "Why are you asking?"

"I just want to make sure I'm there for you and that I'm being a good wife. We've been so busy the past two months. I simply wanted to check in."

I put the car into park and turn to my wife. "You make me happier than I've ever been every single day, just by being you. Never doubt how perfect you are for me or how much I love you. Okay?"

"Okay." She smiles, and my chest aches at how incredibly beautiful she is, inside and out.

"You've changed my life, Alma. I'd have been gone from this world years ago without you. I know it. You saved me in every way possible and gave me this incredible life. I am thankful for you every second of every day."

Tears fall from Alma's eyes again, this time for a different reason. "I'm grateful for you every second of every day too. Thank you for loving me."

"You're easy to love. I should be thanking you." I chuckle as I shift to drive before pulling out onto the street.

"Someday, I hope you realize just how easy you are to love too." Alma smiles and squeezes my hand.

I might never believe that, but as long as Alma loves me, the rest doesn't really matter.

CHAPTER 49

ALMA

*R*adio turned high, windows down, I drive home from tutoring at the Lair. My hair whips around behind me to its own beat. As I extend my hand out the driver's window, the warm sun and air feel good against my skin. Driving with open windows to good music is one of my favorite things. It doesn't get much better than this.

Leo and I have been running the Lair for almost a year now, and it's been an inspiring journey. We work so hard and come home exhausted every night, but it's given us so much. The relationships we've built with these kids are priceless. I get to come home from work each day with gratitude in my heart, knowing that I'm making a difference in someone else's life. I can't save the world, but I can love a child and maybe save them. When they grow up and have children, they'll raise them with a legacy of love and not hurt. They'll break the cycle of pain. It's a positive ripple effect, and it's important.

People loving people will save the world. I know it.

Pulling into the driveway, I spot Ethan's car and smile. He hasn't been over for a while. It will be good to see him. I park the car and check my phone to see if I have any missed texts from Leo. I shoot him a quick text.

Hey, Ethan's here. You heading home soon? Love you. xx

I'm anxious to see how Leo's day has been. I've called him several times today with no response. That happens sometimes when he's working off-site conducting home visits with some of our troubled youth. It's important to check in on our kids at their homes to make sure they're getting all of their needs met. These visits often go in a direction of their own. Leo never knows what he'll find. Sometimes, the family is short of food, so he buys them groceries. He's entered homes that weren't fit to live in and had to hire a cleaning crew and get furniture delivered. Other times, he might walk into something that needs a government agency intervention.

I enter the house to find Ethan sitting at the table with his head in his hands. His face is red and wet from tears.

"Ethan," I gasp. "What's wrong?"

He raises his stare to meet mine. His eyes are haunted and pained. I'm not sure how I know what he's about to say but somehow I do. The deepest parts of my soul shatter because I know that *he's gone.*

I drop my purse, and my hands cover my heart.

"No." I shake my head.

"I'm sorry," he murmurs.

"No," I say louder. "No," I cry as tears start to fall from my eyes.

"I got a call from one of the guys Leo used to run with back before you. He said Leo used today, and it must've been a bad batch or something. He doesn't know, but I wanted to tell you before the cops arrived. I didn't want you to find out that way," he sobs.

"No!" I scream. "It's not true. It wasn't Leo! You're mistaken." My back heaves with sobs, and the room starts spinning.

What is happening? It doesn't make sense. This isn't right.

"I'm so sorry, Alma. I wish it weren't true, but it is. Leo's gone."

"No," I choke out. "No," I beg, praying this reality isn't real. *It can't be. There has to be a mistake.*

"Ethan?" I plead, hoping against all odds that he's wrong.

"I'm so sorry," he repeats.

"No," I gasp and drop to my knees. My face falls, and my entire body mourns.

An eternity passes in the space of a few desperate sobs. In that fraction of time, I die a hundred times over. The pain is so intense that every cell in my body aches. A despair this deep could only be healed by one person, and he's the one who caused it.

Nothing adds up. We were happy. He was happy. Our life was fulfilling. *Why would he do this to us? To me?* He promised me forever, and I counted on it because I can't live this life without him.

Arms pull me from the ground, and I swat them away. I just want to lie on this floor and die. *I can't do this.*

"Come on," Ethan urges, his arms propped under mine. "They're here."

Two uniformed police officers stand at my door, telling me what I already know but can't believe. Words fail me. Shock is my new home.

Ethan says something to the officers and then closes the door.

"What can I do? How can I help?" he asks.

"Leo's family," I mutter before staggering down the hall.

"Okay, I'll tell them." He follows behind me.

"Anyone who matters, please," I request.

People who love Leo should know, but I'm not strong enough to tell them.

"I can do that," he says.

I kick off my shoes and stumble into bed, tears soaking the pillow immediately.

"Are you going to be okay?" Worry saturates Ethan's words.

"No, but you can go. I need to be alone."

I'm not okay. I'm never going to be okay. My mind, body, and soul are shattering into a million pieces, but I need to break alone.

"I'll go. Please call me if you need anything. I'm so sorry, Alma. Truly, I am," Ethan says before he's gone.

I'm not sure how to mourn a loss this devastating.

How do I live in a world where Leo doesn't? How do I breathe when he isn't?

I don't know how I'll ever get past this, and maybe I won't. Some heartbreaks are fatal. Our love was all-encompassing, and now that it's gone, it might take me with it. Maybe I'll let it because I'm not strong enough to fight without it, and even if I were, I don't want to.

CHAPTER 50

ALMA

*L*ying on my side, the soft white comforter wrapped around me, I stare at a spot on the wall beside my bed. It's a small black dot, almost like an ink stain from a ballpoint pen. I can't recall seeing it before, and I don't know how it got there.

I remember when Leo surprised me with these painted walls. I had spent a rare day with my parents and come home to him painting our bedroom. The light blue, almost gray, made me so happy. Such a calming color. Perfect for this space. Soft, welcoming, soothing, and romantic.

The dark blemish bothers me. It needs to be fixed, but I don't know if Leo had any leftover paint. If I try to color-match the paint and the shade is off, it will ruin the wall that Leo gifted me. I'm not sure I can risk it, but imperfection grates on me. He made it perfect for me, and now, it's not.

The alarm on my cell phone sounds, and I reach toward the

nightstand, snatch it up, and turn the intrusive sound off. There are dozens of notifications—texts, social media tags, and missed calls from family and friends. I can't read them all. I don't care what those who claim to love Leo have to say. No one knows him and loves him the way that I do … did … do. I can't wrap my mind around past tense just yet.

It was always meant to be me and Leo against the world. I know him. I know every hidden whisper of his soul—me, no one else. They can't possibly mourn him the way he deserves to be mourned, only I can. Me. Because I am his, and he is mine.

He is mine.

He was mine.

How can I do this? How can I get up and go to his funeral? The task seems too difficult to bear. I'm not strong enough.

Amos's text pops up on my screen as I stare at my screen saver, a black-and-white picture of Leo and me from our wedding. We're so happy in this photo. My back is to his front, his arms wrapped around my waist. His strong hands hold mine against my middle. I'm leaning into his chest, my head tilted back to see him. His face is leaning in toward mine. We both carry larger-than-life smiles. I don't remember what we were laughing about, but it must have been something great. Leo didn't gift the world with his smiles often. Most of them were reserved for me, and I cherished every one of them.

I read my best friend's text.

One step in front of the other. I'll be there soon. xo

Per usual, Amos has a direct link to my heart and knows exactly what I need to hear.

One step in front of the other. I can do that. For Leo, I can do that.

Setting my phone back on my nightstand, I sit up. The room starts to spin, and I close my eyes while my mind settles. The world has been a blur these past few days. I haven't gotten out of bed but a few times. I haven't eaten or drunk anything besides the few sips of water that Amos made me drink. He's been in and out, making sure I'm okay.

Truthfully, I wish I could stay in bed and sleep until the pain resides. I don't want to exist until my soul no longer screams in agony from Leo's absence. I suppose I want to sleep forever. I can't live in a world without his light.

You owe it to him to say good-bye, I remind myself.

Feet on floor. Stand. Walk to the bathroom. Shower. I list off my next steps in my head. *One step at a time.*

I stand and brace myself against the wall until I'm not so dizzy. Spotting the water bottle that Amos left beside the bed, I grab it and force myself to drink it down. I can't mourn Leo properly if I pass out from dehydration.

I amble to the bathroom and turn on the shower. In my hands, I clench the black T-shirt that I retrieved from the hamper the day of Leo's death. I bring it to my face and inhale. Tears well in my eyes. I can hardly smell him anymore.

What has it been, three days? Four? He's leaving me.

I step out of my panties and remove Leo's shirt, pulling it up and over my head. Balling it up in my fists, I press it to my face, trying to find him.

I locate a spot on the shirt that still smells like Leo, and I breathe him in. *Don't leave me,* I beg as tears fall from my eyes. *Stay.* I rock back and forth in the bathroom, now full of hot steam from the shower, crying into his shirt. *Stay with me. Please.*

I love you.

Stay with me.

Lowering the shirt from my face, I hug it to my chest and open my eyes. I need to shower. I can shower.

One step at a time.

When I turn toward the shower, the mirror above the sink catches my eye. I gasp and drop the shirt.

The words *I love you*, written by Leo's finger, appear on the mirror, highlighted by the surrounding glass that is fogged up from the hot, steamy air. I tremble and press my splayed hands against the glass on either side of his words. Beads of condensation start to form, causing the letters to drip.

No.

Something in me breaks, and I howl into the thick air, "You left me! You left me!"

My grasp finds the metal soap dispenser, and I scream as I throw it into his last words. The mirror shatters, and pieces crash onto the counter and the tiled floor.

"You're gone. You left me."

The fight abandons me, and my words are now sobs as I fall to my knees against the tiles. The glass shards crunch beneath me, but I don't feel anything.

The pain and the heartbreak threaten to burst me open from the inside until it's all so unbearable that it vanishes, leaving me numb. He's gone, and I can't feel anything. I look up to the place on the wall where the mirror used to reside, and I panic.

His words. They're gone.

All that remains is the ugly brown backing of the mirror.

No. No. No!

I claw at the glass pieces around me and try to find his words. I can put it back together. Standing, I look on the counter in a desperate search of pieces of the puzzle that contain his message.

"I love you!" I cry out. "I'm sorry. Come back to me."

None of the sharp shards on the granite countertop show Leo's writing, so I drop back to the ground, frantically looking through the pieces on the floor.

I can fix this.

I blink the tears away from my eyes. Blurred visions of glass and bright red smears meet me as I search. I know the blood is coming from me, but I can't address that until I find his words and put them back together.

"Oh my God, Alma!" Amos yells from the now-open bathroom door.

"Help me!" I cry. "I have to find the pieces. Please help me!" I beg him. "He was here a minute ago, and then I broke him, and now, I have to put the pieces back together. Help me find them. Please." I dig around the broken mirror, but his words are gone. "He was here."

"I know," Amos says softly. He grabs my wrists and pulls me up from the ground.

"He was here." My voice breaks. I point to the mirror. "He was here."

"I know," Amos repeats, pulling me toward the shower. He slides open the glass door of the enclosure and steadies my arm as I step in. "I'll be right back. I'm just going to clean this up, and then I'll help you," he says gently. His big brown eyes are wide with some emotion I can't place.

Pity? Love? Maybe both.

Amos shuts the door, and I watch as the red-stained water escapes down the drain. My muscles hurt, and I'm just so tired. I lie down against the warm tiles of the shower. The water beats against my skin in a soothing rhythm, and I close my eyes.

"Come on, Alma. Let's stand up." Amos's words catch me off guard.

How long have I been lying here? I don't know.

I open my eyes to find Amos standing above me, wearing nothing but his boxer briefs. He hooks his arms under mine and pulls me to my feet.

"Let me help you." His words are steady and kind.

I watch, almost as if I were a distant bystander, as Amos squirts shampoo into his hand and begins to wash my hair. He threads his fingers into my hair and massages my scalp before holding my shoulders and leaning me back into the shower spray to rinse. He applies conditioner and repeats the motions.

Taking the loofah, he loads it with my shower gel and scrubs my back, arms, and legs. He squints as he assesses the damage I've done to myself.

"None of them are deep," he says aloud—to himself or me, I'm not sure.

"I'm sorry. I didn't mean to," I tell him, my voice quiet.

I'm starting to feel more human now that I'm clean, and I realize what it must have looked like when Amos found me naked and bloody in a pile of broken glass.

"It's okay. You're okay," he reassures me.

I look up to him. "I don't know if I can live this life without him."

He pulls me into a hug. "I know."

My tears mix with the water as they trail down Amos's chest, and I let his embrace engulf me in a warmth that I so desperately need.

* * *

My breath catches when I see the stylish black dress that Amos laid out on my bed for me. Pulling the towel tighter around me, I hesitantly step toward the dress and gently graze my fingers across the material. A myriad of memories returns at the movement. Amos doesn't know what this particular ensemble means to me or the sentiment it carries. *How could he?*

I close my eyes and remember opening the big white box and then wearing this dress while Leo asked me to be his forever before he removed me from it and made love to me for hours. It feels like it was yesterday. We were so happy, and life was perfect. I'd give anything for that day back.

I suppose most things from here on out are going to carry

325

some sort of memory. Everything in my life has been touched by Leo in some aspect. I have to find a way to go on despite the heartache that the memories bring. This is my new normal.

I put on the dress and slip on some black flats. Stepping over toward the nightstand on Leo's side of the bed, I pick up his wedding ring. I find the wooden box Leo made me and run my fingers across the quote he carved into the top. My knees threaten to give out. I hold on to every ounce of strength I have to remain upright.

Opening the lid, I take a necklace from the box and let the Tiffany's heart pendant slide off the chain, and I replace the heart with Leo's ring. The funeral director asked me if I wanted Leo to be buried with it, and I told him no. I want that piece of him, of our marriage, on me. Leo wouldn't mind. He told me once that I could cremate him and flush his ashes in the toilet for all he cared. I remember gasping and smacking his arm when he said that.

He simply stated, "Babe, when I die, my soul will be wherever souls go. My body is just a shell, and when my soul leaves it, it's useless. I don't care what you do with it."

So, I know that he wouldn't want to be buried with something that held importance to me.

Holding my hand to my chest, I feel his titanium band against my skin, and I sigh before making for the bathroom. The room is mirror free, thanks to my outburst, and now, it's also glass and blood-free, thanks to Amos. I brush my teeth for at least five minutes. It feels so refreshing. I can't remember brushing them since … it happened. I run a brush through my wet hair before twisting it into a low bun. Using my compact as a mirror, I apply some tinted moisturizer to my face to aid in covering up the purple bags under my eyes. After a quick layer of waterproof mascara, I deem myself presentable. Though minimal, the effort is daunting.

I find Amos in the kitchen, dressed in his suit.

"Hey." He smiles sweetly. "You look beautiful."

I shake my head. "Beautiful, no, but hopefully, I look human … enough."

"You definitely look human." He plates a couple of breakfast burritos and sets them down on the table. "You need to eat something."

"I'm not hungry," I protest.

"I understand that, but you've barely eaten anything in four days. You're going to pass out at the funeral. Please eat. For me?" he pleads.

"We're going to be late."

He sets a large mug of coffee and a tall glass of water on the table above the plate. "That doesn't matter. They won't start without you. I'll call and make sure of it. You need to eat something. It's going to be a long day."

"Fine," I relent with a sigh and take a seat at the table.

I bite into the burrito, and though I know from experience that Amos's breakfast burritos are delicious, this one tastes like cardboard. I use the glass of water to help me get it down.

Amos rinses off the pan, dries it, and puts it away before walking over to me.

"Besides the obvious, how are you feeling about today? About seeing everyone?" he questions.

"Really nervous. You saw me in the bathroom. That's me as of late." I put the burrito down on the plate and take a sip of the coffee, which tastes like ass.

"You'll be okay. I'll be by your side the entire time, and if you need to leave, we'll leave. You don't have to stay for the luncheon afterward."

"That's probably a good idea. I can barely stomach any of this." I gesture to the half-eaten burrito before me. "We should go."

"Okay." Amos doesn't argue with me, and I'm grateful.

I just want this day to be over.

He retrieves my phone from the bedroom and puts it into my purse. I'm not sure why since I haven't opened a message from anyone but Amos in four days.

"Phone and purse. Anything else?"

"No."

He extends a hand toward me, and I place my hand in his palm. He leads me out to his car and gets me buckled up in the passenger seat before closing my door and walking around the front of the car to his door.

As he pulls out of my drive, I can't help thinking that I have no idea how I'm going to get through this day. I still can't believe any of this is real. Yet my shattered heart reminds me that it is. I can fall apart when I get home, but somehow I have to make it through today. For Leo, I must.

CHAPTER 51

ALMA

*P*ulling into the Hardings' estate brings a whole new wave of nausea. I hate this place—this glamorous, majestic, lonely, tortured place. In the five years I knew Leo, we were here the same amount. Even once a year was too much. Leo's nightmares following a visit would last for weeks.

It was important to him though to try to mend the severed bonds between him and his family. Despite everything they had or hadn't done for him, he wanted to make it better. He wanted to move forward. He wanted to heal. His heart was always too gentle and pure to be attached to the Harding name.

He saw his mother, brother, and Cat more than once a year but always on safe ground—a restaurant or our home—not here.

"He would hate this," I say as Amos continues down the long driveway.

There are at least a hundred cars parked in the front lawn. Enormous flower displays line the drive. The front yard alone tells me that the Hardings spared no expense for this gathering, and yet I know that the effort is meaningless. This is all their fault.

"He hated extravagant parties. He hated this estate. I can't believe I agreed to this." Disappointment in myself cripples me and adds to the suffocating agony that is my existence.

"It doesn't matter. Leo would be glad that you were spared the heartache of planning his funeral. Who cares what these people do? You can celebrate his life and mourn his loss and honor him in your own way. All he cared about was you anyway," Amos says.

"I should've planned it." My voice is heavy with tears.

"You're doing the best you can, Alma. Leo wouldn't blame you for a second."

I simply nod because that much is true. I could do no wrong by my husband, but it doesn't mean that I didn't want more for his soul's send-off. I don't want this circus. He deserves something real. Amos is right; all Leo cared about was me. I'll find a way to make this better. I'll say good-bye to him in my own way.

Amos parks in the front circle drive. I close my eyes and pull in a deep breath, willing strength to permeate my every cell as the air fills my lungs.

My door opens, and my friend extends a hand. "You ready?"

"No," I sigh, but I exit the car anyway.

We walk through the house until we're in the back of the estate. The lush lawn is so ornately decorated with lovely flowers that it looks like a wedding. There are rows of white metal chairs facing the front altar, where Leo's titanium-colored casket rests. The casket is draped with a spray of white lilies. Next to Leo's casket is a huge canvas painting of him.

Admittedly, the painting is beautiful and captures his smile and the light in his bright blue eyes.

"Alma." Cat dabs her eyes with a tissue before wrapping her arms around me.

I return her hug, my tears falling onto her black dress.

She leads me down the aisle between the rows of chairs. People I've never met whisper their condolences as I pass. Ethan and his family, Ollie, and Quinn sit in the second row, and their presence brings me a semblance of comfort. They knew and loved Leo at least. Leo's parents and brother sit in the front row, and on the other side of the aisle are my parents. Their presence throws me off. The Webers don't participate in something as traditional as funerals. My mom's teary face smiles sadly toward me, and I have to look behind me to Amos to center myself. He nods in reassurance.

This whole march down the aisle is surreal, and it makes my skin crawl. I swallow the nausea in my throat. The dry burrito threatens to surface. Amos takes the seat next to my mother, and I sit between him and the aisle. Cat squeezes my hand before taking her seat across the space, next to Stephen.

A string quartet starts to play a breathtaking ballad, an enchanting tune full of love and loss. It takes everything in me not to crumble at the sound. I press the tissue beneath my eyes as a minister I've never seen before stands on the podium and starts a generic monologue about life and grief. A tiny smile tugs at my heart as I imagine what Leo would be saying about this guy if he were sitting next to me. What a joke.

The quartet plays another song, and then Cat walks up to the podium. She looks at me and presses her lips together in a tight smile.

"I'm not going to talk long because Leo would hate it if I did." She chuckles to herself, and I nod through my tears. "But I have to say something about my brother-in-law and friend. Most people only saw Leo's rough exterior, but to those of us who were lucky enough to be loved by him, there was so much more. Leo was a kind soul, a loyal friend, and so very loving. He had a tremendous fighting spirit, and I know he fought to the end. Leo loved his wife, Alma, more than anything in the universe. He once told me that she filled his soul with life, and it wasn't until her that he truly wanted to live. He would still be here if he could, but life has a way of stealing those who are the most precious and the most gentle-hearted." She looks up to the sky, her hand against her chest. "I love you, Leo, my gentle lion. I will miss you every day. Until we meet again."

As Cat steps down from the podium, tears streaming down her face, she looks to me for approval, and I nod and blow her a kiss. Her words were perfect, and Leo wouldn't have hated them ... too much.

A stringed melody plays again, and I expect the minister to say something in closing, but instead, Mr. Harding walks up to the podium in his suit that probably cost more than my car, a solemn expression on his face and notecards in his hand.

I turn to Cat, wide-eyed, for only she could understand my trepidation in this moment. She appears as equally bewildered and shrugs, telling me she didn't know this was happening.

I steeple my hands in front of my face, my eyes shut, and pray. *Please don't do this. Sit down.*

Leo's dad doesn't have the right to say anything today. He's not up there because he cares. He's up there because it looks good, and he has a reputation to uphold.

I can't sit through this. I squirm in my seat, ready to bolt.

Amos puts his hand atop my leg and whispers, "It's almost over. You can do this."

Peering toward my best friend, I shake my head. *You don't know!* I want to scream to him.

He nods, oblivious to my rising rage.

The music stops, and my stare darts toward Victor Harding.

Please sit down. Can't you even be decent now that he's gone?

Leo's dad starts talking. My breakfast rolls within my belly, and I clamp my mouth shut.

"Leo was a pistol when he was young. Always running through the house, bumping into irreplaceable art pieces, hiding on the grounds when we had to be somewhere. He sure gave me and his mother a run for our money." He chuckles, and there are some laughs among the crowd. "You know what they say, all we can do as parents is provide our children with love and a good example. But children are born with their own personalities, and what they choose to do with them is often out of our control. Regardless, we loved our boy, bruises and all."

I stand from my seat and scream, "No!"

Amos pulls my arm in an attempt to get me to sit. "Alma," he urges, but I shrug him off and march toward the podium.

My entire body trembles with fury. He is not going to make Leo's death about him.

"No!" I scream again, tears streaming down my face. "Sit down!"

Mr. Harding stares at me, terrified, and it gives me the strength to go on.

For Leo.

He was silent long enough, and now, he's gone. I won't be quiet ... never again.

I walk up and snatch the microphone from the podium, and Victor stands there in shock.

I scan the crowd of concerned faces—a few who loved Leo, the rest who didn't know him at all. "Leo is dead because of him." I point to Mr. Harding.

Leo's mom stands from her chair and shouts, "That's enough."

"Oh, I'm not even close to finished. Sit down because Leo is dead because of you, too, and you." I point to Stephen. I ignore the enraged faces of Leo's family, and I look out into the crowd. "Leo was born perfect. He was a gift. He was perfect," I say again, my voice quivering with tears. "His family ruined him. They took this amazing gift from God, and they broke him. His dad physically, emotionally, and sexually abused him for years."

Gasps come from the crowd, and there's a ruckus behind me, which I think is Mr. Harding tripping and falling.

"Imagine the worst possible things that can be done to a child and know that Leo's dad did those deplorable acts to him *repeatedly* … for years. Victor Harding isn't America's heart-throb. He's the devil. A rapist, a molester. And Leo's mom and brother … they knew it was happening. They heard the cries, but neither of them helped. Neither protected him. His own mother let him fall to abuse over and over again, in her own home. How can anyone do that? How can you bring a child into this world and fail him so miserably?" I exclaim, disgust and sorrow in my voice.

"They took this perfect soul and broke him until he was a shell of a person. His dad eventually stopped torturing him, and his mother and brother went on pretending that it never happened, but Leo lived with it every day. He turned to substance abuse because he needed something to dull the internal hell that he faced daily. He had vicious nightmares all the time. He had to relive his pain over and over again. And through all of this, he remained good and kind down to his core. He loved fiercely and fought even harder. He fought every single fucking day of his life with everything he had!" My words come out on a strangled sob. "He wanted to stay here. He wanted a happy life with me. He hadn't used in four and a half years. He had one setback, and it killed him. It was an acci-dent. He wanted to be here! He deserved to be loved. He deserved a life. These people robbed him of that. They didn't love him. I love him!" My chest trembles.

"And he loved me, and now, he's gone," I cry, my voice broken. "Leo didn't die from an overdose. He died because the people who were supposed to love him the most ruined him so irreversibly that he could never fully recover. His innocent life was stolen from him by monsters. Most of you weren't lucky enough to know the real Leo, but for the handful of us that were, he was a gift, a treasure." My voice breaks, and I say softly, "We were truly happy. He was everything to me, my one true love, my soul mate. I loved him, and now, he's gone."

I throw the microphone on the ground, and a loud thud echoes from the speakers. Amos is at my side, wrapping his arm around me and leading me away. I cling to his chest.

"He's gone." My lips tremble, and the absolute sorrow in my soul cries.

"I know," Amos whispers. "I know."

Someone grabs my hand, and I look down to Stephen's grasp on my wrist. Cat sits beside him, her shoulders quaking in silent sobs.

"I was just a kid, Alma," Stephen utters, his voice hoarse.

I shake his hand off of me. "So was he."

Amos and I continue past the crowd. Nervous whispers buzz around me like creepy locusts, and I ignore them.

Screw all of these people. None of them loved Leo.

I loved him.

He was mine.

And now, he's gone.

CHAPTER 52

ALMA

*L*eo's been gone a month. Thirty days. Four weeks. Around seven hundred and thirty hours. And it's rough.

Every morning when I wake, I instinctually reach for him on the other side of the bed, wanting him to fold me into his embrace. Then, I remember, and my soul shatters all over again. I've held a steaming pot of water up to every mirror and window in our home, hoping to find another message from beyond, but I always come up short.

Every minute of every day, I feel sick, my body still in shock at his absence. I have to force myself to eat, and most meals threaten to come up, many succeeding. I'm navigating how to exist in a world where he's not. Sometimes, I think I'm failing. The parts of me that hold on to Leo's existence with every fiber of my being urge me to allow myself some grace. I still feel Leo deep in my heart and soul, and he whispers that

I'm doing just fine. I want to believe it, but it's hard to trust in anything right now.

I'm closed off to the world. I gave the managers at The Lion's Lair a raise and asked them to take over the place for the foreseeable future. I turned my phone off after the funeral and haven't powered it up since. I have no desire to talk to those who were absent in Leo's life. It's just me, in this big house, alone with his ghost and my memories.

Yesterday, I received a certified letter from the coroner's office. Turns out, the cocaine that Leo had taken was a bad batch, laced with fentanyl—proof that he hadn't tried to leave me. He slipped and heartbreakingly purchased a deadly batch. I had known that his death wasn't intentional. I never doubted that for a second, but it still provided a fragment of closure.

The past month has been spent trying to figure out where I went wrong, where I failed him, and what I missed. Were there signs? If so, I didn't see them—a fact that makes me hurt even more. Was Leo struggling, and I didn't notice? He had been meeting with Ollie regularly, so perhaps there was a battle that he was fighting that I wasn't aware of. There were many stints of time throughout our relationship where he saw Ollie more often than others though. So, I didn't question that either. That's a downfall of loving an addict—he had pains and inner struggles that he kept from me. I would've taken all of his hurt away if I could. I would've shouldered them all, if he'd let me. Did he see something during the home visits that tipped the scales and made him break the sobriety he'd fought for all these years? I'll never know, and perhaps that's for the best. What can I do now?

A knock sounds at my door. I mute the bad reality TV I'm watching and make my way to the door. I hesitantly open it. A man I've never seen stands in a nice suit, holding a portfolio.

"Mrs. Alma Harding?" he asks.

"Yeah," I respond.

"Hello. I'm Alan Grice, the Hardings' estate attorney. I have Leo's will and asset information here for you. I've been trying to reach you via phone and email but not had any luck. Please excuse me for dropping by, unannounced."

"Oh, no problem. Please come in." I step to the side to allow him entrance.

I sit across from him at the kitchen table as he removes files and sets them out on the wooden surface.

"Leo came into my office four years ago and set everything up. I just need a couple of signatures from you, and I'll be out of your way."

"What is all of this?" I ask.

"These are Leo's trust and investment accounts. He put them all in your name."

"You mean, our joint bank accounts?" I ask, knowing that my name is already on our checking and savings accounts, which totals a substantial amount of money.

"No, these are accounts that Leo has never made a withdrawal from. He invested the majority of his original trust fund years ago, and they've been building. I don't think he ever had any intention of using the money from these accounts unless he really needed it. He told me that too much money is dangerous. But as they are all in your name, you should have the account information for them. In total, the sum is around forty million dollars."

"Forty million dollars," I choke out.

"Yes," Mr. Grice says calmly, as if that amount were pocket change. "I'll need your signature here and here"—he points to two signature lines and hands me a pen—"to make everything final. All of the information you need to keep track of the investments or make withdrawals or additions is included here." He places his hand on the file. "My information is here as well, and I can help you with anything you might need."

I sign the paperwork.

"And finally, when Mr. Harding came in several years ago to transfer everything over to you, he gave me a letter to give to you upon his death."

I gasp, "What?"

Mr. Grice pulls a sealed envelope out of one of the folders. My name is written on the front in Leo's handwriting, and I immediately start to cry as I take the letter.

"I will see myself out. Please reach out if you need anything. I'm very sorry for your loss, Mrs. Harding."

Mr. Grice retreats, and I'm faintly aware of the door closing in the distance. My fingers tremble, and I clench the envelope.

I stare at my name for the longest time, absorbing every letter. Leo wrote this. I can't believe it. Tears stream down my face, and anticipation invades every pore. I'm about to read Leo's words for the last time.

Finding my courage, I carefully open the envelope. Pulling out the pages, I unfold them and lose my breath when I see the stationery from the hotel on Mackinac Island, the place where we got engaged. Then, I look at the date.

He wrote this the night of our engagement, over four years ago.

My dearest Alma,

You're asleep, drunk off of sugar from our excessive fudge-tasting, and I'm sitting here, watching you breathe, thankful for every breath. The diamond ring I gave you circles your finger, and I've never felt more happiness. In all my life, I never thought I would find someone as perfect as you, and I never thought you'd love me back.

Knowing that you're going to be my wife someday is so overwhelming. I can barely process it all. Yet it's true. I'm going to marry you, Almalee Hannelda Weber, and cherish every piece of you for the rest of my life.

My existence hasn't been easy, but knowing that I get to finish this journey with you makes it all worth it. Any amount of time that

I get with you is priceless. If everything I went through led me to you and our life together, I can't regret any of it. I'd go through it all again just to get another hour with you. Your soul gives mine life. Your love gives me purpose. You give me everything.

Last year, I told you that I didn't think I was long for this world, and it upset you a great deal. I mentioned that when I look into the future, all I see is blackness, and that's still true. If you're reading this letter, it means that I'm gone. I really hope that I'm wrong, and you're reading this letter with a silver bun atop your head, swinging on our porch swing, surrounded by our grandchildren.

I hope I'm wrong, Alma. I truly do. More than anything, I want a long life with you. I want to experience everything this world has to offer. I want the house, the pets, the kids, the adventure, the grand-children—THE LIFE.

From a very young age, I've accepted the fact that I'm going to die young. Most children dream into the future. They can envision what their life is going to be like. I've never had that ability. My future is unknown; it's a blackness that I can't predict. I don't see myself old and gray with a grandkid on my lap, but I do see you that way.

Now that I've found you, the thought of leaving you terrifies me, and I want more than anything to be wrong. I will do everything in my power to stay with you, Alma. I will. But if my fate is a short one, I need you to know that you've made it enough.

I know I tell you all the time, but I don't think you quite grasp how much I love you. There aren't sufficient words that could ever describe it. The closest I can come is to say that I was dying, and you gave me life. I was suffocating, and you gave me air. I was drowning, and you pulled me from the depths of despair. I owe everything I am to you, and I'll pay that debt with my love.

I can face whatever tomorrow brings because I had today. One day of your love is enough. You are my everything. And if you're reading this letter and you're younger than eighty, I'm sorry for leaving you too soon. Please forgive me. Please move on. Love again.

Promise me you'll be happy again. The only thing that terrifies me more than losing you is leaving you alone and sad.

I want you to be happy. You deserve a life bursting with love. You made all of my dreams come true. Know that I was filled with joy and love and gratitude for every day that I got with you.

True love, like ours, transcends time and space. Even if I'm not physically here, I'm still loving you from afar. If you need me, close your eyes and look within. I'll be there. My love will always be there because you own every piece of it.

I love you forever.

Leo

I blink away my tears as I read the last few lines. My eyes swell from crying, and I gasp for breath. I set the letter down on the table and wrap my arms around my middle. Closing my eyes, I search for him.

I love you, Leo. I need you to help me get through this. I'm dying without you. I miss you so much. I love you. I love you. I love you.

I rock in the chair, searching my heart for him. I feel it—the love. My body warms, and my breathing calms. He's here. He's always here.

I can do hard things.

I will survive this.

I am loved.

The thoughts come to me, and I think that maybe my inner strength is cheering me on, but I can't deny that it's him. It's always been him.

CHAPTER 53

ALMA

*L*eo's been gone two months. I still ache for him every second of every day. My body still mourns him, and I can barely hold down food. But I'm trying to live. I'm trying to be happy. It's going to be a while before I can feel happiness, so for now, I'm putting one foot in front of the other. I'm taking it one day at a time.

I'm showing up. I'm leaving the house. Checking on Lion's Lair. Grocery shopping. Cooking. Eating. Trying. I spend more time *not* crying than sobbing, so I consider that progress. I reread Leo's letter each day, and it helps me feel like he's still here. I believe that part of him is.

I've had lunch with Quinn, Amos, Ollie, and Cat over the past month, which is also progress. It's been good to talk to people who love me or Leo. I don't feel as alone as I did, and the truth is that I'm not alone.

The extravagant amount of money that Leo left me is going

to remain untouched—for now. Maybe, someday, I'll use that money to expand Lion's Lair to other cities or use it for other forms of good. At this moment, all I can focus on is getting up, putting one foot in front of the other, and going through the motions, and that's enough.

Standing in front of the new bathroom mirror, I brush my teeth to get ready for the day. My gaze keeps dropping to the spot where Leo's electric toothbrush and charger sat. Two weeks ago, I finally threw them out. Nothing says desperate widow like holding on to an old toothbrush. There's still a water ring against the granite where the toothbrush sat, reminding me that it's been quite some time since I cleaned the bathroom.

You can do hard things, I remind myself.

A small chuckle teases my lips as I think about what my life has come to. I used to love cleaning; it was my happy time.

That's it. I'm going to blare some music and deep clean the house today. It will feel good—or if not good, then normal. I connect my phone to the Bluetooth speakers. An upbeat Post Malone song plays through the house. I reach under the sink to grab the tile cleaner and knock over a box of tampons.

My mouth falls open, and I step away from the sink, hitting my back against the wall.

No, it can't be. It's not possible.

I recall buying the box over two and a half months ago, before Leo's death, but there's no way. It has to be the stress. Women skip periods all the time because of stress, and Lord knows I've been under a lot of it.

But what if ...

I snatch my phone, purse, and car keys and run out of the house.

Fifteen minutes later, I'm home from the pharmacy and in the bathroom, peeing on a white stick. I pace up and down the hall, waiting for the allotted four minutes. Finally, I step into

343

the bathroom and peek at the plastic wand lying on the countertop.

Pregnant.

The single word is displayed clear as day through the oval window.

It can't be. I shake my head and pick up the test. It says *pregnant.* A sob erupts from my throat, and I hold the test as I slide down the wall until I'm sitting on the tiled floor.

I can't believe this.

Tears fall, and my cries are tormented, a mix between despair and joy. I'm so torn. On one hand, I could be carrying a piece of Leo in me right now. On the other, our dream is coming true, and he's not here for it.

I rise from the floor and call my doctor's office. I beg the receptionist to get me in ASAP, and thankfully, there was a cancellation. Jogging back out to the car, I peel out of the driveway and toward my gynecologist's office.

Sitting in the office amid other women—some visibly pregnant, others not—I can't make my tears cease as I wait to be called back. I imagine a collective sigh of relief from the other waiting room occupants when my name is called. After a pit stop to the restroom to pee in a cup, I'm escorted to an exam room.

As soon as the gown is on and I'm sitting in the chair with the stirrups, Dr. Belland enters. There's pity in her eyes when she sees me. She must've heard or read of Leo's passing. She reaches her hand toward me and gently squeezes mine.

"I took a test, and it said pregnant, but that's not possible, is it?" My words come out in rapid succession.

She nods, a tight smile on her face. "You're pregnant, Alma."

I cry harder. "How is that possible? I thought I couldn't get pregnant."

"Well, on the scans, your tubes look almost completely blocked, but it's been four years. Your body changes, heals.

There had to be a small enough opening for at least one egg to sneak through."

I shake my head. "This is unbelievable." Tears fall against my chest, wetting the pink hospital gown. "Am I going to be able to carry it full-term?"

"Well, let's take a look and see. When was your last period?" she asks as she turns on a machine beside me.

"At least two and a half months. I don't remember."

"Go ahead and lie down. We're going to do a vaginal ultrasound to check the baby."

I do as instructed, and she inserts a wand into me. Whooshing sounds come from the machine, and Dr. Belland smiles.

"There's your baby." She points to the screen, and I gasp.

There's a tiny human on the screen. I can see the head, body, arms, and legs. The baby seems to be puckering his or her lips, one arm reaching out in front of its little round belly.

"Oh my God. I can't believe it," I cry in disbelief. "This is such a miracle."

Dr. Belland nods. "It is, Alma." She moves the wand, and another angle comes up. This time, the baby's spinal cord is visible. "I'm going to take some measurements and snap some pictures for you."

She works, pointing out parts of the baby—his or her heart and brain, spine, and limbs—stating that everything looks great.

"Based on the measurements, you're three months along. Your uterus looks great, no visible problems that I can see. Eighty percent of miscarriages occur within the first three months, so your chances of carrying the baby are good. You are considered a high-risk pregnancy based on your history, so I'll be seeing you weekly, but everything looks great, Alma. No cause for concern right now."

She pulls out the ultrasound wand, and I sit up.

Wrapping my arms around my chest, I cry, "Thank you."

She tilts her head and watches me, curiously. "Do you want a hug, Alma?"

"Yes, please." I nod.

Dr. Belland hugs me, and I hold her tight, tears falling onto her shoulder. I wish I were crying with Leo over this joyous news, but it feels nice to hold a real person.

"You're going to be just fine." She pats my back and releases her hold on me.

"Thanks again."

"Days like this are why I love this job." She grins. "I'll see you next week," she says and leaves the room.

I stay seated and cross my arms over my chest, hugging myself once more. I close my eyes and try to feel him.

Thank you for leaving me a piece of you. Keep the baby safe. I love you.

An immense amount of love engulfs me. I think it might be Leo or maybe the love I already feel for this life growing inside of me or perhaps both. For the first time in two months, I smile—a real, genuine smile.

Leo was kind and his soul gentle. I know he fought hard for us, but there are some evils that fragile hearts can't fight forever. Maybe that's why he said he always knew.

I'd give anything to change the past. I'd give anything to have Leo here with me. I don't understand the meaning behind his death, and maybe I never will. I have to stop allowing the questions I can't answer to steal the life from me.

Focusing on the truths will keep me going. Leo loved me, and what we had was a gift. We were happy, and our marriage was special. He was my soul mate, and I was lucky to have found him. I wouldn't trade the time I had with him for anything. This aching sorrow consuming me is a small price to pay for my life with Leo. He was worth it, all of it. He gave me a miracle, and I'm certain that the best parts of Leo are growing inside of me.

Maybe he couldn't stay, but a part of him did. That life, that perfect piece of Leo, is here to save me. And I know I'm going to be okay.

EPILOGUE

ALMA

EIGHT MONTHS LATER

$\mathcal{M}$y life has never been what one would call normal. As original as my name, my story is mine alone. As brutal as it's been beautiful, I wouldn't give up this life for anything.

Soul-crushing love is rare, and I had it. If I'd known that I'd lose him so soon in our marriage, I would've married him all the same. A hundred times over. Five years with Leo is worth more than a million years of regular love. I don't know if I'll ever remarry. How is it possible to promise yourself to someone else when your heart will always be taken?

There is nothing beautiful or poetic in experiencing a great loss, but there is something incredible about surviving it.

The fortune from years ago that's framed above our

wedding photo in my bedroom couldn't have been closer to the truth. There's no doubt in my mind that Leo was meant for me as I was for him. He will be burned into my soul forever. No matter what else I do in this life or who else I love, I will carry him with me—for real love never truly leaves. He will always be a part of me.

The last six months of my pregnancy were a healing journey. The scars over the loss of Leo will never heal fully, but I'm as whole as I'll ever be, and I owe it to her. My miracle.

My pregnancy was typical in all of the usual ways. I was exhausted, bloated, and waddled around like a very unfortunate duck. My friends gifted me with pink everything. Quinn threw me an adorable baby shower. In the later months, my back and hips killed me to the point where sleep evaded me most nights. Instead of sleeping, I would lie in bed and feel her as she jumped and kicked around like a little ninja.

My pregnancy was anything but ordinary in a lot of aspects. I heard morning sickness tapers off for most women, but for me it arrived late, and stuck with me for the remainder of the pregnancy. I threw up daily, like it was my part-time job. My husband wasn't there for the ultrasounds or first visible kicks. I ran to the store on my own at two a.m. for pickles and ice cream instead of sending my husband. Two of my best friends, Quinn and Amos, were in the delivery room with me instead of Leo, but at least I wasn't alone.

All in all, pregnancy was like the rest of my life—heartbreaking and beautiful, at the same time—and I loved every minute of it because it brought me to her.

Love Grace Harding.

Seven pounds, two ounces.

Nineteen inches long.

Most gorgeous baby girl in the universe.

I wanted to find a name that meant lion, so she could be named after her gentle and fierce daddy. In my search, I found that *løve* in Danish means lion. The Danish version isn't pronounced the way *love* in English is pronounced, but I thought it was perfect. It means lion, and if any baby was conceived out of love, it's her. She was wanted more than anything, even when I didn't think the idea of her was a possibility.

My entire life, I've been hard on myself. I wanted to be perfect and right at all times, but that's not how it works. Storms are inevitable—or in my case, catastrophic tsunamis—and as long as I'm trying my best, I need to give myself some grace, to be kind to my heart and gentle with my soul. Love's middle name is a reminder for her to do the same. I want her to try her best and then gift herself with grace.

The one person we all have to rely on is ourselves. These past years have shown me that it doesn't matter how much someone else loves me. I need to be able to love, forgive, and hold myself up. Only I can do that. Only I can keep going when it seems impossible.

I hold Love in my arms. At two months old, she's already developing a personality. I see Leo in her features, and I'm so grateful. She has his deep blue eyes, full lips, and wide smile. I hope she grows up into an incredible soul, just as he was. I spend my days nursing, changing, and holding her. She's the most amazing thing to ever happen to me.

The way in which I adore her is just as powerful as my love was for Leo but different, more intense, because she's mine and Leo's—we made her—and I'm going to protect her with everything I am. She won't go a day without knowing that she's loved unconditionally. She will never be left alone with anyone who could hurt her. Her achievements will be celebrated. I'll show her how to be kind and thoughtful, though if she's anything like Leo, she was born with those traits. I will catch her when she falls until I can't, and then she'll catch herself with the skills she owns because she will be fierce and gentle, like her daddy.

"Mama loves you, baby Love." I grin toward her, and she gives me a hint of a smile and clings to my finger. "Mommy's going to love you so much, you might get tired of me, but promise to show me grace. I just can't help how much I adore you. And when you're a teen, just skip the part where you hate me, okay? My heart couldn't handle that."

She holds my finger tighter, and I take that as a yes.

I lean down and kiss her cheeks over and over again as she makes the cooing noises I love so much.

"You're the best gift that your daddy ever gave me." Tears well in my eyes. "The very best gift."

* * *

TWO YEARS LATER

"Come on, Lovebug. We're going to drop these flowers off with Daddy." I hold out my hand, and Love takes it.

I sigh in relief. She's a very strong-willed little lady—a trait I think she inherited from both of her parents. Her short legs walk beside me as her chestnut-brown ponytail bounces on her head.

We reach Leo's tombstone, and I set the pot of flowers down at its base. Reaching in the bag on my shoulder, I pull out the blanket and spread it over the grave.

"Pic-a-nic!"

"You got it, girlie. We are having a picnic! I have all sorts of goodies in here." I pull out the Tupperware containers of finger foods, which is every meal with a toddler. "Here are some strawberries, cheese, Veggie Straws, and blueberries."

I set Love's sippy cup in front of her as she holds the

container of blueberries in her lap and begins to shovel them in her mouth.

"One at a time, or you're going to choke." I grab a single blueberry and demonstrate.

Love is concentrating on her food. I sit cross-legged in front of Leo's grave. I talk to him every day in my head, his love still very much alive inside me. Though, sometimes, I like to come here and speak out loud.

"It's hard to believe that, next month, you'll have been gone for three years. If I didn't have a visual representation of the passing of time, who's growing like a weed, I wouldn't believe it. Gosh, I wish you were here. I wish you could love her and hold her, and I wish she could know you. You would've been such an amazing dad."

"You'll be happy to know that she's your mini. From your bright blue eyes to your mischievous grin, she's you. She's kind and sensitive, and she definitely has a little temper when things aren't going right. I swear, I'd bet she's your mirror image when you were two. She makes me laugh and cry because, gosh, it's like watching you grow up."

I turn to Love, who has pulled all of her chubby, little toddler-sized Disney princesses out of the bag and is lining them up. They're her favorite toys right now. They're a modern version of the Little People figurines, which were popular when I was a kid, turned into Disney princesses. I got her the whole set when we went to Disney last month, and she's obsessed.

I nod toward Love. "She likes to line up and organize her princesses, which I can't be certain but I think that's one trait she got from me." I chuckle. "She's smart, Leo—like, so smart. You'd be amazed. She's perfect." I wipe an errant tear.

"Leo, I don't know where I'd be without her. She pulled me from my grief and saved me in so many ways. Your letter told me to love again and be happy, and she allowed me to do both.

Thank you for her. Thank you for the greatest gift you could've given me. You left me a part of you, and I get to see you in her every day. I swear, a piece of your soul lives within her too. When I hug her, I feel you. When she laughs, I see you. And I promise you, she's so loved and so happy, and I will never let anyone hurt her."

Love walks over to me and touches a tear on my cheek. "Mama cry." She looks sad.

"No, baby. Mommy's happy. Happy tears." I pull her pudgy, little hand to my lips and kiss the top.

"Happy?" she asks.

"Very happy." I smile.

She retreats, scurrying toward her princesses on the blanket, and then comes back to me. "Mama?"

"Yes, Lovey?"

She gives me the Snow White doll. "White. Mama, white."

"You want me to have Snow White?" I ask her.

She nods, a dimpled smile spreading across her face.

"You want Mommy to have your Snow White even though she's your favorite?" I raise an eyebrow.

She nods again, giggling now.

"Thank you, Love." I hug Snow White to my chest and then pucker my lips toward my daughter. "Kisses?"

She leans toward me and plants a wet kiss on my lips before heading back to the rest of her princesses.

I hold the plastic doll, Love's most cherished possession, against my heart. "I told you she has your soul."

My heart aches with adoration, and my chest fills with love. I close my eyes, my face toward the sky. As the sun warms my skin, I smile with a joy that's soul deep, and I know that wherever Leo is, he's smiling too.

Dear Readers,

Are you okay? That was rough, I know. It broke my heart to write, and I'm sure it was devastating to read. I want to tell you how Alma and Leo came to be and why their story is so special to me.

Leo was modeled after my late father. My dad was abused, same as Leo. His mother and brother knew and didn't protect him. He fought the demons his whole life and battled drug and alcohol addiction. He died too young.

My dad had a kind heart and a gentle soul. Despite everything that he went through, he never laid a finger on me or my siblings. He loved us as best he could. He searched for happiness and love his entire life, but he could never let go of the pain of his childhood.

There are many sides of addiction, and I wanted to show that. Drugs don't define the person; their heart does.

The chapter where Alma broke the mirror after Leo's death was the first chapter I wrote in this novel. The scenes from the death to the epilogue have been in my head for years. I just didn't know how Leo and Alma would get there.

Then, I heard the song "If the World Was Ending" by JP Saxe, featuring Julia Michaels. I listened to that song on repeat for two days, and in that time, the entirety of this book came to me. That's now happened to me twice. My novel *Chasing Memories* came to me the same way—by listening to one song on repeat.

I love that song, and if you haven't heard it, you should listen to it. It is the perfect mood for Alma and Leo's story.

I hope I gave Leo's life justice with this novel, and I pray that, despite the heartache, you enjoyed reading it. It's hard to pick a favorite book from the ones I've written, as they're all special for different reasons, but I really love this one. Leo and Alma will always have a cherished place in my heart. Their love story was incredible, and though I wish Leo's life weren't so short, his love will live on, for those who love us never leave us.

Thank you so much for reading.

Make your journey beautiful.

Love,

Ellie

KINDRED SOULS

ELLIE WADE

PROLOGUE

ALMA

I used to wonder if soul mates existed. Is it really possible for one person to be destined for another? I know now that it's possible, and soul mates are real. I found mine, or perhaps we found each other. Our love was true, raw, and deep—our connection, magical.

He was my everything, and I was his.

Our souls connected, entwining together to form an inseparable bond. There aren't words to adequately describe what this type of love feels like. It's everything I imagined and so much more.

His love permeated every cell of my being, filling me up until I was whole. A simple look from him would leave me breathless. A smile would make my knees weak. A touch would ignite a flame so powerful within that I was sure I'd crumble to ashes.

Every day with Leo was a gift, and I knew it.

He was my forever, yet our forever wasn't long enough.

I heard somewhere that the best of us get their angel wings early, and in Leo's case, this was true. He was so good, and where it mattered the most, he was the best. His heart was pure, and his love was endless. He left me way too soon, but even now, with my heart shattered and my soul crushed, I wouldn't change a minute of our life together. I wouldn't take any of it back to save myself from this pain. Having Leo's love for any amount of time makes all of this worth it.

Each second that passes without him hurts, and maybe it always will. I hope it doesn't because Leo left me a gift, a perfect little Love, and she needs me.

She deserves all of me.

She should have a mother who's whole and present. And I'm trying. They say that time heals all, and I hope they're right. Somedays, I don't know how I'll go on, but then she circles my finger with her tiny little hand, and I know I will. I have to. Perhaps, time will heal me, but I think Love will.

One way or another love will save me. It has to.

CHAPTER 1

ALMA

*C*arrots washed, I shake off the excess water and put them onto the veggie tray. Grabbing a dish towel, I dry my hands and stare out the window above the sink toward the backyard. My daughter, Love, in all of her three-year-old adorableness shoots down the slide of her play structure. Her poofy princess Belle dress flies up as she descends. I can't help but smile, a genuine happy grin.

I may be biased, but my little girl is beautiful beyond words. She reminds me so much of Leo with her dark hair, bright blue eyes, and radiant smile. Her soul is a hundred percent kind, good, and brave—just like her daddy's. The past three years and nine months have been the worst years of my life but also the best. Every day is a true power struggle of opposing emotions. Grief fights to pull me down, but joy always seems to win, filling my heart with gratitude. And, how could it not? I have my little Love.

My mother, Lee-Anne, meets Love at the base of the slide and swoops her up into her arms, spinning her in a circle. Love giggles, and her yellow dress flutters in the warm breeze. My smile widens and I shake my head. Sometimes, I can't believe that this woman before me is my mother. She bears no resemblance to the woman who *raised* me, and I use that word loosely. She's present and sober, two things she never was when I was growing up. She's also widowed.

Two years ago, she showed up on my doorstep a shell of a woman. At that time, I hadn't seen or heard from her since Leo's funeral. She'd never even met Love. She was clinging to a black box, which turned out to hold the ashes of my father, who I then learned had passed of a heart attack. The decades of partying and drugs had been too much for his body.

It's strange, but I feel like at that moment, on my doorstep, was the first time my mother actually *saw* me. She had lost the love of her life as I had lost mine. We had something in common. We both belonged to a club that neither of us had wanted access to.

I took her in and sent her to a six-month rehab facility, where she finally became clean for the first time since my birth. It wasn't easy for either of us. My mother is as stubborn as they come, so she fought the process. Yet after months of rehab, therapy, tears, and long conversations, we made it here. I bought her a condo a few blocks from this house so she has her own space, but she's here almost all of the time. She loves being a grandma, or Gigi, as she prefers to be called. I guess Love saved her, too.

It's surreal seeing my mother sober, caring, and all the things she wasn't for me, but I love it nonetheless. I'm so glad my daughter has her.

A pinky finger wraps around mine, pulling me from my thoughts. "Hey, you," I say, turning toward my best friend Amos.

He pulls me into a hug. "Everything looks great—the decorations, the books, the cake."

"Thanks." I step back from him and look around at the explosion of yellow balloons and everything from Disney's *Beauty and the Beast*, Love's current favorite movie. "It turned out pretty good."

"It turned out perfectly. You're super woman, Mutt." The nickname he's held for me since our childhood makes me smile as he leans in and kisses my forehead. "Has Love seen it?"

"Yes, she was a ball of giggles this morning," I nod toward the window. "She's out there in the fanciest Belle dress I could find in all her princess glory."

"And the weather is perfect." He raises an eyebrow. "So, all of that worrying for nothing."

In Michigan, it's a toss-up whether May second is sunny and eighty degrees or snowy and cold. The weatherman had predicted cold and sleet, but I learned long ago never to rely on the news weather forecasters. They don't seem to be able to predict Michigan weather any better than I could.

I release a sigh. "Yeah, it's all good."

Amos faces me and takes my smallest fingers on each hand in his. "You are an amazing mother, Alma. Truly. Love is so lucky to have you. You've been through so much, and every step you take is with strength and grace. I'm so proud of you. Relax and enjoy today. Your baby is three." He purses his lips together in a smile, swinging our joined hands between us.

I bite the interior of my cheek and exhale. "Yeah, she is. I can't believe it. She's three!" I chuckle. "Where has the time gone?" My smile falters, and unshed tears come to my eyes. "I wish he was here for this." My words are a sad whisper.

"He is," Amos reassures me. "You know he is."

I nod.

"You're doing so great." He squeezes my hands before calling out, "Alexa, play 'Here Comes the Sun' by the Beatles."

The first few notes of one of my favorite songs sound out through the speakers, and I smile.

Amos takes a step back before bending and offering me his hand. "Can I have this dance?"

"Sure." I grin, placing my hand in his. I release a soft gasp when he pulls me to him.

We dance around the kitchen, and I laugh as Amos spins and dips me. Dance therapy at its best. By the time the song is over, all of the pent-up stress and emotions have fallen away, and I'm simply here—present in the moment. As always, my best friend knew just what I needed.

The doorbell rings, indicating the arrival of a party guest.

"Alexa, play the *Beauty and the Beast* soundtrack," I call out. Pulling my hands from Amos's grasp, I plop a spoon into the veggie dip.

"Really?" Amos scrunches his face in a mock protest.

"All day long, baby." I smirk. "Don't worry, by the end of the day, you'll be singing along with the enchanted silverware. Can you get the door? I'm going to go outside and get Lee-Anne and Love."

As I pull open the sliding glass door to the backyard, Amos says, "Alexa, turn the volume down," and it causes me to laugh.

* * *

LOVE LIES asleep against my chest, her sweaty cheek touching my skin. I swipe a lock of her dark hair away from her face.

All of our neighborhood friends with young children left the party a while ago. Just our family—for all intents and purposes—is left.

Leo's mother stands and faces me. "Thanks for the invitation, Alma. I truly appreciate being able to see my granddaughter."

"You're welcome," I say with a forced smile.

It's hard for me to welcome Leo's mom into my home. She wasn't technically Leo's abuser, but she definitely holds a lot of the blame. Even before I was a mother myself, I couldn't wrap my head around how any parent could harm their child. Now that I have Love, it makes me even sicker to think about it, which I try not to do. A part of me will always hold hatred in my heart for Mrs. Harding. I can't help it.

She's tried so hard to be in my daughter's life, and I have empathy for her because I know she means well. She loved Leo in her own way, and maybe she was just weak, but what she did—or better yet, didn't do—when it came to protecting Leo is unforgivable. She'll never have the type of relationship that she wants with Love. She won't be able to take her for sleepovers or have unsupervised visits. Where my little girl is concerned, I'll never leave her safety up to chance. I'll always protect her.

Cat gets up from the couch. "Boo. I guess that means I have to go, too." Bending down, she kisses my cheek and softly kisses Love's head. "Let's get together this week. Lunch or dinner, okay? I hardly got to see you today." She smiles.

"Sounds good. Love you."

Cat has become one of my favorite people. She is like a sister to me and an amazing aunt to Love. Her husband, Leo's brother Stephen, doesn't come around, and I'm perfectly fine with that. Of course, Mr. Harding has never met Love, and he never will.

"I should probably go, too." Ollie, my dear friend and Leo's old NA sponsor, stands to leave.

"Aw, man," I protest.

"I'm sorry. I'm meeting up with someone tonight. But I'll swing by again, soon," Ollie says.

"Promise?" I raise an eyebrow.

"I promise." He winks to me, says goodbye to the others, then follows Mrs. Harding and Cat out the door.

"And then there were three," I say to Quinn and Amos. "Oh, I mean four. Sorry, Lee-Anne," I say to my mom.

Lee-Anne gets up from the couch, "Almalee Hannelda," her voice chastising. "I told you to call me Mom."

"I'm sorry, *Mom*, but a twenty-seven-year habit isn't easy to break."

"More like twenty-five." She turns to address Quinn and Amos. "She didn't say her first word until she was at least two. She was a little slow."

"I was not." I scoff.

Quinn and Amos exchange amused looks.

"Anyway"—she holds out her arms toward Love—"let me go lay her down, and you kids can hang out."

I press my lips against Love's head, giving her a kiss, and I breathe her in. She smells of sugar, vanilla, and sweat—all evidence of a day well spent. "I love you, my little love," I whisper to her before my mom lifts her from me.

Quinn pops up from the lounge chair. "I'll go get us some wine."

"There's some Riesling in the fridge," I tell her.

"Oh, perfect. My favorite. Does that work for you?" she asks Amos.

"Yeah, anything is fine," he says.

Quinn hurries off to the kitchen.

Amos looks around. "It's so strange to see Lee-Anne like this."

"I know." I nod, eyes wide.

"Like who is this woman? *Call me Mom?* She would've whipped your butt if you had dared to call her mom when you were a kid. She's like a real human now, you know? A completely different person." He shakes his head.

"Tell me about it," I chuckle under my breath. "It's like I'm learning who she is for the first time. And you're right. She never resembled a real human when we were growing up. She and my dad lived in their own world that only had room for the two of them. And please," I grumble. "Like she remembers when my first word was. I wasn't slow."

Amos laughs. "Come on, Mutt. You were valedictorian of our high school and graduated from college with honors. No one thinks you're lacking intelligence."

Quinn returns with three glasses of wine and hands them out. She plops down beside me, pulling her legs up onto the sofa. "Oh my gosh. When is the last time the three of us have hung out like this alone together?" she asks. "It's been way too long. Tell me. What's going on in your dating life, Amos?"

"It's pretty boring, I'm afraid. No news to report." He takes a sip of wine.

Quinn scrunches her face in disappointment. "Bummer." She looks at me. "What about you?"

"Me?" I half shriek, almost inhaling wine into my lungs. "You know I'm not dating anyone."

She sighs. "It will be four years this August, Alma. You're only twenty-seven. Leo would want you to be happy, you know that."

My eyes fill with tears, but I refuse to let them fall. I want to yell at my friend and tell her that she's being insensitive, but I know she means well, and she's right. Leo told me that he wanted me to find love again in the letter he left. Of course he would want me to be happy. I simply don't know how to move on from him.

I swallow down the pain. "It's not that easy, Quinn," I manage to say.

She places her hand on my knee and squeezes gently. "Okay." She nods.

"I promise I'll come to you when and if anything happens with my love life. Deal?"

Her smile widens. "Deal!"

"What's going on with you and Beau? I meant to ask you

earlier why he didn't come, but with the chaos of three-year-olds running around, I forgot," I inquire, swirling the white wine in my glass.

"Well, Beau and I are old news." She twirls a strand of her long blond hair around her fingers and shrugs.

"You broke up?"

She nods. "We broke up."

"What happened?" I ask.

"He just wasn't the one, you know? I don't want to settle. I want to ache when I'm away from my man. I want storybook love. I want the happily ever after." She looks around at all the party decorations in the room. A yellow balloon floats near her, and she smacks it. "I want a freaking beast to turn into a prince and buy me a library but with shoes instead of books. Is that too much to ask?"

Amos and I laugh. "No, that's not too much to ask," I say with a grin.

She hits another balloon bobbing toward her. "When did you get these balloons? They're all falling already."

"This morning." I scan the room, taking in all the balloons coming off from their helium high. "The guy at the store offered to put this gel in them that would make them stay on the ceiling for up to three days, but it was another fifty cents per balloon, so I said no."

"It would've been worth the fifty cents." Quinn shakes her head.

"Fifty cents per balloon, and I ordered sixty balloons," I offer in my defense.

"You're a millionaire, Alma. You can swing an additional thirty bucks," Quinn scoffs

"Well, I grew up saving pennies. Being frugal is in my nature. I hate wasting money."

Quinn tips her head back and finishes her glass of wine. "Well, when I find my Prince Charming, he will not be frugal."

"Right. Because he's going to buy you a library of shoes," Amos states, the side of his mouth tilting up.

"Exactly!" Quinn points her empty glass toward Amos. "I'm going to go get more wine. Does anyone want a refill? You know what? Never mind. I'll just bring out the bottle."

CHAPTER 2

ALMA

A little body squirms beside me, waking me from my slumber.

"Momma," her sweet little voice calls my name.

"Lovie." I smile, my eyes refusing to open.

"Momma."

"Lovie."

"Momma," she says, this time squeezing my cheeks between her hands.

"Lovie." I reach out and tickle her belly, causing an eruption of giggles.

Love has a queen-sized bed in her sweet pink, gray, and white room. I transitioned her from the crib right into a big girl's bed. Admittedly, there may have been a slight ulterior motive behind such a large bed, given that each night I crawl into bed beside her. Most days, I'm a stage-five clinger when it comes to this perfect little human. I can't deny it. She's my life-line in this unsettling world.

I open my eyes to find Love's face a mere inch from my own. "How does it feel to be three?"

"Good." She giggles.

"Did you like your party yesterday?" I ask.

She nods her head enthusiastically.

"What was your favorite part?"

"My dess." She grins. The letter 'r' continues to evade her.

"It was a perfect dress for my perfect little princess." I run my fingers through her hair. An odd scent fills the room. "Do you smell something?" I ask Love. "Uh-oh," I say dramatically. "Let's hope Gigi isn't cooking us something. Do you think she is?"

Love nods with a giggle.

"Oh no! What do you think it is?"

"Mud pie!" Love laughs.

"Not mud pie!" I scrunch my nose, and Love giggles.

"With bugs!" she adds, always with a flair for the dramatic.

I stick out my tongue and fall to the side of the bed in mock death. Love bursts into a fit of laughter.

She jumps on me, checking me for life. "Momma!"

I open my eyes. "I'm okay! But I think we better go check on Gigi."

"'Kay!" she jumps off the bed, her long hair flying up as she falls. Her bare feet pitter-patter down the hallway before I'm out of her room.

In the kitchen, I find Lee-Anne in front of the stove, exactly where she shouldn't be. One thing that hasn't changed since her *call me mom now* rebirth is her ability to make edible food. She couldn't cook when I was growing up, and she can't cook now.

"Good morning, Mom. What are you making?" I ask as I fill the coffee pot, side-eyeing the object in the frying pan.

"Pancakes." She gleams proudly.

"What's in them?" I've learned not to accept simple answers at face value when it comes to my mother.

"Well, I created my own recipe. Taking some tofu, I blended it up and mixed it with some almond milk, quinoa, and spices."

"Oh."

She chuckles. "Just give them a chance, Alma."

"I always do," I remind her. I've put more gross things in my mouth since she's been sober than I have in my entire life.

"Sit. Sit," she says excitedly. "I'll bring everything over."

I get Love situated at the table and take a seat. Lee-Anne sets a plate in front of each of us. The pancakes are thin, tortilla-like in appearance, and an unsettling shade of green-ish-brown.

"Try it," she urges eagerly, her eyes gleaming.

I take a bite of the flat patties. They're extremely dense, chewy, and taste like a mix between chalk and paint. At least, I imagine that's what a fried chalk and paint mixture would taste like.

Looking toward Love, I see her chewing slowly, her lips turned into a frown.

I choke down my bite. "What do you think? Do you like them?"

She looks at my mother apologetically and back at me, shaking her head slightly. She wants to please her Gigi but is smart enough to know that eating a plate of this won't end well. We make a game out of Gigi's crazy food by naming it based on what it tastes like. A flax and raisin combo that Lee-Anne made for us a couple of days ago was fittingly nicknamed "mud with bugs."

"What should we call this one?" I ask her, raising my brows with a grin.

"Steet," she answers in a soft voice.

"Street?" I clarify. Love nods, and I burst out in laughter, shaking my head. It's not as if I have anything against healthy meals. I'm all about feeding my daughter nutritious food, but my mother simply has an inability to grasp ingredients that work well together versus those that don't. "Mom, you know it's okay to use the Jiffy mix once in a while."

"But these are healthier than Jiffy mix," she argues, dishing a pancake onto her plate.

"Mom." I take a swig of water to wash the flavor from my mouth. "They taste like pavement. I love you for trying, and we appreciate your hard work, right, Love?" Love nods. "But we're going to have to say no thank you to these pancakes."

"Well, I think they're good," Lee-Anne says before inserting a forkful into her mouth. I study her face for signs of disgust, but she holds strong. I'm sure she's dying a little with each bite, but who knows? She's been eating like this my whole life, so there's a slight chance she could've acquired a taste for the inedible.

"Do I smell food?" Amos asks, entering the kitchen. He's rubbing his hand along the back of his neck.

He and Quinn stayed over last night after some heavy wine consumption. I only had two glasses. I've never been one for hangovers, and now that I get up and run around with a toddler all day, I definitely don't have time for one.

"Yeah, my mom made street pancakes," I say. Lifting my gaze to his, I press my lips in a line.

"Are they related to street tacos?" He raises a brow.

"No, they are more of the pavement variety," I tease. He looks confused. "Love said they taste like you're eating the street, so we're going with it. Mom, tell him what's in them."

Lee-Anne fills Amos in on the ingredients.

He nods with interest and gives my mother an appreciative smile before saying, "I see." He directs his next question to me. "Can I make you something else?"

Amos is one of the best chefs I know. "Yes, please. No offense, Mom."

"None taken. I like 'em," she says with a shrug before taking another bite.

I get up to get some juice for Love and a cup of coffee for me. "Did you see Quinn?" I ask Amos. He's pulling items out of the refrigerator and placing them on the granite countertop—eggs, salsa, garlic, cilantro, cheese, and tortillas.

"No, her door was shut when I came down here. I'm sure she'll be out for a while."

Amos whips us up some breakfast burritos. I consider myself a decent cook. Growing up, I was the one in our household who made anything resembling a meal. Yet Amos takes food to the next level. His food always has an extra ingredient that makes it delicious.

The burritos he's made today are a Mexican variety complete with eggs, beans, rice, and spices, and I love that he added extra cilantro, which is one of my favorite flavors. They are so good that I almost moan when I take my first bite.

"Do you like them, Lovebug?" Amos asks, sitting in the chair beside me with his own burrito.

She nods, her mouth full.

"What do they taste like?" I inquire.

"Yummy," she replies, shoving the burrito into her mouth.

I look at Amos. "Your yummy burritos are a hit." I turn toward Lee-Anne. "Still no offense, Mom."

Rolling her eyes, she tilts her mouth up into a smile as she waves her hand through the space between us.

We're quiet as we eat, all clearly famished, and it's then I realize that I'm not sure how much either Love or myself ate yesterday. The day was packed with games, fun, and cake. There was pizza, and I believe Love ate some, though I don't recall how much. She crashed after her party, and neither of us had dinner.

"I'm a horrible mother," I say aloud. Amos and Lee-Anne both look toward me. "Love fell asleep after her party. I didn't even feed her dinner. How could I forget to feed my child dinner?"

Lee-Anne shakes her head and waves her hand once more. "That happens. It's fine. She ate her weight in cake yesterday, so there's that."

"You know you're an incredible mother." Amos grins, picking up a piece of cilantro that's fallen from his burrito onto the plate. He places it in his mouth. "Stop it. She's perfectly healthy and clearly needed sleep more than dinner after such an exciting day yesterday."

"I guess. I'll have to remember this for next year, though, so it doesn't happen again."

"Why is everyone yelling?" Quinn whines as she stumbles into the dining room, looking worse for wear. Her long blond hair is matted on one side where she slept on it, and her mascara has left a trail from her eyes to her cheeks.

"No one is yelling." I chuckle. "Are you hungry? We have street pancakes or yummy burritos."

"Am I supposed to know what street pancakes are?" she grumbles, holding her fingers to her temples.

"Ibuprofen is in the cabinet by the window, and there's coffee." I raise my arm, pointing toward the cabinet.

"Now you're speaking my language." She sighs.

Quinn joins us at the table, and we finish our breakfast, sipping her coffee with her eyes closed.

"What's everyone's plans for today?" I ask.

"I'm going to go grocery shopping and then to one of those paint classes," Lee-Anne says. "I found a Groupon for one. It's in the basement of one of the restaurants downtown, and we're going to paint this pretty tree with flowers."

"Oh, that sounds so fun, Mom. You'll love that."

"I'm excited. Am I still watching Love all week?" she asks.

"If that still works for you? I can't take her to work this week. My days are jam-packed with meetings. It wouldn't be very fun for her."

"Of course it still works. You know Gigi loves her days with her favorite girl." She smiles toward Love, who grins right back. I'm so grateful that my daughter has her Gigi.

I clear the plates and start to load the dishwasher.

"I think I'm going to go home and take a nap." Quinn scrunches her nose and supplies a guilty smirk, her bright blue eyes barely visible through her squint. "Thanks for last night. It was so great to catch up. We need to get together more often."

"Definitely, at least until you find your prince with a library of shoes. You'll be too busy for us then."

"Well, obviously. Being a shoe princess will be very taxing." She puckers her lips with a nod. She takes a final sip of coffee before making her way around the table to give us all hugs.

Mom follows Quinn out, eager to get to her grocery shopping so she's finished well before her painting class.

"Are you leaving us, too?" I ask Amos.

He leans back in his chair. "No, I thought I'd stay and hang out."

"Yay! Cookie is staying with us." I say to Love, clapping my hands together. She starts clapping along with me.

"Plus, God knows what your mother is going to bring back from the store. I need to stay to make sure you two eat today." He chuckles.

"Yes, we need to eat. After all, we both skipped dinner last night." I grin. "Lovebug, what do you want to do? Do you want to watch a movie and relax a little?"

She nods. "Belle!"

I hold my hands out to the side, palms up. "*Beauty and the Beast*, it is! No take backs, Cookie." I smirk toward Amos.

"Yay." Amos feigns excitement. "At least I know all of the words to the songs, now."

"Yes, and singing along is expected." I wink.

Love runs off to grab her plush Belle doll to watch the movie with us.

"I'm just so glad that we've moved on from Snow White," I tell Amos as I set up the movie. "Snow White's not nearly as good."

"I'd have to agree with you there."

I plop down on the sofa next to Amos and lean up against his side. Love sits next to me and snuggles up against me while clutching Belle against her. Her face lights up as the movie begins to play. It's my favorite part—experiencing life through her eyes. For a moment, grief tugs on my heart as I wish Leo was here with us. I say a prayer for strength, then I let those thoughts go. By the time Belle starts singing about her neighbors' boring lives, all I feel is happiness.

CHAPTER 3

ALMA

Seventy-eight emails, twenty-three voicemails, and a stack of files taller than Love await me when I get to my office Monday morning. I set my coffee down beside the towering pile of paperwork and plop in my chair with a sigh. I'm exhausted, and my day has barely begun.

I love it here. Lion's Lair was our dream, mine and Leo's, and it's more than I could've ever hoped for. We're making a difference in people's lives by keeping kids off the streets, away from drugs, and in school, and I'm humbled by that. Yet I'm tired. It wasn't always this overwhelming. There's so much to do, and I feel like I'm failing.

Halfway through my fourth email, a knock sounds on the office door.

"Alma, there's someone here to see you, a Nate Jackson," Jen, our greeter, tells me.

I stand from my chair, "Nate? Oh my gosh, send him in."

Nate was one of the first teens that Leo and I helped relocate from his abusive home, put into a good foster home, and finally adopted. He, like so many others, is the reason this place was created.

Nate steps into my office, all seven feet of him. "Nate!" I squeal and wrap my arms around his middle.

He hugs me tight. "Hi, Alma. I was passing through town, and I just had to stop in."

I release him from my embrace. "I'm so glad you did. Sit." I motion toward the sofa. "I want to hear everything. You've grown like eighteen feet since I saw you last."

Nate chuckles. "Nah, not that much. But I've grown some."

I take a seat beside him and put my hand on his. "You look great, Nate. You're good?"

"I am." He smiles, a real genuine one, and I'm filled with gratitude.

I press a hand to my chest, tears coming to my eyes. "I'm so glad."

This is just what I needed today, a success story to remind me why our work here is so important.

"Is Leo around? I'd love to see him, too."

My heart plummets into my stomach, and the air leaves my lungs. For a moment, I'm completely immobile—frozen in this alternate reality where Leo's name is spoken in the present tense.

"Alma?" Nate questions, and his voice carries concern.

I shake my head, pulling myself back to the present. "Um." I swallow the lump in my throat, releasing a sigh. "Leo passed away, Nate, over three years ago."

I should have realized he didn't know. How would he? He was adopted by a family in Florida well before Leo's passing. It's so strange to be with someone who, until just now, thought of Leo as a living, breathing person.

"No! Really? What happened?" His face is one of shock.

379

"I know. It's a lot, and I'm sorry." I pull in a breath. "He... overdosed. He had been clean for five years, and he slipped once, and unfortunately, the drug was laced with fentanyl, and it killed him."

I haven't had to deal with this type of encounter for a while now, but after Leo's death, I decided that I was simply going to tell the truth when the topic came up. I'm not ashamed of my husband. He was a good man. Addiction doesn't affect the worst of us. It doesn't discriminate. Sometimes, it pulls down the best of us, and people need to know that. If Leo's story can save even one person or stop one teen from turning to drugs, then his death was not in vain.

Nate raises his arm and clutches the back of his neck. "Alma, I'm so sorry."

"I know." A single tear rolls down my cheek. "Me, too. He would've loved to see you. Who knows? Maybe he can see us. I hope he can, anyway."

"I was looking forward to kicking his ass in a game of one-on-one." Nate chuckles sadly.

"Ooh, if anything would bring him back, it would be a basketball challenge." I smile. "He could never resist competition."

"He thought he was all that."

"That he did." I nod, laughing under my breath.

"You know he wasn't that good."

I grab a tissue and blot beneath my eyes. "Oh, I know." I smile at the memory of Leo on the courts playfully trash-talking the kids like he was an NBA superstar. The teens ate it up and loved the competition, especially since nine times out of ten, they'd kick Leo's butt.

"Remember that game that went on for hours? It was Ollie and Leo against Wiley and me. Every time Wiley and I would get within a point of winning, Leo would raise the ending score so the game would continue, making it go on forever. You finally showed up with pizza to get us to stop playing."

More tears come at the memory, and I wipe my face. "I remember. Gosh, no one ever talks about him. I think it makes them feel uncomfortable, or maybe they don't want to make me sad." I hold up the tissues in my hand. "But it's so nice to remember him."

"He was the best," Nate says.

"He was," I agree. "You know we have a little girl?" I stand and walk over to my desk to retrieve a framed picture of Love. I hand it to Nate. "He never met her, but she looks just like him, doesn't she?"

"Yes, she does," Nate says in awe. "She's beautiful, Alma."

"Thank you." I smile toward the photo in my hand, utter infatuation radiating from me. I'm so in love with this little girl. I put the picture back on my desk. "So tell me about you. What are you up to? What brings you back to Michigan?"

Nate and I chat for over an hour about his life in Florida and reminisce about Leo. It's therapy for my soul. The stress over my growing to-do list has vanished.

"Before you leave, let me take you by June's office. She can set you up with a scholarship to help with college," I tell him.

"It's not necessary, Alma. I qualified for loans. I'll be fine."

"I know you will, but please let us help. The funds are there, and you are more than deserving. I insist. I'm so proud of you, Nate. You don't even know how much your visit has meant to me today. Thank you."

We step out of my office and walk toward June's door.

"You all saved me, Alma—you, Leo, this place."

I take Nate's hand in mine and squeeze. "You saved yourself, Nate. We just gave you the tools."

"June." I tap my knuckles against her door before pushing it open. "This is my dear friend, Nate. He is one of our first success stories. I'd like to get him set up with some scholarships, please, as much as we can."

"Sure thing! Come on in, Nate." June stands from her desk to greet him.

"Make sure to stop by next time you're in town, and the best of luck in college. You will do amazing things, Nate Jackson. I believe in you," I say to Nate before hugging him tight.

"Thank you, Alma, for everything."

I leave Nate in June's capable hands and make my way back to my office to tackle my day, feeling like I can conquer the world.

After just one email into my world conquering, my door swings open. A winded Eduardo swiftly shuts it behind him, a large folder in his grasp. "We need to talk," he whispers, his dark eyes darting from side to side as if he's reassuring himself we're alone. Eduardo has always had a flair for the dramatic. It's one of my favorite things about him.

"Oooh, this sounds serious," I tease.

"It is," he says flatly with no trace of a smile. This gets my attention, and I click out of my email.

Standing, I walk around my desk and motion for him to sit beside me on the couch. "What's going on?"

"Well, it started when I went looking for the invoice for that one bouncy house place that we used last year for the spring carnival. They were really great. Remember? I couldn't find their name or contact info, so I went looking for the original bill. When I was looking through the files, a few things didn't add up. I didn't want to alarm you or bring attention to the situation before I knew for sure, so I've been doing some digging. I had to be very careful so that I wouldn't arouse suspicion and cause a certain someone to cover her tracks. That's why I've been working late this past week, so I could have the building to myself."

I halt his thought process. "Eduardo, spit it out. I'm going crazy here," I say.

He inhales and releases an audible exhale. "Alivia is stealing from us."

"What do you mean?" My brows furrow.

"I mean, she's stolen at minimum two hundred thousand dollars from this place."

"How do you know? That can't be. She's been with us from the very beginning," I protest.

Alivia has been head of finance since we opened. She is a trusted friend and colleague. I'm having a difficult time wrapping my mind around Eduardo's accusations.

"I know, and I'm sorry, but I'm a hundred percent certain. I made sure I had all of the documentation ready before I brought this to you. I have copies of everything. I've only gone back a year and a half, so more than likely, it's probably even more. I don't know when she started."

"Okay, let me see." I nod toward the thick file in his hands.

He takes me through the documentation, and it's blaringly obvious that Alivia has been skimming from the funds with fake invoices for a long time. "I can't believe she did this." I shake my head. "This is a charity, for goodness' sake. She's stealing from kids! Does she have no heart? How did I miss this?"

"This isn't your fault, Alma. You're doing the job of ten people. You can't be everywhere all the time. You trusted Alivia to handle the money and thought she was. You had no reason to investigate. Plus, the way she did it was very crafty. She knew what she was doing."

"Ugh." I slump against the back of the couch. "This makes me sick."

"What should we do?" he asks, looking at me for answers.

"Don't do anything yet. Just act normal. I'm going to consult with legal and see what the next steps should be. I'm thinking I'll get legal and a tech team in here after close tonight to see if they find anything else on her computer or in the rest of the files. I don't want her to think anything is amiss and get rid of any evidence, so be nice today." I hold Eduardo's stare. "Can you do that?"

He waves his hand through the air, rolling his eyes. "I've been nothing but cheerful with that thief for a week. I'll be fine."

"Okay." I nod. "I guess I have some calls to make. Thank you for bringing this to me. I appreciate you, E."

"You know I'd do anything for you and this place." He pats my hand, giving me a sympathetic smile.

I nod. "I do."

Taking the file of evidence to my desk, I pick up the phone to make some calls.

CHAPTER 4

ALMA

*L*ove breathes softly, her arms wrap around her plush princess doll collection, holding firm, even in slumber. She looks like an angel. I smooth down her silky brunette hair and kiss her head.

"I love you, my little Love," I whisper against her head which smells of pineapple and citrus, her new fruity shampoo.

Rolling out of her bed, I quietly exit her bedroom and close the door.

What a horrible day.

I feel so very alone, though I know I am far from it. I have an entire team of people who have become my family. Individuals that would do anything for Love and me. I have more support than many, and I know this. But I don't have my partner, and days like today make that fact all the more blaring. I miss having that person who's mine—my other half, my ride or die.

My soul mate.

I miss facing the challenges of this world with him because everything with him seemed a little less difficult. Now, I must carry the weight of today alone, and it's heavy.

I pick up the trail of toys strewn about the house and toss them into the toy chest. I pour myself a glass of wine and sip it while I load the dishwasher. The kitchen looks like a bomb went off in it, leaving crumbs, flour, and random containers and dishes on every surface. Another thing that hasn't changed in Lee-Anne's rebirth is her housekeeping skills. She's not one to clean up after herself. Horrid visions of her living conditions come to mind as I think back to my impromptu visits to the house where I grew up. *The stuff of nightmares.*

I can't complain, though. She's amazing with Love, and that's all I can ask for. I'm so grateful that I don't have to worry about my daughter when I'm at work. I know she's having a wonderful time with her Gigi. Lee-Anne makes every day an adventure, and Love adores her.

A soft knock sounds at the door before Amos enters, carrying several plastic bags.

"Oh my gosh. What are you doing here?" I ask, overjoyed to see my best friend.

"Your text said you had the worst day ever, and I figured that called for reinforcements." He holds up the bags in his grasp.

I quickly close the distance between us and throw my arms around him. He drops the bags and hugs me back. His embrace and the comfort it brings open the flood gates, and before I realize it's happening, I'm sobbing into his chest.

Amos simply holds me while I cry.

When the tears slow and my breathing steadies, he says, "First things first. What have you eaten today?"

"I had a piece of toast with my coffee this morning," I admit.

He sighs, rubbing my back. "I figured." Stepping back, he retrieves the items he brought and heads into the living room, and I follow. He unloads his items onto the coffee table in front of the couch. "I have grape Faygo pop for you." He hands me a plastic bottle.

"My favorite." I take the beverage from his hand and screw off the cap before taking a long chug. "Ahh." I release an exaggerated sigh. "I already feel more human. Sugar makes everything better."

I sit cross-legged on the rug with the sofa to my back.

"Indeed. But you should eat some actual food today." He's unloading containers of Chinese onto the table. "For dessert, I have both gummy worms and gummy sharks"—he wiggles the plastic bags of candy before me—"and I promise you can have all of the white and red gummy worms." He sits on the floor beside me with the buffet of goodness on the table before us.

"You're the best. Thank you. You don't know how much I needed this." I dig into the veggie lo mein and wrap the noodles around the plastic spork before taking a big bite.

"Do you want me to grab us some real silverware?" he asks.

"No, that's okay. Eating with the plastic spork is half of the fun." I grin. "OMG. This is so good." I shove another huge spork full into my mouth. "I just realized how hungry I am."

"Well, eat up. I got plenty."

The room is quiet save for the slurping of my noodles as I suck them into my mouth at record speed. I finish off the lo mein and lean back against the sofa, my hand splayed across my belly. "Ah-maze-ing." I sigh contently.

"Feel better?" Amos asks.

"So much better. Thank you." I slide my pinky finger through Amos's. Our hands, connected by our smallest fingers, rest between us on the rug. This connection between my oldest friend and me makes the gravity of the day less grave.

"Now that you've eaten, do you want to talk about it?" Amos inquires softly. "Everything okay with Love?"

"Oh, yeah. She's fine, perfect. I barely got to see her today. I only got home in time to tuck her into bed, but she was happy and had a good day with Lee-Anne."

"Your mom fed her appropriately?" Skepticism lines Amos's voice.

"Yeah." I chuckle. "I check in at meal times to make sure she's eating well. Lee-Anne made her some concoction that Love describes as tasting like frogs, so I just had Mom make her a PB&J with apple and carrot slices."

"I wonder what frogs taste like," Amos says in amusement.

"I'm not sure, but Lee-Anne said something about collard greens, kale, and spinach...so the green factor might have made Love think of frogs."

"Gotcha. That makes sense. So I'm guessing it's something with work?"

I nod. "Yeah. You remember Alivia, our head of finance?"

"Yeah."

"Well, apparently, she's been stealing from Lion's Lair for a while, and a lot, like hundreds of thousands of dollars. I'm just sick over it. Most of that money was donated by people wanting to help us make a difference in young people's lives, and she stole it. The crazy thing is that I didn't catch it. Eduardo did." I blow out a breath. "I feel like I'm failing, Amos. I hate feeling this way. I work so hard every day, and I never catch up. There's always more to do. I'm the only parent Love has, and I want to be there for her, more than I am now. Yet these kids at the Lair need me, too. They don't have a Gigi at home snuggling and playing with them, and making a meal full of antioxidants to keep them healthy, even if it tastes like frog. Most of these kids have no one but us. I can't let them down... and I am. I...feel alone, and overwhelmed...and sad." Tears stream down my cheeks once more with the reality of my words.

"Shh." Amos releases his little finger from mine and wraps his arm around my back, pulling me against his side. I rest my head on his shoulder, and he rubs my arm. "Listen to me, Alma. First of all, you are not alone. You have so many people who love you and would do anything for you. You know that."

"I know," I whisper.

"You have to remember that you are only one person. You've always been a perfectionist and given a hundred and ten percent at every task or project put before you. And while I believe you are a superwoman, you still need help. When Love was a baby, you had more support at the Lair, but then Bill moved and Crystal left for that other job, and you didn't replace them, right?"

"No," I admit.

"So your two managers left, and you took on both of their responsibilities, plus Leo's. Right?"

"Yeah."

"And if that wasn't enough, the Lair has grown. You serve more children than you did four years ago. So there's more work and fewer people. First and foremost, you need to hire more staff and delegate the responsibilities."

"Maybe you're right."

"I am right." Amos sounds amused. "If you don't, you're going to burn out, and then you won't be helping anyone. Plus, if you have the staff you need, you'll be able to go back to the tutoring and working with the kids, which is your passion."

"That's true."

"I know you think that no one will do it as well as you can, but I promise you there are really good-hearted and qualified people out there, and we'll find them," he says.

"We'll?" I ask.

"Yeah, I'm going to come work with you."

"What? No. You have a great job, Amos. I can't ask you to give that up for me."

"Let's clarify that with I have a well-paying job, but it's not a great job. In fact, it's boring and tedious. I've been thinking about this for a while actually. I do have degrees in business and finance, after all. I can help you invest and streamline your funds so you can continue all of the wonderful work you do there. Plus, you're a teacher, Alma, and you're running a corporation, basically by yourself. You're doing an incredible job at it but let me help. This is what I've been trained for. I can tighten up your business model, and you can get back to teaching, and we'll both be doing what we love. Quitting my current job and working with you isn't a sacrifice. It's a blessing."

I think about Amos's words. "I would love to be able to work with the kids again in the study room."

"Exactly, and all the other stuff sounds pretty good, too. Right?" There's a playfulness in Amos's voice, and it makes me smile.

"Yeah," I agree.

"So?"

Raising my head from his shoulders, I turn to face him. "Amos Joseph Davis, my one and only Cookie for the past twenty years, will you be my business partner?"

He extends his hand and shakes mine, wearing a wide smile on his face. "Mutt, I'd love to."

I let out a squeal and throw my arms around his neck. He hugs me, laughing against my neck. "You're going to be okay. It's going to be good."

"It's going to be great!" I say. "This calls for the special candy." I grab the bag of blue gummy sharks from the table.

When Amos and I were kids, we were rarely able to find stores that carried these sharks, so it was always a cause for huge celebration when we did. Amos came across a store in downtown Ann Arbor that had them our first month of college, and since then, we have them quite often. Yet they still have a nostalgic quality to them that reminds me of being a kid and sneaking away with my best friend to consume the blue sugary goodness.

I pull two sharks from the bag and hand one to Amos. "To our new partnership," I say, smushing the shark in my grasp against the one in his in an odd gummy toast.

"Cheers," he says, and we both plop the candies into our mouths.

When he swallowed the shark, Amos says, "So this Alivia whore…do you need help with that situation?"

I shake my head. "No, the legal team is taking care of it. She won't be back tomorrow or ever."

"Oh, good. I'll give my notice tomorrow at work, and we'll go from there," he says.

"Yay! Okay. Do you want to stick around for a bit? We could watch *Friends*."

Amos stands. "Sure. Set it up. Let me just clean up some of this first." He starts tossing the empty containers into one of the plastic bags and takes everything into the kitchen. "There's a whole untouched meal in here. I'm putting it in the refrigerator. Make sure to take it to work tomorrow for lunch," he calls from the kitchen.

"Okay," I agree, remote in hand as I pull up a *Friends* episode.

When Amos returns to the living room, I feel like a completely different person from the one I was when he arrived here tonight. As always, Amos knew just what I needed.

He plops down on the couch beside me. "Thank you for saving me, over and over, for two decades now. I don't know what I'd do without you," I tell him in all seriousness.

"Same," he says before kissing the top of my head. "Same."

CHAPTER 5

AMOS

"You took a lunch today, right?" I ask Jen, Lion's Lair's greeter. She's a spunky nineteen-year-old with a megawatt smile, whom I've caught working through her lunch several times this week.

In fact, I've noticed most of Alma's staff going above and beyond their work responsibilities and hours since I started on Monday. Alma has a great group of people here. Save for the one bad apple they had, everyone is wonderful. It definitely feels like a family.

"Yes, Boss." Jen puckers her lips. "I actually took a long one. My boyfriend is home on leave. He took me to Olive Garden for lunch. It was delicious." She rubs her belly for effect.

I lean against the front desk, looking down at Jen. The front of the desk is tall, like one would see at a hotel. Jen sits behind it with a workstation at her height. "Well, good. What branch is your boyfriend in, and when did he get home?"

"Just last night. He's in the Navy. He's stationed in Chicago, which isn't that bad. I normally spend weekends with him, but he's been deployed for six months, so it's been a while."

"Last night was the first time you've seen him in six months?" I ask.

"Yeah." She bobs her head. She reminds me of Tinker Bell with her short blond hair and large blue eyes. I know Tinker Bell well, courtesy of Love. That fairy is one of her favorites.

"Well, what are you doing here?" I say with all sincerity. "You should take the afternoon off and start the weekend early."

"I wanted to, but there's just so much going on here, and with *you know...*"

You know has become the official slang around the office when someone refers to Alivia and her thieving ways.

"Oh, it's fine. It's a Friday afternoon. There aren't any more appointments scheduled. Take the rest of the day off. Go spend time with your sailor. I'll man the desk after I finish lunch," I offer.

"Really? What about the people coming in for the self-defense course?"

"I'll direct them to the gym. No worries."

"Are you sure? That would be amazing."

"Absolutely. Go. I'll let Alma know, but you know she won't mind. Have a great weekend."

"Oh my gosh! Thanks!" Jen retrieves her large purse from under the desk and skips for the door, already on her cell.

I shake my head with a smile and grab the bag of food that was delivered a few minutes ago and the original reason for my visit with Jen.

"Knock, knock," I say as I'm entering Alma's office.

She waves me in with a grin, the office phone pressed up to her ear. "Absolutely. Well, hopefully, her mom signs the form and sends it back. I'm making a note to call you on Monday morning, and we'll go from there. Okay. Sounds great, Judy. Thank you so much."

"Who was that?" I ask as Alma hangs up the phone.

"A social worker at one of the local schools. She has a teen girl she needs help with. The girl's going through a hard time, cutting, a possible eating disorder, bad grades...the works. We think there's definitely some emotional trauma, possibly abuse involved. We've just had a difficult time getting in touch with a parent. I might have to make a home visit next week. Sounds like this sweet girl is going to need a village."

"Then she definitely needs access to this place." I set the bag of food down on the coffee table in front of the office sofa. "I'm so impressed with everyone here, Alma. All of your employees are great and have big hearts."

"I agree." She stands and walks around her desk. She's wearing a formfitting cream pencil skirt with a white top. The auburn highlights are brighter now that it's almost summer, and the sun visits more often. Her hair bounces against her tanned arms as she closes the distance between us. She's elegant, and sexy, and utterly beautiful. "What did you bring me?" Her voice rises an octave, her interest piqued, as it always is when good food is involved.

I clear my throat. "Sushi." I start pulling out containers.

"Uh, I love you. I literally had a dream about sushi last night. I've been craving it all day." She sits on the couch and opens up a container. "It was so weird. In my dream, I was in a minivan with my grandma and a whole bunch of siblings. I don't remember even meeting my grandma. She died when I was young, leaving us the house, which is why I moved in next to you in the first place, and obviously, I don't have any siblings." She picks up a roll of sushi. "But in the dream, I did, and we drove around for hours and hours looking for sushi. Finally, we found a food court that said it sold sushi, but it was like this maze, and the deeper I got into this food court maze, the more worried I got, afraid that I'd never find the sushi." She shrugs and plops the rolled rice into her mouth. "It was strange."

I take a seat beside Alma. "Did you ever get to find it, the sushi?" I ask with a chuckle.

"No." She shakes her head. "I spent the whole night searching for it and never found it. So, I'm serious when I say I woke up craving the hell out of it." She laughs.

"I've been craving it, too. Not to that extent." I grin. "But I thought it sounded good. We haven't had it in a while. Oh, by the way, I sent Jen home. Did you know her boyfriend just got back from deployment?"

"Bobby's back? No, I didn't know. Well, that's great. She should've taken the day off today." Alma puts another sushi roll in her mouth.

"I thought the same thing, but she said that she didn't want to with *you know* going on."

Alma lets out a grunt. "I'm so sick of *you know*. I just wish she'd go to jail already. She deserves to be in jail."

"She will, but it takes time," I reassure her.

"I love these ones with this crunch stuff on top and that kind of spicy orange sauce drizzled on it. I think they're called tiger rolls, right?" Alma asks.

"I think so. Yeah, they're really good."

"This weekend is going to be beautiful. I'm taking Love to the zoo tomorrow if you want to come, then we can continue our *Vampire Diaries* marathon when she's in bed. You haven't voiced whether you're team Damon or team Stefan, and I'm going to need you to do that."

"I'd love to go to the zoo, and I suppose I can stay for your vampire show. But don't you find the whole, '*Dear Diary, today I wanted to suck the blood of a hot girl who looks like another hot girl from a hundred and fifty years ago, but I didn't*,' stuff cheesy and weird?" I chuckle.

"Stop." Alma tosses a napkin at me. "The diary entries aren't that bad."

"They basically are."

"Maybe but Quinn says that the whole *Dear Diary* part of the show fizzles out after the first season. Plus, if Lee-Anne and my dad had been normal parents, and prescribed to social norms, like TV and cable, then you would've been watching it with me when it first aired anyway. So, thanks to Netflix, this is an experience that we don't have to miss out on."

"We are very fortunate," I deadpan. "I have to say, I'm surprised that you're on Stefan's team...and equally surprised that I'm discussing the merits of two fictional vampires." I scoff. "Anyway, I thought you'd go for Damon. He's the bad one, which is kind of how Leo started out. Plus, the actor who plays Damon has dark hair and blue eyes, just like Leo. I just figured he'd be your type."

I've always kept my opinions about Alma's husband to myself. He wasn't who I thought Alma would've been interested in, at least in the beginning. He changed and grew up and was an awesome person most of the time I knew him. But initially, I had my reservations.

Alma is quiet for a moment. "Oh my gosh. You're right. Why am I not team Damon?" She sounds concerned.

"Alma, I'm kidding. You can't compare Leo to a TV vampire. It's not the same. It doesn't mean anything," I remind her.

She shakes her head as if clearing her thoughts. "You're right. It doesn't. It just caught me off guard. I guess I like Stefan's character because he's good and he's not selfish, and he wants the best for everyone. Plus, he is *very cute*." She puts emphasis on the last two words. "What are you doing tonight? We could do dinner with Love and Lee-Anne and hang out after Love's bedtime."

I raise a brow. "By hang out, you mean watch the show?"

"I mean, if you insist, I could be game for that." She shrugs, a sly grin on her face.

"Sure."

"Yay! Okay, well, I'm going to get back to work. I still have a lot of things that I want to finish before I leave."

I catch her stare in mine. "Remember we spoke of delegating? Bruce and Holly were hired for a reason. They were your top two choices after the interviews, and you got them. They're talented and capable."

"Agreed, and I've handed off a lot of the work. I'm simply trying to finish up things I've already started. It would just take more time to go over everything that I've previously done to get them up to speed than to finish it myself." She pauses when she takes in my look of skepticism. "Stop." She chuckles. "I am delegating. The pile of files on my desk is a quarter of what it used to be. I swear. And I've left Bruce in charge of this weekend's activities here, and I'm not even going to check in on him."

"Alright. I'm just looking out for you."

She tosses the empty containers into the trash. "I know. You always are, and I love you for it."

Reaching her office door, I open it to leave before turning to say, "I'm going to grab my laptop and be at the front desk if you need me."

"Why? Oh yeah, Jen. Got it." She waves her hand in front of her and nods. "Okay. I'll see you in a bit."

Before I've closed the door, she's already typing away feverishly against her keyboard with a look of determination on her face. She may have gone to college for a teaching degree, but she makes one hell of a CEO.

* * *

"HEY, MAN," Jude Martinez, an Ann Arbor police officer, greets me.

I pull my eyes away from the computer screen and stand from the desk. Walking around to the front lobby, I shake Jude's hand.

"Everything's all set up for you. A few women are here already."

"Sweet. You gonna help me out again today? Jane can't make it." he says of his partner, a fiery police officer, who normally helps instruct these classes.

"Yeah, sure. Jen went home early today. So, I'll just hang up here until everyone arrives, then quickly change, and meet you in there. How many are signed up today?"

"Fifty."

"Great turn-out."

"Yeah." He nods. "I'm so grateful to have the larger space here. We can run these bigger classes."

Jude heads off toward the gym, and as women start to steadily trickle in, I direct them to the class space.

Alma volunteered the Lair's gym space to Jude a couple of months ago. He runs these free self-defense courses for women throughout the city. They're quite popular and always have a waitlist.

Jude's a cool guy. He says he was raised by women—his sisters, mom, and grandmother—and wants to give back and empower women with the skills needed to defend themselves. He hasn't directly spoken about it, but I get the feeling that one of his sisters went through a traumatic experience involving a man and unwanted contact.

When most of the women have arrived, I put a sign on the front desk with an arrow pointing toward the gym, then change into a pair of track pants and a T-shirt.

I run into Alma as I'm exiting the locker room.

She eyes my attire. "Shooting some hoops?"

"No, Jude's here. I'm going to help him with the class."

Her eyes light up. "Oh, I forgot that was today. I want to go."

"Go change. It's just starting."

Alma and I keep athletic clothes on hand in case we have the time to play with the kids. Shooting some hoops or hitting around a volleyball with the teens is an incredible stress reliever. There's so much that goes into keeping this place running. Sometimes, it's nice to hang out with the kids to keep it all in perspective.

"Alright, I think I will." She raises her brows. "But just so you know, I'm going to kick your ass in there." She shoots me a wink.

"Oh, we'll see," I tease.

"Well, it wouldn't be a very good self-defense class if you don't let me win."

I shake my head with a laugh. "True. I'll see you in there."

CHAPTER 6

ALMA

"*B*ring Gigi another yellow one, baby," Lee-Anne says to Love, holding a bunch of freshly picked dandelions in her hand. She lies next to me on a large blanket.

Love smiles big and runs off into the plush grass. The bright green lawn, in desperate need of a mow, reaches past her ankles. She giggles as it tickles her skin in search of her favorite flower.

I make sure the front yard's landscaping is attended to with regularity, but the backyard is left a little wild so the flowers can grow. Dandelions have always been one of my favorites. I know they're technically weeds, but I think they're too special to be classified as such. To me, they're strong and resilient. In their short life, they bloom a happy yellow and then morph into a fluffy white wishing wand. I spent many hours throughout the summers of my life making wishes, and so much of what I've always wanted has come true.

I lean back on my hands with my face toward the sky, letting the sun's warm rays kiss my skin. I really should start using sunscreen, but I inherited my mother's olive Venezuelan skin tone, and it loves the sun. Lee-Anne hasn't worn an ounce of SPF her entire life, and her skin still looks great, so I'm not too worried about it.

Love returns with another flower and tosses it to my mom before she runs off again.

"I'm going to use these for dinner," Lee-Anne says.

"Of course you are." I chuckle.

"They're great in salads and have astounding health benefits. You should give them a try," she urges.

"I will."

She sighs. "I failed you. I know that, Alma. I was a horrible mother."

"Mom, it's okay. I said I'll try the salad."

She shakes her head. "No, it's not just the fact that your diet is alarming, and sugar is one of your main food groups. It's everything that I did and didn't do. I didn't teach you anything. I didn't guide you or protect you. I was so selfish. Now that Alman is gone, I realize that. I had no one, yet you took me in. You bought me a condo. You provide everything I need, and I don't deserve any of it. I gave you nothing."

I turn toward her, grabbing her hand. "It's okay, Mom. We've been over all of this. It's water under the bridge. I've forgiven you, and we've moved on. You don't have to worry about the past."

"You're such a wonderful mother, Almalee. You're successful, kind, and driven—and you've always been that way. I don't understand how you're so good when your upbringing was so bad."

"It wasn't bad, Mom. Leo's was bad. You never harmed me.

You weren't always present, but maybe that's good. You and Dad weren't in a great place. So, perhaps it helped that you were absent a lot, and maybe I am who I am because of my upbringing. Plus, I wasn't alone. I had Amos." I squeeze her hand. "I'm sorry you lost Dad, but I'm so grateful to have you now. And Love is the luckiest little girl to have a Gigi who loves her as much as you do."

"How could I not? She is perfect."

"She is," I agree.

"Momma! A wish!" Love charges toward me with a fluffy white dandelion in her hand.

"Yay! You found a wish." She plops down in my lap.

"For you." She hands me the wishing wand.

"For me? Oh goodness." I hold the flower in front of my face. "I need to make this a good one." I close my eyes, think of something I want, open my eyes, and blow until all of the willowy seedlings are dancing through the air.

Love giggles. "Good one," she says, imitating what I always say to her when she blows the seeds off a dandelion.

"It was a good one." I nuzzle into her neck and pepper kisses up her cheek. "See if you can find two more so you and Gigi can make a wish."

"Okay!" she cheers before hopping off my lap and running through the grass.

"Amos used to always bring you *wishing wands*." Lee-Anne smiles at the memory.

"Yeah, he did. He knew I loved them."

"That boy would do anything for you, still will."

"Yeah, he's the best."

"You know he loves you," Lee-Anne says, eyeing me to assess my reaction.

"I know. I love him, too."

"No, like *loves* you, Almalee."

I press my lips together in a line and squint in my mother's direction. "If you're suggesting he loves me more than a friend, you're wrong. We're the best of friends, Mom, and have been for twenty years. We have a relationship that's deeper than most, but it's true friendship. That's all."

Lee-Anne shakes her head. "I admit, I don't know a lot. But I know what I know, and that man is in love with you, always has been since you two were young. You may not be ready to see it, but one day, you will. He's a great person, and you'd be lucky to have him. You're too young to be alone for the rest of your life. I had a lifetime with my soul mate, and I'm content being a Gigi and a Mom from here on out. I don't want or need another romantic love. But you, my dear...you do."

"Mom," I protest, her name coming out louder than I anticipated. "Stop. It's not like that. Besides, I've already met and married my soul mate."

"Who's to say that you only get one?" she questions as Love runs up with two more wishing wands and her daddy's smile.

* * *

MY VAMPIRE CRUSH is on the big screen in front of me, wooing his human high school love interest, and I can't even focus. All I can think about is my mother's words from earlier today. Everything feels off. Amos's arm around my shoulder is heavier than normal. I'm aware of his every movement. His chest rises and falls beside me, and as he breathes normally, my lungs ache for air.

I can't think straight or breathe correctly with him so close to me. We're hanging out as we always do, yet it's all different now. Contrasting thoughts duel in my mind. Disbelief and realization battle, and I'm not sure which is stronger.

Lee-Anne is wrong. She has to be. Why did she have to plant those seeds? Now everything feels off, just different.

Amos and I have always been close. He was my everything

when I had nothing. My protector when I was alone. Nothing has changed. When I lost Leo, Amos was there to pick me up. He took care of me as he always has. That is what we do, Cookie and Mutt. We make sure the other is okay—always.

I sit up and scoot away from Amos. Grabbing the remote, I pause the TV and turn to face him.

"Are you okay?" He eyes me curiously.

"When Leo died, you left your job and got another in Ann Arbor. Why?" I ask.

Amos looks confused. "It was a better job," he answers slowly. "Paid more."

"You left your previous job because of me, to be closer to me."

He shrugs. "Yeah, that was a factor, but I was happy to do it, Alma. You were alone and going through a tough time. Plus, the job was better anyway, so it made sense. Is there anything wrong with that?"

"I don't know." I shake my head.

"Alma." Amos reaches for my hand. I cross my arms over my chest and avoid the connection. "What's going on?"

"Why haven't you dated anyone since you moved back to Ann Arbor? You haven't been on a date in over four years."

"So?" Amos's response is short, but his stare lingers on my face.

"You're over here every night. And now we work together. We're together all day long."

"Yeah?" he says slowly. "What's this about?"

"How are you going to find the person you're going to marry if you're always with me?" My voice comes out more shrieky than planned. "I can't be the reason you're alone."

"I'm not alone, though. I have you and Love…and your mother, friends, people at work. It's fine, Alma. I'm happy," he answers.

"It's not enough." I shake my head. "You need more. You're here every night."

"You invited me here." The tone of his voice is deeper. "If you don't want me here, then don't ask me to come over."

"It's not that I don't want you here." I blow out a breath. "I'm not making sense. I don't know what I'm trying to say. I'm sorry. Forget it."

"I don't want to forget it, Alma. Something is obviously bothering you, and I want to know what it is."

I tilt my head to the side. "I don't even know what it is," I say, pursing my lips. "It's just been a weird day. Let's call it a night. Okay?"

Amos nods. "You'd tell me if something was bothering you?"

"Of course," I answer, not certain if I even believe my own words.

Amos puts on his shoes and turns off the television. I follow him as he walks to the front door. Before he leaves, he twists to face me. I hold out my pinky finger, and he grabs it with his.

"We're fine, right?" I ask.

He leans down until his forehead is touching mine. "Always."

CHAPTER 7

ALMA

"They say that malls are dying in America. Do you think that's true?" Cat asks, her heels clicking against the tiled floor as we stroll by the stores. We've been perusing the shops in this place for a couple of hours now. I have no idea how she manages to walk in such high heels for so long.

It's been wonderful to catch up with her. She's the only one from Leo's family I have a real relationship with, and I'm grateful for her. She's such an important part of my life. It's been months since the two of us have been able to hang out. Now that things are calmer at work, and I've hired more help and Amos, I can finally relax—a little, at least.

"I'm not sure. I mean, it makes sense since online shopping is so popular. Brick-and-mortar stores seem like a dying breed," I reply. "I kind of lost interest in the mall when Borders shut down. Do you remember that store? It was my favorite."

"No, I don't. What did they sell?"

"Books."

"Oh. Well, I'm more of a magazine type of girl. Ooh, let's go in here." Cat takes my arm and leads me into a store that smacks me in the face with perfume as we enter. It reeks of oak and spice. I'd have a constant headache if I worked here. "See this shirt?" She runs the fabric between her finger and thumb. "Gorgeous, no? But feel it. The fabric is cheap and scratchy. I would never buy this item. Yet had I only the visual online, I might. One can't clothes shop on a screen. It's not the same."

"It's not, but it's easier," I offer.

"Easy isn't better, Alma." We step out of the foul-smelling scratchy-shirt store and continue our window shopping. "Plus, you never know what you're going to find in a mall. You may want a silk shirt or a phone case or a Christmas ornament or shoes, and it's all here." She grabs my arm, and we halt. "I mean, look at that." She motions toward a kiosk. "They have neon hair extensions. In the mall, someone could walk by that and think, 'Omg. I've always wanted bright green hair extensions, and I never realized until seeing them here just now.' They wouldn't have known to search for those online. The mall surprises you with things you didn't even know you needed."

"That's true." I laugh. "You want to grab a coffee?"

"Yes, I do," Cat agrees. "See, you can't get fresh Starbucks from your sofa as you online shop."

"Another valid point," I say.

"Moscow has incredible and beautiful malls," Cat says, her voice almost dreamy. "One of my favorites is the Aviapark. It has more than five hundred stores on many levels, tons of eateries, and a cinema. In the center of the building is a huge pillar aquarium with the most beautiful fish. The aquarium is twenty-four meters tall, or almost eighty feet in American terms." She winks. "It's big."

"Compared to that, this mall is a joke." I chuckle. Our local mall isn't anything special.

"Yeah, it's quite puny, but it's better than nothing," Cat says before ordering her espresso.

I get a venti skinny chai latte which has been my go-to drink from Starbucks since college and sit beside Cat on one of the sofas around the Starbucks booth.

"Tell me again of your family in Moscow. I know we've talked about it before, but last time, a lot of wine was involved, so some of the details are fuzzy. Your mother is from Italy, and your dad is from Russia?"

"Yes," Cat says. "My mother's family lived in Naples. My grandparents were very poor, and my mother grew up in the slums of Naples. It was a very dangerous place with lots of crime and gangs. The buildings are actually being torn down now because they got so bad. My mother was a waitress at a small place in a nicer part of the city, and that's where she met my father when he was there on business. It was love at first sight, as they say. They married and moved to Moscow, taking my grandparents with them. My grandparents and mother run an Italian restaurant there. They want for nothing and are happy. My father is very successful with his business."

"You started modeling in Moscow?" I ask.

"Yes. An agent recruited me when I was serving him at the restaurant. Waitressing is a lucky profession in my family." She smiles.

"Yeah, I guess so. And you met Stephen at a show?"

She nods. "Yes, in Prague. I thought it was love at first sight. You know? Like my parents had. But now I'm not so sure."

Stephen never comes around, and Cat rarely speaks of him. It wasn't much different when Leo was alive, either. I've never really understood their relationship, to be honest. "Marriage is hard, Cat. It takes work," I say, trying to be supportive though I don't particularly think too highly of my brother-in-law.

"It's more than that, I think. We don't have what my parents or grandparents have or what you and Leo had. There was an initial infatuation, but I don't think it was love. I was so caught up in the excitement of it all at the time. You know? My common sense was clouded by infatuation. Stephen is gorgeous, and he was this successful American businessman. It was all so thrilling at the time, and I fell under the illusion of love. But Stephen is too much like his father. I don't think he's truly capable of real love."

"I'm sorry, Cat." And I am. As great as my indifference is toward Stephen, I realize that Cat loved him at some point. She's a wonderful person, so if she loved him, there must have been a reason.

She waves her hand like it's of no importance. "It's fine. I've known for a long time, years really, but I'm so stubborn and wanted to make it work. I don't want to feel like a failure."

"You're not, and no one would think you are. Maybe Stephen wasn't meant to be your forever. Perhaps you had to experience this chapter of your life to prepare you for the next?" My mouth tilts up in a sympathetic smile.

"That's a good way to look at the world, Ms. Alma." She grabs my hand and squeezes gently before releasing.

We sit in silence for a few minutes and observe as the mall-goers pass by, people watching at its finest. My stomach grumbles, reminding me that I'm hungry.

"I bet your mother's restaurant serves amazing food," I say, wishing I were there at this very moment.

"The best." Cat chuckles and stands from the sofa. "Let's get you some food."

"I am a little hungry," I admit, quirking an eyebrow up. "Anything close to your family's Italian food nearby?"

Cat scoffs. "There's not similar food anywhere in this state.

There are mall pretzels, though." She nods toward the pretzel place down the corridor from us.

"I guess that will have to do." I sigh.

"You would love Moscow. You and Love should come home with me and visit my family someday," Cat offers.

"That would be incredible. I love traveling, and I'd love to meet your family. Do you think you'll ever move back?"

Cat tosses her empty espresso cup in the trash. "I'm not sure. I guess we'll see where this next chapter of my life takes me." She smiles.

I scan the area as we make our way toward the pretzel place. I wonder if we're the subject of anyone's people watching. The two of us are quite a pair—me in my leggings, T-shirt, and Converse, and Cat in her designer dress and heels. My hair is tossed up into a messy bun while Cat's is long, shiny, and perfectly straight. She seriously doesn't have a hair out of place. She's as beautiful on the outside as she is on the inside and, in my opinion, deserves more than Stephen. She's worthy of epic love, and I hope she gets it.

"Are you thinking about making any changes with Stephen in the near future?" I wonder.

"I haven't made up my mind," she responds thoughtfully.

"I get that."

Cat's not the type of person to jump into anything without thinking over every aspect of her decision.

"Tell me, Alma," Cat says. "What's the next chapter of your life going to look like?"

I shrug. "I have no idea."

"I hope there will be another great love for you." She presses her lips in a line.

"Well, that seems to be the consensus as of late. Everyone wants me to move on, but I just want Leo back." Emotion swells within my throat, and I swallow. "I know that's never going to happen, but by moving on, it's like closing the door to that chapter of my life, and I don't want to. I wasn't ready for Leo and my chapter to be over, and I don't know if I ever will be. I'd rather have him in memory than not at all."

Cat halts and turns to face me. "You'll always have him in your heart and memories, Alma. Moving on won't change that. You can visit him in your dreams every night until your last breath. But you only get one life, and you deserve the best that it has to offer."

"So do you, Cat."

She nods. "I can't disagree with you there."

CHAPTER 8

AMOS

I often think about when I fell in love with Alma, and the honest truth is that I've always loved her. There isn't a memory of Alma in my mind that isn't shrouded in adoration.

From the first moment I saw her, something drew me in. We were young, only seven. She was sitting on the ground covered in mud and playing in the dirt like she wouldn't rather be anywhere else. Her mother was screeching out the lyrics to some Spanish song from the kitchen window. There were boxes on her porch and debris in her yard. Yet amidst all the chaos that surrounded her, she was mesmerizing. I didn't know what I was feeling, but I knew I needed her in my life.

She's been a constant in my life from that moment on. We've shared everything. Every goal. Every desire. Every accomplishment. Every fear. She was by my side through it all.

There isn't anything I wouldn't do for her, and I know she'd do anything for me.

Somewhere through the years, our relationship became so cherished that neither of us dared to jeopardize the status quo. There's been an attraction on both of our parts. I've felt it from her as she's felt it from me. Yet we ignored it because romantic relationships fail, and our friendship was never worth the gamble.

Alma is and always has been my soul mate.

I loved her then. I love her now. I'll love her forever.

There was a time when I thought our souls were destined for eternal friendship and nothing more, and I was okay with that because, above all, I want her to be happy. And she was. She was thrilled with her life and her marriage.

A hidden part of my soul crumbled when she married. The pain was so raw that I thought it would destroy me, and I couldn't confide in the one person I always had. I needed Alma more than ever, but she was no longer mine.

Fake smiles and forced conversations were the new normal for months. I buried the ache and regret. There were so many what-ifs.

What if I had just told her that we were meant to be together? Kissed her? Held her? Any action on my part before him could've prevented it all. I was so terrified to lose her that I did nothing and ended up losing her anyway.

Time and perspective heal—at least, for me, it did. I saw her smiles and true happiness and couldn't wish anything else for her. I reminded myself that I still had Alma in all of the ways I always had. She was my best friend, and she always would be. Our souls would forever be bonded in that way, and that was enough.

I would take away her loss and pain if I had the power to do so. I wish she had the father of her child here with her now, I truly do. I would give her the world if I could, and he was her everything. Yet he's gone.

But I'm here, and I love her and her daughter.

After Leo's death, I didn't anticipate this. As much as I've always loved Alma, I could only hurt for her loss and be here to support her. There were no ulterior motives or hidden agendas. There was only friendship. I was fulfilled being Uncle Cookie to Love and best friend to Alma.

Something is changing, though. I can't put my finger on it, but I can feel it around me. The air between us is unfamiliar. It's charged with a glimmer of something resembling a future, different than the one previously laid out for us.

If I'm not mistaken, this change has been brewing for a while now. I can't ignore it, not this time. Perhaps enough time has passed, and Alma's heart is starting to open again. If history has taught me anything, it's that everything can change in the briefest of seconds, and I can't risk losing her again.

CHAPTER 9

ALMA

"*A*wesome, two blues," I say with excitement, staring down at the card that Amos just picked up. "Good card, Cookie!"

Love claps her hands and giggles. She loves playing Candy Land, and we always make a big deal when we pick up a card with double colors.

"Yes." Amos cheers and moves his little boy playing piece two blue spaces up on the board.

"I have kale smoothies," Lee-Anne sing-songs from the kitchen, carrying in glasses of creamy green liquid. She sets them down on the table next to the root beer floats that I made everyone before we started the game.

Can't blame her for trying. "Thanks, Mom."

"Thanks, Gigi," Love says, and Quinn and Amos both offer their gratitude as well.

I take a quick swig of the green stuff and wash it down with a gulp of root beer. Satisfied, my mom retreats from the table.

"Okay, your turn, Quinn," I say.

Quinn picks up a card. "Oh, I got Queen Frostine!" she says and wiggles triumphantly in her chair. Queen Frostine is the coolest card and very close to the end of the path on the board, almost always ensuring a win.

"Oh, that's Love's card," I tell her.

"What do you mean?" She furrows her brows.

"Queen Frostine is Love's favorite, so whoever draws her card gives it to Love so she can visit her. Queen Frostine reminds us of Elsa, and Love adores Elsa, right, Love Dove?" I smile wide toward my daughter who is looking at Quinn expectantly with a big smile on her face.

Quinn frowns. "But that's not how the game is played."

"I know. We play it a little differently. We cheer when we get our favorite colors or doubles, and we visit our favorite people. Love always visits Queen Frostine and Princess Lolly while I visit Gramma Nut and Jolly, but we never visit Lord Licorice." I say the last name in a spooky voice. "Do we, Love?"

"No, he's mean." She pouts out her lips.

I nod in agreement. "Yep, Lord Licorice is mean so we don't visit him," I say matter of factly with a shrug.

"But Queen Frostine is near the end, so whoever gets her will most likely win," Quinn argues with a whine.

"Yeah, but that's okay. We all get to visit King Kandy at the end. The King likes to throw a big party when all the kids get there, and everyone gets to eat lots of candy."

"He's nice," Love agrees with a nod, her long brunette piggy tails bouncing a happy dance against her shoulders.

"Alma, you have to teach your daughter how to lose. It's not healthy for someone to win all of the time. Game nights with my family were cutthroat, and my older sisters never took it easy on me, but it made me stronger," Quinn protests.

"Quinn, give the three-year-old the princess card." Amos scoffs with a shake of his head.

Quinn looks from me to Amos, clutching the card in her hand. "You all are serious?"

We nod, our lips pressed in a line.

"Ugh." She groans before plastering on a fake smile and handing the card to Love. "Here's Queen Frostine."

Love takes the card from Quinn's hand and skips her character piece over the colorful path until she reaches Queen Frostine's spot.

"Make sure you ask her what she's going to wear to King Kandy's party," I say to Love. "Oh, and ask her what her favorite candy is. Remember last time she said gummy bears, but that other time she said chocolate? See what she thinks today."

"Okay!" Love grins and moves her character pawn in front of the queen. She starts talking rapidly under her breath.

"Sorry, Quinn. Love and the queen are besties. But you can go again if you want." I nod toward the stack of cards.

Quinn picks up a card. "Well, seeing that I didn't get to move, I'd hope so." She looks at the card. "Oh, I got Gramma Nut."

I hold out my hand, palm up.

"Really?" she snaps.

"Well, I have to ask her what she's making for the king's party because I don't want to bring the same candy. That'd just be embarrassing." I pucker my lips and raise my eyebrows.

Amos laughs, and Quinn smacks the card down in my hand.

Quinn picks up another card. "I got a red." She looks around the table. "Does anyone own reds?"

"Nope," I say cheerily. "That's all you. Red is one of our least favorite colors."

"Great," Quinn mumbles and moves her pawn forward a

space. "I don't know if I like game night with the Harding girls."

"What are you talking about?" I gasp in mock protest. "We throw a party at the end, and there will be candy."

"Real candy?" Quinn squints, wearing a frown.

"Of course." I smile sweetly.

"Fine," Quinn mumbles.

The four of us move our playing pieces back and forth on the multicolored path, depending on which character we're visiting while Lee-Anne catches up on her latest binge on Netflix. She's enjoying watching a lifetime of shows that she missed out on as well. At least once a day, she tells me how incredible TV is.

Most days, I look around at my support system, and I feel so blessed. I'm so thankful to have my mother for the first time in my life. I'm grateful that Amos and I are still inseparable and that Quinn and I have stayed in touch after college. Love has so many people who adore her, and I couldn't wish for anything more.

Eventually, all of us make it to King Kandy's party at the end of the Candy Lane. Standing from the table, I grab the basket of treats from the top of the refrigerator and set it on the table.

"Your choice of sweets for the party," I say.

Love stands up on the chair, leans over the table, and pulls a container of mini M&M's from the basket. She loves all things miniature. I grab a bag of my trusty gummy worms.

Quinn holds up a package of seaweed crisps. "Why are these in here?"

"My mom." I chuckle. "She's always trying to trick us into eating her food."

Quinn exchanges the seaweed for a Twix bar while Love and Amos negotiate some trades with her chocolate pieces and his gummy bears.

"Lovie, do you want to take the basket to Gigi to see if she'd like a movie snack?" I ask.

Love nods and bolts into the living room with the goody basket in hand.

Quinn takes a bite of her candy bar. "I think I'm going to have to eat my Twix and run. I have a presentation to do for the staff meeting on Monday, and you know how much technology hates me."

Quinn has moved up in the fashion world over the past few years. She started as a personal shopper and glorified fitting room attendant, and now she's the department store manager.

"No worries. I'm glad you could come over," I say.

We chat for a few minutes before Quinn heads out. Amos helps me clear the table, and he starts loading the dishwasher. I wipe the counter with a rag. It's littered with vegetable fragments from Lee-Anne's kale smoothie preparation. The wall behind the blender is splattered with green.

"How'd you get stuff on the wall, Mom?" I call out but am met with no response. The TV is now blaring a song from *Tangled*, a new movie that we've recently added to our rotation. In all honesty, it's my personal favorite princess movie to date. Love and I adore Max, the horse in the movie. "It's like she didn't even put the top on the blender," I say to Amos.

"Some things never change." He chuckles.

After the kitchen is presentable once more, I pick Love up from the sofa, despite her protests, and take her upstairs for a bath. After she's squeaky clean, we brush teeth, get into our jammies, climb into Love's bed, read books, and finally lie down. I hold her in the darkness as stars from her night-light dance on the ceiling.

"One more story, Momma." she requests, her little voice soft and tired.

"Which one?"

"A Daddy one. Your Moana day," she urges, referring to our

419

wedding. Moana, another favorite Disney princess, lives on an island much like Hawaii, so I'm sure Love is picturing a scene straight from the movie.

"Okay, well, Daddy and I waited until Mommy was all finished with school to get married. When I graduated, Daddy was so happy, and he wanted to spend forever with Mommy. We were in love and didn't want to wait to get married, so we flew to Hawaii."

"You were pwincess?" Love asks.

"I was. I had a beautiful dress."

"Daddy was pwince," she adds. The fact that Leo and I were royalty is her favorite part of this story.

"He was. He was the most handsome prince in the whole world, and I was the happiest princess. We stood on the beach and promised to love each other forever and ever."

"And then you swam in your dwess?"

I hug her tight. "I did, and it was magical."

"I miss Daddy." She repeats this sentiment often, and it breaks my heart. It's so unfair that she didn't even get a chance to know him.

"I do too, sweetie. Everyday. But he's our angel, right? He's always watching out for us and protecting us, and even though he can't tell you himself—he loves you from Heaven. He loves you so much."

"Okay." She nods against my chest.

Her breaths even out as I continue to hold her against me. I run my fingers through her soft hair and close my eyes. I picture Leo in my mind. His hair, the exact shade as Love, and his eyes, too, a bright sky blue. Thanks to his precious mini in my arms, I'll never forget his hair, eyes, or smile. I know it's crazy, but I swear she's starting to laugh like him.

I imagine a time that Leo and I were together, and I go over every detail in my mind—what he looked like, smelled like, felt like, and what he said, how he sounded, all of it. I think of as many details as possible, and then I hold on to them as tightly as I can.

After Leo's death, every detail was so clear, so real that I felt like I was there, with him, at that moment. Yet now, it's getting more difficult to see the details. The image is blurry, and it's like my senses are blocked. I can no longer imagine the little things like the smell of his cologne or the feeling of his skin as he held my hand in his. Now, instead of remembering what it was like to be at that moment with him, it's as if I'm looking at a picture of us. And the photo isn't clear.

I don't want to forget a second of my life with Leo, yet I am a little more each day. Maybe when they say that time heals, they mean that time forces one to forget. Staring at a muted photo of my husband doesn't hurt as much as feeling him around me. At the same time, it's much more painful because the knowledge that I'm losing him all over again is more than I can bear. The universe stole his body and soul from me, and now it's pulling away my memories.

Stay with me.

Please.

Stay with me.

CHAPTER 10

AMOS

*L*ee-Anne and I finished watching Love's Rapunzel movie. I don't know why we didn't turn to something else after Alma took Love up to bed. I think it was part laziness and, quite honestly, mostly due to the fact that it's a good movie. Granted, it's Love's new obsession, so I haven't yet watched it a hundred times like I have the others. But it's enjoyable enough that two grown adults kept watching long after the three-year-old of the house had gone to bed.

As the ending credits rolled, Lee-Anne said her goodbye for the evening and left for her condo. I offered to drive her, but she insisted on walking the few blocks home, if that is what one would call it. She's only ever there to sleep. Most nights, Alma suggests her mom take one of the guest bedrooms here, but Lee-Anne always insists on sleeping at her place.

I suppose I'm only ever at my place to sleep, as well. To know Alma is to love her, and I want to be with her all of the time. Now that Lee-Anne is finally in a place where she can have a relationship with her daughter and granddaughter, she probably never wants to leave, either.

Alma has been upstairs for a while, which usually means she's fallen asleep, and on those nights, I see myself out. Given the fact that it's still relatively early for a Saturday night, I wait for a bit.

The Detroit Tiger's baseball game is finishing up when Alma emerges from the second level.

"Hey," she whispers, clearing her throat. "Sorry. You didn't have to wait."

She rubs her face, and her eyes are a little puffy.

"I don't mind. Lee-Anne and I had to finish *Tangled*, and I wanted to watch the end of this game, anyway."

"You did not finish watching that cartoon with my mother?" Alma laughs.

I shrug. "I know. It's a little pathetic, but it was good."

"It is? Right?" She disappears into the kitchen. "I'm grabbing some water. Do you want anything?"

"A water would be great. Thanks."

She returns, setting two waters down on the end table before plopping down beside me. "If you think we're watching baseball, you are sadly mistaken."

"I know." I grin. "I was just watching it while you were upstairs. Shall we continue with your dreamy vampires?" I reach for the remote.

"Yes, please."

I scroll through Netflix to find the episode that we left off on.

"Do you think Quinn is happy?" Alma asks.

"Yeah, don't you?"

To be fair, I don't spend much time analyzing Quinn. I would consider Quinn a friend but only through Alma. I've only texted or called her in the past seven years if I needed something for Alma. I wouldn't say that I regret my time with Quinn freshman year, but I know now that my decisions regarding her were fueled by unsettled feelings for Alma, and admittedly, jealousy.

Alma turns toward me. "I don't know. She's been difficult to read lately. I mean, she ended things with Beau after dating for over a year. At one point, I thought she would marry him. And she didn't go into details about the breakup either. It was all very vague. She's spending her Saturday with us playing Candy Land instead of going to a club with her other single friends. Then she went home to work. It's just different for her. Don't you think?"

"I wouldn't worry about it," I say, tucking a loose strand of hair that's fallen from Alma's ponytail behind her ear. "She's still in her twenties. This is the decade when we all figure everything out. She's probably just transitioning from who she was to who she wants to be. Everyone changes from the person they were in college."

"You're probably right," Alma says, satisfied. "Though you haven't changed much since college. I don't think I have either, really, if you don't count the fact that I'm a widowed mother."

"We haven't changed because we're old souls. You and I have always known who we were and who we wanted to be."

"That's true," she agrees. "How'd you get so smart?"

"I guess I was just born this way," I tease.

"Me too." she turns back toward the TV and leans into me.

I wrap my arm around her shoulder and click the remote, turning on her show.

We sit facing forward, but I can't concentrate on the episode. My senses have a sole focus. *Alma.* My side burns beneath my shirt as her body leans against me. When I inhale, I smell the sweetness of her shampoo. My heart beats a needy rhythm within my chest as the blood races through my veins. I work to steady my breathing, but everything about her is intoxicating.

I've always felt that she was my soul mate, my other half. And for years, every time I've had the overwhelming urge to kiss her, I focus on the invisible barrier between us. It's there for a reason, and there's always a reason. Or at least I thought they were valid explanations as to why a friendship was all we could have. I'm done with excuses and baseless logic. We're single. We're adults. And I love her. I don't want to live the rest of our lives with this barrier between us when I know that what lies beyond it is breathtaking.

I pause the show. "Alma?"

"Yeah?" she twists to face me.

Everything that I've been wanting to say to her eludes me, and I'm left speechless. Years of fear over losing her, and the closeness we share, paralyzes me.

What if she's not ready?

What if she doesn't feel the same as I do, and I jeopardize everything?

I can't lose her.

I move my head from side to side. "It's nothing."

She reaches toward me and grasps my face in her hands. "What is it? You can tell me." Genuine concern lines her expression, and I want to say so many things.

My heart pounds in my chest, and I can feel the thrumming through my body. The beats echo in my ears.

She holds my gaze in hers. "You know you can tell me anything," she says, leaning her forehead against mine.

In this space of shared breaths, desire overrules concern, and on instinct, I move closer until my lips are on hers. The kiss is hesitant and soft. It's short, just one peck, but the contact sends a jolt through me. I pull away slightly, my lips a vibration from hers, and wait. There are no words spoken as her hands remain on my face.

The air between us is heavy and charged. I press my lips against hers once again, this time with more resolve. The kiss deepens as my hands circle around her back, pulling her closer. I lick against her lips, requesting entry, and her mouth parts ever so slightly, allowing me access. She releases a slight whimper as my tongue enters her mouth. The kiss is everything I knew it would be and so much more. It's utter perfection.

A weight lifts off my chest as our lips move together, our tongues entwined in a dance they were destined for. I'm happier than I've ever been…and then I feel it, the moisture on my skin as the warm tears roll down her cheeks. I pull away, and my chest aches when I see the pain on her face. I feel sick when I realize it. *She doesn't feel the same.*

She drops her hands and presses her fingers against her trembling lips as the tears fall faster. There's so much regret and sorrow on her face. It's palpable, creating a bubble of thick air pregnant with grief around us.

Her name is on the tip of my tongue.

She shakes her head, dropping her hand. "I can't," she says through a sob. "I can't forget. I'm sorry. I'm so…" She swallows hard "Sorry." She chokes out before jolting up from the sofa and running up the stairs toward her bedroom.

Elbows on my knees, I clutch my hands together and press my forehead against my fist.

What did I just do?

CHAPTER 11

ALMA

I can still feel his kiss. I hold my fingers against my lips, willing the sensation of his mouth on mine to vanish. It's too much.

Leo was my first—everything. He's the only man to ever touch me, to kiss me.

Until now.

I can never again say he's my one and only, and that reality hurts. Heartache pours from me as wet tears course down my face.

I lie in my giant bed. I've rarely slept here since Leo's death. It's too hard. The bed feels empty without him beside me. The vast, hollow space threatens to pull me down into an abyss of solitude that I'll never escape. Leo stares at me from the bedside table. The two of us smiling on our wedding day. Within the walls of the frame, we're safe, happy, and have our whole lives before us. At that moment in time, I could've never imagined the path I was destined for.

The thing is, I know, with every fiber of my being, that Leo wouldn't want me to walk through this life alone. He's never coming back, and he would want me to move on. I should move on. It's been almost four years. I need to move on. But I simply can't. I still love him too much. Betrayal emits from my pores, and shame holds me hostage. I feel like I cheated on Leo.

I kissed another.

I kissed *Amos.*

Yes, Amos initiated the kiss, but I didn't stop it. I should have. The truth is, there's a small part in me that wanted it, if only to see how it would be. I admit I've been curious throughout my life. Amos is absolutely beautiful, inside and out, and I've loved him as long as I can remember. If he wasn't my sole companion and only real family growing up, we might have dated when we were younger. Yet he was always too important to risk. Growing up, if my attraction for him surfaced, I'd push it down. Always.

I never wanted to jeopardize what we had. Amos, and our relationship, saved me in every way possible. Everything I am today is because of him. Everything I've accomplished is because he believed in me. I was never afraid of falling because I knew he'd catch me. His love and devotion gave me a life outside what was intended.

I'm eternally grateful for Amos, and I love him beyond measure. Even still, though, my heart belongs to Leo. I don't know how to get past that. In another life, Amos could've been my other half, but in this one, it'll always be Leo.

It's true that I'm young and I should move on, but what's true and what's possible isn't up to me. Some things just are.

I hug Leo's pillow to me. It's long lost all scents of him. There are few physical signs of him left anymore. All I have are my memories, and they're fading. Closing my eyes, I picture our wedding, our first Christmas, Leo's graduation, Mackinaw Island when he proposed, and the day we got the keys to Lion's Lair. I play the highlights of our life on a reel and picture every detail I can. I recall what he was wearing, how he felt, how he smelled, and what he said. I remember everything I can and then I imagine it again and again and again.

I remember him and our life together because I can't forget. I won't.

* * *

It's the eyes. *They stare into my soul, and all I feel is happy, whole, and loved. My surroundings are blurry but I don't want to leave this place. I want to stay here and look into his beautiful deep brown eyes forever.*

I jolt awake with a gasp, my hand to my chest, and take stock of my surroundings. I'm in my bedroom. Leo, and his stunning blues stare at me from my bedside table. My heart beats rapidly against my chest.

Breathe.

My dream, the details are lost, but the feeling lingers, that of happiness and love. It was just Amos and me.

I jump out of bed. Love and Lee-Anne can be heard downstairs. I brush my teeth and make my way toward the giggles. My mother's Spanish music is playing from the speakers. I remember this song from when I was a child. It's one of Shakira's earlier albums.

Love and Lee-Anne are dancing in the living room. Each of them is shaking their hips, Love in her princess jammie dress and Mom in a bright purple jogging suit. I halt at the foot of the stairs and just watch them. *Pure joy.* Every day is an adventure with those two, and as Love grows, so does my mom. I feel like I'm getting to know her true self a little more each day. I hope that my dad can see her from wherever he is. I like to think he'd be over the moon happy to see how well she's doing. I only wish they could've both gotten clean earlier, and that I could've known him too.

"No one told me I was missing a dance party!" I shout over the music, a big grin on my face.

"Come, Chiquita!" Lee-Anne waves me over. "Estamos bailando."

"I see that," I say. "I want to dance, too." I grab Love's hands and twirl her around. She laughs as her nightgown spins in a circle around her.

The three of us dance to songs, the lyrics of which I can only pick out bits and pieces of, and it's freeing. It's fun and happy and exactly what I need. Finally, Love plops down on the rug, done with dancing. I turn down the music, scoop Love up, and together we sit on the sofa.

"You're here bright and early, Mom."

Lee-Anne takes a seat on the other end of the couch. "I didn't sleep well last night and was up with the sun. So, I just came over."

"I didn't sleep that well last night, either," I admit. "You know what I think we need today? A little vitamin D therapy. Maybe a girls' day to the beach?"

"Beach! Beach! Beach!" Love claps her hands.

"That sounds fun," my mom says. "No Amos?"

"Not today. It'll be just us girls. We can pack a picnic, sand and water toys and make a whole day of it."

"I love pic-a-nics!" Love squeals.

I hug her tight. "I know you do, little Love."

"I'll make breakfast first," Lee-Anne offers.

"Nope." I shake my head. "It's a girls' day of fun, which means no cooking. Let's go to the Gandy Dancer down by the tracks to eat. They have the best Sunday brunch. We'll bring the cooler and pick up sandwiches, sides, and drinks from

Zimmerman's after brunch for our picnic. There are some healthy and delicious options at both of those places," I say.

"That's true. I do enjoy their food."

"Then it's settled. We just need to gather the beach stuff."

The three of us jump off the couch ready to start the day. Despite the events of last night, and the broken sleep that followed, I'm consumed with an excited energy.

One of the many things that my time with Leo taught me was the beauty of Michigan. Prior to college, I hadn't visited most of the state in which I live, including the five Great Lakes that border the state. Leo and I traveled a lot throughout the five years we were together. That time together made me fall in love with nature and the peace that it can bring. I need that serenity today.

I don't think we'll venture out to one of the Great Lakes, as they are a bit of a drive. One of the local lakes will work just fine.

CHAPTER 12

ALMA

*W*ater slides up onto the beach, filling the moat around the sandcastle we built. Love's plastic Snow White figurine stands atop the lump of sand protecting the castle from intruders. Ariel and a few of her princess friends bob in the sandy water filling the moat.

Love sleeps soundly beneath the beach umbrella. The day at the lake has wiped her out. Mom and I sit on the vibrant-hued blanket, our arms propped up behind us, legs out in front, as we soak in all of the sun's rays. I can almost see my skin tanning as the streams of light heat my legs. I'm obsessed with the sun probably more than someone who lives in Michigan should be. We can go weeks without a glimpse of it during the winter months, but our summers make up for it.

"I never took you to the beach when you were young." Lee-Anne's voice is low. "I can't believe that." She looks over toward her sleeping grandbaby. "She had the best day. I don't think her smile faltered for one second. I never gave that to you, that joy."

She shakes her head, her lips tilting down, and looks back toward the water.

I don't offer a response.

These declarations are something that Lee-Anne does quite often. Sometimes I tell her that it's okay and it's in the past. I turned out fine, and I forgive her. She knows all of this. There's nothing she can do to change it now. A part of me thinks these random pronouncements are her way of coming to terms with who she was then compared to now. She regrets so much. Truthfully, my heart breaks for her. If I suddenly woke up twenty years from now with Love grown, and me having missed most of it, I'd be beside myself with grief.

I opt to cut Lee-Anne's self-reflection short. "Amos kissed me last night," I blurt out, my voice shaking.

She gasps and twists her body to face me. "What? When? How? Did you kiss him back?" she spits out the questions in rapid succession.

I sigh and shrug my shoulders. "After you left. We were watching a show, and then he seemed to want to talk about something important, and before I knew it, his lips were on mine."

"Did you kiss him back?"

"Yeah." I squint. "I guess. Yes, I did, but then I was crying, so he stopped. I told him I couldn't do it, and then I ran upstairs, and he left." I blow out a breath. "Then I dreamed about him and I together, which freaked me out. So, now...we're here."

"So you're hiding from him? Has he called?"

I shake my head. "He's giving me space and time to process everything, I'm sure. And I'm not hiding, per se. I just needed a day to decompress and clear my head."

"Well, what are you thinking?" Pulling her knees up to her chest, she wraps her arms around them.

"First, that you were right." I scoff. "There are clearly feelings there."

"Well, obviously, Almalee."

"He was my second kiss, Mom. I've only ever been with Leo, and it felt wrong, like I was betraying him. It hurt." My voice cracks.

"You've only been with one person?" Lee-Anne's question carries an air of astonishment.

"Yeah, I thought you knew that."

"Whoo!" she exclaims, her eyes wide. "You are nothing like me, Chiquita. I was fooling around with boys when I was fourteen. Your father and I would sleep with other couples quite often, in fact, all together."

"Mom!" I protest. "Great. Now, I can add orgies to the list of things I did not need to know about you and Vati. Seriously, Mom. Don't you think that list is already long enough?" I shudder.

"Alma, if there's one thing I've always been with you, it's honest. I'm not going to change now. You're a grown woman. You can talk about sex without freaking out." The corner of her lip tilts into a smile.

"Yes, Mother, but there is something called *too much information*. I don't need to know everything. Okay?"

"Well, I couldn't tell you everything if I wanted to, anyway. Your father and I were always high on something, so the details are a little foggy, at best."

"Bummer." I chuckle under my breath.

I could live a lifetime without the added knowledge I now have of my parents. But I have to give it to my mother. Moments ago, I was on the verge of tears. Now, the conversation isn't as difficult.

Lee-Anne taps my knee. "Okay, so—you and Amos—you do understand that you did nothing wrong. You're young. You can and should move on. Leo would want that for you and for Love. Right?"

I simply nod, the lump in my throat returning.

"Almalee, mi amor, look at me," Lee-Anne urges. I turn to face her, my lip quivering. "It's okay to move on. It's okay."

"I don't know how to move on when I still love him so much," I admit.

"Baby, you're always going to love him, and that's fine. You'll never replace Leo. He is a great love of your life, your husband, and the father of your little girl. I promise you will love him forever. Yet you can have another great love, a man who is here and can love you back, a man who can hold you and kiss you, and adore your daughter. Your next love will need to understand that he shares your heart with Leo. And if he's the one, he'll be understanding of that."

"I can't ever forget, Leo, Mom." I shake my head, my eyes filling with tears.

She squeezes my knee reassuringly, "You never will. Some details may fade, but you'll always remember the stuff that matters. I promise you."

I pull in a deep breath through my nose. My chest rises as I turn toward the blue water. The soft waves lap against the sandy beach.

"I don't know how to love someone else the way I love Leo," I whisper.

"You'll never love someone the way you love Leo. You'll love him differently, unique to him. It won't be the same, but it will be amazing, maybe even better."

"No," I protest.

She holds her hands up in surrender. "Okay, we won't say better...just different but equally as wonderful. Falling in love is magical, mi hija. Open your heart so you can feel it again. Do you think you could love Amos as more than a friend?"

"Maybe. I've had feelings that've leaned in that direction... when I was younger. I mean, I love him already. So much."

"Well, he's very handsome," she says. "Always has been."

"Yes, he is," I agree.

"He's smart, kind, and understanding. He adores both you and Love. He's always taken care of you." She pauses. "I know I missed a lot, Almalee, but I never missed how much that boy loved you, cared for you, and protected you."

Reaching to my side, I trace my finger along the sand and draw a heart. "He did. Always."

"This hurts me to say, but I think you're who you are today because of him, not your father or me."

"Yeah," I agree softly. "I think I want to try. I'm just afraid of losing him. I've had him my whole life. I don't know what I'd do if I didn't. We don't know if we're compatible romantically. What if it doesn't work out and it's so awkward that I lose him?"

"Nope," she says adamantly, the 'p' sound echoing off her lips. "That would never happen. He's your soul mate, Alma. You two have been drawn to each other since you were itty bitty. He's destined to be in your life always, in one way or another. You won't lose him. But if you're worried. Talk to him. Tell him your fears. He'll understand."

"He always does," I admit. No one has ever understood me the way that Amos does. "I'm going to try." I nod my head with determination.

"That's all you can do."

"I just wish I didn't have to. I wish Leo were here with me." I press my lips together.

"Wishes are a powerful thing. They can lift your spirits high when you're dreaming of an enchanting future. But if you're wishing for the impossible, your life is going to slip through your fingers while you're waiting for something that can never be. Don't waste your life on a dream. Soak up the magic. Live. Life moves too fast, and you don't want to miss it."

I cover my mom's hand with mine. "You know, you might not have been there for me when I was young, but I can't imagine a better mom to be here for me now. The universe must've known that I'd need you the most as an adult. I want you to know that you make our life, mine and Love's, better every day with your presence. I'm so grateful for you. Love is so lucky to have the best Gigi ever. I love you, Mom."

She presses her trembling lips together as a few tears roll down her sun-kissed cheeks and nods.

A groggy toddler voice catches our attention. "Momma."

"Hey, baby. Did you have a good nap?"

She nods and stands from the beach blanket. "I firsty."

I hand her a juice box, and she crawls into my lap. I tuck her hair, stringy with sunscreen residue, behind her ear and kiss her head.

"It's almost dinnertime. Are you ready to get going, or should we take one more dip into the lake?" I ask.

The mention of leaving has rejuvenated my sleepy girl. She pops up from my lap, drops her empty juice box, and extends both of her hands. Mom and I each take one and follow her toward the water.

Love giggles as the waves tickle our feet. The sand squishes beneath my toes, grounding me to the present. This right here —the tiny hand in my grasp and the happiness in my soul—is why my heart beats. I have an incredible life, and I'm going to cherish every minute of it. I look at my mom, whose wide smile mirrors my own. There's a world of magic destined for me, and I'm ready to soak it all in.

CHAPTER 13

ALMA

*M*y chest tightens when I don't see Amos's car in its usual place in the parking lot of Lion's Lair. He always beats me here in the morning.

I had intended on calling him and maybe having him over last night, but the long day at the beach zapped all of the energy from me. We were all exhausted when we got back. After our shower, Love and I crashed hard. The second my head hit the pillow, I was out. Lee-Anne even stayed over, which she never does. The task of walking a few blocks to her condo was too daunting.

I unlock the front doors and start prepping the building for another day. Jen wanders in a few minutes later.

"Good morning, Alma," she sing-songs.

"Hi, Jen. How was your weekend in Chicago?"

"Amazing!" she squeals, thrusting her arm out to show me her hand. "I got engaged!"

"Oh my goodness!" I cheer and take her extended hand in mine to check out the ring. It's a green stone surrounded by silver vines. It makes me think of nature and fairies, which is perfect for Jen. "It is so you. I love it."

"Isn't it? It's an emerald. I never wanted a diamond, you know? Green has always been my favorite color...so, it's just perfect."

I pull her over to the sofa in the front lobby. "Tell me everything. I need details."

"It was so romantic," she dives into the proposal.

I listen, nod, and smile. Yet with each passing minute that Amos doesn't show, I become more worried. I try to stop my gaze from darting to the front door every two seconds, but it's all I want to do. I should've sent a text, at the very least, to Amos yesterday. I think I messed up.

When Jen's story ends, I pull her into a hug. "I'm so happy for you, Jen."

"Thanks, Alma."

I excuse myself and hurry to my office. Pulling my cell phone from my purse, I type out a text to Amos.

Hey! I'm sorry I didn't call yesterday. Mom, Love, and I spent the whole day at the beach. Love and I were passed out by seven. Lol

His response is almost immediate.

No worries. Sounds like you had a fun day.

Yeah, it was great.

I stare at my screen, but he doesn't text anything else. Eighty-five minutes—fine, seconds—pass, but I can't take it anymore.

Um...are you coming to work today?

Yeah, when I'm finished here.

Where?

Remember I had a meeting with the Howard Corp. this morning? You know...they want to donate a crap ton of money to the Lair. Ringing any bells? Lol

I sit back in my office chair and look down toward my desk calendar. It's huge, old-school, and redundant since I have a Google calendar, too. But there's something about a big ole visual right in front of me that I love. Penned in with a fine point, hot pink Sharpie is Amos's meeting with the Howard Corp. Had I bothered to open my calendar in my phone or computer this morning, his meeting would be scheduled in there as well.

I TEXT BACK.

Oh, that's right.

Everything okay?

He asks.

Perfect. I'll see you soon. Love you.

Love you, too.

Well, apparently, Amos and I are fine, and I'm going crazy. We're not even dating, and I'm already losing it. That can't be a good sign. I'm twenty-seven years old, and I don't know how to do this. It all just happened with Leo. He pushed me up against a few walls and kissed me. I convinced myself that I hated him until I couldn't ignore the lust anymore and caved to his charm. We dated and fell in love. That's my complete frame of reference.

I don't know how to start something with someone I've loved for two decades.

There isn't time to mull over it now. Jen messages me to let me know that my first tutoring appointment is here. Now that school is out for the summer, our days here are pretty busy with kids. Our recreation and food programs, especially.

I meet Jezebel in one of the tutoring rooms.

"Hey, Jez," I greet her. She has to take summer school for math since she failed the subject this past seventh grade school year. The two of us meet every morning to go over the concepts for the day before she heads to school for her class.

"Hi, Alma." She gives me a weak smile.

"Uh, oh. What are we doing today?" I raise a brow.

"Fractions," she grumbles. "It's so stupid, too. When in my life am I ever going to have to know how to multiply a stupid fraction? Never."

"Fractions come in handy with cooking and recipes," I offer.

"I hate cooking. I'm just going to get fast food for dinner every night or pizza when I'm older. So, I'll never need fractions."

I sit down beside her. "Well, I'm not sure how much you'll use them when you're an adult, but you'll definitely need to understand them for the next five years of school until you graduate, and more if you go to college."

"I'm not going to college."

"You might, Jez. You're a smart girl. You have time to decide what you want to do when you're older, but I can guarantee that the next five years will be a lot easier if you grasp these concepts now. Seventh-grade math is all about learning the fundamental skills that will help you in future math classes."

"I'm stupid. I can't do it, Alma." She drops her forehead to the desk.

"You are anything but stupid, Jezebel. You are so smart, but your brain thinks in words and colors. You have an artist's brain. You're creative. Math is more analytical thinking. There are set steps, and once you understand the steps, you'll get it. Plus, you know all of your multiplication facts and fact families. Right?"

"Yeah." She sighs.

"Well, that's basically all you need to know to multiply fractions. Here." I open the dry erase marker on the table and start writing on the board in front of us. "Let me show you the tricks." I shoot her a wink. "You'll have this down in no time. I promise."

Jezebel and I work on fraction multiplication until she has to go. She hugs me before she leaves, a beautiful smile present on her face.

"I knew you could do it," I whisper as I hug her back. "See you tomorrow."

"Thank you, Alma."

"Have a great day, Jez. I'm so proud of you."

She waves and runs out the doors to catch the bus.

Jen informs me of my next appointment. "Simon is a no-show."

"Really?" I sigh. "That makes me worried. I better go call to make sure everything is okay. Ring down if he comes in late."

"Will do."

"Thanks, Jen."

Just as I finish leaving a voicemail for Simon's mother, Amos steps into my office.

"How'd it go?" I ask.

"Great. They're giving us double what we thought they would." He grins.

"You're joking."

"I'm not. The money is in the account. I input our banking info right there at the meeting, and they initiated the transfer."

I jump up from my desk chair and run over to Amos. He wraps me in a hug. "That's amazing, Amos. I don't know how you pulled it off."

"I told ya, I saved them a lot of money when I worked with the firm. They owed me. Plus, it's a great write-off that will help them with their taxes this year. So, it's a win-win."

"That money will cover everything that Alivia took, pay for all of our legal fees dealing with her, and still leave a large sum to put toward the Lair. This is incredible, Amos."

"Yeah, I'm pretty pleased."

"Ah, you're the best. Thank you. Thank you. Thank you." I rock back and forth, hugging him tight.

"It is my job," he says.

Taking a step back, I stare up into his big brown eyes. "I'm sorry."

"For?"

"For running upstairs and leaving you alone after that moment and for not contacting you yesterday. I'm sure you were worried all day. I shouldn't have made you go through that, and I'm sorry. I just needed..."

"Time," he answers for me, complete understanding in his eyes. "I get it, Alma, and you have nothing to apologize for. It's me who should be apologizing. I shouldn't have kissed you out of the blue like that. I'm sorry. Let's just forget it happened and move on. Not a big deal." His mouth tilts into a meek grin.

I shake my head. "It's a big deal to me, and I can't forget it."

"Alma," he pleads, dropping his head.

Lifting my arms, I cup his face with my hands. His expression is one of hesitant confusion. My heart hammers against the walls of my chest, and my mind works in overdrive as I try to calm my racing nerves. I pull in a fortifying breath and stand on my tiptoes. Eyes closed, my lips press against his. He's still, his body tight and assessing, but his lips are soft and warm. I push down the impending panic and concentrate on this moment, this kiss, and this connection. Nothing else.

I focus on Amos. I lean against him, my hands splayed across his chest. The hurried rhythm of his heart plays a song of love and desire against my palms. Electricity jolts through my body, bringing me to life. When I block out the noise and live in this moment with these lips and this man, it's perfection. Every cell in my body fills with an energy I haven't felt in years. I want to cry and scream and cartwheel around my office all at once. I feared I'd never feel this—desire—again, but here it is.

I moan into his mouth as the kiss deepens. His tongue dances with mine as if he's been waiting his entire life to do so. I grasp the base of his neck and pull him toward me, wanting to take the kiss deeper. I need more.

"Alma, Simon's mom is on line three." Jen's voice sounds from the phone's speaker, startling Amos and me. We jump apart, eyes wide.

I swallow hard. "Okay, tell her I'll be with her in one minute," I call out.

Pressing my hand to my mouth, I look at Amos.

His lips tilt up at the corners. "That should've been our first kiss," he says with a satisfied smile. Words fail me as my heart continues to beat wildly in my chest. "Alma, will you go on a date with me tonight?"

I nod. Just once.

He steps toward me and wraps his pinky finger around mine before leaning down and kissing my forehead. "I'll pick you up at seven," he whispers against my skin, and then he walks out.

I head over to my desk, where Leo's picture is staring up at me. Hysteria builds within, but I will it to stay down, deep where I can ignore it. I shake my hands out to my sides and rotate my head around in a circle, blowing out a long breath.

Picking up the receiver, I hit line three. "Hello, Ms. Fredericks. I'm so glad you called," I say. I swivel my chair around so my back is to the desk.

I can't look toward Leo right now because I don't have the time to deal with the fall that will inevitably come.

CHAPTER 14

AMOS

$\mathcal{T}$he day at the Lair was jam-packed with appointments and activities as most Mondays are. I only saw Alma in passing and from a distance the rest of the day, but that was probably for the best. I know this is difficult for her. She's still in love with Leo, and I can't fault her for that. She'll need time to process our relationship every step of the way. She's never been one to leap into anything without thinking it through.

For me, I'm done deliberating because I've been thinking about what it'd be like to be with Alma for years, and it's something I want, something I've always wanted. There was a moment when I thought I pushed too far, too fast, and lost my chance. But the kiss in Alma's office proved the opposite.

It's time.

A part of Alma will always love Leo, and that's okay. She loves me, too. We've loved each other for twenty years, maybe not in the same way that she loved her husband, but it was a true and deep love nonetheless. The foundation has been laid. We're already friends, partners, and family. I'm ready for more, and I think with time, she'll realize that she is too.

I pull into Alma's driveway and turn off the car. She pays a boy in her neighborhood to cut the grass in her front yard every Monday, and I'm pleased to see that he was a no-show today. There are dozens of round white dandelion flowers peppered across the grass. I pick a handful before stepping onto the front porch and ringing the doorbell.

This is new. I've always just walked right in. A nervous and excited energy takes over me. This is our first date. I've been out with Alma thousands of times but never like this.

Alma opens the door, a shy grin present on her gorgeous face. She's wearing a light yellow sundress. Her skin has darkened a shade with the summer sun. She's never been one to wear a lot of makeup because she's never needed to. She's the most beautiful woman I've ever seen. She looks like a goddess with her golden dress, shiny long chestnut locks, and big brown eyes. Her full lips have a light layer of lip gloss that I'm dying to kiss off, but I don't.

"Hi," I say instead, a short, sweet, and simple greeting. No pressure.

"Hi." She grins.

Lee-Anne stands a few feet behind with Love on her hip. They are both grinning wide. Love waves wildly.

"Hi, Love Dove," I say to her and wave back.

"Hi, Cookie!"

"Mrs. Weber." I nod, greeting Alma's mom.

"Have fun, you two." She smiles.

"Bye!" Alma waves before closing the door behind her.

"Why does it feel like we're in high school and your mom is seeing us off?" I chuckle.

"Because she didn't get the normal mother experiences

back then, so she's making up for it now." Alma shakes her head.

I hold out the bouquet of dandelions in my hand. "For you."

She presses a hand to her chest. "You brought me a bouquet of wishing wands?"

"It was a selfish move, really." I raise a brow. "I was hoping to sneak in a wish for us."

She nods with a small smile on her face and hands me a dandelion. She pulls another one from the group and holds it in her other hand. "Make a wish," she says.

She closes her eyes to think of her wish. I stare right at mine. We both blow the tiny little seeds into the summer air.

I extend my hand, and her fingers slide through mine. It feels natural and right—a perfect fit. When we've reached the car, I open her door and close it once she's seated. The drive to the restaurant is a short one. It's a local fondue place where the meals are dipped in cheese and the desserts are dipped in chocolate—a dream come true for Alma. Another draw to the restaurant is the secluded seating. The restaurant is darker than most, and each round booth is set back into the wall, hidden from view. When seated, it feels like you're the only ones at the restaurant. Given there's going to be some deep conversations tonight, I thought it'd be perfect.

Alma extends her skewer with steamed broccoli and dips it into the creamy cheese pot in the center of the table. The flickering of candlelight dances against her skin, making her even more beautiful.

"This is amazing. I mean, a whole meal dipped in cheese." She plops the cheese-covered vegetable into her mouth.

"Right?" I agree.

The dinner conversation is light, and more or less, normal. Alma and I talk about work, and Love, and Lee-Anne. If it weren't for the kiss in her office earlier, this would feel like any other meal we've shared together over the years. Yet the vibrations from that kiss are still being felt. So, though sitting here with Alma is the same as always, it's also vastly different. The air between us is buzzing with newness and excitement despite the fact that we're both pretending it's not.

When the server brings out the pot of melted chocolate and tray of cake squares and fruit for dipping, something changes. The dessert is a signal that the night is nearing a close. It's a catalyst to the conversation that we need.

"We should talk," Alma says. Her tone has morphed from casual dinner conversation to concern.

I nod. "Okay."

"First, what is it that you want to happen here? Where do you see this going? What do you want?" she asks.

"You," I respond simply. "In all the ways I can have you. I just want you."

She stares at her plate as she stabs a piece of pound cake. "What if we don't work out, Amos?"

"We will."

She raises her doe eyes to meet mine. "But what if we don't? I can't lose you. I need you in my life, forever. I'd never risk our friendship."

"I promise that you will always have me in your life. We've been inseparable for all these years. Nothing will change that."

"You're absolutely positive?" She chews on her bottom lip. "Because I cannot live my life without you in it. I need you. Love needs you. Romantic relationships don't always work, Amos. As much as we may want it to. What if we fail and can't get back to where we were as friends?"

I set my elbow on the table and hold my smallest finger out to Alma. She wraps her pinky around mine. "I am yours forever in whatever way I can have you. You will never lose me. Pinky promise."

Our hands remain connected in the center of the table. I slide the rest of my fingers through hers. Hands clasped together, she nods. "Okay. There's something else." Her voice is barely a whisper now. "I still love him." She shrugs, and tears fill her eyes. "I'll always love him, and I know that's not fair to you, but I can't help it."

I squeeze her hand in mine. "It's okay. I understand. Of course you'll always love him. There's room in your heart to love us both."

She moves her head from side to side, and a tear rolls down her cheek. "I'm sorry. I don't want to ever make you feel less than or second best, and I'm afraid I will without meaning to. You deserve so much. You deserve an epic love, Amos." She looks down at the table. "I had an epic love." She sighs. "It's not fair of me to take that from you because I'll never be able to give you that."

"It's okay. I know what I'm getting into, Alma."

"When Leo died, a part of me did, too. I'm broken...I mean, you know. You've seen me. Surely, there's someone whole who could give you everything that I can't."

"She wouldn't be you." I release her hand and scoot around the booth until I'm beside her. She twists to face me. "I'm not asking you to marry me. I'm not making you promise me forever. I'm just asking you to try. One date, one day at a time. Here, let's try something. I need you to clear your mind. Don't overthink anything. Just be here with me. Can you do that? Look at me." I tilt her chin up. "It's just you and me. Okay?"

She nods.

I cradle her jaw, drawing her lips to me, and kiss her softly. Her lips move against mine, and she sighs. I pull away. "What did you just feel?"

She licks her lips. "Good."

"What else?"

"I felt...desire."

"Okay." I lean forward and plant a soft kiss on her collar-bone. She releases a small gasp. My lips move up her neck, peppering kisses against her skin. She tilts her head to the side, allowing me access. "Does this feel good?" I whisper when I reach her lips.

She bobs her head in affirmation.

"There's something here, Alma," I say before kissing her lips. "I feel it, and you do, too. There's never going to be a perfect time. There's never going to be a moment when you don't love him, so we can't keep waiting for that. It's been almost four years. Your heart is big enough to love us both, and I'm okay with that. I'm okay with anything as long as I have you. You say you're broken, but to me, you're perfect. You always have been."

Dragging my thumb across her cheek, I wipe an errant tear. "Can we try?"

"Yeah," she says quietly, chewing on the side of her lip.

"Yes?" I chuckle. "You're sure?"

"I said yes." She scoffs. "I'll give you today."

"And maybe tomorrow, too?"

"Okay, tomorrow too." She circles her arms around my neck. "Well, you can't say I didn't warn you."

"I'm not scared," I say.

"God, I am." She laughs, and the sound is beautiful.

"I'll catch you if you fall. Always have. Always will."

She swallows. "I know you will."

I kiss her. It's a short kiss, but it's everything because she's mine. She may not see it yet, but she's mine forever.

Finally.

CHAPTER 15

ALMA

*A*mos takes my hand as we leave the fondue restaurant. I rub my stomach with my free hand. It hurts, it's so full, but I might've been able to fit a few more bites in. The food was fantastic.

"So, where are we going?" I ask.

We stroll through Ann Arbor past many of the University of Michigan campus buildings. This place was Amos's stomping ground for four years during his undergrad. I'm actually not too familiar with U of M's campus. As close as it is to Eastern's campus, where I went to college, I didn't spend much time here. Amos always came to me.

"We're just walking," he says with a grin.

My hand in his feels nice, comfortable. Amos has always made me feel safe.

We veer off the sidewalk when we reach a small park. It's

quaint with a handful of old oak trees, some bushes, and a bench.

The sun is setting as Amos leads me across the grass. "I always passed this place on the way to Econ sophomore year. Out of all the parks in Ann Arbor, it's not usually a very populated one. It's kind of tucked away from the busyness of campus," Amos says.

We reach the back of the park, and he leads me around a huge old oak, the width of which is at least two of me standing shoulder to shoulder.

"I used to come here to read or study on nice days," he continues. "There was always a couple back behind this tree kissing. Every day, a different pair. It was annoying at the time because leaning against the base of this tree would've been the perfect reading spot. Besides annoyance, I can't deny that I felt a little jealous, and to be completely honest, I pictured you and me here, together. The thought was fleeting, and I pushed it away the moment it surfaced because you were taken and happy...but it was there—for a moment." He pauses and steps toward me.

I lean back against the hard bark of the broad oak. "You brought me to the college kids' make-out spot?" I raise a brow and drape my arms over Amos's shoulders.

Amos drags his bottom lip through his teeth and takes me in. Lifting his arm, he wipes a piece of hair from my face and tucks it behind my ear. "I never thought I'd be here with you." His voice is low and reverent. He chuckles under his breath. "I almost can't believe it." His deep brown gaze captures mine. I've always known that Amos loved me, but now, looking into his eyes, I'm starting to realize just how much and in what way. The intensity of his love lights my core aflame and causes pressure to build within my chest.

His lips, perfectly full and inviting, call to me. I run my

thumb over them, and he kisses it. Amos has always been beautiful, but up close, like this, he's even more so.

His fingers circle my wrist, and he lowers his mouth to my skin. His eyes hold my gaze. Leisurely, he peppers kisses on my hand and up my arm, over my shoulder, and up my neck. He takes my head between the palms of his hands, closes the gap between us, and kisses me so softly that my lips quiver against his. His mouth worships mine in its own time, savoring the connection. An intense and visceral need consumes me, and I pull his head closer, needing more. A myriad of emotions course through me as he claims my mouth with his tongue. I focus on the ones that bring me joy at this moment.

He kisses me thoroughly against the tree where hundreds of college students have done the same, but I can guarantee that none of them were kissed like this. Pulling away, he nuzzles his nose against my earlobe.

"Better than my dreams." He kisses the base of my neck and steps back, a smile forming on his face, lighting up his eyes. The love I see dancing in his gaze makes my heart twist a little.

I circle his waist with my arms and hug him, resting my face against his chest. My entire body hums over the kiss. An awareness of something greater saturates the air, and deep within is the knowledge that if I'm brave enough to accept it—it'll change my life.

* * *

"Do you want to come in?" I ask Amos. We stand on the front porch. He faces me, and his hands hold mine.

He shakes his head. "No, I don't think so. I mean, don't get me wrong. I want to, but it's probably not the best idea on a first date." He quirks a brow and scrunches his nose, causing me to laugh.

"Come on. Love and Lee-Anne will want to see you anyway." I tilt my head, motioning toward the entry door.

"No." He grins. "Tell them we'll all do dinner tomorrow. Tonight was a big deal, our first date. You need time to decompress. I want to do this right. I want this to work, Alma."

"You're afraid of me getting scared and freaking out?" I ask, my lips puckering as my eyebrows rise.

He levels a gaze at me, one full of understanding and adoration. "A little bit. Yeah," he admits. "I know this is a big deal for you, and I get it. We should take things slow."

"Okay, if you're sure."

"I'm sure." His lips press against mine in a chaste kiss. "I had fun tonight. I'll see you tomorrow."

"Bye." I wave. He gets in his car and drives away, and I already miss him.

Love runs toward me when I open the door, and I scoop her up in a hug. "Hey, Love bug. How's your night been with Gigi?"

"Good! We had worms and tomatoes for dinner!"

"Worms and tomatoes?" I scrunch up my face.

"Also known as spaghetti." Lee-Anne laughs.

"Did it taste like spaghetti?" I ask, amused.

"Yes," Lee-Anne states. "It was very good. I actually pureed the carrots and spinach before adding them to the sauce, so she didn't even know they were there."

"I'm sure it was delicious!" I squeeze Love.

"Where's Cookie?" Love asks.

"He had to go home but wants to have dinner with us tomorrow. So, tell me, what else did you do while I was gone?"

"We colored," Love says.

"You did? Let me see." I set Love down, and she leads me to the table where dozens of crayons and pieces of paper are scattered about. She shows me all of her creations before running off to pick out which bath bomb she wants after I tell her it's bath time.

Lee-Anne grabs my wrist. "So, how was it?"

"It was really great." My lips press together in a smile. "He took me to that fondue place downtown. The meal was amazing, of course. We talked a lot about everything. After dinner, we walked around town, and that's about it."

"You fooled around a little, right?" Lee-Anne looks mildly disappointed with the details of my night.

"Yes." I chuckle. "There was kissing."

"Well, it's something," she states.

"Mom." I smack her arm playfully. "It was our first date."

She rolls her eyes. "Please, Almalee. You and that boy have been on hundreds of dates."

"As friends. It's different," I say, picking up the crayons from the table and placing them in their box.

She smiles. "Well, I'm just glad you went and had fun, and that you're trying." She grasps my arms and squeezes tight. "This is good." She drops her hands. "I should go and let you have time with Love before bed."

"Okay, well, you know you're welcome to stay," I offer, as I always do.

"No, I should get home, but I'll see you bright and early in the morning." She leans in and kisses my cheek. "Buenas noches, mi amor."

"Night, Mom. Thanks for watching Love."

"Anytime."

I follow her upstairs. While she says goodbye to Love, I take off my dress and throw on my leggings and tank top. Stepping into the bathroom, Love has her bath bomb basket out. Each multicolored bomb is set out in a straight line across the tiled floor.

"Did you decide which one you want tonight?"

"This one!" she holds up a multihued purple bomb in the shape of a mermaid tail.

"Ooh, great choice."

I run the bath, and Love steps in. She giggles as the mermaid tail starts to fizz vibrant colors in the water.

"Momma, what's a date?"

"What?" I question.

"Gigi said you and Cookie were on a date."

"Oh." I nod in understanding. "Well, a date is when two people go out together to do something fun, like dinner or a movie."

"Like the beach?"

"Exactly. We had a beach date yesterday. Tonight, Amos and I went on a dinner date."

I feel like I should talk to her about Amos, but I don't know how to approach it. He spends most days over here already, so that wouldn't be anything that I'd need to run by her. Amos and I have always been affectionate toward each other, so even that wouldn't be a change. She's never seen me romantically date a man before so she doesn't have a frame of reference for how it differs from the life we already share with Amos.

"I really like Amos," I tell her.

"Me too!" she exclaims, swishing her Ariel doll in the water.

That works.

CHAPTER 16

ALMA

*T*he Lair was insanely busy today, so basically, the same as any other day. I was able to share a few stolen glances with Amos as we passed in the hallway on our way to separate meetings. The goose bump-inducing electricity of a new relationship lingers in the air. That spark is thrilling, bursting with a possibility that wasn't there before.

I found myself nervously anticipating our shared moments, however brief they were. There wasn't time for anything substantial in terms of our newly budding courtship. The day was absent of kisses and deep conversations, but it was exhilarating just the same. The idea of something greater, alone, made the world seem a little brighter.

I'm noticing things about him, too. Perhaps, I didn't allow myself to see his little traits that make my heart beat faster before. Self-preservation at its finest. The absence of these minute details enabled me to live in the friendship zone without question. And, man…I was happy there, in that place of security and comfort and unconditional love.

But now…

It's irrevocably changed. It's different, and despite the promise that our friendship is untouchable, should our relationship go south, I know the change is permanent. Some things can't be unseen. Unfelt.

I watch the muscles in his forearm move, ever so slightly, as he chops onions into slices on the cutting board. His skin is perfection, smooth, and a deep espresso. My fingertips tingle, the desire to trace the lines and ridges of his body calls to me.

Pulling my bottom lip between my teeth, I admire Amos's mouth. His lips, full and inviting, have always been gorgeous, but I'm just now noticing the way his bottom lip is slightly larger, a little more plump. It's like a siren calling out to me, and I can imagine pulling it into my mouth.

He smiles wide, laughing with Love, who sits on the counter watching him prepare dinner. Nothing is more devastatingly beautiful than Amos Davis in a full-blown smile. He wears his black-rimmed glasses that make him even sexier.

"You're gonna cry." Amos smiles to Love.

She folds her arms over her chest. "No, you are."

I click a mental picture of the sight before me. My two favorite people.

"Why are we crying?" I lift a brow.

Amos's lips tug up at the corners as he turns toward me. "The onions. I told Love to back up because they might bother her eyes and make her cry, but she says she's too tough for that," he says in jest.

"I very tough," Love states.

"You are," I agree. "You're my super tough, princess girl."

I stand opposite Amos on the other side of the countertop and wrap my arms around Love. "These onions are pretty mild, so we should be okay, but there are some types that make Mommy cry every time."

"Not me," Love protests.

"Okay, not you." I kiss her temple and raise my eyes to meet Amos's. "Dinner smells delicious. I can't wait to eat."

He's making fajitas, and the spicy scent throughout the kitchen is intoxicating.

"All in good time." He grins before swiping the vegetables from the cutting board into the frying pan. The slices of steak and chicken are in another skillet. He's keeping the veggies away from the meat so that Lee-Anne can eat them. He's always been so considerate of others.

Sometimes the smallest gestures, the ones that take no real effort just the courtesy to make them in the first place, are the greatest acts of love. I think the world has lost a little of that kindness, but Amos is one of the good ones. His heart is unyielding in its desire to serve others, and he's always been that way.

"Love, you want to help me set the table?" I ask.

She nods and stands on the granite with her arms extended. I scoop her up and swing her off the counter. "No feet on the counter, Love bug."

"We may sit on the counter but not stand," Amos teases.

"Exactly. Butts are fine. Feet cross the line. It's called logic." I eye him, my lips puckered.

He chuckles. "Of course. Solid logic there."

I hand Love the plates, and she carries them to the table. I reach for the knob to the silverware drawer, and my arm brushes Amos's, sending a buzz over my skin. I lift my gaze toward him, and his eyes lock on mine, a knowing smile on his face. He looks to Love, who's occupied at the table, and presses a gentle kiss to my lips.

My mouth stretches into a grin, and I quickly grab the silverware I need. The wide grin never leaves my face as I help

Love with the table setting. A small part of me feels silly, my behavior and feelings reminiscent of a thirteen-year-old girl with her first crush. Yet a much bigger part couldn't care less if I resemble an entire cheer squad of teen girls with crushes. I'm ridiculously happy.

Table set, I make my way into the living room where Lee-Anne gawks at the TV, an old episode of *Survivor* on. It's her current binge show. She's on season three, I believe.

"You know, I don't understand why they complain so much. So they can't shower and have to eat bugs and grass. I could do that. Hell, I have done that. Your father and I spent some time in very free and natural communes. I swear, we had a friend once who went months between showers. I could win this show."

"I'm sure you could, Mom."

"Look at this guy." She motions toward a bright-eyed, curly-haired hottie on the screen. "Is he not the most adorable guy you've ever seen?"

"He's pretty cute," I admit.

"His name is Ethan. Whew, he's a beautiful man. Too young for me, of course, but very attractive."

"This was filmed a long time ago, Mom. I think he's actually in his late forties right now, but I believe he is happily married."

"Hmm." She sounds disappointed. "How do you know about Ethan? You haven't watched this, have you?"

"No, but I've read about him or seen him in the news here or there over the years. These contestants are pretty much celebrities when they leave the show."

"Well, I really like him. I hope he wins the million."

"Maybe he will," I say, leaning over the back of the sofa. "Dinner is almost ready. Amos has the veggies cooking now, and he made some black beans. Anything else?"

"Yes, can you get out my chia and flax tortillas from the refrigerator. I'll use those."

"Sure." I push off the couch and head back toward the kitchen. Love is sitting at the table, her tongue sticking out of the corner of her mouth as she tries to fold a cloth napkin. "What are you doing?" I question with a chuckle.

"Making chickens."

"You want the napkins to be in the shape of chickens? I don't know, Love Dove. That's pretty hard. I can't even do that. Why don't you go pick out a special ring for everyone's napkins?"

She looks up from the piece of cloth in front of her, eyes wide and excited as if she's just remembering the drawer of napkin rings that we've acquired over the past couple of years. Darting from the table, her little feet pad across the tiled floor until she reaches the drawer. It's a treasure chest of large rings. Love and I picked out each one on our adventures, with a good portion acquired at the local art fair. Some are wooden, painted in vibrant colors, others are shaped from metals, and a few are ceramic—all of them special to us.

My parents didn't believe in waste. I didn't grow up with paper towels or napkins, and it's one thing from my youth I've carried into adulthood. However, unlike my childhood where the same towel was used to dry off after a shower, wipe the kitchen counters, or clean my face, I've invested in a variety of colorful cloth squares to use at meals.

Love chooses four hoops and eagerly carries them to the table. She begins to pull the cloth through the first one.

"Which holders did you pick?" I ask her.

"The penguin, pink flower, banana, and pig," she says proudly.

"Oh, great choices."

Amos is plating up the food. I grab my mom's tortillas from

the refrigerator. "Mom would like her chia and flax tortillas. But I will be sticking to the processed white flour ones." I grin.

"I think I will too." He puts a stack of tortillas in the warmer and places them in the microwave. "I'll just warm these up, and then we're ready."

"Pause your love affair with Ethan, Mom. It's time to eat." I call out loud enough so that my mother can hear over the grunting contestants completing a physical challenge on the TV.

"Should I ask?" Amos questions with a smirk.

"*Survivor.*"

"Ah." He nods in understanding.

We sit down in the dining room and dish the food onto our plates. I look around the table and can't help but think how perfect this picture is. Love two fists her tortilla, holding it tightly as she determinedly takes a bite. Mom jammers on about Ethan, the survivor's athletic ability. *He's a professional soccer player, you know?* While Amos plays a flirtatious game of footsie with me under the table.

I'm drowning in this blissful utopia, and I don't want to come up for air. I need the baggage and emotional realities of this entire situation to stay far away, up in the clouds where they can't touch me. This. These people. This feeling. I need it more than my next breath.

Lee-Anne finishes her summary of the most recent episode of *Survivor* and dishes some black beans onto her flax and chia wrap.

"Mom, tell us something you're grateful for today," I say to the woman who barely knew me just a few short years ago. The woman who I can say I love now more than I ever have.

We started these grateful dinner time chats a month ago. I don't remember to do them every night, but I'm trying to stay consistent. I'm slowly building traditions into Love's life, as I think of them, one's that will help her become a healthy and happy woman someday. I want her to have everything I didn't and truly feel that she's loved unconditionally. I want to give her the childhood that I dreamed about, and it's never been about material things for me. It's about time with the ones we love and knowing that we're valued and cherished. My parents never made me feel like my existence mattered, and I need Love to know, that, for me—her existence is everything.

She saved me.

She was a parting gift from her dad that gave me the strength to continue living when I wanted to give up. She allowed me to feel joy when I was surrounded by darkness and love when my heart was shattered from pain. She's my miracle, and every second with her is a blessing.

Lee-Anne sets down her glass of water. "Well, today Lovie and I went walking through town, and there's this new shop with all sorts of things. It's very eclectic and hip. Anyway, they had a glass jar of this lavender spice that I've been searching everywhere for. I couldn't believe it. Right there, on the shelf with the candles and notecards, was a bottle of this spice that I've needed for so long." She clasps her hands together. "Anyway, I sure am grateful for it."

"That's awesome. What's the spice for?" I ask.

"Cookies."

"Cookies?" I look at Amos and Love with a confused expression. "But you don't bake."

She shrugs. "I know that, but I saw this cookie recipe in one of those magazines you brought me...the Oprah one, or maybe that Southern one. Anyway, the picture made the cookies look so delicious, and I've been wanting to make them with Love ever since."

"Well, okay. That's fantastic, Mom." I turn my attention to Love. "What makes you happy today, Lovie?"

She scrunches up her nose and holds up the pink piglet

napkin holder that she chose for herself and giggles under her breath.

"Oh." I splay my hand across my chest. "Perfect. That would make me happy, too. What's your favorite part?"

"His nose," she answers in her sweet little voice.

"Oh, I love pig noses, too." I look at Amos. "And you?"

"This right here. Having dinner with my favorite girls is the highlight of a pretty awesome day. What about you?"

"I'm grateful for you." I smile toward Amos. "For making an incredible dinner for us, and to Gigi, for taking such good care of my Love Dove while I work so I can help other kids that need me, and I'm thankful for Love and the best hugs in the world." I smile toward my daughter, and she returns it with one of her own.

"She really is the best hugger." Lee-Ann smiles toward her grandbaby, and Amos and I nod in agreement.

An hour after we've finished eating, I take Love upstairs for her bedtime routine while Amos cleans the kitchen, and Lee-Anne sneaks in another episode of who she started calling "her Ethan" over dinner.

Bath time, stories, and bedroom snuggles eventually culminate with a sleeping three-year-old, and I head downstairs.

Lee-Anne stands and flips off the TV with an exasperated, "Man, that was intense."

"Did your guy survive tribal council?" I ask.

"Yes, he did," she says relieved. "Alright, mi amorcito, I'll see you tomorrow." She kisses my cheek before heading out.

"Night, Mom."

Amos enters the living room with two glasses of wine. I take one and have a sip. "Thanks."

Setting the glass on the end table, I fall into the sofa, and Amos follows suit, plopping beside me. He takes my hand in his and threads our fingers together. His thumb runs back and forth along the top of my hand.

"Today was good," he states.

"It really was."

"So, date number two is in the books." His intense brown stare captures mine.

My eyes dart to his lips and back to his eyes. "It didn't even feel like a date. It just felt...normal and good."

"Did you expect different?" His mouth tilts into a grin.

"I don't know." I press my lips together. "I guess, I thought it might be weird in some way, or at least I was worried that it might be."

"Nothing's changed, Alma. It's us."

I smirk and quirk a brow. "Well, a little has changed." When Amos doesn't respond, I continue. "I see these"—I brush the thumb of my free hand over his lips—"a little differently now."

He kisses the pad of my thumb before giving it a nibble. "Yeah, maybe a little has changed."

He cups my chin and leads my mouth to his as we lean toward each other. I groan at the contact, the intense desire to kiss him all day escaping in a verbal release. The sound fuels Amos's movements, and he deepens the kiss. I pull my hand from his and press my palms against his shoulders, pushing his back against the couch cushions. I swing my leg over his lap and straddle him, our lips never separating.

Circling my arms around his neck, I push my body as close to his as it will go, and we kiss, and kiss, and kiss.

And it's perfect.

At this moment, I pray the clouds will stay far away. But I'll have to come up for air eventually, and when I do, I can only hope it doesn't rain.

CHAPTER 17

AMOS

Opening the door to Alma's office, I find her in conversation with Brooke, our outreach counselor. She's standing, bent over the table, pointing toward some papers. They're discussing some of the children we serve and their needs.

Every time I lay eyes on Alma, I'm captivated by her.

Her beauty. Her heart. Her drive.

She's amazing.

The formfitting skirt she's wearing clings to her curves, and the sight of it makes me all sorts of heated. I can't deny that I've had my share of daydreams in which I remove her attire and take her on the office table. I would never act on these desires for multiple reasons, but one can dream.

This empire of good that she and Leo built years ago is awe-inspiring, and the way she's run the charity since his passing is incredible. She's fucking incredible.

466

I can't help but feel that I'm not meant to be here. It's nothing that Alma or anyone has done. The whole staff is exceptional and welcoming. It's simply that Leo exists every-where within these walls. This entire place was their dream, and I'm late to the party—his party. Lion's Lair will always belong to Leo, and I'll forever be second place to him. I can't compete. No one stands a chance against a beloved legacy. And I have to be okay with that because there's nowhere else I'd rather be.

Our days here are often busy, and we don't exactly get a lot of one-on-one time but just knowing that Alma is under the same roof as me makes me happy. Being close to her is what I want. What I need. I'm not a weak man. Growing up with my father ensured that fact. I'm strong enough to come to work every day with a hint of vulnerability surrounding me if it means a life with Alma.

Second place is better than no place at all.

Alma looks up from the table, noticing me in the doorway for the first time. A smile spreads across her face. She wraps up the conversation with Brooke.

Brooke collects the papers on the table and taps them into a stack before sliding them into a folder and excusing herself from the room.

"Hi," Alma says, closing the gap between us.

I push the door closed behind me. "Hi, beautiful."

She drapes her arms around my shoulders. Leaning down our lips meet in a gentle kiss. I breathe her in, wanting so much more than a peck on the lips.

"I wanted to talk to you about this weekend," I say.

"Yes?" She lifts a brow.

"Let's get away for a couple of nights. Just you and me. I've already spoken to your mother, and she can stay at the house with Love. We'll be gone Friday night and Saturday but can come home early Sunday so you won't miss Love for the whole weekend."

The joy on her face from seeing me just seconds ago falls. Her features tighten with visible panic.

"It's just two nights. One full day. I think it will be good for us." I take her hands in mine and run my thumbs across her skin in a soothing rhythm.

She shakes her head and presses her lips in a line. "I don't know, Amos. I've never spent a night without Love in her entire life. I don't know..." She chews on the inside of her cheek.

Her response isn't surprising. In fact, it's what I expected. I know leaving Love will be hard for her.

We've been officially dating for over a month now, and truth be told, not much has changed in our routine, save for some awesome make-out sessions. We do the same things we've done since she lost Leo. I spend my evenings with Alma, Love, and Lee-Anne. There are princess movies and toddler games. Meals, and laughter, and snuggles. Excursions to the beach, or the zoo, or the library. It's all perfectly wonderful as it's been for the past four years. At night, when Love sleeps, and Lee-Anne returns to her condo, Alma and I sit on the sofa and talk, watch TV shows, and kiss.

Every day is some version of the one before.

I simply feel that we need to take this relationship to the next level if we're ever truly to know whether it will work. Alma has only been with one man, and my heart has to find out if she's capable of loving two. For each day I spend with her, I fall deeper in love. The uncertainty of our future is a constant dagger to my chest, a never-ending worry. *Will she love me? Can she?*

I'm going to love Alma until the day I die. There's no question about that. The hesitation comes in when I start to wonder, in what way? How is she going to allow me to love her?

A night or two away is what we need. We would benefit from a day when it's just us, in a neutral location, where we figure out what our future looks like. It's impossible to delve deeper into our relationship when we're forever surrounded by his memory.

I knew when I initiated this that it would require patience and understanding. I'm not here to judge Alma or the way in which she moves on. But I truly feel that getting away would help her.

It would help us.

Yet it's not my decision to make.

"I know it's a lot to ask, but I think we need it. We need time for us, away from our lives here to figure things out," I say, my voice gentle.

"I thought things were going well between us?" Alma asks softly, her eyes cast downward.

"They are. God, they are." I squeeze her hands. "The past month has been wonderful, some of the happiest moments in my life. But I think it's time to explore what more looks like for us. You know? I want *more* with you, Alma. But I want to do it right. I think a night away from our usual routine would be great."

Alma closes her eyes and pulls in a steadying breath. "I can't leave Love." She opens her eyes and holds me in her conflicted stare. "I can't be apart from her. I know it's silly, and parents spend nights without their kids all the time, but I can't. The thought of not holding her while she falls asleep makes me ill. Panic runs through my veins simply thinking about leaving her for that long. I know that someday I'll have to be ready. It's just not now. I'm sorry."

"It's okay." I circle my arms around her, pulling her into a hug. "I completely understand."

"I love you." She says the three little words that we've said to each other thousands of times in our life, yet this time, they sound like a consolation prize to a heart that I'll never own.

"I love you." I kiss the top of her forehead.

"My house for dinner?" she asks.

"Of course."

"I'll get there, Amos. I will." She steps back with a shy smile.

"I have no worries." I lie.

She glances at the clock on the wall. "I'm due in tutoring, but I'll see you tonight?"

I nod. "Absolutely. I'm meeting Shady on the courts in a few."

"Oh my gosh. Tell him I said hi. I'll try to sneak down to see him before you're done. I haven't seen him in a while."

"I will."

She gifts me with a grin and a quick kiss, and she leaves the office.

I grab my gym bag from my office and change into my shorts and a T-shirt. When I'm finished lacing up my tennis shoes, I head down to the gym. A good game of basketball actually sounds great right about now.

Shady, legal name William Smith, is already on the courts shooting hoops. I'm not sure where Shady's nickname came from, but the first time I met him, he asked me to call him such, so I do.

"Hey, Shade," I greet him.

"Big A! What's up, man?" He slaps my hand with his and leans in for a shoulder bump. Admittedly, I'm not a huge fan of the nickname that he has for me, but I don't have the heart to have him call me anything else. His face lights up when he calls me by the name. So for the shade-man, I'll be Big A.

He tosses the basketball to me. "Ready to get your butt kicked?"

"I'll have you know that I've been practicing since last week, and I think I'm going to win this one," I respond.

Shady laughs. "Not a chance."

Playing one-on-one is a great exercise, and the truth is, I need the workout and the endorphins it brings. Alma's rejection stung. I had hoped she'd...try. That's not fair because she is trying. I'm just so close to having her and very afraid she's going to slip away.

I said I was good with any future, as long as she's in it—in one way or another. But I know now that's not true. I don't want a future when she isn't mine, and there's not a damn thing I can do about it. It's all up to her. All my cards are in. I'm in—completely.

I just pray she'll jump in with me.

CHAPTER 18

ALMA

I light the last candle and look around the room. The entire main level of my house is glowing with flickering candlelight. It's beautiful.

There's soft, melodic music playing on the speakers, adding to the romantic vibe.

Earlier in the week, when Amos asked me to go away with him, I wanted to, desperately. It's true that we need to switch things up from the norm. I've been keeping our relationship in the shallow end, afraid to take it deeper. The truth is, I'm terrified, and maybe it's silly, but it's the reality of it.

This past month has been incredible, and I feel happier and more whole than I have in a long time, but I'm still scared. I want to love another and let Leo go. I know that's the healthiest course of action. But I'm also terrified to let him go because I still love him so much.

I can't live in the past, and I can't bring Leo back. For

myself and my daughter, it's important to move on and create a future for the two of us, one filled with immense joy and one that's based in reality and not a desperate longing for the impossible.

It's time, and I'm ready.

Retrieving the bottle of wine from the kitchen, I set it on the coffee table in front of the couch, next to my best attempt at a charcuterie board with meats, cheeses, crackers, and fruit.

The stage is set.

I asked Amos to come later tonight. I spent the evening with Love after a long week of work. Her sweetness filled my soul, and I needed it—that reset button.

There's a light knock on the front door, and I can't help but smile. Amos never knocks, has never had to. He's always been welcome within these walls. That simple act alone tells me that he's nervous, and I hate that I've made him feel that way. I hope tonight proves to him just how much I love him and how ready I am to move forward with him.

I swing the door open with a grin. "Knocking?"

He shrugs, the corner of his mouth tilting up. "It just felt right."

"Well, it's wrong." I link our pinky fingers and pull him through the threshold. "Don't knock. Never knock."

He chuckles softly. "Well, okay then."

I throw my arms around his neck and raise my lips to his. The moment our mouths meet, a delicious vibration courses through me, and I'm finally ready to feed my insatiable hunger. My body is on alert, the signs of want pounding across my pebbled skin with each heartbeat. *I need him.*

Amos pulls away, breaking our connection, and I gasp at the loss of contact. He leans his forehead against mine, his breaths heavy. "If that's the welcome I get by knocking, I'll always knock." His voice is deep and husky, and his breath ragged.

"I'm sorry," I whisper as I pepper kisses over the skin of his neck. "I'm sorry I said no to this weekend."

"Hey," he says, concerned. Grasping my shoulders, he pushes me a step away so he can look into my eyes. "You have nothing to be sorry for. You weren't ready. It's okay. I told you from the beginning that I'm here for you, and we'll take this at your pace."

I take his face in my hands. "I am ready, though." My thumbs pull his bottom lip down, and he hisses at the contact, his eyes rolling back.

"Alma," he says, looking around the candlelit space. "This is all incredible, and you are amazing. I love you so much. You know that. I will wait an eternity for you. I'm sorry I tried to rush you...I wasn't thinking clearly. Everything you've given me in the past month has been more than enough."

I reach for the button to his jeans, and I unclasp it. "I said I'm ready." My voice strains with need as I pull his pants and boxers down his muscular legs. He springs free, and my mouth falls slack, the vessel within my chest pounding rapidly at the sight.

I drop to my knees and grab him at the base, pulling his impressive length into my mouth. Amos hisses under his breath, a few choice expletives fall from his lips as his fingers slide through my hair. His skin is soft, and I moan around him as I take him as deep as I can. My tongue circles the tip.

"Alma." Amos moans, his hips pick up pace as he pushes harder into my mouth. "Fuuuck." The deep timbre is pained as the two of us get lost in the carnal need of the moment.

I can't think straight. I'm fueled by the all-encompassing desire to push Amos toward the brink until he collapses in ecstasy. I need his release more than I need my own. The wetness between my legs soaks my panties, and my body hums with pleasure.

"Wait." He gasps, pushing me away. "Not yet."

In a blur of frenzied movements, he kicks off his pants and removes his shirt until he's standing naked before me. My mouth falls slack at the site. He's a vision of perfection. His body is one of the most beautiful things I've ever seen. He makes quick work of removing my clothes.

We stand before each other bare and vulnerable, and needy. He traces the skin of my neck, down over my collarbone, until he's cupping my breasts.

"I'm in awe of you," he chokes out. "Utterly stunning."

His hands continue their descent, tracing lines over my ribs and across my stomach. He continues downward until his fingers move against the bundle of nerves between my legs.

I whimper at the touch and claw at his arms to steady myself. He continues rubbing, walking us back toward the sofa, his mouth kissing mine. I feel the fabric of the couch against the back of my knees and fall onto the cushions. Amos's fingers enter me, and I moan into his mouth. My legs begin to shudder with his presence. His fingers enter me and then pull out to rub my clit and enter me again in an intoxicating rhythm.

His lips leave mine, and he whispers against my mouth. "I feel like I've been waiting my whole life to taste you."

He kisses down my body until his face hovers between my legs. He plunges two fingers into me as he starts licking me in long, slow strides.

"Oh my God." I sob into the lust-filled air, and I reach for Amos's head, holding it as he moves against me. "Amos," I cry as his tongue picks up speed.

His fingers fuck me, rubbing toward my front wall as his tongue assaults me with pleasure. It's too much. Too amazing.

My nerves light, burning through every cell of my body. The build is intense, bordering on painful. I need this release more than I need my next breath. It hurts...so good. His tongue moves faster, and his fingers pump harder. I cry out, and my body begins to shake with anticipation as the release builds. He moves his free hand to my breast and tugs on my nipple.

And I explode. Lightning ignites and burns through my body from my toes to my head. I lose all sense of reality and get lost in the feeling and sensations encompassing me. A strangled moan leaves my lips, and my body quivers its release.

Amos kisses me as the final tremors leave me. "That was fucking amazing. Better than I could've imagined, Alma. So good. You are everything. Fuck, I need you so much."

"Take me." I sigh, still weak and sated from one of the best orgasms I've had. "Take me," I repeat.

"Do you have a condom?" Amos asks.

I shake my head. "We don't need one. I don't want anything between us."

Neither of us has been sexually active in years, and we've both been tested since then. Right now, I need to experience all of Amos with nothing between us.

He groans at my response and kisses me once again before lifting me onto him. His back against the sofa, I straddle him. We both watch as he pulls me over him. The connection is beautiful and so incredibly hot. We look good together.

"I love you," he says, looking up from our connection.

"I love you," I answer.

Our eyes stay locked as he begins to move. He grasps my hips, lifting me up and down onto him. In this position, he's so deep. I chew on my bottom lip and focus on his beautiful face. I'm drowning in love and lust, and pure satisfaction. I want to live in this feeling. I want Amos inside me all day long. God, it's incredible.

"Fuck, this is amazing, Alma." he groans, his thoughts mirroring my own.

"It is," I say on an exhale.

I start bouncing onto him, aided by his hold on me. We

make love harder and faster. Our skin slaps against one another, the sound echoing throughout the space. He takes my nipple into his mouth and sucks. I kiss his neck and suck on his earlobe. We whisper words of adoration, and it's perfect.

"I'm gonna come. Hop off," he grunts.

"Wait," I plead. "Touch me."

He strokes my bundle of nerves, and with a bit of pressure and a couple of flicks of his fingers, I'm screaming out a release. He pumps harder against me and moans as his body shakes against mine.

I fall against him, our skin slick with sweat, our breaths heavy.

"We could live a thousand years, and I still wouldn't get enough of you." Amos kisses me softly, his arms holding me tight.

I know exactly how he feels.

We remain connected and kiss softly amidst the candle-light. Skin on skin, we make out until my lips ache, and then we kiss some more. Our skin is still slick with sweat, warm from the heat in the room and our frenzied lovemaking. I can feel Amos hardening again inside me.

Amos breaks the kiss and lifts me off him. "Come on," he says gently. Grabbing my hand, he leads me upstairs and into the bathroom. He doesn't let go of my hand as he turns on the shower. He pulls me into the shower, and I stand beneath the spray of the warm water.

Squirting some body wash on my loofah, he lightly runs it along my skin, cleaning me. I squirt soap in my hand and run the suds over the ridges of his muscles. We kiss beneath the water and caress each other's skin. He makes me feel cherished and loved.

His soapy fingers reach between my legs and start rubbing my spot. It's sensitive from my two previous orgasms, but with some gentle coaxing, it starts to accept Amos's touch. I lean back onto the tiled wall and close my eyes. The hot water hits my side as Amos's hand moves between my legs. He sucks my breast into his mouth, and I take in all the sensations, the collection of movements enchanting. He teases my nipple, pulling it harder into his mouth, and his hand picks up speed while the fingers on his free hand enter me. I'm spiraling into an orgasm in seconds, moaning into the steamy air.

He pushes me flush against the back of the shower and hikes one of my legs around his hip to enter me. I lean into his chest and lick his taut nipples as he enters me again and again. Hard and fast, my back hits the wall as he pounds into me. He pulls my clit between his fingers, and I explode along with Amos. We let out a collective moan as he empties himself inside me once more.

"You're so perfect." He kisses my neck. "Fucking perfect."

"That was amazing," I respond.

"We don't ever have to go away. Work can have your days, and Love can have all your free time—just promise me your nights."

"You have my nights." I pull his tongue into my mouth. "Take them all."

He plays with my breasts, tugging and pulling. "We fit so well together, Alma," he says between kisses. "It's like your body was made for me and mine for you. I've never had this." His tongue dances with mine. "I don't want to ever be without you. Now that I know how we are together, there will never be anyone else for me."

The steam from the shower blankets me in warmth while Amos blankets me in love. It's been so long since I've had this —this feeling. Hope. Love. Physical satisfaction. I forgot what it felt like to be sated and adored.

Amos turns me around and pulls me to him, my back to his chest. He steps under the spray and kisses my neck as water cascades over my skin. He slides his hand down my waist.

"You're so beautiful, Alma."

He lowers his fingers until they're once again between my legs. *I physically can't do this again.* Every inch of my body aches with sated sensation, and my muscles burn from use. I don't have energy for another orgasm, yet as Amos strokes me, my body comes alive once more. I arch my back, turning my face to the side, my cheek against his muscled chest, my breaths quicken.

"You're so responsive, Alma. You and I are going to have so much fun." He nibbles my neck.

I freeze at his words. A cold blast of déjà vu hits me as echoes of another voice whisper the same thing. I push Amos's hand from me and step away.

"Alma? What is it?" Concern lines his voice, his eyes wide.

The tiled walls of the shower blur as tears come to my eyes. Visions of me naked, here, blood trickling down my legs invade my memories, and with them come the pain I felt at that moment.

So much pain.

I press my palms to my chest, hoping to relieve the ache.

"Alma?" Amos holds my arms. "What is it?"

He was there too.

A broken mirror.

A lost message.

Pain and loss and despair.

And Amos.

He was there, but he was helping me survive the misery, and now he's trying to make me forget the love.

I love Leo.

Lust-filled visions of the past hour flash through my mind on a reel, and I clutch my stomach, the urge to vomit strong. *I moved on.* Leo is no longer the only man I've ever loved or the only man I've slept with. I forgot him. During my time with

Amos and the lust-fueled ecstasy we shared, I completely forgot him.

Guilt consumes me, and I fall to my knees against the tiled shower floor. The blood is absent, but the agony is the same as it was that day.

Devastating.

All-consuming grief.

He's gone, and I'm forgetting him and enjoying it. *It's not right.*

"Alma." Amos lowers to his knees. "Talk to me."

I raise my face, soaked with tears and shame. "Please go," I beg.

"Alma."

"Go! Please. I need to be alone. Just go, Amos!" I cry.

His face is filled with indecision. "Let me help—"

I cut him off. "Go, now!"

His chest deflates, and the pain on his face is visceral, but he nods once and stands before stepping out of the shower.

I huddle in a ball and let the hot water pelt my back.

I don't know what to do.

It can't always be like this. How can I move on when it hurts this much? Grief, shame, and sorrow are my enemies. They can't give me Leo back, and they make any attempt at closure so incredibly painful that I'm bound to be alone forever.

I know Leo wouldn't want that for me. But I don't know what else to do.

CHAPTER 19

AMOS

It went against everything in me to leave her, crying alone in the shower, but she told me to. I had to listen. I knew it wouldn't be easy dating Alma. Though knowing something and living through it is very different.

Last night went from the best night of my life to one of my worst.

I can't stop thinking about us together. We were perfection. I've had sex plenty of times with several women, but it never came close to that. What I experienced with Alma was more than sex. It was an out-of-body experience with more satisfaction and love than I've ever felt. Nothing will ever top that connection, and I believe that wholeheartedly, deep within my soul.

At twenty-seven years old, I felt true love for the first time.

I'm mad, though I have no right to be.

I'm hurt, though I know her rejection isn't personal.

I'm angry with a man who's dead for holding Alma captive when I simply want to love her. Nothing about this is fair or easy.

She texted me this morning and told me that she needed time.

Time? For what?

To convince herself that a lonely widow is all she's meant to be? I can fight with everything in me, but I can't make her love me the way I love her. I can't make her forget him if her heart won't allow it. I can't make her move on or be happy if she's not ready. It's out of my hands.

I love her more than any man has loved a woman. I've protected her my whole life. I was her stability in a childhood that was anything but stable. I loved her unconditionally with my entire soul when no one else, not even her parents, did. I loved her until she felt strong, confident, and ready to take on the world. And she did. She's done amazing things for so many children.

She's been my other half before I knew what that meant. She stole my heart decades ago and never gave it back.

And I don't want it back.

I want her.

I need her to love me, and as pathetic as I may sound, not even in the same way in which I love her. If she can't love me with as much depth as I do her, I'd be okay, as long as she loved me enough to let me in. To be a real part of her life. To share a bed and a future with. I don't need all of her love. I just need enough of it.

Just a fraction of Alma's heart is a gift.

I've been lying here all day, in my lonely ass apartment, thinking about what I should do next. What's my next move? The truth is, I don't think I have one. I've shown her my love for years. I've put that love into words and laid it all out on the table as of late. I made love to her with my body, heart, and soul—and she was affected by it just as much as I was.

She knows.

She knows the entirety of my heart and intentions. There's nothing else I could do or say that would make it more clear. It's her move. She's either in or out, and only she knows which one.

I've always been a strong man, and very little has rattled me in life. Nothing really, save for Alma. Yet when something bothers me, it's Alma I talk to. She's always been my confidant. Ironically, I'm hurting more than I've ever hurt, and I can't talk to the one person I need to.

It's a bleak position to be in.

My cell rings, and I look to see that it's my mother. I send the call to voicemail, not in the mood to talk to her right now. She immediately rings back.

I release a sigh, and this time, I answer.

She's frantic. Her sentences are practically incoherent, but the words—Dad, heart attack, and hospital—are pretty clear.

"I'm on my way, Mom," I reassure her.

Five minutes later, I'm in my car and on my way home. The drive is a little over an hour from Ann Arbor, which gives me time to think. Dad, heart attack, and hospital. One would think those three words would elicit some sort of reaction in me.

Yet they don't.

My dad loves me in his own way, or at least I think he does. Yet he's never once showed an ounce of affection toward me. He's been cold, distant, and hard my whole life. Visiting my parents has never been an enjoyable experience. I wish things were different, but my dad is who he is, and I don't see that changing anytime soon.

I do feel sadness for my mother. The fear of losing my dad was tangible over the phone. For whatever reason, she loves him—in her own way.

I stopped going home a couple of years ago. I visited for years out of obligation, but it dawned on me that, as an adult, it's my choice as to what behavior I accept. I couldn't change the way my father treated me, but I could stop putting myself in the position to be treated that way.

My mother has driven to Ann Arbor a few times to see me over the years, but the relationship I have with my parents is anything but ideal.

My mom throws her arms around me and bursts into tears the moment I see her at the hospital. I rub her back as she cries into my chest in the hall outside my father's room. He's visible through the glass windows of the hospital door. He's lying in bed, in a hospital gown, with wires and tubes connected to his chest and arms.

"What did the doctor say?" I ask when her sobbing abates.

"They think he'll be okay. They want him to have surgery to clear the blockage from his artery. They say he needs to eat better and have less stress. You know your dad. I don't know how that is going to work. He only wants steaks, fried foods, and fatty carbs, and he hasn't had a non-stressful day in his life. I don't know what I'm going to do." Her voice is desperate.

"Mom, only Dad can make the choices to live a better life. You can't force him. The doctor can tell him the facts, and you can support him in healthier decisions, but ultimately, it's on him."

"I know. I'm just afraid that he won't change. He's always been so stubborn."

"If he wants to hold on to a toxic life because he's stubborn, then that's his choice. He knows the consequences. You can't change people, Mom. You can only support them."

"I won't be able to live without him if he doesn't get better." Her voice becomes frantic again.

"First of all," I say, rubbing her back, "he's still here now. But if you lose him someday, you'll be okay because you're strong, Mom. You don't give yourself enough credit, but you are."

"Thank you for coming home." She sniffles. "I know he's not your favorite person."

"He's still my dad, and I came for you."

My comments result in a small grin from my mother. "You're the best son a mother could ask for."

We stand side by side. My arm wraps around her back and holds her shoulder as we look in at my father. "It's weird seeing him so fragile, isn't it? Doesn't even look like him," she says.

"It doesn't."

"His surgery is tomorrow. Would you be able to stay with me? Maybe until he comes home in a few days. I don't want to be alone right now."

"Sure. Of course, I can do that." I kiss my mom's temple. "Let me just tell work that I'll be out this week."

"Okay," she responds as I step away and pull out my phone.

Calling Alma, *work*, doesn't feel right. Yet I do work for her, so it's accurate. I haven't told my mother about Alma and me yet, and I'm not rushing to tell her anytime soon. At least, not until I know we're going to work. I couldn't bear the condolences from my mother if we didn't.

I pull out my phone and text Alma.

HEY, I need to take a few days off work this week. Maybe most of the week. My father had a heart attack, so I'm home helping my mom.

HER RESPONSE COMES QUICKLY.

WHAT? OMG. I'm so sorry. I can come and see you today or tomorrow? Yes, I'm coming. I can help you with whatever you need.

. . .

I DON'T KNOW what to feel about her text. She was screaming at me to leave her alone last night, and now she wants to come help. I'm sure it's the best friend in her, and I appreciate it, but it's not needed.

No. Don't come. We're fine. Enjoy your weekend with Love. I'll text you when I know when I'm coming back.

ARE YOU SURE?
  I'm sure.

OKAY. Please let me know if you need anything. Xo

I STARE at her last text. *Xo?* We're not *xo* type people. We're *Love you* type people. Always have been.

I shake my head. I can't worry about it now. My mother is literally shaking.

"Mom, when's the last time you ate?"

She moves her head from side to side. "I don't remember."

I hold out my hand. "Come on. Let's go get some food."

* * *

THE NEXT MORNING, Dad goes into surgery without a kind word coming out of his mouth. Can't say I'm surprised. He is who he is, and if a near-death experience isn't going to change him, nothing is.

"How long do you think the surgery will last?" I ask my mom.

"The surgeon said three to four hours if all goes well. But it will be some time after that before we can see him," she responds.

"Do you want to go do something?"

"I think I'll just wait here. I don't want to be too far away from your father."

"Okay, then we wait. Let me at least get us some good magazines." I tap my mother's knee and promise to return soon.

I'm not sure what it is that my mother enjoys reading. Her whole life has been my father. So I grab one of everything remotely interesting that the gift shop has to offer. I also get a couple of bottles of sweet tea, chocolate bars, and potato chips.

Stepping out of the gift shop, bags in hand, I see her at the reception desk. Tanned skin, perfect curves, long, dark waves that cascade down to the middle of her back. My heart picks up speed, love rushing through my veins at the sight of her, no respect for the gravity of two nights ago. I can't feel this way when she and I may not make it as a couple, but my body doesn't listen. It's instinctual, and I crave everything about her.

As if she feels my stare, she turns to face me with a meek smile on her face.

She walks toward me, bags in hand.

"Hi. Are you doing okay?"

"Yeah, I am."

She lifts the bags in her grasp. "I didn't know what you needed, so I brought a few things. I got some sweet tea because I know it's your mom's favorite, and some candy bars for her sweet tooth, and some chips in case she needs something a little salty after so much sweet. I also got her some magazines to read while she's waiting. I don't know what she likes, so I bought everything they had." She sets the bags on the ground and pulls out a bag of Famous Amos cookies. "And I got these for you. I'm sorry." She shakes her head, a frown on her face.

Years back, Alma decided to gift my namesake cookies when we were at odds, which doesn't happen very often. I press my lips in a line, thinking of how I should even respond. She's so thoughtful and caring. The contents of our bags mirroring each other shows just how in sync and similar we are.

I take the bag of Famous Amos cookies from her extended hand. "Thank you. I appreciate it but not necessary."

"It is, though. I was horrible to you. I'm so sorry."

I sigh. "Let's deal with that later," I say, knowing that if my father wasn't in the hospital undergoing open-heart surgery, we still wouldn't be talking. There's no point in forcing a conversation that she isn't ready to have, especially not here. "Mom will be excited to see you."

"Amos." Her voice cracks. "I'm sorry."

"I know you are. It's okay. You'll figure it out, and it doesn't have to be today." My lips curve into a ghost of a smile, reassuring her that I'm okay even if I'm not.

She lowers her chin in a nod and retrieves her bags before following me to the waiting room.

"Alma," mom says, a sincere smile finding her face. "It's so good to see you."

Alma hugs my mom. "I'm sorry to hear about Mr. Davis."

"Yeah." Mom shrugs and shakes her head. "It's going to be fine. He has a world-class heart surgeon working on him now, and then he'll be fine, just fine."

"I'm so glad." Alma takes a seat between my mother and me. She hands the bags she brought over. "I brought some snacks and reading material. Maybe it will help pass the time."

"You're so sweet. Thank you, dear." She looks inside the bags and pulls out a sweet tea and candy bar. "Would you two like some? Alma brought plenty to share."

"I'm good. Thank you," Alma and I say in unison.

"Okay. Well, if you change your mind, let me know. So, tell me, Alma, what have you been up to? I haven't spoken to you in so long. You still running that place that helps kids? How's your daughter? Your mom? I heard about your dad's passing. I'm so sorry about that."

Alma grins sweetly, "Thank you. My mom is doing great. We're closer than ever. She is over at my house every day and lives only a few blocks away. Yes." She nods. "Love is three now and perfect in every way. I'm still running the Lion's Lair, and it's going fantastic. Amos has been a big help with that."

"How's that?" she asks, looking from me to Alma.

Alma looks at me, confused, and then back at my mom. "Well, he works there now. He's my partner at the Lair."

"He didn't tell me that. How wonderful. So, then you two get to see each other quite often. You were always inseparable as children. I'm glad to see your friendship has lasted all these years."

"Yeah, me too," Alma says in a cheerful voice, though I can hear the worry in her words.

"So what do you do at work?" Mom asks.

Alma supplies her with uplifting anecdotes about some of our children at the Lair, and Mom listens intently. The conversation is easy as Alma catches my mother up on the past several years. She leaves out the part about us dating just as I have.

Mom reaches for another candy bar and pulls out a stack of magazines.

"What do you have?" Alma eyes the bags at my feet.

"Take a look," I tell her.

She looks inside and scoffs. "Almost identical. Great minds think alike."

"I guess they do."

"You don't have to stay. It's going to be a long day, and

you're looking at the gist of it right here. We have everything we need. I know you want to get home to Love and spend the rest of your Sunday with her. I appreciate you coming, but you should go." I squeeze her knee, reassuring her of my sincerity, though touching her feels wrong with how things ended the other night.

"Okay. I just wanted to make sure you were both okay."

"You have, and we are. You can go home."

She nods and stands, offering a goodbye to my mom before the two of us walk toward the hospital entrance.

We stop and step off to the side of the exit door. Alma turns to face me. "I hope you know that the other night had nothing to do with you and everything to do with me. You were incredible."

"I appreciate what you're doing, but it's not necessary. I don't need my sexual skills complimented. It's not about that." My words come out harsher than I'd like.

She drops her head. "You're mad. You deserve to be. I treated you so…"

I press a finger beneath her chin and lift her face, locking her gaze with mine. "I'm fine. Don't worry about it. Okay?"

"I told you I was broken." Her chin quivers beneath my touch. "You deserve so much better."

"Hey, stop." I pull her into a hug, wrapping my arms around her, and she nuzzles her face into my shirt. "I don't want to do this here. You said you needed time. Take the time. We don't have to decide anything this second. You know where I stand. You know how much I love you. Now, you have to figure out what you want."

She nods against my chest. "Okay."

Alma turns and takes a step toward the door as panic rises within me. Regret over my recent words and feigned acceptance set in. I can't allow her to walk away from me, thinking

I'm okay letting her go. I reach out for her hand and pull her back to me.

I cup her face in my hands. "Just know that I'm all in. You are the only one for me. I will fight for you for the rest of my life if that's what it takes because you and I are destined to be together. You're my soul mate, Alma. I've known that since I was seven. You're my other half, my kindred spirit. I don't want this life without you. We are so good together, in every way. Friday night was the culmination of twenty years of love and should show you that. But I can't compete with a ghost. There are no winners in that scenario. You have to let go enough to let me in, or it won't work. It just can't."

She drops her chin. "Okay," she says again.

"Think about it, Alma. Really think about what you want in this life because you're young and there's so much in store for you. An exciting new chapter could be starting right now, but you have to be brave enough to turn the page." I swipe my thumbs against her soft cheeks. "I love you," I say before I pull her into a kiss. It's not a long one, but it carries the hope for a future on our shared breaths, and it's powerful.

"I love you," she whispers across my lips before she turns and walks away.

Please let it be enough. I think as she disappears through the doors. *Let it be enough.*

CHAPTER 20

ALMA

I cried the whole way home from the hospital on Sunday, my heart tearing in two. I've skated through the week in a daze, my mind always somewhere else. Memories of Leo came back to me in vivid detail—all of them, just when I thought they were fading.

There isn't a choice, not really. Only one scenario makes sense, and my brain knows this. I can't turn away from the chance at an incredible life with an epic love because I'm afraid to let my first love go. *It's time.* It's been time, but that doesn't make it any easier.

If Leo and I had ended on bad terms, gotten a divorce, or grown apart—it'd be a different story. It's a struggle to love another when I'm still so in love with him. If it were anyone but Amos, I wouldn't. I'd rather live in the memories alone.

But it's Amos.

And he's worth it.

He's worth fighting for, and the crazy thing is that I'm only fighting myself and my own inability to let go.

As I pull away from work, my car drives as if on autopilot. I don't register where I'm heading until I'm there. I put the car in park, turn off the engine, and stare ahead.

LEO DAVID HARDING
  Beloved Husband
  YOU ARE BURNED INTO MY SOUL FOREVER.

TEARS COURSE over my cheeks before I reach his tombstone. My heart breaks at the sight, as it always does. Love and I come here every once in a while to talk to her daddy, and when we do, it's not as hard as it is now. I know that if Leo is listening, he'd be able to listen to my thoughts regardless of where I am. Still coming to the cemetery makes me feel closer to him. I have this idea in my head that if he's going to hear me anywhere, it'd be here.

I kneel at his gravestone.

I pull in a breath. "You told me to move on. You want me to be happy. But why is it so hard? Why do I feel that I'm betraying you and what we had? Love deserves a father figure in her life, and I deserve a companion. It makes sense. But it's so fucking hard, Leo." I sob into my hands. "It's so fucking hard to let you go."

The ache within my chest is unbearable. Loving Leo, my soul mate, has become a life sentence—one I can't escape no matter how hard I try.

"I need you to help me. Give me strength. Let me let you go," I choke out. "I have to let you go."

Even as I say the words, they feel like lies coming from my mouth. I lie down on the soft grass in front of the gravestone and cry.

"You're never coming back," I whisper. "I love him, you know? Maybe you always knew. You had a way with reading people like that. In the beginning, you were so jealous of him, and I couldn't understand why. Perhaps you saw it before I did."

My hand slides out to my side, running the blades of grass between my fingers. "I think I could love him the way I loved you, and that thought terrifies me. You are my soul mate. What does it mean if I can love him in equal measure?"

Who says we get just one?

The thought sounds within my mind, loud and clear. I can't tell whose voice it is. Mine? Leo's? My mother's? It doesn't matter though because I finally hear it.

Who says we get just one?

I sit up. "I can have two epic loves. Can't I?"

I wait for a response that doesn't come.

As always, when I truly need Leo, I close my eyes and focus deep within. I breathe in and out, a steady rhythm and I concentrate on the beats of my heart, the sounds of the birds and bugs around me, and the gentle whooshing of the summer wind. I go into myself for minutes, an hour—I lose track of time. I block the negativity of the world out and breathe. The ache in my chest finally lessons and I know Leo lifted it from me, as if to say, *It's okay to let me go.*

"I will love you, forever." my voice trembles. I stand and peer down at his grave. Kissing the tips of my fingers, I press them against the stone. "Forever."

I turn and walk toward my car. Opening the door, I put one leg inside, and return my attention back toward Leo's resting place. "Goodbye, my love."

I drive away from the cemetery, broken and shattered but stronger and lighter, at the same time. The weight in my chest has truly lifted.

It's taken four years but I finally said goodbye.

CHAPTER 21

ALMA

"*I* think that Ariel is right..." I look at the overturned cards on the table and pick one. "...here!" I say, revealing Princess Tianna in her green ball gown.

"No." Love giggles. "Momma, she's right here." Love turns over the Ariel card.

"Oh." I feign surprise. "There she is. I'm silly."

"Momma silly." Love shakes her head and collects the Ariel matches from her Memory game.

"You got the match so you can go again," I tell her.

I watch as Love bites her tongue in concentration and studies the cards on the table. It's so incredible watching her little brain work. She's so smart, and astonishes me every day. I used to bite my tongue when I was concentrating as a child. I'm so giddy when I discover something about her personality that comes from me. She's her daddy's mini, no doubt, and I love it. I'll always feel him here with me, through her. Still, it's fun when random traits of mine shine through in her personality.

We finish the princess Memory game and make some ice cream sundaes to take outside. It's a beautiful, hot and humid, Michigan summer day.

Perfect for ice cream sundaes.

When we've eaten until our hearts' content, I turn on the sprinklers.

"Come on." I reach my hand toward Love. "Let's rinse off all the stickiness."

"Momma. My dress." She holds the skirt of her floral sundress.

I bend my knees so I'm face-to-face with her. "Let's go run through in our clothes. Who needs a swimsuit. Right?"

"Right!" She takes my hand, and we race through the oscillating sprinkles, laughing the entire time.

I close my eyes as the water pelts my face. The spray is chilly, but the sun quickly heats my wet skin. Arms out to our sides, we spin in circles under the water. There's nothing I love more than living life through my daughter's eyes. When I'm with Love, I'm happier than I've ever been. Each day as her mother is a blessing.

Soaked and exhausted from laughter, we plop down in the grass, just out of reach from the sprinkler.

"It's itchy, Momma." she scratches at her arms where the blades of grass meet her skin.

"Come here." I pull her onto my chest and wrap my arms around her. "Better?"

"Yes." She rests her face against me

I hold her tight. "Do you know that I love you more than anyone else in the entire world?"

"Yep!"

"Do you know that you're the absolute love of my life?"

"Yep!"

"Good. Never forget it. No matter what you grow up to be, who you grow up to love, or what you do in this life...I will always love you. Always. Always. Okay?" I tell her this type of stuff all the time, and perhaps it's a little deep for a three-year-old, but I want it to be so ingrained in her that she'll never question it. "You, Love Grace, are the best thing to ever happen to me. I love you, forever."

"I love you, Momma. You the best."

"No, you are."

"You are," she snaps.

"Never. It's you."

"You!" She laughs.

"Okay, fine." I hug her tighter. "We're both the best."

"Okay." Love agrees. "Both best."

"Are you excited for your weekend of fun with Gigi?" I ask, pulling a wet strand of hair from her face.

She nods her head with enthusiasm.

"She always makes everything so fun. Doesn't she?"

"Gigi the best, too." Love notes.

"She is. We're all amazing. Aren't we?" I kiss her head.

I took the past two days off from the Lair and spent every waking moment with Love. Truth is, I needed it. I needed her, and the utter innocence and happiness she fills me with. She's the best therapy there is.

Everything at work is running smoothly, and I figured what's the point in being the boss if I don't take some time off here and there. After Leo's death and during Love's first year of life, I was home a lot. Since Lee-Anne has been helping me with Love, I've been working more than ever, and I'm not doing it anymore—at least not so much. I have a collection of brilliant and capable co-workers who are able to run the place without me there every moment. Love's only going to be this little once, and I need to cherish it.

Amos is coming back tonight, and I'm going to surprise

him with a weekend away. We've hardly spoken this week, just a few texts here and there. He's been home helping his parents and giving me space to think about what I want.

I already know what I want.

It took me a while to accept it, but I'm ready.

I can't sacrifice time with Love for Amos. I know that about myself. She's my number one. She has to be. But I can still have a meaningful relationship. Amos is right. She'll be fine spending a night or two away from me. These past two days of uninterrupted quality time with Love have helped ease my guilt.

I'll get better at delegating my time. When Love was born, it was she and I against the world. At the time, I was struggling to simply exist, and she was my anchor. Every day doesn't have to be a battle. It's okay if I simply—live.

Let go.

Smile.

Just be.

Be present. Be joyful. And be without worry.

I can do that, and this weekend, with Amos, I will.

"What's going on out here?" Amos's voice startles me from the snuggle session in the grass.

I sit up, and Love hops off me.

She runs to Amos and jumps into his arms, giving him a big, wet hug. "Cookie!"

"Hey, Love bug. What are my girls doing?"

"Ice cream and sprinklers," Love says excitedly.

"Wow. Looks like I missed a fun day." He kisses her on the head and sets her down on her feet.

"Hi." I reach him and press my lips to his. "I missed you," I say against his mouth before kissing him again.

"I missed you." He sighs, a hint of relief present.

"Everything okay at home?"

He nods. "Yeah, Dad's home and resting, grumpy as ever

but recovering nicely from surgery. I enjoyed my time with Mom before he came home from the hospital. It was great."

"Good. I'm so glad. You're home early? I thought you'd be getting back tonight?"

"Well, there's only so much time I can handle with my father. It was time to come back." He scans my wet attire. "You said you needed to see me. Was it an invite to whatever this is?" He chuckles.

His question sparks an idea, and I look down to Love. "What do you say? Should we show Amos what we're up to?"

She grins and bobs her head.

"You might want to toss your wallet and phone over there." I point toward a dry patch of grass.

Amos does as instructed, and I thread my fingers through his. Love holds his other hand, and we run through the sprinklers. Amos releases cries of mock protest, which causes Love to laugh harder. We dance, and spin, and run in circles through the spray. Water soaks my face making it hard to see straight until we're once again exhausted and fall onto the grass.

Love plops on my stomach.

"There you go," I say. "Now you're fully up to speed on our day. Well, besides the ice cream and games, of course."

Amos lies beside me and wraps his pinky finger around mine. "I missed ice cream and games?"

"I'm afraid so, but I think we left you some ice cream."

"We did," Love chimes in. "There's a lot!"

"Oh, good," Amos responds.

We lie in the grass, eyes closed, as the sun warms our skin. After a few minutes, Love's breathing evens out.

"She's out," I whisper and turn my face toward Amos.

"I stopped by at the Lair first. They say you've been home," Amos remarks, quietly as not to wake Love.

"Yeah, I took the past two days off for Mommy and Love time."

"That's good, Alma." Amos smiles.

"It's been great. I think I want to start taking a day off during the week to be with her, at least until she starts school. I don't want to miss anything."

"You should. You have a team of people running the Lair, Alma. It doesn't always have to fall on you."

"I know. There are just so many kids who need help and not enough time in the day to do everything that needs to be done."

"Unfortunately, in our business, there will never be enough hours in the day. You have to take comfort that you're helping as many as you can. You can't save the world, but the kids you do help—you're saving them. And all of your staff has huge hearts. They don't work as hard as they do because you're there all the time. They work so hard because they care, and that won't change if you take a day off."

I nod, knowing he's right. "There's another reason I spent the past couple of days home with Love."

"Yeah?"

"I planned a weekend away. Just the two of us."

Amos's eyes widen, and the corners of his mouth tilt up. "You did?"

I bite my bottom lip, "I did. I'm sorry I said no before. This week apart was good for me. I've been able to put some things into perspective, and I'm ready."

He lifts a brow. "You sure?"

"I am."

He closes the distance between our mouths and kisses me. "I love you, Almalee Hannelda."

"I love you," I answer.

"Where are we going?"

"It's a surprise."

"Okay." He smirks. "I like that."

Amos scoots up close beside me and kisses me slowly and

quietly. His lips are magical, and it takes everything in me not to deepen the kiss.

"I should go in and shower," I say when his lips leave mine. "And you should go home and pack."

"What do I need to bring?"

"Whatever you want, really. Maybe a bathing suit."

"I can do that." He stands and lifts Love from me. There's a pool of sweat on my chest where her face was. He holds her in his arms, and we walk into the cool air-conditioned house.

Lee-Anne sits at the table reading a magazine. The easy smile on her face is a little too perfect. I can only imagine she witnessed Amos and my kissing session in the grass and is all too pleased.

"Hi, Mom. I didn't know you were here."

"Yep, just got here. Wanted to be here while you got ready for this weekend."

Amos lays Love down on the couch.

"Well, she is excited about her weekend with you," I tell my mom.

"Oh, I'm excited, too. I have so many things planned. She's going to be having so much fun. She won't have time to miss you."

I let out a chuckle. "Well, I'm glad. I'm going to go shower," I say to my mom before waving goodbye to Amos. "I'll see you soon."

"Can't wait."

Me either.

CHAPTER 22

AMOS

I wind the car through the narrow drive. A forest of tall pines lines either side of the road, creating a beautiful canopy of green over us. Moments later, the house comes into view. Huge and white with dozens of grand windows, the house is exquisite and impressive as it overlooks the white sand and crystal blue water of Lake Michigan.

"How did you score this place?" I ask Alma as I put the car in park, knowing a rental this beautiful would book up two years in advance.

"Well." Alma grins proudly. "You know, Ms. Betty?"

"Our psychologist, Ms. Betty?"

"The very one." Alma nods. "It's hers! She said it's always rented except for the weekends that she's up here. She and her wife Florence were supposed to be here this weekend but had to fly to Florida instead. One of their daughters needs help moving or something. So, when I mentioned that I was looking for a place, she offered it to us."

"Wow. This place is incredible." I step out of the car and look out toward the crashing waves of the lake.

"Yeah, did you know that Florence is a heart surgeon at the University of Michigan hospital?" Alma asks.

"No, I didn't."

"Me either. I can't believe that's never come up."

I grab the bags from the trunk. "I can't believe they don't live up here full time. How could you own such a beautiful home and not live there?"

"I asked Betty. She said that they both adore their jobs in Ann Arbor, so they can't move up here just yet."

"That makes sense." I give Alma a kiss. "Let's go explore."

The interior of the house is just as beautiful as the exterior. A white stone fireplace, dark wooden floors, cream walls with blue accents, and contemporary but elegant features make the huge home feel sophisticated and beachy at the same time.

I drop the bags in the bedroom and follow Alma onto the deck. The calming sounds of the waves and the wind whipping through the trees are some things I'd never grow tired of. The house is set up on a hill away from the private beach. The plot of land is large enough that we can't see any other homes from the deck, which is rare on Lake Michigan.

Alma and I lay against the cushions of the padded lounger and stare out toward the water. "You should buy a place like this. It's heaven on earth," I say.

"I really should."

"You have the money. Why not use it toward something this amazing? Love would love it here."

"She would," Alma agrees. "She adores the beach. I love the Great Lakes. You know I'd never been to one until college? Leo showed them to me."

"I remember," I say.

"I'm sorry. I shouldn't have said that."

"No." I grab her hand. "I'm glad you did. You need to be able to talk about him. He's a huge part of your past and Love's dad. We can't pretend he never happened, and I know you'd never want that. I understand that you were in love and married before. It's okay."

She squeezes my hand and lets out a sigh. "You're so good to me."

"Are you really okay?" I ask her, remembering how things ended last weekend after we'd made love.

"I am," she says, her voice steady. "I promise."

"I believe you, but I worry. I don't want to do anything that might upset you. Last weekend was…" I search for the right word to use.

Alma finishes my sentence for me. "Needed." She shrugs. "I needed to know what it felt like to be with you so I would know how right it was. I needed the guilt so I could get past it. I needed to let go."

"And did you?"

"I think I did. I feel lighter and happy. I'm sure our future won't be without struggles. I'm a work in progress, but I hope we're worth it."

I bring her hand to my lips and kiss her soft skin. "You're worth everything to me, Alma. Everything. I'll never stop fighting for you."

She presses her lips together in a smile and lowers her chin. "I know, and I'm fighting for you, too. I want you to know that I truly am."

We get lulled by the melody of the water and sit in silence for several minutes.

"So last weekend was good for you?" I quirk a brow. It's a self-indulgent question, but I want to hear her say it. I need to know that I made her feel as good as she made me feel.

She releases a light-hearted chuckle. "Yeah." She scoffs. "It was…God, Amos…it was incredible."

"Were you surprised?" I wonder.

"Maybe a little," she admits. "I guess I thought it would be good, but it was greater than any expectation. It's like…"

"We're meant to be." I finish her thought.

"Yeah," she says softly. "I also wondered how we'd never done that before. I mean, you and I were hormonal teenagers together, and we never tried to see what it'd be like. It's kind of shocking when I think about it."

"It is, but it wasn't our time. Our friendship was more important than anything then. It was the thing that supported us both and gave us the strength to be and do what we dreamed. And truthfully, if we had, we would've never stopped, and then you wouldn't have Love."

"That's true. I suppose life has its own agenda. And just so you know." She rotates her body so she's leaning into me. "It won't end the same way. This time."

Her words cause an ache within my chest. Simply thinking about the finale in the shower unsettles me in a way that's hard to process. I swallow and pull in a breath. "Okay."

"It won't. I promise."

I nod and kiss the top of her head.

She must sense my hesitation. "I hurt you, and I'm sorry. I didn't see those emotions coming until they were there, but I've dealt with them. Amos." She holds her palm against my cheek and turns my face toward hers. "I'm good….now."

"Okay," I reassure her. "I'm glad."

I focus my gaze back on the water and allow the lull of the waves to relax me once more.

Alma kisses my neck softly at first. I close my eyes as her lips start to move with purpose, nibbling and sucking against my skin. Immediately, I'm painfully hard within my shorts. She's making the move, and I didn't realize it until now, but I needed her to. I had to know that she was ready. I couldn't survive being a regret, not again.

My skin itches with want when she pulls her lips from me. She stands. Her hooded eyes bore into mine. Her full lips, slightly parted as she pushes the straps of her dress down her shoulders. The dress falls and pools at her feet. I gnaw at my bottom lip as she unclasps her bra and frees her breasts.

"Alma," I say on exhale as she begins to shimmy out of her panties.

She stands before me completely bare. Her long brunette hair feathers across her skin, lightly blowing in the lake's breeze. The sun is setting on the horizon, and the sky is alive with shades of blue, purple, and pink. Her body creates a perfect silhouette against the bright orange sun. For a moment, I'm unable to move, captivated by her beauty. She's so insanely gorgeous, it's unreal. She's my living dream. Her body is perfection, but her soul is more.

I hold her stare as I unbuckle my khakis and release myself. I kick off my shorts and boxers and pull my shirt over my head.

"Come here." My voice is gravelly from lust. "I need to taste you." I hold my hand out, and she takes it. Pulling her toward me, I lie flat on the large lounge chair.

Alma hesitates.

"Straddle my face, baby. Don't be shy," I urge her.

She climbs across me and puts a knee on either side of my face. I reach for her hips and pull her down onto me. We groan in unison as my tongue takes the first taste. I start licking faster, greedy for more—more of her sounds, her movements, her body. Grasping her thighs, I rock her back and forth against my face.

"Amos," she calls out, her voice shaking.

I pick up the pace and make love to her with my mouth,

licking and probing and sucking until she's shaking and screaming my name.

She scoots down my body and falls onto me, breathing heavily. I kiss across her skin, over her shoulders, and up her neck until I'm at her mouth. I lick the seam of her lips, and she opens, allowing me entrance. We kiss, our tongues dancing wildly with one other. She holds my face, and I grasp her hair, pulling her face tighter against mine. I can't get enough of her. I'll never have enough of her.

Releasing a hand from her hair, I grab my shaft and run it along her wet opening. She moans at the contact. "Are you ready?" I say into her mouth.

"God, yes," she groans.

Grabbing her hips, I lower her onto my length. She whimpers, and the sweet sound makes me want to come at this very moment. I start lifting my hips toward her, and I pull her against me. "Does that feel good?" I grunt.

She presses her face against my neck. "Yes. Yes. Yes," she answers, her words breathy.

Circling my arm around her back, I flip us so that her back is against the cushion, and I'm above her. Tilting back, I grab her knees and push up and out, so they're at her side, opening her wide. I pound harder, able to go so deep in this position. Alma cries out a sob of pleasure. She's grabbing at my arms as I enter her again and again.

"Oh, fuck me. Yes. Oh, yes." She moves her hips to meet me thrust for thrust.

She lowers her hand between her legs and feels at the base as I enter her. Collecting wetness on her fingers, she starts to rub herself. The sight is my undoing, and I pump harder, chasing my orgasm. As her eyes roll back and she starts to tremble, I pound my release inside her. We're a collection of moans and sobs as we find our high together.

I fall onto her and kiss her lips. "God, I fucking love you."

"Our bodies were seriously made for one another, Amos," she says between kisses. "I will never get enough of you. I don't want to do anything this weekend that doesn't involve you inside me."

"What about cooking? We have to eat." I say, holding her face in my hands as my lips continue to worship her mouth.

"I'll cook the food while you fuck me." She circles her tongue around mine.

"I'd say that sounds like a plan, except you usually prefer I do the cooking," I tease.

She giggles. "That's true. Okay, new plan. You cook and make love to me at the same time."

"Well, I'll do my best."

CHAPTER 23

ALMA

I stand wearing only Amos's T-shirt and my panties and lean against the open sliding glass door of the deck. The water is so beautiful, and the sounds of the waves alluring. The lake breeze blows against my skin. I could get used to lake life. There's no air conditioning in this place as it's not needed. Michigan doesn't get hot enough in the summers to warrant it, especially here where the windows are always open, inviting in the fresh, cooling air from the water.

Amos walks up behind me and pulls my hair to the side, kissing my neck. "Lunch is ready."

I pivot around to face him and drape my arms over his shoulders. Standing on my toes, I give him a gentle kiss. "It smells amazing."

Wearing only his boxer briefs, he leads me to the table where a bowl of freshly cut fruit and a plate of French toast sits. The spread is simple, but I know it'll be delicious. The food resembles a breakfast, but I was craving French toast with fresh maple syrup, and so Amos delivered.

Sitting at the table, I start dishing up. My body is tired, but my soul is alive and happy. Last night and this morning were spent making love to Amos in every position and place this house has to offer. We're like desperate honeymooners who can't get enough of one another, and I'm definitely not complaining. Sex with Amos is unbelievable.

"What are you thinking about?" he asks, his mouth in a smirk as he plops a strawberry in his mouth.

"Nothing," I say meekly, peering down to my plate.

He shakes his head with a chuckle. "You've never been able to lie. You know that?"

I shrug. "So, you can't prove a thing." I scrunch up my nose.

He nods knowingly. "I was thinking about it, too."

I press my lips together in a grin.

"I can't imagine Betty here after we've had sex on every surface," Amos says.

"Well, she rents this place out a lot, and I know others are doing it here as well. I suppose it goes with the territory of rentals. The professional cleaners that come in after each stay probably give Betty and Florence a little peace of mind."

"Do you think others have done it there?" He raises a brow and nods toward the cream sofa in front of the fireplace.

"Probably."

"What about there?" He motions toward the wall between the bookshelves that made a pleasant backdrop for wall sex last night.

"I don't know." I chuckle.

"There?" He looks at the large silver Viking range where I took him in my mouth as he made eggs this morning. My heartbeat quickens at the memory. "What about here?" He runs his hand across the table where his mouth worshiped between my legs until I was screaming after we consumed said eggs.

"Amos," I protest, my voice coming out in a whimper. "My French toast." I supply the only argument I have.

"Eat," he urges. "I'll watch," he says as he frees himself from his boxers. Circling his fingers around his shaft, he starts to rub up and down in long and leisurely motions.

My mouth falls slack at the sight, and a rush of need soaks my panties.

"You play dirty." I push away from the table and stand, stepping out of my satin fabric covering me.

"Your shirt," Amos says, moving his hand against himself with more fervor as he pulls his bottom lip between his teeth.

I rip off my shirt, leaving me completely bare, and I straddle him in the chair. His hands grab my ass cheeks and squeeze as I sink onto him. We release a collective moan as I start bouncing against him, my orgasm instantly starting to build. He releases his hold on my ass and threads his fingers through my hair, pulling my face toward his. He kisses me hard and rough.

Our lips crave more.

Our tongues explore, deep.

The kiss is intoxicating and almost painful in its all-consuming desperation.

I ride him, my relentless need urging me faster.

He pulls his mouth from mine and sucks at my breasts, pulling my nipples into his mouth.

"I'm close." He draws out.

"Me, too," I whine against the sweat-soaked skin of his neck.

He lowers a hand between my legs, and with a rub and pinch, we're moaning out our release together.

Still atop him, I lean against his chest and catch my breath.

"How are we going to go back to real life where we can't fuck at the dining table during every meal?" He bites my shoulder playfully.

"I know," I agree. "How are we going to go to work this week when I know that you're not going to press me against the wall and pound into me?"

"I mean, I could?" He quirks his brows and supplies a playful smirk.

"Yes because that would be completely appropriate and professional." I chuckle.

"You do own the place," he kids.

"And as the owner, I have to hold on to a shred of scruples." I kiss his forehead.

He peppers kisses against my arm. "Can I ask you something?"

"Always."

"You're not on birth control, right?"

"No." I shake my head.

"And we're not taking any precautions?" He eyes me in question.

I've thought about this a lot, but I never talked it over with Amos, which I realize isn't right.

"Well, they say Love was a miracle baby. I still have a lot of scar tissue and blockage from the accident. The chances of conceiving another baby naturally are low, but it could happen again because it happened once. I guess, in my mind, I figured if it happened at some point, it was meant to be. But I should've talked about it with you. I'm sorry. It's not likely that I'd get pregnant, but what if I did? What do you think about that?"

Amos smiles. "I think that'd make me a very happy man."

"Really?"

"Of course. You and me, we're forever. We've always been. And now that we've added this"—he nods toward where we're still connected—"I'm even more sure of it. I never want to love a woman, kiss a woman, or touch a woman if that woman isn't you. You've owned my heart since we were seven, and you'll own all of me until my last breath. We can take it slow and do it on your terms when you're ready, but we're forever."

"Mutt and Cookie against the world?" I grin.

"Then. Now. Always."

I lean into him and hug him tight.

"I'm hungry," I add.

"Well, here." Reaching around me, he stabs a piece of toast with his fork and brings it around to my mouth. "Let me help you with that."

A trickle of syrup falls against my chest as I bite the French toast. It's cold and soggy but still good. Amos repeats the movement, placing another piece in my mouth, and another trickle of sticky maple syrup falls to my chest.

"I'm getting all sticky," I protest with a giggle.

He leans down and licks a glob of syrup that's fallen on my breast.

"You're just spreading it. You know?" I laugh.

"Well, finish eating, and we'll get cleaned up." He puts the full fork into my mouth again.

"Maybe I should do it." I protest with a wide smile across my face. I chew the huge piece of soggy bread in my mouth.

He shakes his head. "No, I'm committed now."

Amos finishes feeding me and then takes my hand as he leads us outside. We run down the wooden steps leading to the white sandy beach. I look around the grassy sand dunes, making sure we're indeed alone. I don't want to scar an innocent child out building a sandcastle.

We're alone, just Amos and me. There's nothing but grassy dunes, porcelain-colored sand, and blue waves as far as the eye can see. This property is heaven on earth.

"You ready?" Amos nods toward the water.

I pull in a breath, knowing the water will be cold. Lake Michigan is so big, and frozen for much of the year. It warms up in the summer months but is still pretty chilly compared to other bodies of water.

"Yeah." I squeeze his hand.

Hands clasped, we run into the waves. I shriek as the cool water assaults my skin, taking my breath away.

"Come on," Amos urges, pulling me in deeper. "You'll get used to it."

He's right. After a few minutes, the water feels relatively warm, or perhaps my skin has gone numb, but either way, it's pleasant. The lake feels like an ocean in that it's so big, one can't see the end past the horizon. It feels infinite. Unlike the water of the ocean, this water is void of all salt.

I lie back and float atop the bobbing water as the sun warms my cool skin.

"You're right. I need to buy a home on the lake." I mutter.

"Right?" Amos floats beside me.

We swim and kiss and play in the waves, skinny dipping at its finest.

Eventually, we decide to head back up to the house. I dash across the sun-baked sand because the bottoms of my feet protest the heat.

One of the cool features of the house is an outdoor shower. It's a large square built from the same wood as the deck. The wooden walls are chest high so one can take in the surroundings as they shower.

"My lake house is going to have one of these," I say, stepping beneath the warm spray of the shower.

"Definitely."

"What game should we play when we're finished?" I ask.

We searched the house for games last night and came up with Star Wars Monopoly and Harry Potter Clue. I'm convinced that past renters left them. I can't imagine Betty and Florence playing either.

"I'm thinking Clue," Amos says. "We're more apt to finish

that game. Monopoly can take forever, and we tend to get distracted."

"I have no idea what you mean." I feign ignorance.

"No?" Amos squints accusingly.

"Nope." I pop the 'p' with the shake of my head.

He puckers his lips and joins me beneath the water. "Maybe I should remind you?"

"I think that'd be wise." I circle my hands around his waist and splay my palms against his muscled back.

He crashes his mouth against mine, and I dig my nails into the skin of his back, pulling him closer.

Amos cradles my jaw in his hands. "I will never tire of loving you, Alma. Never."

"Promise?"

"Absolutely."

He kisses me with fiery abandon. "Thank you for this weekend. Thank you for loving me enough to let go."

Dueling emotions get lodged in my throat, and I can only nod in response. This happiness is something I never thought I'd feel again, and here I am in this utopia with Amos. I'm overwhelmed with love and using all the leftover strength I can muster to keep the guilt buried. It has no place here, not anymore.

I said goodbye.

This is the new start to the rest of my life.

He slides his hands under my thighs and lifts me off the ground. I wrap my legs around him as he pushes me back against the wooden wall of the shower. Dropping one of his hands, he guides himself into me.

I hold on tight as Amos assaults me with pleasure. Tears fall down my cheeks, dissolving in the steamy spray. This is everything I needed and never knew I wanted. I am loved and safe. An awareness of something greater permeates every pore as I realize I'm no longer alone.

I'll never be alone again.

The vessel within my chest twists with overwhelming acceptance and gratitude. I'm loved, and Amos will make me happy for the rest of my life if I let him.

His mouth finds mine once more as he thrusts into me below. He kisses me thoroughly and completely, not leaving any room for doubt. A torrent of emotions is crashing down on me, but the one that speaks the loudest is love.

Simply love.

CHAPTER 24

AMOS

The three-hour drive back to Ann Arbor from the weekend at our Lake Michigan oasis is a quiet one. We're both lost in our own minds. At least, I know I am.

This weekend was incredible. It was Alma and me being a couple with no other distractions. It was neutral ground without past memories for Alma to compare to. I knew when I asked her to go away last week that it would be what we needed, and it was.

I know that Alma and I work as a couple. I know we're meant to be together. It's just the ghosts of daily life, and the routines and familiar locations of the past that keep her guilt at the surface. I feel for her. I don't know what it's like to move on when I'm still in love with someone else. I don't know what it's like to lose someone in the way in which she did. It carries a weight that I'll never bear, and I'd take it from her if I could.

But this weekend was a breakthrough. It was tangible—the

difference in mindset. A decision has been made, and I couldn't be happier.

I'm not naïve enough to think that we're going to go back home and be met with the perfection of this weekend. There will be challenges. I'm hoping that the past two days we spent together will be a reminder of what we're fighting for—a relationship they write about, an epic love story.

"Are you hungry?" I ask. "I could stop and get something before we get back?" Our fingers cling to each other between the seats.

She squeezes my hand. "No, I'm good. I just want to get home."

"To see Love?" The question is rhetorical.

"Yeah—gosh, I miss her. The closer we get to home, the antsier I get to see her."

"Well, I'm proud of you for going away and spending a weekend apart. I know she had an amazing time with Lee-Anne."

"I'm sure she did." The side of her lip tilts up.

"Thank you again for this weekend. It was..." I hesitate, needing the right word to describe how much it meant to me. "...perfect." It's generic, but it's true. Everything about the past two days was utter perfection. I've never been happier.

"Stop thanking me." Alma shakes her head. "You were right. It was needed, and it was perfect. I loved every minute of it."

I veer off the highway onto the ramp that leads to Alma's neighborhood.

"We should do it once a month. Get away, just me and you," I suggest.

"Whoa, boy." Alma chuckles. "Let's slow down a bit there."

"Every other month?" I raise a brow.

"We can work up to once a quarter," Alma acquiesces.

I nod, pleased. "I can agree to four times a year. Remember, you can take time off during the week to hang out with Love. I mean, that was a great plan."

"It made leaving a little easier."

I pull into Alma's drive, and before I have the car fully in park, she's out and running into the house. My chest fills with pride. I always knew she'd be a fantastic mother, despite not having a good example of what one was growing up, and it's heartwarming to see it in action.

After retrieving the bags from the trunk of the car, I make my way inside. Love and Alma, arms wrapped around each other, sit on the sofa. Love is telling Alma all about her worm dinner. I grin. I can only imagine what healthy concoction Lee-Anne came up with.

"Did you two have a good time?" Lee-Anne asks with a knowing stare.

"We did. It was great."

I set down the bags, and she hands me a cup of tea. "Try this. It's hibiscus tea. Did you know that hibiscus is very good for you? It gets all the free radicals out of your body and prevents cell damage. It's excellent for your immune system."

I thank her and take a sip of the tea. I'm actually not sure what she means about free radicals, but I don't dare ask.

"So?" she questions.

I bob my head in affirmation. "It's great. Thanks again."

"Just so you know, I've been telling Almalee that you two are a good match. I've known it for years. It's been obvious since you two were little."

"Well, thank you," I reply, not quite certain how to respond.

She waves her hand toward the teacup and nods. "Okay. You drink the tea, and I'm going to go and let you all have the rest of the day together as a family."

"You're welcome to stay for dinner. I can make one of your favorites?" I offer.

She shakes her head. "No way, José. I'm going to go home. You three need your space." She taps me on the arm.

Lee-Anne excuses herself to say goodbye to the girls, and I take Alma's bag up to her room. Flicking on the light switch, I scan the space. It's exactly as it was four years ago when I picked out a dress for her to wear for the funeral. Pictures of Alma and Leo are everywhere—on the dresser, the walls, and the nightstand beside the beds. I doubt anything has been moved since his death, a sad shrine to her lost marriage. I turn the light off and shut the door.

"Maybe we should have Amos pick? He can be the tiebreaker." I hear Alma say to Love as I descend the steps.

"Pick what?" I ask.

At the sound of my voice, Love jumps up from the sofa and runs toward me, tackling me in a hug.

"Hey, Love Dove. I missed you." I kiss the top of her head. "Do you and your mom need help with something?"

"Yes! Movie night," Love answers.

Alma pulls up the Disney Plus channel on the TV. "We're having a debate. I think we should try out a new movie, maybe one we haven't seen before, like *Toy Story* or *Cars*, but Love wants to watch the *Beauty and the Beast* again."

"I love Belle!" Love argues. "I don't like cars."

"How do you know? You've never seen it," Alma says.

"I want Belle," Love protests.

"See?" Alma looks up at me. "We need a tiebreaker."

"I don't know if I feel comfortable being the tiebreaker." I look around and spot a box of crayons spilled onto the table. "How about we leave it up to fate?"

Walking over to the table, I snatch up the red and yellow crayon and hold them out. "Red is for *Cars* and yellow is for?" I look toward Love, eyebrows raised.

"Belle!" she answers.

"That's right. Belle." I smile down at her, and she jumps up

521

and down. "I'm going to put a color in each hand behind my back, and you can choose. Whatever color is chosen is the winner. Deal?"

Both of my girls nod, wearing identical goofy expressions. Alma likes to think that Love takes after Leo in everything, and in many things, she does. But she has so much of her momma in her, too.

Holding the crayons behind my back, I mix them up. "Okay, Lovie. Pick a hand." I hold my closed hands behind my back.

Love eyes my arms carefully as if she can see through me to the color. "This one." She points at my right arm.

I pull my right arm out from behind my back and hold it out. Turning my hand over, I slowly open my fingers, revealing the yellow crayon. Love jumps up and down, shrieking with happiness.

"*Beauty and the Beast* it is!" I call out, and Alma shakes her head with a laugh.

Love runs around the living room. The yellow princess sundress she's wearing flies out behind her as she giggles in victory.

"What would you ladies like for dinner?" I ask.

"Tacos!" they shout in unison.

I chuckle. "Well, at least we agree on that."

Alma follows me into the kitchen as I start removing ingredients from the refrigerator.

She stands in front of me and drapes her arms over my shoulders. "Did you move the yellow crayon to the hand she picked? Was that a setup?"

I lean down and give her a chaste kiss. "I'll never tell."

"I knew it." She shakes her head.

"What?" I shrug, feigning innocence. "She picked the yellow crayon."

Alma drops her hands and leans against the granite countertop. "She'd like other movies if she watched them."

"But listen." I nod toward the living room where Love is dancing and singing her rendition to the song from the movie, "Be our Guest."

"Yeah, I know. She's obsessed. And, you're a softie." Alma opens the bag of tortilla chips. Retrieving a corn chip, she dips it into the salsa and plops it into her mouth. "Just so you know, I'm glad you chose her even if I have to watch that movie for the millionth time. She's lucky to have you."

I pour the can of black beans into a small pot and sprinkle in some seasoning.

"Will you stay with me tonight?" Alma asks.

"Are you sure? Won't you be sleeping with Love?" I wipe my hands on the towel and turn to face Alma, taking her hands in mine.

"I'm sure. I'll lie with her until she's asleep, and then I'll sneak out. It's time."

"Okay, if you're sure." I kiss her gently. "I'd love to stay over."

Alma presses her lips together in a grin and lowers her chin in approval.

"I'll finish up here. I'm pretty sure the song she's on is a duet." I motion toward the living room. "She needs you."

Alma lifts her arm and circles her hand around the back of my neck as she pulls me down for another kiss. "I'm so lucky to have you," she whispers against my lips.

"The feeling's mutual."

CHAPTER 25

ALMA

*T*he light blue-gray walls are gone, and I can't deny that it hurts. Leo painted our bedroom walls with the perfect shade. He knew I'd love that calming color, and I did. And now…like so many other things, it's gone.

But it has to be.

The night that we got back from Lake Michigan, I asked Amos to stay over. When the time came for bed, I couldn't bring him into my bedroom. I couldn't sleep with Amos in a room that Leo built for me, in the bed that we conceived Love in. I simply couldn't.

So we slept in one of the guest bedrooms and have been ever since. The guest bedroom is nice and comfortable, but it's not my room. I can't be afraid to sleep in my room.

The truth is, I've barely slept in it since the funeral. I started sleeping elsewhere in the house until the thought of going back to my bedroom was too much.

Now, it looks nothing like it did. I hired a company to come in and redesign the space. I wanted it inspired after Betty and Florence's lake house. I supplied the designer with pictures from the lake house, and they did the rest.

Everything is new—the color of the walls, the curtains, the furniture, the moldings, and the bed. It's all new. It was either make it so that I could stand to sleep in the master bedroom or get a new house. The point being, I need to move on.

I love this house, so this will have to do.

The walls are now a cream, and the accents in the room are brighter blues. It's whimsical, romantic, classy, and nautical all at once, just like the lake house. It's perfect, and Amos is going to love it. He has no idea that it's been worked on as the work crew is gone by the time he comes over at night.

I wonder if there's a term that means one's heart is breaking from sadness and happiness all at once? Of course, there's *bittersweet,* but that doesn't fully capture how I'm feeling right now. It's so much worse than bitter and so much greater than sweet. My heart tears open with the intensity of both emotions as I stare at the framed picture of me, Amos, and Love, on the dresser. It's one of my favorites, taken this summer. The three of us are squished in tight. Large, happy smiles grace our faces. We're a family, and truth be told, we've always been.

Amos has been there for me since day one. He held my hand as I gave birth to Love. He changed diapers and rocked her in his arms so I could get a nap in when she kept me up all night. He's cleaned her up and bandaged her cuts and boo-boos. He makes her laugh and cooks her dinner. He loves her, and he loves me. We appear to be a family because we are one.

Love may never know her biological Daddy, but she'll never go a day without love from a man who loves her just as much as Leo would if he were here.

In a life with so much heartbreak, there's an exponential

amount of love. It's all around me. It's in the children's faces at work. It radiates from my friends every time we're together. It flows through my mother in every act she does for Love and me. Amos has given me all of his love, freely and often, since he was seven. Life isn't fair, but I can't deny that it's beautiful. It didn't work out the way I thought it would, but it's still working out pretty well when I stop and truly look around at the blessings in my life.

So my heart hurts. It aches with so much loss but even more love. And I'm grateful.

"Alma?" Amos calls from downstairs.

I close the door to my bedroom and rush down the stairs.

"Hey! What are you doing here?" I ask before standing up on my toes and giving him a kiss.

"Well, I just finished my home visits for today, so I thought I'd swing by and see what you were up to. Where's Love?" He looks around.

"Oh, she just left. Lee-Anne is taking her to the herb store and then to the park."

"Well, that sounds fun."

"I'm actually glad you stopped by. I have a present for you."

"You do?" He quirks up a brow.

"Yes." I grin. "I was going to show you tonight, but since you're here, you might as well see now." I extend my pinky, and he takes it in his and follows me up the stairs.

"You ready?" I ask, my hand on the knob of the bedroom door.

"Um, sure." Amos chuckles.

I swing the door open and stand to the side to watch Amos take in the new space.

He looks from me to the room and back to me again. "Alma..." he breathes out.

"Come on." I pull him over the threshold. "I know that it's silly that we've been sleeping in the guest bedroom."

He shakes his head. "No, it's not silly. I completely understand."

"I know you do, and that's one of the many things I love about you. But I couldn't avoid my bedroom forever, so I had it remodeled. Everything is brand new. New bed, chair —everything."

"It looks like the lake house." He moves slowly around the room.

I grin. "Yes. That was the design inspiration. I wanted it to be our space. I wanted a room that would bring joy to us and remind us of our incredible weekend together. A place that was just ours to make new memories together."

"I love it," he says, picking up the framed picture on the dresser.

"You do?" My voice raises an octave.

"I really do. It's perfect, Alma. Just perfect."

He steps over to the bedside table where I have a four-picture collage strip framed. It's the two of us from our senior year in high school.

"The photo booth from the movie theater," he recalls.

"Yep. We were there seeing the last *Harry Potter* movie."

"I remember. Good thing we had these taken prior to the movie. Your eyes were a puffy mess afterward."

"I know." I sigh. "So many good wizards dead."

He shuts the bedroom door.

"So new everything?"

"Everything," I say.

"I wonder if the bed works?" He takes a step toward me, and an immediate need for him rushes through me.

"I wouldn't know." I shrug, feeling my cheeks flush. Goose bumps trickle across my skin.

Standing before me, he laces our fingers together and trails kisses along my neck. Eyes closed, I sigh as his mouth cherishes my skin in soft lingering pecks.

"I love our room." Amos's hot breath flutters against my neck, the heavy combination of his words and movements skew my equilibrium, and I sway.

"I love you," I breathe.

He releases my trembling hands and guides me down onto the bed. His deep brown gaze sears into mine, only breaking the connection to remove our clothing. He stands before me a picture of perfection. He exudes masculinity. Every cell in my body craves him, and every rhythmic beat of my heart wants him.

He lowers to his knees and trails kisses along my inner thigh until his mouth is at my core.

"Wait." The command a shaky inhalation. I pull at his arms. "I need you, now."

He climbs up my body and rests his forearms on either side of my head, boxing me in. The heat from his skin burns against me as a fiery need ignites within.

His gaze holds mine as he enters me. I draw in a deep breath as he fills me so full. So completely. The sensation is exquisite. He hisses as he starts to move.

"I love you, Alma." He kisses me.

"I love you," I say, and he kisses me again.

We stare into each other's eyes as his hips move faster against me. There's so much in his beautiful depths, so much love, and loyalty, and hunger for me. I need Amos in every way possible, and I know that I always will.

I raise my arm and move my thumb against his parted lips. The movement causes a growl to erupt from him, and he crashes his lips to mine. He ravishes my mouth with his as he thrusts harder and deeper into me. He takes the kiss deeper. His tongue dances with mine with greedy abandon.

I'm addicted to everything about Amos. The way he loves me. The way he makes me feel. The way he cherishes and looks after me. The way he understands me. The way he knows my mind, body, and soul deeper than I know myself. He's become someone I can't resist, and he'd never hurt me.

He's my ultimate protector. My lover. My friend.

My stomach tightens, and the familiar pull grows within as Amos takes me higher and higher.

He threads his fingers through mine and holds them against the bed over my head. His voice raspy and tight with need pleads, "Don't look away. Keep your eyes open. I want to see you fall." His words are my undoing, and my mouth opens in a sob as I start shaking. My body trembles with enormous jolts of pleasure, electricity lighting every piece of me aflame.

Amos's mouth falls slack, and he moans, his face almost pained as he releases inside me. It's one of the most beautiful sights I've seen.

As the tremors rolling through me abate, Amos falls atop me. I can feel his heart thrumming wildly against my chest.

He kisses the side of my face. "It works," he says, the timbre of his voice all husky. "The new bed. It works."

I laugh and push his chest. He rolls off to lie next to me.

"Yeah, I'd say it works just fine."

The room is quiet save for our sated breaths, our pinkies connected between us. "I think you should move in. Officially. You're here all the time anyway. What's the point of paying for your apartment?"

I turn on my side. Elbow bent, I prop my head up on my hand. Amos turns and mirrors me.

"It hasn't been that long, Alma. Only a couple of months. We have all the time in the world. We don't have to rush."

"It's not rushing, though. We've barely spent more than a few hours apart in years. You're always here, and I want you to be. You only go to your place to sleep, occasionally, and change clothes. Life is short, Amos, and I want to surround myself with those I love. I don't want to wait for some pre-determined amount of time until it's *suitable* for us to live together. I've lost enough, and I simply want to be happy. *You* make me happy. You make Love happy. Your place is here." I hesitate. "I mean, if you want it to be."

"Stop." He thumps my nose playfully with his finger. "Of course I want it to be."

"Yeah?" I raise a brow.

"Yeah. I'll bring over my stuff this weekend."

"Good." I kiss him and stand from the bed.

Amos sits up. "Wait." His voice carries a hint of panic. "Where are you going?" He traces his finger along my waist and up to my breast before pulling on my nipple. "Come back here."

"No." I giggle. "They're going to be back soon."

"So? The door is closed. And it's not like Lee-Anne doesn't know we're sleeping together."

"Of course she knows but let's not give her a reason to bring it up. I mean, unless you want to hear a completely graphic and inappropriate story about her and my dad going at it because you know that's where the conversation will lead." I eye him.

He jumps from the bed and pulls on his boxers. "Oh, no. You are so right. She'll go there."

"Absolutely she will. She loves talking about their sex life for some reason. I walked in on enough of it when I was a kid. I don't need to hear about it now."

Amos pulls on his shirt as I finish buttoning my pants.

"So basically, that was fun, and we're never doing it again," he teases, causing me to laugh.

"Stop. We can. Now that you're living here, we'll just have to have a few guidelines and boundaries, is all. Mom is good about giving me my space when she thinks I need it."

"That's true. She is."

I cradle his face in my hands and pull him into a kiss. "And now that you're living here, we're going to be doing that a lot."

"Promise?"

"Definitely."

* * *

LEE-ANNE HAS LEFT for the evening, and Amos is back at his place retrieving some clothes. Love and I sit at the table, our hands each in our own tub of colorful foam.

Every now and then, I pretend I can keep up with the Pinterest moms and do a project from the site. Tonight's adventure turned out to be quite easy and incredibly satisfying. I put some dish soap, water, and food coloring in a metal bowl and beat it on high with the mixer until it turned into foam. I made several different colored batches, and now we're swirling them together and building peaks and valleys in the most colorful and sensory-pleasing way.

"Oh, I love that. Are you making a pink mountain?" I ask as Love piles more pink fluff into the same spot.

"Yup." She nods. She peers into my bin. "I yuv your torna-do." She motions toward the tall multihued shape I twisted into a cone.

Tilting my head to the side, I look at the shape Love pointed out. "You're right. That's totally a tornado. I didn't even realize. You're one smart cookie."

Appearing satisfied, Love goes back to building her mountain. My use of Amos's nickname reminds me of the question I asked him earlier today.

My romantic relationship with Amos has been a natural progression, and one that hasn't sparked any questions from Love. The reality is that he's always been in her life, and for the past three years, he's been here hanging out with us more than he's not. Amos and I have always had a physical friendship—hugs, kisses on the head, and clasping pinkies have been our norm. Over the past couple of months, the affection has increased to include hand holding and kisses on the lips.

"I wanted to talk to you about something," I begin, feeling a lot of pressure to do this right.

Love continues to swirl the foam around and squish it through her fingers. So I continue. "Lovie, I love Amos." The declaration comes barreling out of my mouth along with any hopes of successfully working the topic into the conversation. *Smooth.*

"Me, too," she says without skipping a beat.

"Right." I chuckle. "Well, Mommy used to love Amos like a friend, but now I love him like a boyfriend."

She nods. "I know. You kiss on the yips."

My heart expands in my chest, and I smile wide. Gosh, I love this girl. "Right, and how do you feel about that?"

"Happy."

"Oh, good. It makes me happy, too," I admit. "So you like that Amos is Mommy's boyfriend?"

She nods.

"Wonderful. Okay." I let out a relieved sigh. "Now, what would you think if Amos moved into our house and lived here with us all the time?"

Love turns to me, her little eyebrows furrowed as if she doesn't quite understand the question.

"So his clothes would be here in the closet. He would sleep here every night and get up here every morning. He wouldn't leave to go back to his house. He would live here like you and me do, and we would share our house with him. And after I tuck you in at night and you fall asleep, I would go to sleep in my bedroom and share my room with Amos." I swallow and wait for her reply.

"Will he make me bwekfast?" she inquires in a sweet voice.

"Oh, yeah. He can make you breakfast or any other meal whenever you want."

She nods satisfied. "I yike it."

"You like that he's going to live here?"

"Yes!"

"So it will make you happy if Amos lives with us and is Mommy's boyfriend?"

Love nods again. "Can he make me pancakes?"

"Sure. He can whip up some pancakes in the morning. Do you want blueberries, or…"

"Chocolate chips!" She claps her hands together, and bits of foam fly through the air.

I kiss her head with a laugh. "Then it's settled. Tomorrow, Amos will make chocolate chip pancakes for my girl."

Love goes back to playing in her tub of foam, and my heart's content.

CHAPTER 26

AMOS

The five-foot-tall golden "2" and "8" balloons are positioned in the foyer, ready to greet the party-goers as they enter. Lee-Anne has Alma and Love whisked away on a 'girls day of fun' as a cover while I get the party ready.

Alma's never had a surprise party, and this one will definitely be a surprise, given that her actual birthday was a couple of weeks ago in July. She spent the day of her twenty-eighth birthday with me, Love, and Lee-Anne, hanging out at the house, playing her favorite games, eating her favorite foods, and relaxing with her favorite people. It's what she asked for, and it's what she got.

I wanted to do something else, some more to celebrate her. The anniversary of Leo's death is coming up in a few weeks, and in a way, I suppose, I want to pull the focus from that or at least turn the sad energy into a celebration for Alma. She's spent so much time these past four years honoring Leo and grieving. It's time she's celebrated for the incredible person she is. She survived a tragic event while growing a healthy baby inside her, made sure the Lair thrived, and has been the best mother to Love. She loves everyone around her fiercely. She's superwoman, and I fall deeper in love with her every day.

Bringing everyone she loves together to celebrate her is the least I can do.

All of our co-workers from the Lair are here and past college friends including Quinn and Ethan. I invited Ollie, Cat, and Leo's mother as they all care for Alma. The collection of loved ones mingle in the backyard as I wait for the girls to get back from their adventure.

Finally, they do.

Alma steps in the door and eyes the balloons. "What is this?"

I extend my hand, taking hers in mine. "Close your eyes."

"Okay," Alma says with a giggle and does as instructed.

Lee-Anne holds Love on her hip and follows us as I lead Alma through the house to the back deck. I motion toward the hushed crowd, and they yell out a collective, "Surprise!"

Alma opens her eyes with a gasp. "What?" She chuckles, her eyes sparkling.

The core group of people she cares about stands before us on the glittery white dance floor, cheering.

The backyard is draped in a canopy of twinkle lights creating a magical feel to the space. I hired a company that set up a bar, complete with a champagne fountain. The party designer set up an elegant food and dessert station, complete with food and goodies from Alma's favorite restaurants in Ann Arbor.

Our friends stand beneath the canopy of lights on the dance floor. The space resembles a princess fairy ball with incredible food served on fancy white plates.

"Happy Birthday." I smile.

Alma turns to me in disbelief. "But my birthday was a couple of weeks ago."

"That's part of the surprise." I smirk.

Her mouth breaks into a smile, the one that never fails to make my heart stutter. She levels a gaze at me, one full of complete adoration, and takes my face between her hands. "You are too good to me, Amos," she says before capturing my lips in a kiss.

The group of partygoers goes quiet, and Alma tenses. Her mouth freezes against mine as we realize what we just did and how much of a surprise it must be.

The summer has been such a whirlwind of new love and experiences for us that Alma hasn't gotten together with her friends to tell them about our new adventure together. We've talked about the fact that we need to tell people but never got around to telling anyone as we were completely captivated with our life in our happy little bubble.

"I flipping knew it!" Quinn yells as the group starts to cheer again.

Alma removes her lips from mine and looks over the deck railing. "Surprise. We're together," she says sheepishly, gliding her fingers through mine and raising our joined hands in the air.

More hoots and hollers emerge. Alma laughs and turns back toward me, burying her face in my chest.

We make our way down the steps of the deck to greet everyone.

We come to Cat and Mrs. Harding first. Alma says, "Hi. Is this weird?"

"Gosh, no!" Cat pulls Alma into a hug. "You deserve to be happy. This is great."

Mrs. Harding shakes my hand. "Thank you for inviting me, Amos. I'm so grateful."

I nod in response.

"Happy late Birthday, Alma." She gives her an awkward side hug. "You know he'd want you to be happy," she says with a tight grin.

"I know. Thank you," Alma says.

"I was hoping to spend some time with Love," Mrs. Harding asks hesitantly.

"Of course. You'll find her next to the dessert table." Alma chuckles. "She loves to dance. If you tell the DJ to play a song from the *Beauty and the Beast* soundtrack, you'll make her day."

Mrs. Harding's face lights up. "Oh, I'll do that. Thank you," she says before scurrying off to see Love.

Quinn tackle hugs Alma and me, squeezing us tight and rocking us back and forth. "I knew you two would end up together. A squared, together, forever." She takes a step back with an approving smile on her face. "I always knew it, even in college. Remember I kept asking you why you weren't with Amos? There's always been this energy between you, like the two of you are one person—an extension of each other." She holds a hand from each of us in hers. "This is right." She nods. "Meant to be. I'm so happy for you." Her stare connects with Alma's. "You deserve all the happiness in the world."

Alma circles her arms around Quinn, and the two of them hug. "Thank you," Alma says quietly. "That means a lot."

"I need to know all the details, like how and when?" Quinn says.

"Okay, let me make my rounds and say hello to everyone here. Then Amos and I will fill a plate with tacos, which I see eyeing me over there." Alma nods toward the food table. "And we'll meet you at one of the back tables and give you all the details."

"Every last one?" Quinn raises a brow, a smirk on her face.

"If you really want them." Alma shakes her head with a laugh.

"Oh, I do."

Hand in hand, Alma and I make our rounds, chat with our friends and thank them for coming. Alma's smile doesn't leave her face, and I'm content. This is exactly what I wanted for her, a night when she could feel special and see just how much she means to those in her life.

On our way to the food table, the first few notes of the *Beauty and the Beast* ballad plays. Mrs. Potts, aka Angela Lansbury, starts to sing, and Alma grabs my hand and pulls me onto the dance floor.

Beside us, Mrs. Harding holds Love, and the two sway to the music. Leo's mother is experiencing true bliss with her granddaughter, a little girl version of her late son, and my heart goes out to her. Her role has been anything but acceptable in her son's life. Yet I can't help but feel sorry for her just the same. She reminds me of my own mother, kind but weak. There's no excuse for her not protecting her son, but I feel for her and can't help thinking she's somehow a victim, too.

I look at Alma, her beautiful browns sparkle beneath the twinkle lights, and she stares up at me with so much adoration. She's strong and kind. She'd never let harm come to her daughter. She's had trials in her life but has never used them as excuses to be less than the person she's destined to be. I don't know what makes the difference between a mother like Alma and a mother like Mrs. Harding.

Alma lifts up on her toes and places a soft kiss on my lips. "You know this could be our song in a way?"

"I'm a beast?" I quirk a brow.

"Gosh, no," she says. "You're obviously the beauty, and I'm the beast."

"How is that even possible?"

"I was broken, covered in layers of hurt and grief. You were patient and loved me, giving me the support I needed to shed the layers one by one until the beast of sorrow released me, allowing me to be here with you in this world of immense happiness. You loved me when I was shrouded in pain. You've always viewed me through rose-colored glasses. You've never seen the ugliness."

I pull her closer and kiss her forehead. "You're wrong, my love. There's never been ugliness to see. That's all in your head. To me, you are and have always been the most beautiful woman in the world."

She presses her cheek against my chest, and we dance.

The song ends, and an upbeat tune plays through the speakers.

"Ready for your tacos?" I ask.

"Always." Alma follows me to the food table.

In my peripheral, Quinn waits at a table, wineglass in hand.

I eye Quinn. "That conversation is going to be uncomfortable. Isn't it?"

Alma laughs. "Oh, yes. She won't have a filter just because you're there."

"Maybe I should give you two some alone girl time," I offer.

"You're more than welcome to sit with us, but I won't pretend the awkwardness of the conversation won't give you nightmares," Alma teases.

"Yeah, I'll go check on your mother and visit with the crew from work."

"It's probably best." She chuckles, placing a handful of cilantro on her corn tortilla.

I kiss her temple. "Have fun."

"Love you," she says.

"Love you."

CHAPTER 27

ALMA

*L*ove walks between Lee-Anne and me, holding our hands as we stroll through campus. It's been a while since I've been back to Eastern. This place holds so many memories—each one more beautiful and heartbreaking than the last.

My mother has never seen the campus or where I spent four years of my life as she and my father weren't around when I was in college. She admires the brick dormitory as if it's the Sistine Chapel or something.

"It's just dorm rooms, Mom," I say with a laugh.

"I think it's a very nice building, Almalee."

I shake my head.

"Come on, this way." I lead us past the dorms to the old frat house where I saw Leo for the second time.

I entertain my mother with a few PG stories from those

first few parties. It's so crazy to think back to those moments when it was all starting.

We cross the street.

"And this was our first house," I say to Love. "Your daddy lived here first, and then I moved in."

"Oh, this is beautiful." Lee-Anne's voice is in awe.

"I agree with you there. Leo had it restored and remodeled. It's a special house, that's for sure."

"You lived here with Daddy?" Love asks.

We stand on the sidewalk facing the front porch of the grand home.

"We did. It was a happy place. We had Amos, and Quinn, and Ethan, and Aunt Cat over all the time. We celebrated holidays here, and lived here when we were first married. I loved it."

"I wonder who lives here now?" Lee-Anne says.

"I don't know." I look at my first home with Leo with fond nostalgia. I hope that whoever lives here now is as happy within those walls as I was. "We should go. Aunt Cat should be at the restaurant about now."

I lead them down the block from the house.

"This Coney Island was where Daddy and I had our first date. It was his favorite place to eat. You'll love it," I tell Love. "A sweet man named Luca owns it, and he makes the best chili cheese fries in the world."

The bell chimes over the door as we enter. Luca stops what he's doing and calls out, "Alma, my love! It's been too long." He rushes over to me and hugs me tight. I wrap my arms around him and cling to this comfort from my past. Luca was a friend to Leo when he needed one. He gave me a job when I needed one. He has one of the biggest hearts of anyone I've met in this life. I haven't seen him in years, and it's as if no time has passed.

Luca steps back. Holding my shoulders, he assesses me. "You look good. Happy."

"Thank you. You look good, too."

"Who'd you bring with you today?" he asks.

"This is my mom, Lee-Anne, and my daughter, Love."

Luca crouches to Love's level. "She's his spitting image," he says, unshed tears in his eyes.

"She is," I agree.

He holds out his hand to shake Love's. "Your daddy was my favorite customer and a good friend."

Luca stands and addresses my mother. "And now I see where Alma gets her great beauty from." He reaches for my mother's hand and kisses the top of it, causing her to blush.

"You know what Leo would be saying to you right now?" I quirk a brow toward Luca.

"Oh yes, I do." He nods. "He'd say, 'Luca, stop being creepy and bring us chili cheese fries and Cokes!'"

I throw my head back and laugh. "That's exactly what he'd say, and you sound a lot like him."

"Well, let me get you to your seat. I believe a member of your party is already here." He motions toward the back booth where Cat stands, waiting for us.

She's more casual than normal with a black tank top and ripped skinny jeans. Though the black leather stiletto-heeled boots she's wearing probably cost a pretty penny. Even dressed down, she's prettier than anyone in the room.

She gives my mother and Love hugs before pulling me into a long one. "I can't believe it's been four years today."

"I know," I say softly. "It's hard to believe."

"Are we all getting the Leo special?" Luca asks.

"Yes!" I say, "Well, except my mom. She'll probably need a menu. She's not a Leo special kind of girl."

Lee-Anne chats with Luca, and I slide into the booth across from Cat with Love at my side.

"It's strange being back here, no?" Cat asks.

"Yeah, it is, but nice, too."

More and more, I'm finding that my memories surround me with a cloak of peace when they come. They no longer hurt as they once did. I'm able to look at the past with gratitude and love. Even with my ending with Leo being what it was, I'd never change our time together. I'm lucky to have had him for the time I did.

"He sure is a nice man, and cute, too. Don't you think?" Lee-Anne asks as she slides in beside Cat.

"Yeah." I grin. "He's awesome. You know he lost his wife and son years back? It's heartbreaking."

"That is sad. I wonder if he has friends to talk to. It's important to have a community. You know? When I lost Alman, I had you and Love, and I don't know how I would've been able to make it without you."

"Everyone in town knows and adores him. It's been at least eleven years since he lost them. I think he's doing well."

"Oh, I'm sure he could use a friend." Lee-Anne ogles Luca where he stands behind the counter.

I look at Cat and shake my head with a grin. Maybe my mother isn't as resigned to being alone for the rest of her life as she's declared.

Luca delivers our Cokes and my mother's water. He makes sure to tell Lee-Anne how important it is to be hydrated, and she agrees adamantly with him.

He returns shortly after delivering the drinks with plates of chili cheese fries. He sets a plate of cheese fries down in front of my mother.

My eyes go wide. "You're going to eat processed cheese and fries?"

"I couldn't do the chili. I won't eat meat, but I figure for one day, today, here...I can do cheese for Leo," she says.

"Wow. You surprise me every day, Mom."

Luca sets bottles of ketchup and his freshly made ranch dressing on the table.

"This is perfect," I tell him. "Thank you. I'm sure Leo is smiling down from heaven."

"I know he is, my dear." Luca gives me a warm smile and retreats from the table.

"Okay," I say to Love. "Your daddy had a specific way to eat these. First, you scoop up a fry and make sure it has chili and cheese on it. Then you dip it into the ranch, and then the ketchup." I demonstrate the technique before putting the fork full into my mouth. "Perfect!" I say through a mouthful of food, causing Love to laugh. "Your turn."

Love follows my example and takes a bite.

"So?" I ask expectantly.

"Yummy!" She giggles.

"Yes." I give her a high five. "Your daddy would be so happy. He could seriously eat this for every meal."

"It looks absolutely disgusting." Lee-Anne scrunches her nose.

"Just try it, Mom." I grin.

Lee-Anne follows suit and takes a bite of the fry. Disgust is written all over her face, and I hold in my amusement.

"Do you yike it?" Love asks her.

Lee-Anne nods, her eyes wide. Cat and I laugh out loud, unable to hide our amusement at the clear torture this meal is for my mother.

"Everyone likes it!" I tell Love.

"Yay. Daddy's happy."

"He sure is, Love Dove. He's so happy."

The four of us eat and reminisce. I don't fail to notice that Lee-Anne picks at the sides of her plate where the fries without anything on them reside. Truthfully, I didn't expect her to try the dish, to begin with, and Leo wouldn't have cared either way. It's sweet that she's trying, though.

"Does Daddy get fries in heaven?" Love asks.

"I think so. I think all of his favorite things are up in heaven with him. I think he gets to watch over all of his favorite people on earth and keep them safe, like a guardian angel. I think he's completely happy and free."

"Me too," Love says.

"Me too," Cat says, tears in her eyes.

"Me too," Lee-Anne agrees, a loving smile on her face as she looks off to the side, lost in her own thoughts.

I believe my words to Love with everything I am. There's no scientific proof that heaven exists, but I believe deep in my heart that it does. I have faith that it's real, and that's the thing about faith—I know it to be true, though I have no evidence of it. It just is.

Leo is free and happy.

I'm certain of it.

CHAPTER 28

ALMA

"*I* love you so much." I pull Love in for a hug. "You are going to have so much fun." Leaning in, I pucker my lips, and Love comes in for a kiss.

"Let me make sure everything's in order," Amos says from beside me. Love turns her attention toward him. "Backpack?"

"Check!" Love cheers, taking part in a ritual that she and Amos already did back at the house. I find it cute and oddly comforting.

"Purple power bow?" He quirks a brow.

"Check!" Love taps the top of her head, where a bow is wrapped around her ponytail.

I'm not sure when it happened, but sometime within the past month, she's moved on from her Belle obsession and is now riding the Rapunzel train. The movie *Tangled* has edged out *Beauty and the Beast,* and I have to say that it's a much-needed change. I was starting to dream about dancing forks.

"Smile?"

"Check!" Love flashes her smile.

"Kind heart?"

She places a hand on her chest. "Check. I will help anybody who needs a friend."

"Good, Lovebug." Amos shoots Love his beautiful smile, and then he shrugs and looks at me. "I think she's ready."

I nod. "I can't believe it, but I think so, too."

"You're just so big, Lovie." Lee-Anne bends down to Love's level and gives her a hug. "I can't wait to hear all about your adventures."

"Wait!" a voice sounds in the distance.

"We're here!" another yells, and I twist to see Cat and Quinn running up the sidewalk that leads to the school.

They both appear to be dressed for work in fancy skirt suits. Cat's jogging in heels across the pavement, clutching her giant purse to her chest.

"What are you two doing?" I laugh when they reach us.

"Sorry. There was an accident..." Quinn presses her hand to her chest.

Cat finishes the sentence. "On the highway, coming in from the east."

Quinn chuckles, out of breath. "Yeah, I was just sitting there in traffic and look over to see this one"—she hooks her thumb in Cat's direction—"putting on makeup."

"It's been a hell of a morning already," Cat explains. "But I wasn't going to miss Lovie's first day of school!" She crouches down and hugs Love.

"Me either," Quinn says, mirroring Cat's affection.

"Awe, you didn't have to come. I would've sent pictures," I say.

"I had to see the big event in person," Cat exclaims, and Quinn adamantly agrees.

"Speaking of," Amos says under his breath. "I think her teacher is waiting for her."

I look in the direction that Amos indicates, and sure enough, Love's teacher, who looks as if she's barely out of high school, waves in our direction. We've stood here for a good fifteen minutes taking photos and watching the other kids make their way through the doors of the brick building.

I'm unable to delay the inevitable any longer. It's Love's turn.

"Oh, wait. I promised I'd get a picture. Everyone get together," Cat says, and we quickly comply as she holds up her phone to snap some group photos.

Love's teacher crosses the parking lot to greet us. "Is this Love Harding?"

"It sure is," I say with pride.

"Great. Are we ready?" She looks toward the five sentimental-eyed adults when she asks this question.

"Yeah." I nod. "She's very ready."

"I love you, baby. Have a great day!" I say to Love. Her teacher takes her hand and leads her toward the school.

The five of us stand on the sidewalk, facing the school, our arms raised and hands waving. Amos has his phone out recording Love's walk into the school. The group of us must surely look silly, but we're Love's people, and when I stop to think about it—she has some pretty amazing people in her corner.

Love skips beside her teacher, her long, wavy ponytail bounces against her glittery Rapunzel backpack. She's so happy, joy radiates from her. She doesn't look back toward me as they enter the school, and though it breaks my heart a little, it fills me with pride. My little girl is so strong and brave. At three, she's bolder than I am in many ways.

The bright red door of the school closes behind them as the cars from the parent drop-off loop clears.

"She's not old enough. I should get her back," I blurt out, feeling panicked.

"She's going to be great," Amos reassures me.

"How is this happening already? She's still a baby. She's not ready for school." My voice comes out a tad shrieky, but I couldn't care less. My Love just walked into the school, practically all by herself, and I'm feeling a little light-headed as my heart races.

"She looked pretty ready to me," Quinn points out the obvious.

I blow out a breath. "I know," I grumble. "I'm just not ready."

"It's only a few half days a week. She'll be great." Amos pulls me into a side hug and kisses my temple.

A muted sob sounds to my side, and I pivot to see Lee-Anne crying into a handkerchief.

"Mom?" I question, dragging out her name.

"I'm sorry. She's just so little." She sniffles, raising her arm toward the school and dropping it back to her side.

I wrap my arms around my mother. "She really is, but it's only three half days a week." I echo Amos's words from moments ago.

Clinging to Lee-Anne's embrace, I still can't wrap my mind around the fact that my daughter is ready for preschool. When I close my eyes, I can imagine the day she was born as if it were yesterday, and I feel it all in vivid colors. The sound she made. The way her warm, slippery body felt in my arms after she first came out. The way she smelled. The way her cute little lips puckered when she looked into my eyes. Everything about her was perfect, a miracle.

"We can do brunch if you want? I don't need to be at work right now," I offer.

Lee-Anne shakes her head and wipes the cloth beneath her eyes. "No. I'm fine. I have somewhere to be."

"Where?" I question, dropping my embrace. Taking a step back, I study my mother.

"It's nothing. Just breakfast with a friend."

"With who?" I ask, knowing that she doesn't have any friends in this city.

She brushes off my question and says a quick goodbye to the group before scurrying off after reminding me, once again, that she'll meet me here to pick up Love at eleven.

"That was weird," I observe quietly as Lee-Anne retreats.

"Sounds like she has a man friend," Quinn says.

"Oh, definitely," Cat agrees. "Listen, I have to run. I'm catching a plane to LA in a bit. I have a shoot."

"Oh? With who?" I ask.

She twists to the side to show us her rear. "Let's just say that this ass is going to be representing some way too expensive jeans in the near future."

"Nice." I grin. "Thank you for coming. I'm sure it meant a lot to Love."

"Wouldn't have missed it." She kisses each of my cheeks. "We'll catch up when I get back."

She supplies a quick farewell to Amos and Quinn and is off, speed walking back in the direction from which she came.

Quinn takes my hand. "I could actually go for a girls' brunch. I have some things I want to talk to you about."

I look at Amos in question. "Go." He nods. "I can take care of anything that comes up at the Lair."

"That ten o'clock appointment with Earl from the sport's therapy clinic?" I say.

"Handled." He leans in for a kiss. "Have fun."

"Great!" Quinn squeals, looping her arm through mine. "Bye, Amos!" she says as she leads us toward her car.

Quinn drives us to a bougie restaurant in Ann Arbor that has fancy seating, complete with padded faux leather white chairs and black cloth umbrellas shielding us from the September sun.

We catch up over mimosas and veggie and feta-filled omelets.

"So, you and Amos are doing well?" she asks.

I stab a strawberry with my fork. "Yeah, very well. He's officially moved in. Let's be honest, he was practically living with me already. Now, it's official."

She swirls the bit of orange juice left in her champagne flute. "Still, that's a big step. You're feeling okay about everything?"

"I am. It's been amazing. And"—I scrunch up my face—"I'm actually seeing a therapist to work through the lingering Leo guilt. Like four years overdue. Right?"

"Oh, Alma." She places a hand on mine. "That's so good. I'm glad. I'm sure it helps to have another person to listen, validate, and help you sort out all the deep stuff."

"It's been great. While I'm there, it feels like chatting with a friend. After I leave, I notice my perspective shift a bit and feel lighter, somehow. You know?"

"That's the sign of a good therapist." Quinn grins. "No one wants to go somewhere and feel judged. The most beneficial healing is done when you don't even realize it's happening."

"I agree. Otherwise, I'd overthink it all."

"Yep." Quinn nods, her long blond hair bobbing against her shoulders. "That's so great, Alma. I'm so happy for you."

Quinn stares at her plate, flicking around a piece of onion that's fallen from the omelet.

"Is everything okay with you?" I raise a brow. "Sounded like you wanted to talk about something earlier?"

She lowers her fork to her plate and drops her hands to her lap. She chews on the corner of her lip and levels her gaze at me. "There's someone."

I set my fork on the table and give my full attention to Quinn. She seems nervous. "A guy, someone?"

"Yeah." She pulls in a breath. "I think I like him a lot."

"Okay," I draw out, squinting toward her. "I'm sensing a but?"

"I think I like him a lot, but I don't want to." She pulls her bottom lip into her mouth, raking her teeth over the skin beneath her lip. "He's an addict. Or was, though I think they still use present tense, so technically is. I don't know."

I wait, knowing she'll continue.

"He's clean and has been for fourteen years. He's a little older than me. I've been attracted to him for a while but haven't acted on it. You know? I mean, after what you went through...I don't ever want to love an addict. It's too hard. I admire you so much, Alma. I think it's incredible—what you went through and how you came out of it stronger than before —but I don't think that's me. It would destroy me. I know it. I can't take that risk."

"Yeah." I sigh, not knowing what to say.

"He could stay clean, of course, and we could be happy. Yet there would always be that fear in the back of my mind that he'll relapse. Leo was clean for four years, and he relapsed. It could happen." Quinn looks at me expectantly.

"It could," I admit. "That's the thing. You never know. Four-teen years is a long time to be clean to falter, but it happens. Though, it may not. You really like him," I state.

"I do. God, I mean, we've had this flirtation thing going for a few years. Every time I give in to it just a little, I'm drawn toward him like a magnet. Seriously, everything about me craves everything about him. I've been fighting it because I'm so scared. I talked to a couple of my sisters, and they told me to run far away from him and fast. But they don't understand."

"It sounds to me like you're wanting me to tell you to go for it," I say.

Quinn shrugs. "Maybe I am but at the same time, I'm hoping you don't."

"I can't tell you what the right answer is, Quinn. You just have to follow your gut and your heart. Is this guy worth it? Is the possibility of something great worth the possibility of something horrible? Only you know that answer."

"Would you change anything? If you knew then what you know now, would it have mattered?" she asks.

I shake my head. "No. I wouldn't have changed a thing. He was worth it."

CHAPTER 29

AMOS

*L*ove is dressed in toddler skinny jeans and a festive flannel shirt. She's wearing a big orange ribbon in her hair to match the flannel and skips around in her knee-high brown boots. She's straight out of a Gap ad and adorable. Growing up, Alma had a simple fashion—shorts or jeans, and a T-shirt.

She's different now. As her confidence has grown throughout her twenties, her clothing choices have changed and matured, making her even sexier.

Alma comes down the stairs wearing the same outfit as Love, sans the bow.

I shake my head with a chuckle. "Well, look at you."

She shrugs, smiling bright. "I thought it'd be cute in the pictures, and..." She extends her arm out in front of her displaying a similar flannel to what she and Love are sporting. "...I got this for you."

"Oh." I nod. "So…we're all going to match?"

"Yep!" She hops toward me and holds out the shirt. "Do you love it?"

"It's definitely familiar, like I've seen it twice already today." I grin.

"Try it on." She hands me the shirt. "Please." She throws in the last word in the sweet tone she uses that I can't resist.

I put the flannel on over the T-shirt I'm already wearing and button it up. I hold out my arms and do a spin for Alma to see.

She squeals, her hands on her face. "You are so adorable. Yes! It's a winner." Standing on her tiptoes, she presses her lips to me. "We are going to be the cutest ones there."

Lee-Anne arrives, wearing the same flannel as Alma with some moderations. Lee-Anne's version has slits cut into it along the bottom hem. I'm assuming she was going for a flirty and free look, but the dangling fabric reminds me of a scarecrow's outfit. Unlike Alma's skinny jeans, Lee-Anne's are complete bell bottoms, probably from the nineteen seventies. She's sewn sunflower patches all over the front of her jeans, completing the look.

"Alright, Gigi's here. We're ready to go!" Alma calls out and heads out to the car.

There are several pumpkin patches in the area, but we drive out of town a little ways, stopping at one that has a petting zoo, pony rides, freshly made apple donuts and cider, and a hay maze, in addition to the giant field of pumpkins.

Alma is full-fledged paparazzi as she snaps photo after photo of Love with the pumpkins—Love looking at the pumpkins with curiosity, Love using the pumpkins as a chair, climbing the pumpkins, and attempting to lift the pumpkins.

"She's just so adorable, isn't she?" Alma says in awe.

"Yes, she is, babe, and I think you've captured it all." I release a chuckle.

We follow Love through the patch as she looks for the perfect carving pumpkins.

"Michigan autumns are so amazing. Can you imagine living somewhere without apple trees and pumpkin patches? That'd be so sad." Alma says. "Plus, the backdrop of the changing leaf colors. It's all so magical."

"Yeah, the fall is pretty great, but I'm sure people in other states don't think about it much. I mean, you can't miss what you've never had, I suppose. Like Floridians, I bet they have orange festivals or something instead, and while we have the beauty of each season, they have the backdrop of the ocean. They probably wonder how people could live up north where it's cold, and there's no ocean. It's all relative," I say.

"True," Alma says. "The cold's not amazing, but the snow is pretty."

"It is."

Alma stops walking and crouches down. "Lovie, smile," she says and snaps another picture. "We should get some family shots," she says to me.

The three of us pose on the pumpkins while Lee-Anne snaps pictures. Then I get some good shots of just the girls. We ask a stranger to take a few of the four of us.

"So many framers," Alma says, flipping through the photo gallery on her phone. "We should do a whole wall in the entryway of autumn pictures."

"Sounds good," I agree.

When Love has picked out the perfect pumpkins for all of us, I load them into the wagon and set Love atop them, pulling her toward the main building.

I leave the girls at a picnic table and go inside to pay for the pumpkins and get some donuts and cider. When I return, Lee-Anne is telling Love all about the glorious benefits of the pumpkin seed.

"Now, when we get home, we can pull the seeds out and

bake them. Pumpkin seeds are very yummy and so healthy. They're really high in fiber, which helps your body. Plus, they have a lot of antioxidants and are high in magnesium. They help the heart, and bladder, and prostate," Lee-Anne adds proudly.

"Mother." Alma groans. "I don't think Love needs help with a prostate, and she doesn't know what half those words are. Just say, *they're healthy*. Is it that hard?"

"Uh-huh." Love pouts. "I want a postate."

"No, a prostate is something that boys have that girls don't," Alma explains to Love.

"I want one, too," Love says defiantly.

I can't help but laugh. Alma is raising Love to believe she can do anything in this world, which is the right way to raise girls but growing an organ just isn't one of them.

"Who wants donuts?" I cheer, putting an immediate halt to Love's previous focus.

She stands up on the chair of the picnic table and cheers. "Me! Me!"

"Okay, I got a special one just for you, my Love." She smiles wide and takes the freshly made warm donut from my hand, a look of wonder on her face as she takes a bite.

I hold one out to Lee-Anne and see the torment in her eyes as she decides if this donut is worth breaking her sugar ban for. "You know you want it, Lee-Anne." I laugh. "All fresh ingredients, made just now, no preservatives."

"Oh." She groans, taking the donut from me. "You sure know how to sweet-talk a lady, Amos Davis."

I slide onto the picnic table bench next to Alma and hand her a napkin and apple cinnamon donut before pulling the paper cups out of the bag and pouring the apple cider.

The four of us eat our treats and watch as the kids in the distance climb on top of the huge hay maze. Though the painted sign above the giant pile of straw says, *Hay Maze*, it's more like a tall pile of straw bales, stacked high with a large tunnel running through it.

Bees circle the table around us, waiting to drink the sweet cider from an abandoned cup.

"Don't be afraid of the bees," Lee-Anne tells Love. "Bees are our friends and champions for Mother Earth. We couldn't live without bees." Lee-Anne reaches her hand out toward a bee on the wooden table and rests her hand next to it. The bee climbs up onto her fingers and walks across the top of her hand. "See, he's my friend."

Alma and I exchange looks and shake our heads with a smile.

Love's face lights up, and she admires the bee on her Gigi's hand.

"Yes, bees are our friends, but we still have to be careful around them," Alma tells Love. "They can get scared easily, and if they are frightened, they'll sting, and it doesn't feel good."

Alma's words stir something in Love, and she moves her face away from the bee. "Joey got stung by a bee at school and cried," Love says with a look of worry.

"Yeah, it hurts a little when a bee stings you, like a pinch. So, it's better to give them their space when you can," Alma says. "Plus, bees have an important job, so we want to leave them alone to do it."

Lee-Anne nods in agreement, shooing the bee from her hand. She takes a bite of her donut and proceeds to tell Love all about the wonders of pollination. Love listens in awe as Lee-Anne describes the bees jumping from flower to flower and plant to plant.

If Lee-Anne gets her way, I'm sure she'd want Love to grow up to be an environmental activist, saving one tree at a time much like Alma and I protect children. Whatever Love grows to be, it's going to be amazing. The way she listens to stories, such as this one, that should be over her head and asks appropriate questions as to how everything works shows the brilliance of her young mind. She's smart, compassionate, and strong-willed, which, in my opinion, are the makings of a powerful woman who will do incredible things. And I have no doubt she will.

"Are you ready to go climb?" Alma asks Love when we've finished our donuts.

"Yes!" she answers.

I load the pumpkins into the trunk of the car and join the girls on the straw mountain. We climb, and laugh, and roll down the hill. Lee-Anne snaps some more pictures as Love, Alma, and I kick our arms and legs in and out like we're making snow angels in the loose straw at the base of the hill.

It's another incredible day with my family.

And they are...*my family*, and deep within my heart, I know that will never change.

CHAPTER 30

ALMA

*A*utumn passes in a whirlwind of cherished moments. Everything has fallen into place effortlessly. From the second I roll out of bed in the morning, Amos is there to greet me with a kiss and a warm cup of coffee. It's so natural that it's as if it was always meant to be this way.

The daily pain has vanished, and the guilt has subsided. I thought that Love had saved me from the ever-present heartache. The second she came into this world with her stormy blue eyes, chubby cheeks, and the spirit of her daddy, I felt relief. I looked at her, and unconditional love permeated every crevice of my soul. She healed me and pulled me back from the dark abyss that was threatening to consume me.

I think now that my love for her was so powerful that it pushed everything else down. I loved her so much that it was hard to hear the other noise. It never went away, though. The way in which Leo's death shattered me left a permanent imprint. My daughter outshined that darkness, and in that way, she did save me.

From the moment I saw her heartbeat on that ultrasound, I've been living for her.

Smiling for her.

Laughing for her.

Loving for her.

It took Amos's initial kiss and declaration to show me that I'd lost myself. I was no longer living—for me.

I am more, in this life, than Love's mother. Yet my position in that role is what I clung to. It was my sanity.

The possibility of more made me face the demons.

The emotional fallout of a traumatic loss just doesn't go away. It's always lurking just under the surface, leaving its stain on every move I make. It's sneaky in that it coats life with just enough darkness to dull the beautiful moments. I thought I was healed because I lived a life with so much beauty. But I was experiencing it through muted senses clouded by a sadness that stayed just out of reach.

Amos's love ripped me right open, leaving me vulnerable and, for the first time in a long time, aware.

How was I supposed to heal from a pain I didn't know I carried?

It's taken a lot of self-reflection, strength, and determination, but I think I'm finally getting there. The colors of life are more vibrantly hued. Moments are crisper. The beauty is more powerful now that I'm experiencing it without the cover of grief.

It hasn't been easy. Death is permanent and unsettling, and the trauma from it has an unrivaled staying power. It's a daily decision to be brave and avoid sinking into the what-ifs and if-onlys. I can rationalize it all every moment of every day, and it won't change the outcome. Or I can choose to be present and live every day to the fullest.

It was a conscious effort to let it go and say goodbye. Now, I can be fully present for each incredible moment that's yet to come.

Our dwelling of three has become my happy place. In truth, this home has been my favorite place in the world since Leo surprised me with it years ago. It has a great vibe and has always radiated joy. The family within these walls looks different from the couple who ate takeout on a blanket on the floor in the library a lifetime ago. Yet it's just as precious of a picture.

Amos's transition from best friend to boyfriend has been seamless, at least once I accepted it. Love hasn't seemed fazed by the change in the slightest. In fact, she seems happier than ever. I suppose for her, Amos is the only father figure she's ever known.

My mother has picked up quite a few hobbies, supposedly —at least, *something* is occupying her time. She's here for Love every day that I work. That hasn't changed. Although we still see her a lot, she's not here from morning until night like before. I thought, maybe, she was giving Amos and me some space, but I think it's more than that.

I'd bet that she's dating, and I have a feeling that it's Luca. She won't admit it, and I'm not sure why. I sense that she hasn't let my father go, not fully, and the guilt is weighing on her. I've known that feeling, and it's one she'll have to work through. I hope she does find love again. She's still young and should be happy.

I love when my mother is here with us, but it's been pretty great spending so much quality time with just Love and Amos. We're building something pretty special here.

The trial against Alivia, the Lair's previous finance manager, is over. My lawyers made it as painless for me as they could, and I appreciate them so much. Alivia ended up pleading guilty in order to lessen her jail time from twenty years to ten. She's also been court-ordered to pay the Lair back three hundred thousand dollars. I hate that it happened in the first place, and that someone I considered a friend is going to be in jail for a decade. None of it sits well with me, but the law is what it is and stealing was Alivia's choice. I'm simply glad it's done and resolved.

Love's at my side, the two of us cuddled up together beneath the comforter. She leans into me, her eyes focused on the flat screen on the opposite wall. There's a cartoon playing on low volume. I brush my palm over her silky hair and kiss her head. Her hair smells of the natural fruity shampoo we use.

Amos walks in with a wooden tray. "Are my girls hungry?"

Love bolts up, sitting tall. "Yes," she says with a giggle. No matter how many times Amos serves us breakfast in bed, Love is as excited as always.

He pulls the legs of the tray out and sets it down over Love's lap.

"For my littlest princess, I have chocolate chip pancakes, a bowl of fruit, and orange juice." Love picks up a blueberry and tosses it in her mouth. "For my other princess, there's a large cup of coffee, fruit, and toast with grape jelly." He leans in and presses his lips to mine. I sigh as he lingers for just a second.

"I was in the mood for grape jelly toast today," I say in awe, picking up the warm mug of coffee. "How'd you know?"

"Last night, when I ran out to grab a couple of groceries, you made a comment about the jelly getting low and possibly picking up some more. So I knew it was on your mind," he says.

"You're too good to us," I tell him with all sincerity. "I love you."

"Me too," Love agrees, her mouth full of pancakes.

"I love you." He leans in kisses the top of my head. "And I love you." He repeats the movement, kissing the top of Love's head.

He slides in beneath the blanket next to Love and extends his arm across the headboard. His hand rests against my shoulder, his thumb tracing lazy circles over my T-shirt.

"In about an hour, the parade will be on," he says.

"What pawade?" Love asks.

"The Thanksgiving parade. I used to watch it every year with my mom. There are all sorts of floats, giant balloons, and marching bands. You'll like it."

"I want to watch the pawade." Love nods.

"Okay, we'll switch the channel when it's time," he tells her.

"Momma. Did you watch it with Gigi?" Love asks.

"No, Lovie. Gigi and your grandpa weren't really into watching TV. But I'm excited to watch it today."

Amos picks up a piece of melon from the tray and pops it in his mouth. "There's a parade in Detroit every year, too. We should drive down there in a few years, when Love is a little older, and watch it live."

"I wanna do that," Love agrees.

"Then it's a plan, Stan," he says.

"I'm not Stan. You're Stan." Love laughs.

"Okay, I'll be Stan," Amos agrees.

The cartoon on the television changes to the parade, and the three of us remain snuggled beneath the blanket. It's the perfect morning, and I'm so thankful.

* * *

"THE ONLY THING we're missing is the rolls." I search the kitchen of the Lair. "Did the bread delivery not arrive?" Thanksgiving dinner needs rolls.

Jen comes flying into the kitchen, a giant bag of rolls in each hand. "I have the rolls. Eddy says he's sorry he cut it so close."

I take one of the bags from her. "Yes, Jen! You saved the day.

Okay, let's get these in the serving tins and out to the tables. People will be arriving any minute."

Love enters the large kitchen, wearing an adorable dress in autumn colors of yellow, burnt orange, and red, complete with a poufy skirt and a bow tied around her waist. She's so precious. I reach into my back pocket and pull out my phone.

"Look at me, Love bug. I need to get a picture. You're the most beautiful little Thanksgiving princess I've ever seen."

She poses, her hands on her hips, and gives me a big smile as I click a picture.

"Perfect," I say.

"Can I help, Momma?"

I scan the space. "Um, sure, baby. Let me see." I snatch up an extra packet of napkins from the counter. "Can you go find Amos and give these to him? It's a very important job."

"I can do it!" She grins, taking the napkins from me.

"Thank you for being such a great help," I say as she runs out of the kitchen with purpose, holding the napkins tightly against her.

I wipe my hands nervously against my apron as I go over the to-do list in my head. Thanksgiving at the Lair is one of the biggest events we throw each year, and one of the most cherished. Everyone, from the guests to the staff, loves this day.

"We're ready, boss," Gustav, one of our volunteers, says.

"Yes? It's that time?"

"It is. Guests are waiting outside. All the food is out, warmers plugged in, tables set, drink station ready. It looks great."

I blow out a breath. "Okay, let's do this." I pat him on the shoulder and follow him out of the kitchen.

The huge gymnasium is decked out in autumn fanfare. Each table has a pale cream table linen and is decorated with a yellow, orange, and red floral centerpiece. Festive gourds, multicolored squashes, and mini pumpkins circle the flowers.

Everything is so pretty. It could be a fall wedding. And all of it was donated by the wonderful people in our community.

I find Love fussing with some flowers and take her hand, leading her toward the door where people are starting to come in. Amos is already there, along with a line of staff and volunteers.

We welcome the families as they enter, each face—so special to me. Some of these people have been with us since the beginning, while others are new. They've allowed us into their homes and trusted us with their children. They've been open and vulnerable, showing us their flaws and being receptive to help. They've changed my life for the better. Our goal here is to help as many children and families as possible, but the truth is we do it because it fills us up and makes us all feel good. To be able to do what I do each day is something I never take for granted.

"Is this Leo's girl?" a woman who I haven't seen in a few years asks.

"It is." I nod. "This is Love."

The woman crouches down before Love. "You look just like him," she says in awe, tears filling her eyes. "Just like him." She stands and addresses me. "Thank you for the invitation. I had nowhere to go this year. I lost my Benny, in the same way you lost Leo, a year ago." Her voice cracks. "I have no one, and this means so much."

My lip trembles as tears fill my eyes. "I'm so sorry," I say, wrapping the woman in a hug. "I'm sorry. I loved Benny."

Benny came to us at the beginning. He was bright, a talented artist, funny, and kind...and now, gone. That thought is paralyzing. We worked with Benny for years. We must've failed him somehow.

I hold his mother as grief consumes me.

"It wasn't your fault." She rubs my back. "It wasn't mine. It just was. My boy wasn't meant to be here long, and that's just something we have to live with. We all tried, and he was so loved. I came to tell you that he was here years longer because of you and Leo. I know that to be true. You gave me years with my son. This place is special, and it makes a difference. For all the Bennys, there are a hundred others that make it because of you. I came here today to thank you. I never thanked you. I was too proud, but you and Leo and this place were a blessing to my Benny. I need you to know that."

I give her a tight smile and a nod. "Thank you, and thank you for coming."

As the rest of the crowd trickles in, I'm inundated with hugs and blessings. Just this one day could fuel my soul forever. I love these people. It's the most fun seeing our past kids that have grown up and moved on from the program.

Of course, Love is a hit. She's going to be flying high for days from the number of compliments she's getting. I love sharing her daddy's legacy with her.

When everyone is seated, we deliver a little gift bag to each person in attendance and thank them again for coming. The bags are filled with fun finds—soaps, scarves, cookies, candles, jewelry, muffins, and other goodies donated by our local vendors. Additionally, each bag contains a gift card to a Michigan-based store with everything from groceries to toys and clothes. I'm hoping the card will help alleviate some stress for these families as Christmas approaches.

Music plays as people eat and chat. Laughter can be heard all around us. It's perfect.

After everyone clears out, we package up the remaining food and load it into my car, where I'll drop it off at the local food bank.

"Let me drop it off, and you can get home to help your mom with the meal," Amos says, setting a large tin of mashed potatoes into the trunk.

"Are you kidding? If anyone needs to help Lee-Anne, it's

you." I chuckle. "You know you're more talented than me in the kitchen."

He takes hold of my hips. "You don't give yourself enough credit. You can make some great meals, and Thanksgiving food is your specialty." He kisses me.

"Okay, but you know what I mean. You'll still be better and more organized and calm when dealing with my mother." I grin. Amos has the patience of a saint.

"Fine." He places his lips against my forehead. "I'll help your mom with dinner so something at your Friendsgiving is edible." He chuckles.

"Exactly my point."

"Is Love going with you or me?" he asks.

I look over to where she's leaned against my car, picking at the ribbon on her dress. "Take her with you. Let her go home and relax. She's exhausted. It's been a busy day."

"Okay, sounds good. See you at home." He kisses me again. I love the way he says *home*. He extends his hand. "Ready, Love Dove? Let's go see what Gigi is cooking up."

Love perks up and runs over, placing her small hand in his.

"I'm going to drop this food off, and then I'll see you at home. Okay?"

"Okay, Momma."

I watch as my whole heart walks away, and the pressure in my chest threatens to burst. I'm so in love. With him, and her… and this life.

CHAPTER 31

ALMA

I bid Frank, the chatty food bank manager, farewell and step out into the alley behind the building. Before getting into the car, I dial Amos. The call goes to voicemail, so I hang up and dial my mother.

She picks up on the third ring. "Hey, Mom. Can you ask Amos if he needs me to pick up juice for the punch? I know we were low and can't remember if he grabbed some or not."

"Isn't he at the Lair with you?" she asks.

"No, we finished up, and I was dropping food off..." My blood goes cold, and my entire body freezes. Dread pulls at me with its icy claws. "Amos isn't back yet?"

"No, it's just me so far."

"Is Love back?" I snap.

"Love's with you," she states, her voice raising in question.

"I gotta go," I blurt out before hanging up and dialing

Amos's number again. He should've been home a while ago. Once again, I'm sent to voicemail.

My hands shake as I pull up the GPS app on my phone. Warning bells are screaming in my head. Something's wrong.

Amos and I have had GPS apps on our phones for years. I rarely use it, but it comes in handy if I'm at work and wondering if he's finished up with the home visit. I can click on the app and see where he is, so I don't call and interrupt him if he's still there. Or if he's working off campus or at a meeting, and I want to know if he's on his way home so I can warm up dinner.

My phone moves slower than usual as I frantically pull up the app and click on Amos's picture. He shows up on the map, a mile from the Lair. He's not at a store but at a residential intersection. Tears fall onto the phone's screen, and I jump into my car and start the engine.

He's not far, only a few minutes, but the drive toward his little dot on my GPS is agonizing.

"It's fine," I tell myself. "They're fine. They're good. Everything's okay." I talk to myself as I get closer to Amos and Love.

As I approach, the lights of the police car and ambulance cause panic to choke me, and I gasp for air as I pull up behind the police cruiser.

Throwing the car in park, I fling my door open and run toward Amos's car. The front of the other car is crushed, and I want to crumple from fear, but I force myself to keep going. I need to find them.

On the bank in front of the ambulance, Amos stands in the grass, Love on his hip, as he talks to an officer. I run toward them and tackle them in a hug. Tears of relief flow.

"Oh my God. What happened? Are you okay?" I take a step back and pull Love's arm out, checking her for signs of damage.

"We're okay," Amos reassures me. "Just a little fender

bender. The stop sign took most of the force as she hit it. She just tapped our back corner. It was nothing. I'm sorry. I was going to call, but I've been talking to the officer and exchanging insurance information."

I pull Love from his arms and take her in mine. "Are you sure she's okay? Should we have her checked out?"

Amos rubs his palms against my arms. "She's fine. I promise. I'm serious when I say it was nothing. My car is barely dinged."

"Why is there an ambulance?" I ask.

"I think the driver of the other car might go in. She may have hit her head. They're not sure."

I look over to where a woman leans against her car. She stares off into the distance and then stumbles to the side a bit.

My eyes go wide as a fury unlike I've ever know envelops me. "Is she drunk?"

"Yeah." Amos sighs.

I hand Love to Amos and storm toward the woman, ignoring Amos as he pleads for me to come back.

"What the fuck is wrong with you?" I scream, inches from the woman's face. "You don't drive drunk! You could kill someone! There are children and families on the road. You could've ruined my life! Could you live with yourself if you killed someone's child? Do you even care? How could you be so selfish!" Rage rises with each word. She could've taken everything from me, yet she stands here unaffected. *I hate her.*

Amos grabs my arm and pulls me back. "Come on, Alma. Let's go home."

"Get a fucking Uber next time!" I screech as Amos pulls me away.

"I hate her." I cry into his chest. He hugs me with his free arm. Love sits in his other, and her little hand pats my head.

"It's okay, Momma."

"I know, baby, and I'm so glad. Mommy's just scared. I'm sorry for yelling." I swallow hard. "Let's go home."

Our house is full of conversation and laughter as we enter. Leo and I started doing Friendsgiving dinners in college, and it's something I've done ever since. I don't cook often, but the few dishes I do well are Thanksgiving-themed. Getting together with our friends after everyone's respective family meals has always been so fun.

I left Lee-Anne with step-by-step instructions for meal preparation today, but even still, I have no idea what kinds of dishes to expect.

"Happy Thanksgiving." Quinn hugs me. "Thank goodness I brought like half of the dishes this year. Do you realize that your mom put some kind of Atlantic seaweed in the stuffing 'to make it healthier'?" Quinn lifts her fingers in an air quote.

"I figured she'd pull something like that." I force a grin.

"Are you okay?" she asks.

"Yeah, I just need a minute."

I greet Ethan, Ollie, and Cat before heading up to my room and closing the door behind me. Covering my face with my hands, I allow the tears to explode, and my body shakes as the adrenaline and fear subside.

The door to my room opens and closes, and in a moment, I'm wrapped in Amos's embrace.

He kisses my head and holds me tight. "It's okay."

"I know," I choke out. "I was just so scared. I can't lose you. I can't lose her. I wouldn't survive that."

My therapist says that those who experience a tragic loss can suffer from PTSD and fear death for years. Existing in this bubble of debilitating fear, I believe her.

"When you weren't home, and the lights, and the ambulance," I cry.

"I know." He rubs my back. "We're okay. You're not going to lose us."

Tilting my head up, I take his face between my palms. "I'm so in love with you, Amos Davis. I don't ever want to live without you."

"You won't." The corner of his mouth tilts in a grin. "You're stuck with me, forever."

"Promise?"

"Always."

"You know what I'm most thankful for today, on this day of gratitude?" I say, rubbing my thumbs over the skin of his cheeks.

"What's that?"

"You." I kiss him gently. "Everything I am is because of you. Had we not moved in next to you when I was young, I don't know where I'd be today. You're so patient and kind. You've been my friend and my number one support always. You gave me strength when I felt weak. You gave me confidence when I felt lacking. You loved me when I felt unlovable. You've been there for me, always knowing exactly what I needed, through everything. I don't know what I did to deserve you, but I do know that I can't live this life without you." I shake my head, new tears filling my eyes. "Not ever. Okay?"

"Never." His beautiful browns capture mine, and as he kisses me, I pray he holds on forever.

* * *

We sit around in the living room, our bellies stuffed with food, most of it delicious. Amos leans back against the corner of the couch, his arms wrap around me as I sit on his lap. Love nuzzles against me, her eyes closing in sleep as she sits on mine. The three of us are mildly obsessed with each other, and I wouldn't want it any other way.

A plate full of Lee-Anne's seaweed and ginger cookies sits on a platter on the coffee table in the center of the seating area.

"Never have I ever ridden on an elephant," Quinn says and looks around the circle expectantly.

"Oh, man," Cat says, scrunching her nose. She reaches out and picks up a *cookie*, and plops it in her mouth. Her face scrunches up in disgust as she chews.

We're not drinking wine tonight as Ollie's here. He would be fine if we drank, but I just don't feel good about it. I love and respect Ollie so much. He was an incredible friend and mentor to Leo. He's been clean for so long, and hopefully, he'll be clean for the rest of his life. The least we can do is not chug alcohol in his presence. Besides, forcing people to eat Lee-Anne's health *cookies* is so much more fun. My mother's been on a real seaweed kick lately. It's her new miracle health food of choice. I can only say that a seaweed-ginger patty tastes exactly like one would imagine—not good.

"When did you ride an elephant?" Amos asks.

"When I was eighteen. I went to India on holiday with my parents, and they paid for us to take rides at this one park. It was like a zoo." She smiles, content. "Gosh, that seems like forever ago." She swallows. "Okay, now that's down." She puckers her lips. "Never have I ever shoplifted."

Ollie groans and reaches for a seaweed crisp. "What can I say? You all know I used to be a little shit."

As he crunches down on his cookie, Lee-Anne takes one from the plate.

"Mom." I laugh.

She shrugs. "I've had my moments of being a little shit, too."

My friends laugh.

Ollie turns to my mom. "Do you want to ask the next question, or do you want me to?"

"You go ahead." She nods.

"Okay, never have I ever eaten snails," he says.

"Lame," Quinn teases.

Ollie laughs. "I'm sorry. My crowd back in the day wasn't

about socializing before getting wasted. We just got wasted. I'm new to this scene. Anyway...snails?"

Cat, Ethan, and Quinn, all sporting frowns, take a crisp.

"It's like the question doesn't justify the punishment. You know?" Quinn says before turning to Lee-Anne. "I mean, no offense." She motions toward the cookies.

"Spring break cruise, escargot appetizer," Ethan says by way of explanation. "I'll go. Okay." He extends his joined hands out in front of him, cracking his fingers. "Never have I ever danced...let's say, *tangoed* with two men."

"Ethan." I throw a pillow at him. "There's a kid present."

"First, she's sleeping, and second, I used *code*." He smirks.

"Well." I quip. "There's a *mom* present," I say right as I turn to see Mom grabbing a cookie and plopping it in her mouth.

The room explodes with cheering and laughter. I stare at Lee-Anne shaking my head.

"What, Almalee? You knew that. I'm pretty sure you walked in on that a few times."

"Mother!" I groan. "Your granddaughter." My eyes widen.

Mom flicks her hand in the air. "She's sleeping. Lighten up, mi amor."

Amos's chest vibrates beneath me in a chuckle.

"You better watch it, mister." I throw a mock glare behind me.

He kisses my cheek. "You have to admit, no one can ever claim that your mom's no fun."

"That is true."

Ethan points toward Cat. "You guys, Cat's eating a cookie," he blurts out.

"Oh, I'm not alone," Mom adds with a sly grin.

Cat shrugs. "Europe. After a show," she offers. "I was young."

"Never have I ever graduated from high school," Lee-Anne says to a round of grumbles. She knows that everyone in here besides her and Love have graduated from high school and therefore must eat a green pattie.

Ethan snatches a seaweed cookie. "I thought you were cool, man." He shoots a playful glare toward my mom.

"Seriously, though. Not cool, Lee-Anne." Quinn sighs, grabbing another cookie as she presses against her belly. "Is anyone else starting to feel ill?"

"You all should thank me. Do you know how many vitamins and antioxidants you're getting in these? They're good for you," Lee-Anne says.

"You know what I miss?" Ethan looks around. "Remember the days when Friendsgiving ended with, you know, pumpkin pie or cake or any dessert really that wasn't made from ocean weeds."

"There's an apple cobbler, a chocolate pie, and a pumpkin pie cooled in the oven," Amos says with a chuckle.

"Fuck yeah." Ethan stands, clapping his hands. "That's what I'm talking about."

"Whipped cream is in the fridge, and vanilla ice cream is in the freezer," I add.

"Game over." He heads toward the kitchen. "I need to wash down all these vitamins with some sugar."

There's a collective round of agreement as people stand and stretch.

The doorbell rings, and we look around at each other.

"Is anyone expecting someone?" I ask.

Lee-Anne gets up and straightens her shirt. "I am, and he's a little early."

My brain races as a broad smile finds my face. "Mom! Who is it?"

She ignores my question and heads to the door.

I turn to Amos and nod toward Love. "Babe, can you?"

"Absolutely." He takes Love from my arms as I slide off his lap.

I follow Lee-Anne to the door to find Luca standing on the threshold. "I knew it! You know she's been keeping you a secret?" I blurt out before second-guessing my enthusiasm. Maybe they're just friends, or maybe he didn't know that she's been secretive.

He quickly saves my nerves. "Yes, I know. She told me."

"Well, come in, Luca." I stand back, welcoming him in. "Happy Thanksgiving."

I introduce Luca to everyone and leave him in the kitchen dishing up some cobbler. I pull my mom aside, retreating to the now vacant living area.

"Mom. I'm so happy for you. You know I want nothing but joy for you, but Luca's had a hard road with loss. Does he know...about...?" I struggle with how to phrase my question without hurting my mother.

"Does he know that I was a horrible mother to you? Yes. Does he know that I'm a recovering addict? Yes. Does he know that I'm a little out there and free-spirited? Yes. I'm not trying to hurt him, Almalee. We've been talking, as friends, since August. I've told him everything. It's not my intention to hurt or deceive him in any way. At first, it was nice just having a friend, someone besides you, Amos, and Love. It's slowly turning into more, though, and that's why I thought it was time to invite him over."

I take her hands in mine and squeeze. "Okay, that's good. That's great, Mom. I'm so happy for you."

Her face drains of color, and she looks panicked.

"What is it?" I ask.

"I haven't told him about the more than one guy at a time thing. We haven't gone into detail about that kind of stuff. You don't think they're going to tell him?"

I chuckle. "No, Mom. They would never say anything. We may be a crazy group, but we have manners."

"Oh, okay." She nods, relieved, and squeezes my arm. "I better get in there."

"Okay."

She retreats to the kitchen as Amos joins me, his arms free of a sleeping three-year-old.

"She all set?" I ask.

He nods. "She's all tucked in and sound asleep."

I drape my arms around his neck, and he grabs my waist. "It's been a long day," I observe, thinking about the many ups and downs of the day.

"It sure has. So, Luca, huh?"

I press my lips together and bob my head. "Yeah, I guess so. Who would've thought?"

"I'm happy for her," Amos states.

"Me too."

"He'd be a great addition to the family you've built here."

I listen to the laughter coming from the kitchen. "Yeah, he would. It's a beautiful little family, don't you think?"

"The best."

CHAPTER 32

AMOS

*M*y heart is full with nothing but gratitude. Every morning I wake up and can't believe this is my life. It's a storybook existence, really—the perfect picture. When I was young, I never voiced my desire to spend forever with Alma, not even to myself, until a lifetime with her wasn't a choice.

I thought I lost her forever, at least, in that way. Sitting here now…it's surreal.

She looks adorable in her bright green jammies that resemble a North Pole elf's outfit, complete with a golden belt made of pajama fleece, a green-and-white-striped shirt, and slippers with a pointy tip. The Christmas pajama choices this year were rough, and Alma wasn't a fan of any of them. We narrowed it down to this pair, a blue pair with Santa flying a jet, and a red pair with Mickey Mouse. Ultimately, the decision was left to Love, which is why we're all dressed like elves around the Christmas tree.

We're all wearing the chosen jammies, and in all fairness, the ladies all look cute. There's no doubt that I cringe every time I walk by a mirror but I'd wear a plastic bag if that's what Alma wanted.

Love opened her gifts from Santa, a pink Huffy bicycle complete with tassels dangling from the handlebars and a white wicker basket up front. She especially loved her stocking with all of its little treasures and candies. Alma and I had so much fun picking out goodies for Love's stocking. She's at the age where everything, no matter how small, is the greatest gift in existence. I love seeing the world through her eyes, and I hope she always views her surroundings with wonder. In many ways, Alma still does. It's one of the things I love about her. The other day, Alma was more excited about the aluminum foil swan that the server made for her leftovers than the ritzy dinner that preceded it.

"Should we let Gigi open one?" she asks Love.

"Yes!" Love cheers, grabbing a present wrapped in silver with sparkly green holly, which is the designated Gigi wrapping paper. All of our presents are wrapping specific. Alma thought this would be a good idea, so Love could hand out gifts even though she can't read the names.

Lee-Anne opens a book, and she gasps. "I love it." She smiles.

"It's all the edible plants that grow in Michigan, where they can be found, and what their health properties are," Alma says as Lee-Anne flips through the pages.

"This is so thoughtful." Lee-Anne opens her arms for a hug, inviting Alma and Love into her embrace.

Alma's parents weren't big into holidays and rarely celebrated any of them. It's fun watching Lee-Anne experience many aspects of life for the first time these past couple of years. She's in awe of the person and mother Alma has become. Pride radiates from her every day, as it should. Alma is incredible.

We go around the room, each of us opening a present, one at a time. We didn't go overboard with gifts. Each person has a few meaningful presents—Love, of course, has a few more.

Love rips the paper off her collection of Disney princess Barbies and screams, holding the box up in the air. "Yes! Yes! Yes!" she chants, jumping up and down.

"Do you love them?" Alma throws her head back in laughter.

"I yuv them so much!" Love squeezes the box. "Yes! Yes! Yes!"

I laugh. "Which ones did you get, Lovie?"

She sets the box on the floor and looks at the dolls. With her pointer finger, she begins naming them off, "Punzel, White, Belle, Jasmin, Rora, Ariel, Rella, and Tiana."

"Oh, Tiana is your favorite," Gigi says.

"Yep," Alma says. "You have your past, current, and future favorite princesses. So you can play with them all whenever you want."

"Thank you." Love hugs the box again. "I yuv them, Momma."

"I know you do, Love," Alma says. "What a great Christmas morning. We are all so blessed and lucky. Aren't we, Lovie? We have a great family."

Love nods at her mother's words, though her focus is on the box. Her tongue peeks out of her mouth as she tries to open it.

"Need help?" I ask.

She jumps up and hands me the box, and I help her open it and pull out the dolls.

"You know, Lovebug. We forgot that one present we got for your Mom, the secret present," I say in a whisper.

Love's eyes go wide, and she drops the dolls and looks back and forth between Alma and me.

"You want to help me go get it?"

She nods and jumps up.

"There's one more present that I forgot to put under the tree. We'll be right back," I say to Alma and take Love's hand.

We hurry to the guest bedroom and pull the large wrapped box from the closet.

"Remember what we practiced?"

"Yes." Her voice squeaks.

"Are you excited?" I chuckle, clasping a silver necklace around her neck.

"Yes!" She holds the charm of her necklace and smiles.

"Okay, let's go!"

I hold the present, and Love follows me down the steps. I set the box at Alma's feet.

"Oh, it's big." She grins.

"Open it!" Love bounces.

Alma undoes the bow and pulls the silver top off. "Oh my goodness. It's a treasure trove." She starts pulling items from the box. I tried to incorporate two decades of memories into the box. Alma pulls out the bag of gummy sharks and other favorite candies from our past. There's a framed picture from senior prom, and our college acceptance letters. I purchased four bags of gummy worms and removed all of the red and white ones, putting them in their own separate bag. "They're all red and white." Alma laughs. "You're the best."

She continues to make a fuss over the other contents in the box. There's a bumper sticker with the name of the place we stayed at on Lake Michigan six months ago. There's a key chain with a roller coaster, representing our first roller coaster ride at Cedar Point in Ohio. Many of the items, like the tie-dyed scrunchy that she holds now, I found in my old room when I was home for a week after my dad's surgery.

"It's my favorite scrunchie ever. Where'd you find this? I haven't seen it since I was twelve."

"Mom had a whole box of little things that she found of ours from around the house. It was in there, along with some of the other things. I found many of the memories in the box we made for our time capsule that we never buried, the one I kept under my bed. We kept adding things to it, but never ended up burying it. Remember? The college acceptance letters, a bunch of pictures, and your charm bracelet were in there."

"This is incredible. So many wonderful memories, Amos. What's this?" She picks up the leather-bound book at the bottom of the box. There are hundreds of yellow sticky notes sticking out from all sides marking pages.

"That is one of the journals I kept in high school, and each Post-it note is stuck to a page where I wrote about you."

She flips through the book in awe. "That's like every page."

"Pretty much, yeah. Read the page with the pink sticky note."

She thumbs the pink piece of paper and opens the corresponding page.

"Out loud," I urge.

She clears her throat and starts reading.

Today is Alma's birthday. She's sixteen. I made her a picnic in the backyard with all of her favorite things, including enough candy to keep her content for a while. I burned her a CD of all of her favorite songs, and she loved it all. It was an incredible day and will probably be one of my most favorite days ever. She found two white and whispy dandelions in the backyard and gave one to each of us. She told me to close my eyes and think about my deepest desire in the whole world and to make that my wish. I didn't have to think about it because I already knew. I wished for her. We both closed our eyes and blew the white seeds from the flower into the summer air, and I wished for her. Not now, and maybe not for a long time, but someday, I want to spend my whole life with her. She has a life to live and dreams to accomplish. We both do. But someday, she'll be mine forever. I guess, for me, she already is, but when the time is right, I'll ask her, so she'll know. When that day comes, she'll say yes because there aren't two people more destined for each other than she and I. She was mine from the first moment I saw her, and I know that I'm hers, too.

Mutt and Cookie Forever.

TEARS FALL down Alma's cheeks. "You wrote that when you were sixteen?"

I nod and drop to my knee. Alma covers her mouth with her hands.

I take in my soul mate—no makeup, hair in a messy bun, wearing elf jammies—and she's the most beautiful person I've ever seen.

I turn to Love and motion for her to stand beside me. "Yesterday, I spoke with Love and gave her a necklace." Love holds up the silver Tiffany necklace with the dandelion charm hanging from it. "The necklace represents my promise to Love." I look away from Alma and turn to her daughter. "I promised her that I would love and protect her always. I promised her that I would support her and be her number one fan forever. I told her that I know she has a daddy in heaven, but wanted to know if I could be her daddy on earth." Alma sobs from the sofa. "And what did you say, Love Dove?"

"Yes." She nods excitedly and throws her arms around me. I hug her and kiss her cheek. "Then what did I ask you?" I say to Love.

"If you could marry Mommy."

"And what did you say?"

"Yes!" She giggles.

I chuckle and squeeze Love tight before letting her go to face Alma once more. Pulling the diamond ring from my elf slipper, I hold it up before her. "Almalee Hannelda Weber Harding, will you please be my wife?"

She gasps as tears course down her cheeks and nods. "Yes," she sobs. "Yes!"

She slides off the couch and wraps her arms around me and Love and cries. After a few minutes, she leans back, and her tear-soaked face smiles the biggest, most gorgeous smile I've seen. "I love you so much."

"I love you," I say before crashing my lips to hers. The kiss isn't nearly as long as I'd like, but with Love at our side, it's long enough.

"Put on your wing, Momma," Love says.

Alma holds out her hand, and I slide the ring onto her finger.

It's a perfect fit.

I knew it would be.

CHAPTER 33

ALMA

*W*e lean over the countertop, staring into a mug. Inside the ceramic cup sits a chocolate sphere, an Andes mint cocoa bomb. Apparently, Quinn has tried them all, and the mint chocolate is the best.

"You ready?" she says to Love.

Love shakes her head and peers into the magical mug.

Quinn slowly pours heated milk over the bomb until it opens and *explodes* with a heaping pile of cocoa powder and mini marshmallows.

A round of *oohs* and *ahhs* and *whoas* sound out.

"Isn't that so cool?" Quinn ask.

"Yes!" Love agrees.

"Now you just stir it." She inserts the spoon and mixes the drink before sliding it to Love. "And it's perfect."

"Thank you!" Love exclaims as she brings the mug to her lips. "Yummy," she says, her upper lip covered in chocolate.

"That looks yummy." I chuckle. "Thanks, Auntie Quinn."

Quinn shrugs. "Cocoa bombs are all the rage. There's this lady by my parents' house who makes them, and I swear my sisters are single-handedly paying this woman's mortgage with their cocoa bomb orders." She grins and taps the fancy gift box she brought with five other cocoa bombs inside. "I brought you the Reese's cup, strawberry-white chocolate, birthday cake, another mint, and then a regular chocolate to try."

"You're the best. Thank you," I say.

"Well, I have to run. I have other people to visit, but you enjoy your cocoa, Love bug." She leans over the counter and gives Love a kiss on the head. "I love you, and Merry Christmas."

"I yuv you, Quinny," Love says.

Quinn gives me a big hug. "Merry Christmas. And once again, congrats on the engagement. I love you."

"Love you too, and thank you."

She hands out two more hugs and declarations of love to Lee-Anne and Amos before heading out.

"We should dance," Lee-Anne exclaims. "Luca introduced me to this incredible song. I had no idea Christmas music could be so fun." She looks up at the ceiling as if addressing a higher power. "Alexa, play Trans-Siberian Orchestra, 'Christmas Eve/Sarajevo 12/24.'"

The first few notes of the song begin to play over the speakers, and Lee-Anne takes Love's hand and pulls her into the living room. Love giggles as her gigi spins her around in a circle.

I take Amos's hand. "You ready?"

"For you, always," he says as I lead him to the living room.

The four of us dance and spin. We take hold of each other's hands and twirl around together in a four-person circle. When the heavy drumming in the song plays overhead, Lee-Anne starts beating pretend air drums with a determined ferocity, and Love follows suit.

Amos chuckles from beside me, his eyes on the world-class drummers.

A bell chimes and I turn to Amos. "Was that part of the song or the doorbell?" I squint.

"I think that may be the doorbell."

Love and Lee-Anne, unfazed by the chime, continue their routine as I open the door.

"Merry Christmas!" Cat cheers, holding a tall stack of presents.

Leo's mother stands beside Cat with an equally tall tower of presents. "Merry Christmas, Alma. I hope it's okay that I'm here."

"Of course, come in." I step to the side as they enter.

Amos takes the presents from them and places them in front of the Christmas tree as the two women watch Lee-Anne and Love with amusement.

The song ends, and the room is suddenly quiet.

"Love, look who's here," I say. My daughter gasps and runs into Cat's arms.

"Grandma Harding and I brought you some Christmas presents. Do you want to open them?" Cat asks, and Love nods wildly.

"Can I get you something to drink? We have punch, water, champagne?" I ask.

Both women request a glass of champagne. I retreat to the kitchen as Love squeals, opening her first gift. Lee-Anne follows me into the kitchen and fills herself a glass of water.

"You know the more people there are to love your daughter, the better it is for her. There's no such thing as too much love," she notes.

"I know."

"She loves her and wants to be in her life. That's not a bad thing."

"I know," I repeat, pulling the bottle of champagne out of the refrigerator.

"But you're still so mad. I can see it," Lee-Anne says, taking a sip of her water.

I set the bottle down. "Yes, I'm mad, Mom. No, I haven't truly forgiven her."

"There's room in your heart for forgiveness, mi amor. You forgave me for all I've done. Why can't you forgive her?"

Tears come to my eyes, and my lips tremble. I pull in a breath, willing myself not to cry and shake my head. "It's different. You and her are not the same."

"Maybe not. Her history of wrong is different than mine, but we were both wrong. We both let our children down. We both failed in our role as mothers. We'd both take it back if we could. Wrong is wrong, mi amor. Forgiveness is a gift to yourself. Life is too short to hold hate in your heart." She raises her hand to my cheek. "You know this."

I nod, wiping the errant tear that's escaped from my cheek.

Lee-Anne presses her lips together in a slight grin and leans in to kiss my cheek before joining the others in the living room.

I quickly pour the champagne into the glass flutes. Blowing out a breath, I walk into the living room with a smile.

Love gets way more presents than she needs, but she's happy.

We visit with Cat and Mrs. Harding for a while, and then they stand to leave. I walk them to the door, and Cat hugs me tight.

"I'm so happy for you. Congratulations."

"Thank you. Love you."

"Love you. Let's get together soon, no?"

"Absolutely."

Cat looks at Mrs. Harding, "I'll meet you in the car."

"Thank you for allowing me to come over." I open my mouth to speak, and Mrs. Harding raises her hand. "Please, let me finish," she says with a sad smile. "I know you're angry with me, and you have every right to be. I failed my son. This is true. I wanted out, but I was afraid. I thought 'who's going to want me'?" Her eyes fill with tears. "I'm not strong like you, Alma. I'm weak, even now. I should leave him still, but I can't. I don't know who I am without him, and I'm afraid to be alone. It may sound silly, but it's the truth. Yet I loved Leo. I truly loved him. I'm sure that doesn't make sense to you, given what happened, but I loved him and miss him every day. My heart hurts that he's not here, and the guilt that I'm to blame consumes me. I've carried that guilt for years, and I'll never shed it. As long as I live, I'll be drowning in regret. But Love." She looks toward her granddaughter, who's on the floor with Amos as he puts together her new dollhouse. "She's a part of him. She's so much like he was, and it's more than just her appearance. I see Leo in her, and I want to do it right this time. I want to love her the way I should've loved him, the way in which you love her."

She quickly wipes a tear from her face and shakes her head. "I want to know her. Truly know her. She'll never see my husband. I'll never put her in harm's way, but I want to see her more than on her birthday and Christmas. You don't owe me this, of course, but I'm begging you to consider."

"Okay," I say.

Mrs. Harding's eyes go wide in surprise. "Okay?"

"Yes." I swallow. "You can see her because you're right. She carries him with her. I see him all the time. I'm working on forgiving you, and I hope that someday I'll be able to say that I have. When I think about everything in Leo's past, I get so mad because I don't understand why you didn't protect him. And you're right—you're nothing like me. I would die before I let anything happen to my daughter. My purpose on this earth is to protect her. You failed. You failed him, and you are partly to blame for why he's not here." I shake my head. "I may never understand your past or your reasons, but I understand what it means to love someone, and my daughter deserves to be loved and feel love from the people in her life. We'll talk about the perimeters, the obvious one being that she will never see him, but yes—you can have a relationship with her. You're her daddy's mother, and she should know you."

"Thank you, Alma. From the bottom of my heart, thank you." Tears of relief roll down her face.

"You're welcome." She pulls me into a hug. "Merry Christmas," I say with a forced smile that I hope seems genuine. "Thank you for coming over. Love is in heaven with all of her presents."

She takes hold of my hand. "I hope you take comfort in knowing that you're the best thing to ever happen to him, the very best." She sighs and leaves me with a small grin, a real one this time, before retreating from the house.

"Everything okay?" Lee-Anne asks as I watch Cat back out of the drive.

"It will be, Mom." I lean my head against her shoulder.

We watch as the car's taillights disappear around the corner. I close the wooden entry door. "What a day, huh?"

"Indeed but such a magical day. Who knew Christmas could be so great?" she says.

"Well, not you and Vati." I chuckle.

She shakes her head. "Seriously. What were we thinking back then?"

"That's a conversation for another day." I kid. "Are you going to see Luca?"

Lee-Anne nods. "Yeah, he's at his sister's house now. I was just getting ready to head over there. I figure Love's going to crash any minute now, and then you and Amos are gonna want to start celebrating your engagement." She wiggles her brows.

I smack her lightly on the arm. "No, Mom. We are not going there."

"You're still not okay with talking about your sex life?" she questions in a serious tone.

"Mother, I will never be okay talking about that with you."

She shrugs. "Someday you will."

"No, I won't."

"Oh, you'll lighten up, mi amor. You'll see."

I laugh. "Oh, Mom."

* * *

IT WAS the longest and most fantastic day. I waited what seemed like an eternity to have Amos all to myself. Ever since this ring circled my finger, I've wanted to attach my body to Amos's and only come up for air.

However, Christmas was packed with fun, firsts, and family. We enjoyed delicious meals and made holiday-shaped sugar cookies. Amos wanted to show Love all of the classic Claymation Christmas movies, but I said I didn't think she was there yet. Truthfully, I had a difficult time getting through them when I watched for the first time in college. So, we settled on *A Charlie Brown Christmas*, and then switched over to a couple of Disney Christmas cartoons.

Our friends dropped by sporadically throughout the day, and we exchanged gifts and spent time together.

And now finally—it's just Amos and me, and this beautiful ring. I hold out my hand to admire it.

"You like it?" he asks.

"It's perfect," I say. "Everything about today was absolutely amazing. I can't believe Love kept your secret."

"Me either," he says with a chuckle. "That's why I told her

last night. I figured I'd have a good twelve hours until she spilled the beans. It helped that her mind was on Santa and presents once morning came."

"True."

The fireplace is on, and the Christmas tree lights sparkle in front of the big picture window. It's festive and romantic all at once. We lie naked and sated atop the fluffy area rug in front of the fireplace. Propped up on pillows, we stare into each other's eyes.

"I can't believe we're getting married."

"I can." He smiles smugly. "When do you want to do it?"

"Whenever. I would go to the courthouse tomorrow if you wanted."

"No. That wouldn't make you happy. We need some kind of wedding, even if it's something small. But I know you're going to want Love to be part of it, wear a big poufy dress and throw some flowers."

"Oh, you're so right. I need a wedding. She's going to look like an angel. Spring maybe? When it's warmer. Maybe on Lake Michigan?"

"That could definitely work." He presses his lips to mine. "For the record, I'd go to the courthouse tomorrow to marry you, too."

I run my finger across his lips. "I was able to read a couple of passages from your journal today. I can't believe you wrote so many nice things about me."

"Can't you?" He raises a brow.

"I mean, yeah, of course I can. It's just crazy that we've loved each other for so long and never tried getting together, even when we were teens."

He shrugs. "Like I said, you were too important to lose. It was never worth the risk."

"You'll never lose me."

"I'm counting on it," he says. Pulling my bottom lip through his teeth, he sucks it into his mouth. "Do you remember making a dandelion wish on your sixteenth birthday?"

"I do, actually. I remember almost everything about that day. You made it so special for me."

"Do you recall what you wished for?"

I nod. "Yeah, I wished to be happy, just like I was on that day, when I was grown."

"And your wish came true?"

"Yes and no," I say. "That wish was exceeded by a long shot. I'm exponentially happier than I was on that day. I didn't know this level of joy existed."

"I'm glad. I'm beyond happy, too." He kisses the tip of my nose. "Do you want to go upstairs?" he whispers, trailing kisses down my neck.

"No." I run my palms up his bare chest, feeling his muscles between my touch. "I want to stay here by the light of the Christmas tree. It's been the best Christmas ever. We should stay in theme."

"Okay." Amos chuckles. "Whatever you want, my beautiful girl."

We explore every inch of each other's bodies. We make love again by the light of the fire, and it's incredible. Every moment with him always is.

I stare into the fire, my cheek against his chest as I draw lazy circles over his skin.

"Is it weird that you lost your virginity with one of my bridesmaids?" I ask, amused.

Amos pulls in a breath and throws his forearm over his eyes, and groans. "We've gone six months without bringing that up," he says. "I was hoping it'd never come up."

"It's not a big deal. I mean, we weren't together or anything then. Is it ever weird, though?"

"No, it's really not. I don't think about it, truthfully. It feels like a lifetime ago. I don't see her in that way anymore. I haven't since freshman year. Now, she's just your bestie Quinn. Nothing more."

"Well, she's one of my besties. You're my ultimate bestie." I tilt my face up toward his.

"This is true." He presses his lips to mine. "Besties for life."

"For life."

CHAPTER 34

ALMA

The airy hum of the waves sounds through the space as glowing rays of sunshine peek through the windows. With the windows open, I can feel the light breeze on my skin.

"It's a perfect day," I say, my face contorted into an awful expression as it always does when I apply mascara. I swipe the wand across my lashes.

"It really is. It's beautiful." Quinn stands in front of the floor-to-ceiling window that overlooks the lake from the master bedroom suite. "Everything is stunning out there, magazine-worthy."

"Yeah, Clare did it all," I say of the wedding planner. "She made it so easy. I told her my vision, and she brought it to life."

We found this stunning home on Lake Michigan. To give credit where credit is due, I suppose, Mrs. Harding found it. She got wind that Amos and I were looking for a large home on the lake to rent for our wedding, and she found us this one. Apparently, it belongs to some actor that Victor Harding has worked with in the past. One call from Victor and the house was gifted to us for the week. The actor is rarely in Michigan, and the house sits empty most of the year.

I was hesitant to take help from the Hardings, but Amos convinced me to rise above my pride by reminding me it's the least they can do. Mrs. Harding is trying to do right by Love and me. I have to give her that.

The past several days have been one giant slumber party. Our closest friends and family have been staying with us at the house. Our days have been filled with delicious catered meals, games, and fun in the pool. We've played Euchre, our favorite card game, every night, and Amos and I are the reigning champions.

A spa company came in to pamper the girls with facials, manis, and pedis while the guys played a couple of rounds of golf at a nearby course. The past few days have been some of the best in my life, and today, on the white sand, I'm marrying my best friend. Our friends and family will head out tomorrow, and Amos and I will stay here—just the two of us, as a married couple the rest of the week. It's surreal.

"Look, who's hair is all finished?" Lee-Anne leads my little four-year-old into the room. Love smiles big, her hair curled into ringlets that bounce as she walks.

"Oh my goodness. Love Dove!" I shriek and walk over to her.

She wears a muted pink princess dress straight from a fairy tale. The bodice is a shimmery pink fabric with an adorable heart-shaped hole cut out in the back, and the skirt is the puffiest pink tulle.

I take her hand in mine and twirl her around. "You look like a princess."

"I know." She giggles. "I yuv it, Momma."

"I love it, too."

She runs her hand over the satin fabric of my dress. I went with a simple, elegant, formfitting dress. The skirt flows to my feet with a slit up one side. It's soft and comfortable, and perfect for a beach wedding.

"You look like a pwincess, too." she says.

I opted to wear my hair down in loose waves. The theme of the attire is classy and simple, save for Love, who gets to be the most beautiful princess there is. Cat and Quinn have pale sky blue dresses with plunging necklines and flowy simple full-length skirts. The flowers are every assortment of soft pink hues. The guys will be in light gray suits.

"And Mr. and Mrs. Davis just arrived," Lee-Anne says. Amos's parents weren't part of the three-day slumber party but were invited to the wedding ceremony, same as a few close friends from the Lair.

"Oh, great. That means everyone's here, and I think we're pretty much ready. Are the guys ready?" I ask.

"They sure are." Lee-Anne nods. "I'll tell Clare."

Grabbing some tinted lip gloss from the dresser, I lean toward the mirror and run it along my lips, finishing with a smack. "This is happening." I blow out a breath.

The reflection staring back at me is one I know well. The truth is, I've had to figure myself out. My adult life has been one moment after the next of looking deep and discovering who I am and how I'll carry myself in various situations, and there have been quite a few heavy ones.

I wouldn't recognize that girl who stepped onto Eastern's campus almost nine years ago. Though, at nineteen, I'd been through more than most that age, I'd never had to carry the weight on my own. I'd always had him.

I'm proud of the person I am today. The reality is I've been through hell and back. And, I've remained kind and caring. I love fiercely without reservations. I'm strong, and I can take on whatever life chooses to throw my way.

Except I don't have to because I'm not walking through this life alone.

I still have him.

My constant, and now my forever.

"You're perfect, absolutely stunning." Cat stands at my side, a serene smile on her face.

"Thank you."

She tilts her head, resting it atop mine as we stare in the mirror. "I'm so happy for you and grateful I get to celebrate this day with you. You know you're like a sister to me."

"I feel the same," I tell her.

Quinn joins us on my other side. "You're like a sister to me...well, except I enjoy your company more than I do some of my actual sisters." She chuckles. "And I'm glad I get to be here for this one."

She's speaking of my Hawaiian elopement with Leo. She wasn't happy not being a part of my first wedding, and I get it. Someday when Quinn settles down and finds the one, I hope I'm there to celebrate with her.

The mention of my first wedding is met with fondness, a nostalgia toward an incredible moment in my life. Thinking about my time with Leo no longer brings me crippling grief. Our life together was short, but it was wonderful, and I'm so grateful to have been loved by him. This past year with Amos has guided me toward a new level of healing. Not everyone finds their soul mate in this life, and I've found mine—twice.

My mother was right. We don't all get just one.

Leo was, without a doubt, the love of my life. His soul was destined for mine, as mine was his. It was an epic love, and as the years pass, I will always regard it as so.

Amos, too, is the love of my life. Our spirits danced when we were mere children, connecting our souls together for eternity. Our relationship is based on over two decades of aston-ishing moments, companionship, and unconditional love. He, and Love, and the family we've built are my happily ever after.

Maybe it was always destined to be this way.

I can't pretend to understand why life happens how it does, but I know that we are capable of tremendous love. Just when I thought I couldn't possibly love another, my heart grew, allowing for another epic love to take hold.

"Gorgeous! Gorgeous! Gorgeous!" Clare scans the room, pointing at all the women in it with her perfectly manicured finger. "We look ready. Are we ready?"

"We are," I say.

"Perfect. The violinists are playing, guests are seated, and Amos is waiting at the end of the aisle. I'd say, let's get this party started." She motions for my mother to join her. "Mother of the bride first, then we'll have the models in blue, princess Lovebug, and then the stunning bride. Sound good?"

We line up, according to her direction, and follow her out of the house, and stand off to the side of the aisle behind a cover of trees as she sends us down one by one.

When it's just Love and me, I crouch to her level. "Are you ready? You excited?"

She holds her baskets of petals and bobs her head.

"Thank you for being my princess today. You make this day perfect. I love you so much, baby girl."

"I yuv you, Momma." She kisses my lips.

Clare waves Love over, and my little miracle stands in the center of the sandy aisle, constructed with flowers on either side, and she looks so big and beautiful.

There's an intense warmth in my chest as a gentle breeze hits my face, and I feel it. Just like in my darkest moments when I needed strength to continue and would look inside myself to be met with comfort. I press my palm to the skin above my beating heart, and a wave of happiness and love consumes me. An overwhelming sense of peace takes over as tears fill my eyes.

This is exactly where I'm supposed to be.

Love faces me and smiles. I wave proudly, and she turns toward the beach and takes a step. Her hand reaches into the flowers and tosses them to the ground at her feet.

I take her place in the floral flanked sandy walkway.

The sight before me is breathtaking. It's everything I've been dreaming about, executed to perfection. The backdrop of Lake Michigan, in all its magnificence, is simply amazing. Amos waits, his hands crossed at his front, beneath the floral arch.

Handsome, strong, smart, brave, kind, and loving.

Amos is everything.

Most importantly, he's mine.

And I'm his.

Forever.

EPILOGUE

FIVE YEARS LATER

AMOS

*L*ove looks at me worried, as her mother, on the loveseat in our bedroom, groans in pain. I open the doors of the dresser quickly, tossing some essentials into a bag. This should've been done already, and I internally chastise myself that it's not. Alma's four weeks early, having just hit the thirty-six-week mark yesterday. We knew that twins usually come early, but neither of us thought they'd arrive a month early.

"Dad," Love says, fear in her voice. "Is this normal? Is Mom going to be okay? Are the babies going to be okay?"

I close the dresser drawer and turn to her, pressing my palm to her cheek. "She's going to be fine, Lovie. This is very normal." I chuckle. "She was just as vocal when she was having you. And the babies will be in great hands. Please, don't worry."

I remember the day that Alma gave birth to our daughter in vivid detail, like it was yesterday. I was in awe of her that day, as I am every day. My wife is a force to be reckoned with, always has been. She's a fighter, a champion with a heart of gold.

I fling the strap of the bag over my shoulder and take Alma's hand, pulling her from the sofa. Alma's free hand presses against her huge belly as she focuses on her breathing methods.

"Gigi and Luca will be here any minute, and I'll text you with updates. Okay?" I say to Love.

Love nods. "Okay."

"I'll feel much better when I get an epidural," Alma says through labored breaths. She turns to me, her eyes wide with fear. "Do you think it's going to be too late for an epidural? The contractions aren't far apart."

"I'm not sure. We'll have to see when we get there." I lead her down the steps.

Lee-Anne and Luca come in through the front door just as we reach the main level.

"Oh my goodness. Can't believe it's time!" Lee-Anne rushes over to Alma and pulls a brown bag from her purse. "Here, honey. I got you some skullcap and catnip, which will help relieve pain naturally. There's also some chamomile to help with pain during labor. I've included some dry chamomile that you can mix in food, like oatmeal, or there's tea in case that's easier."

"Mom." Alma groans, swatting at the brown bag as another contraction comes on.

I take the natural remedies from Lee-Anne and shove them in the duffel bag at my side. "Thank you, Lee-Anne. We appreciate it. We'll be in touch."

"Wait." Alma stops in the threshold of the front door. "Love." She beckons.

Love runs over to Alma. "I love you so much." Alma kisses Love's cheek. "Don't worry. Everything will be okay, and you're going to be the best big sister. Take care of Gigi while we're gone. Okay?"

"Okay, Mom. I love you," Love says as we exit the house.

The ride to the University of Michigan hospital is a short one, just a few minutes. Alma is immediately wheeled into a room and checked.

"Can I get my epidural now?" she asks after a particularly rough contraction.

"Yes, and we have to hurry. You're almost ready to push," the doctor says. "The epidural is crucial in case we have to move to the operating room. We'll try for a natural birth, but twins often end up needing to be delivered in the OR through a C-section."

"No," Alma protests and then looks at me.

"It will be okay." I rub her sweaty hair away from her face and kiss her forehead. "Do you want some catnip?" I raise a brow, and Alma throws me a death glare. "Sorry. No more jokes." I kiss her again. "You're going to do great. I know it. You're strong, and you can do this."

"I know." She pulls in a breath.

She bares down, her eyes scrunch tight as she whimpers in agony through another contraction.

"It's not too early, is it? Our babies will be okay?" Tears roll down her face.

"They're going to be just fine," I say to reassure us both.

The anesthesiologist enters the room, and I stand back as he inserts a giant needle into her spine for the epidural.

After years of making love without protection that resulted in no pregnancies we decided to see a fertility specialist last year. It turns out, Love was, indeed, a miracle. After the doctor told Alma that chances were very low she'd ever conceive again naturally, we opted to move ahead with IVF. Eight months ago, they implanted two tiny frozen embryos—part Alma and part me—into Alma, and both babies made it all the way here on their own little miracle journey.

We didn't find out the gender of the babies, opting to wait until the birth to see. Life has so few opportunities for true surprises anymore, so we thought, why not?

It's surreal to think that Alma and I are going to be parents to three kids. Three beautiful blessings.

The room is a whirlwind of activity as nurses enter and prep the space for the arrival of the twins. The bottom portion of the bed is removed, and Alma's legs are put into stirrups. Our doctor, masked and gloved up, sits at the foot of the bed, a bright light propped up behind him.

A nurse lifts Alma's gown and squirts some gel on her round belly. "We need to see what position the babies are in." She holds the ultrasound probe against Alma's skin, and we all look toward the machine's screen. The nurse smiles. "Both babies are vertex, heads down, so that's great, Alma. That gives you a high chance for a natural delivery."

"Yes, very good news," the doctor states at the end of the table. "Everything is in line for a seamless delivery. You ready to start pushing?"

"Yeah." Alma's voice quivers.

"It's time." I circle my arm around Alma, and she leans her forehead against my chest. I kiss her head over and over. "You're going to be great. I'm so proud of you."

She nods against me, crying as another contraction hits.

Time passes slowly. Seconds feel like minutes as the nurse instructs Alma to hold each push for a count of ten. Through it all, Alma is amazing, and eventually, they're here.

A boy and a girl.

A perfect little set.

The doctor places the babies on Alma's chest, and we cry, overjoyed and humbled by their presence and health. The sight of them takes my breath away. These tiny humans are a part of me. The love of my life and myself—with help from science—made them, and they're perfect.

"I love you so much," Alma says to the babies, running a finger across their cheeks. "Your daddy loves you so much."

The babies cast their eyes toward Alma's face, the sound of her voice luring them in. "Did you see that?" she asks. "They're looking at me. They're already so smart."

"They're perfect." I kiss her temple.

* * *

THE BABIES HAD to stay at the hospital for a week until their oxygen levels were stable and they could maintain their temperatures outside of the incubator. After seven long days, the doctor was confident that they were ready to be discharged.

Friends and family were able to visit sporadically while we were in the hospital, but I love having our family home, all under one roof.

Our son is named Asher, which means happy and blessed. Our daughter is Alana, meaning valuable and precious. And they are all those things. We now have our own little A squared team.

"I love their hair!" Love chuckles, running her hand over Alana's fuzzy black hair. She stares down at her sister with such wonderment.

"I know, right? They're so adorable." Alma sits beside Love on the sofa, holding Asher and admiring his equally impressive pouf of black hair.

Love kisses Alana's head. "I didn't have this much hair?"

"No." Alma grins. "You were almost bald. Some wispy

brown pieces were covering your head, but not this much. Your hair started really growing when you were about six months old."

"I wonder if it's going to stay curly," Love says, twisting a piece of Alana's hair between her fingers.

"We'll see." Alma shrugs. "Babies change so much."

"They're just so cute. You make the most adorable babies." Love looks at Alma and me.

"That's all your mom," I say. "You were just as precious. Still are." I shoot her a wink.

"They're going to love you so much," Alma tells Love. "They're lucky to have you. You're going to be the best big sister."

Lee-Anne enters the living room, followed by Luca. She hands me a reusable cloth bag that smells like the spice cabinet in the kitchen.

"All the natural remedies and lotions from gas to diaper rash," she tells me. "Now, let me see my babies!"

Over the next hour, all of our best friends arrive to visit with the babies. Newborns sure are magical, awe-inducing little things. There's nothing else quite as precious.

Catered food arrives, and we eat and celebrate the healthy birth of the twins.

There's so much love here in this home. It's all Alma. She's fostered these relationships and built this community. And now our children have all these people to love and protect them as they grow. What a gift.

Most days, I wake up and still can't believe that this is my life. It's more than I could've ever dreamed. I got it all, and I don't take any of it for granted. I remember what it felt like when Alma wasn't mine, and that makes every single moment with her brighter, every day of our life an adventure.

Alma means soul, and it's fitting really since she owns mine.

Everything I am is so entangled with everything she is. I'd be lost without her.

She's my best friend. My lover. My partner.

My soul mate.

Had things been different and had we not ended up together, I would've survived, but I wouldn't have truly lived. For how does one live without the other half of their soul?

I'm eternally grateful that I'll never have to find out.

* * *

ALMA

"Get them ready!" Love calls out from the other side of the room, holding the two most annoying toys in the world up in the air. The all-encompassing turtle toys shake in her grasp. They're neon turtles with every known texture, made from patches of squishy, crinkly, scratchy, and soft fabric. The turtles light up and play repeating music that make one's ears want to bleed.

But the twins love them to the point of obsession.

I look at Amos, who holds Alana, and he nods.

"You got this, buddy," I say to Asher, setting him down on all fours just as Amos sets down Alana.

Love wiggles the two toys, the loud music catching their attention. She sets them on the floor, and the babies are off, crawling toward their turtle.

We cheer them on in an adorable little baby race. We make bets on which baby will arrive first, but their cuteness factor will—of course—make them both winners.

"Come on, Ash!" Love cheers on her brother. "Let's go, baby girl." She smiles toward Alana.

The pudgy twins make grunting noises as they crawl, causing us all to laugh. The ability to crawl is a recent endeavor, and it takes much effort on their parts. Asher is ahead of Alana by a few inches when he suddenly stops, seeing a piece of lint on the rug. He squeezes the fuzz between his fingers and raises his hand to his mouth.

"Love," I call out, motioning toward Asher.

"I got it," Amos says with a chuckle and runs toward Asher, pulling the lint from his drooly fingers before it reaches his mouth.

Alana makes it to her turtle and sits back onto her diapered bottom and starts chewing on its nose.

"Aw, Ash. You had it, buddy." Amos picks him up and kisses his head.

"Girls rule, right Aly?" Love holds out her hand to Alana. "High five?"

Alana looks at Love's extended hand and then back at her turtle, failing the new skill that Love's been working with her on.

"She'll get it," I tell Love and plop down on the sofa, exhausted. Raising three humans is no joke. I'm tired all the time, but I wouldn't trade a second of it. I'm the happiest I've ever been. Plus, eventually, the twins will start sleeping through the night. Soon, I hope.

A steamy cup of coffee appears before me, and I look up to Amos, holding it out toward me.

I gasp with glee and take the mug from him. "Thank you, babe. You're the best."

He leans in for a kiss. "I love you. Is there anything else you need?"

"Just you." I grin.

"That I can do." He sits down beside me, and I lean into him.

The twins play on the area rug. Asher swats his turtle against the base of the end table over and over again, each time switching the song the toy plays. Alana lies on her back, apparently deciding that now is a good time to see if her foot fits in her mouth.

"Mom, can I show you the new dance I learned?" Love asks.

She's not allowed on social media yet, but her best friend learns all these dances from a popular app and teaches them to Love. When the girls hang out, all they want to do is dance.

"Of course! Let's see it."

Love turns on the music and starts dancing. She bites down on her tongue in concentration, and I hold my smile as not to embarrass her, but I think it's so cute when she does that. It's something she's been doing since she was the twins' age.

She finishes the routine, and Amos and I sound our approval.

"Awesome."

"Love it."

"Thank you. Oh, there's another one, too. I don't know it as well, but I'm still pretty good."

"Alright, let's see it," Amos says.

Love begins another routine, and I wiggle closer to Amos, loving the way the warmth of his body feels against mine. Amos is my safe place, my home, and in truth, he always has been. I'm so fortunate to be able to navigate this life with him.

Sitting here, watching my babies—all three of them—in their happy places fills me with joy. The twins, in all their pudgy-legged, teething, drooling glory, flinging around their most prized possessions while my little pre-teen perfects the most absurd dances like her status in life depends on it is my paradise. The fact that I get to experience it all with Amos is a gift from the universe.

Life is unpredictable, brutal, and beautiful all at once. Sometimes it seems to take as much as it gives. This moment, right here, though, in my happy place with my favorite people, makes all the heartache worth it. I can't change the past, but I can appreciate the present, and I do. I'm so grateful for every day.

I've been fortunate in this life to have two soul mates.

It's a crazy notion, but I know it to be true. In my heart, I believe this was my path. I was destined to love them both.

One helped me grow into the woman I was meant to be. He showed me a love with unimaginable devotion and passion. He taught me how to forgive despite the struggle. He proved that even those with the darkest demons can shine the brightest light. Because of him, I learned to judge less and listen more. Through him, I learned to live every day to the fullest and to love my people with my whole heart because life is short and precious. He started us on this path of service so I can live my life knowing I'm making the world a better place, one child at a time. Most importantly, he gave me my daughter and the strength to live without him.

The other has been my rock for as long as I can remember. He loved me when I felt unlovable. He was my family when I had none, and my strength when I felt weak. He never let me falter, my steady rock through every moment of my life. He lifted me up and put me first throughout our entire lives. He loved me quietly until he could love me loudly. He's my forever person. Steady, strong, resilient, and faithful in his affections. With him, I'm never afraid. Beyond unconditional forever love, he's given me peace.

He's given me two little miracles and Love an incredible father—and a home where we'll all grow knowing that he's there loving us and protecting us...Always.

Dear Readers,

I hope you adored Alma, Amos, and Love's HEA as much as I do! Admittedly, it was hard to let go of Leo. **tears** I had a difficult time with Alma moving on but she deserves a lifetime of happiness, and Amos is just the man to fill her life with joy.

When I was writing Bared Souls, I knew that Amos was in love with Alma, and I knew that after Leo's passing they'd be together. I hadn't planned on writing their story but I received so many reader messages asking me to, and I'm so grateful. It seriously fills my soul with so much happiness and gratitude when I receive messages from readers. This industry can be hard, and those messages keep me going. So, if you're someone who reached out to me…thank you! Thank you for embracing Leo and Alma in the way that you did, and wanting more.

I honestly wasn't sure how Bared Souls would be received. A part of me thought people would hate it as it touches on some difficult topics but I felt compelled to write it. It's been a therapeutic journey, and I'm so humbled that it affected so many of you in the way that it did. And now, with some gentle urges from you all, it's turning into a series!

The next book is Quinn's story, Captivated Souls. Cat's book is Destined Souls. All six books in the series are available now.

I hope you enjoyed the "bonus scene" in the Bared Souls portion of this duet. I wanted to write a new chapter for this duet, and a bunch of readers asked for Alma's graduation.

Thank you again for all your love and support. It means the world to me.

Thank you so much for reading.

Make your journey a beautiful one.

Love,

Ellie

ACKNOWLEDGMENTS

I want to thank my readers so very much. Thank you for reading my stories and loving my words! I wouldn't be living this dream without you. Thank you from the bottom of my heart!

To my girls—Gala, Suzanne, Amy C., Kylie, Amy E., and Kim—You all are so awesome. Seriously, each of you is a gift, and you have helped me in invaluable, different ways. I love you all so much. XOXO

To my cover artist, Letitia Hasser from RBA Designs—Thank you! Your work inspires me. You are a true artist, and I am so grateful to work with you. People do judge a book by its cover, so thank you for making mine *gorgeous*! XO

To my editor, Jenny Sims from Editing4Indies—Finding you was a true gift, one that I hope to always have on this journey. Thank you for always fitting me in! I am so grateful for you and everything you have done to make this book the best it can be. XOXO

Lastly, to my loyal readers—I love you! Thank you for reaching out, reviewing, and sharing your book recs with your friends. There are seriously great people in this book community, and I am humbled by your support. Your messages breathe life into my writing and keep me going on this journey. Truly, thank you! Because of you, indie authors get their stories out. Thank you for supporting all authors and the great stories they write.

You can connect with me on several places, and I would love to hear from you.

Join my readers group: www.facebook.com/groups/wadeswarriorsforthehea

Find me on Facebook: www.facebook.com/EllieWadeAuthor

Find me on Instagram: www.instagram.com/authorelliewade

Find me on TikTok: https://www.tiktok.com/@authorelliewade

Visit my website: www.elliewade.com

Sign up for my newsletter: https://app.mailerlite.com/webforms/landing/y8i5t2

Remember, the greatest gift you can give an author is a review. If you feel so inclined, please leave a review on the various retailer sites. It doesn't have to be fancy. A couple of sentences would be awesome!

I could honestly write a whole book about everyone in this world whom I am thankful for. I am blessed in so many ways, and I am beyond grateful for this beautiful life. XOXO

Forever,

Ellie 🖤

OTHER TITLES BY ELLIE WADE

The Flawed Heart Series

Finding London

Keeping London

Loving London

Eternally London

Taming Georgia

The Choices Series

A Beautiful Kind of Love

A Forever Kind of Love

A Grateful Kind of Love

The Soulmate Collection

Bared Souls

Kindred Souls

Captivated Souls

Fated Souls

Destined Souls

Entwined Souls

The Heroes of Fire Station Twelve

Fragment

Found

Stand-alones

Chasing Memories

Forever Baby

A Hundred Ways to Love

Boxed Sets

The Flawed Heart Series

The Beauty in the Journey Collection

The Choices Series

Cherry Blossom Grove

Ellie Wade's Sweet Collection

Licorice Wishes

ABOUT THE AUTHOR

Ellie Wade resides in southeast Michigan with her husband, three children, and three dogs. She has a master's in education from Eastern Michigan University, and she is a huge University of Michigan sports fan. She loves the beauty of her home state, especially the lakes and the gorgeous autumn weather. When she is not writing, she is reading, snuggling up with her kids, or spending time with family and friends. She loves traveling and exploring new places with her family.

Made in the USA
Middletown, DE
13 December 2023

44482491R00371